HARLEQUIN · FIVE DECADES OF ROMANCE · CELEBRATES

LIMITED COLLECTOR'S EDITION 2 IN 1

LAVYRLE SPENCER

SWEET MEMORIES

JAN FREED

ONE TOUGH TEXAN

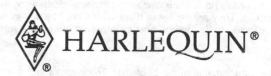

HARLEQUIN®

TORONTO • NEW YORK • LONDON
AMSTERDAM • PARIS • SYDNEY • HAMBURG
STOCKHOLM • ATHENS • TOKYO • MILAN • MADRID
PRAGUE • WARSAW • BUDAPEST • AUCKLAND

ISBN 0-7394-0455-5

HARLEQUIN 50th ANNIVERSARY LIMITED COLLECTOR'S EDITION VOLUME 2

Copyright © 1999 by Harlequin Books S.A.

The publisher acknowledges the copyright holders of the individual works as follows:

SWEET MEMORIES
Copyright © 1984 by LaVyrle Spencer

ONE TOUGH TEXAN
Copyright © 1999 by Jan Freed

Printed in U.S.A.

Table of Contents

Sweet Memories   9
LaVyrle Spencer

One Tough Texan   307
Jan Freed

Sweet Memories
LaVyrle Spencer

Chapter One

At last, Jeff was coming home, but he wasn't alone. Watching the big-bellied jet taxiing to a stop, Theresa Brubaker felt two conflicting emotions—excitement that her "baby brother" would be here for two whole weeks, and annoyance that he'd dragged along some stranger to interfere with their family holiday. Theresa never liked meeting strangers, and at the thought of meeting one now, especially a *man,* a nervous ache grabbed her between the shoulder blades. She worked her head in a circle, flexed her shoulders and tried to shrug away the annoyance.

Through the soles of her knee-high snow boots she felt the shudder and rumble of the engines as they wheezed a last inflated breath, then whistled through a dying decrescendo and sighed into silence. The accordion pleats of the jetway eased forward, its mouth molded against the curve of the plane, and Theresa riveted her eyes on the doorway set in the wall of glass. As the first footsteps of disembarking passengers thudded down the tunnel, she self-consciously glanced down and made sure her heavy gray wool coat was buttoned up completely. She clutched a small black leather purse against her left side in a way that partially concealed her breast and gave her reason to cross her arms.

Her heart tripped out a staccato beat of anticipation—*Jeff. My crazy clown of a brother, the life of the family, coming home to make Christmas what all the songs said it should be. Oh, there's no place like home for the holidays.* Jeff—how she'd missed him. She bit her lower lip and trained her eyes on the door as the first passengers debarked: a young mother carrying a squalling baby, a businessman with a topcoat and briefcase, a bearded, blue-jeaned ski bum hefting a blue satchel boasting the word Vail, two long-legged military men clad in dress blues and garrison caps with visors set squarely across their eyebrows. *Two long-legged military men!*

"Jeff!" Her arm flew up joyously.

He caught sight of Theresa at the same moment she saw his lips form her name. But sister and brother were separated by a fifteen-foot-long ramp and handrail, and what seemed to be one-quarter of the population of Minneapolis greeting incoming arrivals. Jeff pointed her out while she read his lips again— "There she is"—and shouldered through the crowd toward the crown of the ramp.

She was scarcely conscious of her brother's companion as she flew into Jeff's arms, lifting her own around his neck while he scooped her off the floor and whirled her in a circle. His shoulders were broad and hard, his neck smelled of lime, and her eyes were suddenly swimming with tears while he laughed against her temple.

He plopped her onto her feet, smiled down into her joyous face and said gruffly, "Hiya, Treat."

"Hiya, snot-nose," she choked, then tried to laugh, but it came out a chugging gulp before she abashedly buried her face against him again, suddenly conscious of the other man looking on. Beside her ear, she heard the smile in Jeff's voice as he spoke to his friend.

"Didn't I tell you?"

"Yup, you did," came the stranger's voice, rich and deep. She backed up. "Tell him what?"

Jeff grinned down teasingly. "That you're a sentimental fool. Look at you, tears flooding everything, and all over my dress blues." He examined his crisp lapel where a dark blotch showed.

"Oh, I'm sorry," she wailed, "I'm just so glad to see you."

She dabbed at the tear spot on his jacket while he touched her just beneath an eye.

"You'd be sorrier if you could see how those tears make the freckles you hate so much stand out like new pennies."

She slapped his finger away and dabbed at her eyes self-consciously.

"Don't worry about it, Theresa. Come on, meet Brian." Jeff clapped an arm around her shoulders and turned her to face his friend. "This is the light o' my life, who never let me chase women, smoke pot or drive when I drank." At this last, Jeff winked broadly. "So let's not tell her what we did last night, okay, Scanlon?" He squeezed her shoulder, grinned down fondly while his teasing did absolutely nothing to disguise the deeper note of pride in his voice. "My big sister, Theresa. Theresa, this is Brian Scanlon."

She saw his hand first, with long, tapered fingers, extended in greeting. But she was afraid to look up and see where his eyes rested. Thankfully, the way Jeff had commandeered her shoulders, she was able to half hide behind him with one arm about his waist while extending her own hand.

"Hello, Theresa."

She could no longer avoid it. She raised her eyes to his face, but he looked straight into her eyes, smiling. And what a smile!

"Hello, Brian."

"I've heard a lot about you."

I've heard a lot about you, too, she thought, but answered gaily, "I'll just bet you have. My brother could never keep anything to himself."

Brian Scanlon laughed—a pleasant baritone rumble like a soft roll on a timpani—and held her hand in a hard grip, smiling at her from beneath the horizontal visor of his military hat that made her suddenly understand why some women shamelessly chase soldiers.

"Don't worry, he only told me the nice stuff."

Her glance fluttered away from his translucent green eyes

that were far more attractive than in the photographs Jeff had sent, then Brian released her hand and moved to flank her other side as they headed away from the gate area toward the green concourse, still talking.

"All except for a couple of stories about our nasty childhood pranks, like the time you stole a handful of Grandpa Deering's pipe tobacco and taught me how to roll it up in those white papers that come with home permanents, and we both got sick from the chemicals in the paper when it got in our lungs, and the time—"

"Jeffrey Brubaker, I did not steal that tobacco. You did!"

"Well, who found the leftover papers in the bathroom vanity?"

"But who put the idea in my head?"

"I was two years younger. You should have tried to talk me out of it."

"I did!"

"But that was after we got sick and learned our lesson."

All three of them dissolved into laughter. Jeff squeezed her shoulder once more, looked across the top of her head at Brian and set things straight. "I'll be honest. After we got greener than a pair of garter snakes she'd never let me smoke again. I tried it more than once when I was in junior high, but she squealed on me every time and managed to get me grounded more than once. But in the end, she saved me from myself."

To Theresa's left, Brian's laugh rolled like faraway thunder. She noted its full, mellow tone, and now, when she spoke, that tone became every fuller, richer.

"He did tell me about another incident with home permanents when you gave him one against your mother's orders and forgot to set the timer." While he teased, he studied her hair. Jeff had said it was red, but Brian hadn't expected it to be the hue of a poppy!

"Oh, that," she wailed, hiding a cheek behind a palm. "Jeff, did you have to blab that to him? I could have died when I took those curlers out and saw what I'd done to you.''

"*You* could have died? Mother was the one who could have died. That time it was *you* who should've gotten grounded, and I think you would have if you hadn't been eighteen already and going to college.''

"Let's finish the story, little brother. In spite of the fact that you looked like an explosion in a silo, it got you that spot in the band, didn't it? They took one look at that ball of frizz and decided you'd fit right in.''

"Which also put you beyond mother's good graces for the remainder of the summer, until I could prove I wasn't going to start sniffing cocaine and popping uppers every night before we played a gig.''

They had reached the escalator to the lower level where the luggage return was located, so were forced to break rank while riding down.

Studying the backs of the two heads below him, Brian Scanlon couldn't help envying the easy camaraderie between sister and brother. They hadn't seen each other for twelve months, yet they fell into a familiar groove of affectionate bantering as if they were good friends who saw each other daily. *They don't know how lucky they are,* he thought.

The revolving luggage carousels were surrounded, for holiday travel was at its heaviest with only a couple days left till Christmas. As they waited, Brian stood back and listened while the two of them filled in each other on family news.

"Mom and dad wanted to come and pick you up, but I got nominated instead because today was the last day of school before vacation. I got out at two, right after the Christmas program was over, but they both have to work till five, as usual.''

"How are they?''

"Do you have to ask? Absolutely giddy. Mom's been baking pies and putting them in the freezer, and worrying about whether pumpkin is still your favorite and dad kept asking her,

'Margaret, did you buy some of those poppy-seed rolls Jeff always liked?' And mom would lose patience and say, 'Willard, that's the third time you've asked me that, and this is the third time I'm answering. Yes, of course I bought poppy-seed rolls.' Yesterday she baked a German chocolate cake, and after all that fussing, came out and found dad had taken a slice from it. Boy, did the fur fly then. When she scolded him and informed him she'd baked the cake for dessert tonight, dad slunk off and took the car to the car wash and filled it up with gas for you. I don't think either one of them slept a wink last night. Mother was absolutely grumpy this morning, but you know how she gets when she's excited—the minute she sees you it'll dissolve like magic. Mostly she was upset because she had to work today when she'd rather have stayed home and gotten things ready, then come to the airport herself.''

It was plain to Brian that this homecoming had taken on premiere proportions in his family's hearts, even before Theresa went on.

"And just guess what dad did?"

Jeff only smiled a query. Theresa tipped him a smile with hidden meaning. "Get ready for this one, Jeff. He took your old Stella up to Viking Music and had new strings put on it and polished it all up and brought it out to the corner of the living room where you always used to leave it."

"You're kidding!"

"God's truth."

"Do you know how many times he threatened to turn both me and my fifteen-dollar Stella out of the house if the two of us didn't quit bruising his eardrums with all our racket?"

Just then a duffel bag came circling toward them, and Jeff shouldered forward to grab it. No sooner had he set it behind him than a guitar case followed. As he leaned to snag it, Theresa exclaimed, "Your guitar! You brought your guitar?"

"Guitars. Both of ours."

She glanced up at Brian Scanlon, remembering he, too,

played. She caught him studying her instead of the luggage return, his eyes the hue of rich summer moss, and Theresa quickly dropped her gaze.

"Can't let those calluses get soft," Jeff explained, "and anyway, two weeks without pickin' would be more than we could stand, right, Scan?"

"Right."

"But I promise I'll pick a few on the old Stella, just for dad."

A second guitar came bumping down the conveyor belt, followed by another duffel bag, and Theresa watched Brian's shoulders stretch his blue uniform jacket taut as he leaned to retrieve them. A young woman just behind Brian was giving him the once-over as he straightened and turned. The end of the guitar case caught her on the hip, and Brian immediately apologized.

The blonde flashed him a smile, and said, "Anytime, soldier boy."

For a moment he paused, then politely murmured, "Excuse me," and shouldered his duffel, glancing up to meet Theresa's eyes, which slid away shyly.

"All set?" She directed her question at her brother, because Brian made her uncomfortably aware of how inordinately pretty his eyes were for a man, and ever aware that they never dropped lower than her coat collar.

"Yup."

"Homeward bound. Let's go."

They stepped beyond the sliding doors of Minneapolis—St. Paul International into the crisp bite of December cold. Theresa walked between them again as they entered the cavernous concrete parking lot. But when they approached the correct row, she announced, "Dad and I traded cars for the day. I have his wagon, he has my Toyota."

"Hand me the keys. I'm dying to get behind a wheel again," her brother declared.

They loaded guitars and duffel bags into the rear and clambered inside. Through the fifteen-minute ride to the nearby suburb of Apple Valley, while Jeff and Theresa exchanged pleasantries, she tried to overcome her resentment of Brian Scanlon. She had nothing against him personally. How could she? She'd never met him before today. It was strangers in general—more particularly *male* strangers—she tried to avoid. Somehow she'd always thought Jeff guessed and understood. But apparently she was wrong, for when he'd called and enthusiastically asked if he could bring his buddy home to spend the Christmas holidays, then explained that Brian Scanlon had no family, there'd been no hesitation from Margaret Brubaker.

"Why, of course. Bring him. It would be just plain unchristian to make a man spend Christmas in some miserable barracks in North Dakota when there are beds to spare and enough food for an army."

Listening on the extension phone, Theresa had felt her heart fall. She'd wanted to interrupt her mother and say, Just a minute! Don't the rest of us have any say about it? It's *our* Christmas, too.

There were frustrations involved with living at home at age twenty-five, and though sometimes Theresa longed to live elsewhere, the certain loneliness she'd suffer if she made the move always gave her second thoughts. Yes, the house belonged to her mother and father. They could invite whom they chose. And even while Brian Scanlon's intrusion rankled, she realized how selfish her thoughts were. What kind of woman would deny the sharing of Christmas bounty with someone who had no home and family?

But as they drove through the late-afternoon traffic, Theresa's apprehension grew.

They'd be home in less than five minutes, and she'd have to take her coat off, and once she did, it would happen again, as it always did. And she'd want to slink off to her room and cry...as she often did.

Even as the thoughts flashed through her mind, Brian said in his well-modulated voice, "I certainly want to thank you for letting me come along with Jeff and horn in on your holidays."

Theresa felt a flush of guilt working its way past her high gray coat collar, and hoped he wasn't looking at her as she politely lied. "Don't be silly. There's an extra bed in the basement and never a shortage of food. We're all very happy that Jeff thought of inviting you. Since you two started up the band together you're all we hear about when he calls or writes. Brian this and Brian that. Mother's been dying to get an eye on you and make sure her *little boy* has been traveling in good company. But don't pay any attention to her. She used to practically make his girlfriends fill out an application blank with three references."

Just then they drew into the driveway of a very run-of-the-mill L-shaped rambler on a tree-lined street where the houses were enough alike as to be almost indistinguishable from one another.

"Looks like mom and dad haven't gotten home yet," Theresa noted. A fresh film of snow dusted the driveway. Only one set of tire tracks led from the garage, but a single pair of footprints led up to the back door. "But Amy must be here."

The doors of the station wagon swung open, and Jeff Brubaker stood motionless beside the car for a moment, scanning the house in the way of a man seeking reassurance that none of the familiar things had altered. "God, it's good to be home," he breathed, sucking in a great gulp of the cold, pure Minnesota air. Then he became suddenly effervescent, almost jogging around to the tailgate of the wagon. "Come on you two, let's get this junk unloaded."

Thinking ahead to the next five minutes, Theresa appropriated a guitar case to carry inside. She didn't know how she'd manage it, but if worse came to worst, she might be able to hide behind it.

At the sound of the tailgate slamming, a gangly fourteen-year-old girl came flying out the back door. "Jeffy, you're home!" Smiling with a flash of tooth braces, Amy Brubaker threw her arms wide with an open gesture Theresa envied. Not a day went by that Theresa didn't pray her sister be granted the blessing of growing normally.

"Hey, dumpling, how are ya?"

"I'm too big for you to call me dumpling anymore."

They embraced with sibling exuberance before Jeff plopped a direct kiss on Amy's mouth.

"Ouch!" She jerked back and made a face, then bared her teeth for inspection. "Look out when you do that. It hurts!"

"Oh, I forgot about the new hardware. Let's see." He tipped her chin up while she continued curling her lips back as if not in the least daunted by her unattractive braces. Looking on, Theresa wondered how it was her little sister had managed to remain so uninhibited and charmingly self-assured.

"I tell everybody I got 'em decorated just in time for Christmas," Amy declared. "After all, they do look a little like tinsel."

Jeff leaned back from the waist and laughed, then quirked a smile at his friend. "Brian, it's time you met the rambunctious part of the Brubaker family. This is Amy. Amy, here he is at last—Brian Scanlon. And as you can see, I've talked him into bringing his guitar so we can play a couple hot ones for you and your friends, just as ordered."

For the first time, Amy lost her loquaciousness. She jammed her hands as far as they'd go into the tight front pockets of her blue jeans and carefully kept her lips covering the new braces as she smiled and said almost shyly, "Hi."

"Hi, Amy. Whaddya say?" He extended his hand and smiled at Amy with as charming a grin as any of the rock stars beaming from the postered walls of her bedroom. Amy glanced at Brian's hand, made an embarrassed half shrug and finally dragged one hand from the blue denim and let Brian shake it. When he released it, the hand hung in the air between them for a full fifteen seconds while her smile grew and grew, until a reflection flashed from the bars of metal spanning her teeth.

Watching, Theresa thought, *oh, to be fourteen again, with a shape like Amy's, and the total lack of guile that allows her to gaze point-blank in unconcealed admiration, just as she's doing now!*

"Hey, it's cold out here!" Jeff gave an exaggerated shiver. "Let's go in and dig into mom's cake."

They carried duffel bags and guitar cases into the cheery front-facing kitchen of the simple house. The room was papered in an orange- and gold-flowered pattern that was repeated in the fabric inserts of the shutters on the windows flanking the eating area, which looked out on the front yard. An ordinary house on a street with others just like it, the Brubaker home had nothing exceptional to set it apart, except a sense of familial love that Brian Scanlon sensed even before the mother and father arrived to complete the circle.

On the kitchen table was a crocheted doily of white, and in the center sat a pedestal plate bearing a mouth-watering German chocolate cake under a domed lid. When Jeff lifted the lid, the gaping hole came into view. In the hollow wedge was a slip of folded paper. He took it out to reveal a recipe card from which he read aloud: "Jeff, it looked too good for me to resist. See you soon. Dad."

The four of them shared a laugh, but all the while Theresa stood with the broad end of Jeff's guitar case resting on the floor at her toes, and the narrow end shielding the front of her coat. She was the delegate hostess. She should ask for Brian's jacket and hat and make a move toward the hall closet.

"Come on, Brian," Jeff invited, "see the rest of the place." They moved to the living room and immediately four raucous, jarring chords sounded from the piano. Theresa grimaced and glanced at Amy who rolled her eyeballs. It was "Jeff's Outer Space Concerto."

They drew deep breaths in unison, signaled with nods and

bellowed simultaneously, "Je-e-e-eff, knock it off!" While the sisters giggled, Jeff explained to Brian, "I composed that when I was thirteen...before I became an impresario."

Theresa quickly hung up her coat in the front-hall closet and hustled down the hall to her bedroom. She found a pale blue cardigan sweater and whisked it across her shoulders without slipping her arms into the sleeves, then buttoned the top button at her throat. She glanced critically in the mirror, realigned the button-and-buttonhole panels so the sweater covered as much of her as possible, but found to her dismay it did little to disguise her problem. *Oh God, will I ever learn to live with it?*

Her usual, end-of-the-day backache plagued again, and she sighed, straightening her shoulders, but to no avail.

The house tour had stopped in the living room where Jeff had found his Stella. He was twanging out some metallic chords and singing an offbeat melody while Theresa tried to bolster her courage and walk out there. Undoubtedly it would be the same as it always was when she met a man. Brian Scanlon would scarcely glance at her face before his eyes would drop to her breasts and he would become transfixed by them. Since puberty she had relived those awful moments too many times to count, but Theresa had never become inured. That horrifying instant when a man's eyebrows twitched up in surprise, and his lips dropped open while he stared at the outsized mammary glands that had, through some unfortunate freak of nature, grown to proportions resembling volleyballs. They rode out before Theresa like a flagship before a fleet, their double-D circumference made the more pronounced by her delicately boned size-nine frame.

The last time she'd been introduced to a strange man he was the father of one of her second-grade pupils. Even as a parent, the poor man hadn't been able to remember protocol in his shock at glimpsing her enormous breasts. His eyes had riveted on them even while he was shaking Theresa's hand, and after that there'd been such awful tension between them the conference had been a disaster.

If she had carved a notch on her bedroom dresser every time that had happened down through the years, there'd be nothing before her now but a pile of wood chips. Now meeting the apprehensive eyes of the woman reflected in the mirror, Theresa quailed with all the familiar misgivings. Red hair and freckles! As if it wasn't enough that she'd been cursed with these mountainous breasts, she'd landed hair the color of paprika and skin that refused to tan. Instead it broke out in brilliant orange heat spots, as if she had an incurable rash, each time the sun grazed her skin. And this hair—oh, how she hated it! Coarse, springy ringlets that clung to her scalp like a Brillo pad if cut short, or if allowed to grow long, developed untamable waves reminiscent of those disastrous messes fried onto women's heads in the early days of the century before hot permanents had been perfected. Detesting it either way, she'd chosen a middle-of-the-road length and as innocuous a style as she could manage, brushing it straight back from her face and clasping it at her nape with a wide barrette, below which the "tail" erupted like a ball of fire from a volcano.

And what about eyelashes? Didn't every woman deserve to have eyelashes that could at least be seen? Theresa's were the same hue as her hair—pale threads that made the rims of her eyelids look pink and sickly while framing eyes that were almost the identical color of her freckles, a pale tea-brown. She thought of the dark spiky lashes and the stunning green of Brian Scanlon's eyes, and her own drooped to check her sweater once again, and tug it close together, as Theresa realized she could no longer avoid confronting him. She must return to the living room. And if he stared at her breasts with lascivious speculation she'd think of the strains of her favorite Chopin Nocturne, which always had a calming effect upon her.

Amy and Jeff were sitting on the davenport while Brian faced them from the seat of the piano bench. When Jeff caught sight of her, he thwacked the guitar strings dramatically, and let the chord reverberate in fanfare. "There she is!"

So much for slipping quietly into their midst.

Brian was no more than five feet away, still wearing his formal garrison cap. She was conscious of a wink of silver on the large eagle medallion centered above the black leather visor as his eyes swerved her way, directly on a level with the objects of Theresa's despair. Her pale brown eyes met his of sea green. The certainty of what would happen next seemed to lodge in her throat like a pill taken without water. *Now!* she thought. *Now it will happen!* She steeled herself for the sickening embarrassment that was certain to follow.

But Brian Scanlon relaxedly stretched six feet of blue-clad anatomy to its feet and smiled into Theresa's eyes, his own never wavering downward for even a fraction of a second or giving the impression that it even crossed his mind.

"Jeff's been demonstrating the old Stella. She doesn't sound too bad."

Aren't you going to gawk like everybody else? She felt the blush begin to tint her face because he *hadn't* looked, and to cover her fluster grabbed onto the first words that entered her mind.

"As usual, my brother thinks of nothing but music." Theresa strove to keep her voice steady, for her heart was knocking crazily. "And here you sit with your hat and jacket still on. I'll show you where you'll sleep, since neither one of these two had the courtesy to do it."

"I hope I'm not putting anybody out of their bed."

"Not at all. We're putting you on a hideaway bed in the family room downstairs. I just hope nobody puts you out of yours, because it'll be in front of the TV and fireplace, and dad likes to stay up at least until after the ten o'clock news."

He didn't look! He didn't look! The exaltation pounded through her brain as Theresa led the way back through the kitchen to the basement door that opened into the room just behind the stove wall. Oddly enough, she seemed more aware of Brian Scanlon because of the fact that he'd assiduously remained polite and refrained from dropping his eyes. She took his guitar and he his duffel bag, and she led him downstairs into a large basement area with a set of sliding glass doors facing the rear yard. The room was paneled in warm pecan and carpeted in burnt orange that burst into a glow as Theresa switched on a table lamp.

Brian watched her hair light up as she paused above the lamp, then scanned the room, which contained a country pine coffee table, a cushioned davenport and pillowed rockers in the Colonial style. A fireplace was flanked by a television set, and at the end of the room where Brian stood, a thick-legged kitchen set of glossy pine was centered before the sliding glass door.

"Mmm...I like this room. Very homey." His eyes came back to settle upon Theresa as he spoke.

He seemed the type who'd prefer art deco or chrome and glass, but an appreciative reaction riffled through Theresa, for her mother had largely let her choose the colors and textures of the furnishings when they'd redecorated two years ago. It wasn't her own house, but it gave Theresa a taste of home planning, making her eager for the day when she could exercise her own tastes through an entire house.

Brian noted her tightly crossed arms beneath the baby blue sweater and the nervousness that was absent only while her sister and brother were close by.

"I'm sorry it has no closet, but you can hang your things up here." She opened a door leading to an unfinished portion of the basement where the laundry facilities were housed.

He crossed toward her, and she stepped well back as he popped his head around the laundry-room doorway, one foot off the floor behind him. There was a rolling laundry rack with empty hangers tinging in the air currents from the opening of

the door. "There's no bath down here, but feel free to use the
upstairs tub or shower any time you want."

When he turned to her, his eyes again rested directly on hers
as he noted, "It sure beats the BOQ on base, especially at
Christmas time." She was conscious of how crisp and correctly
knotted his formal navy blue tie was, how smoothly the dark
blue military "blouse" contoured his chest and shoulders over
the paler blue of his shirt, of how flattering the square-set cap
was to the equally square-cut lines of his jaw.

"BOQ?" she questioned.

"Bachelor Officers' Quarters."

"Oh." She waited for his eyes to rove downward, but they
didn't. Instead, he began freeing the four silver buttons bearing
the eagle-and-shield U.S. Air Force insignia, turning his back
on her and taking a stroll around the room while freeing the
"blouse" and shrugging out of it. He slipped his hat off the
back of his head with a slow, relaxed movement, and she saw
his hair for the first time. It was a rich chestnut color,
trimmed—according to military regulations—far too short for
her taste, and bearing a ridge across the back from the band of
his cap. He turned toward Theresa again, and she noted that
around his face the chestnut hair held the suggestion of waves,
but was cut too short to allow them free rein. It would be much
more attractive an inch and a half longer, she decided.

"It feels good to get out of these things."

"Oh, here! Let me hang them up."

"Just the blouse—I mean the jacket. We get in trouble if we
hang up our caps."

As she came forward to take his jacket, he extended his cap,
too, and its inner band was still warm from his head. As she
scuttled away around the laundry-room doorway again, that
warmth seemed to singe her palm. When she tipped the cap
upside down to lay it on the rack above the clothes bar, a spicy
scent of some hair preparation found its way to her nostrils. It

seemed to cling to the jacket, too, as she threaded its shoulders over a hanger and hooked it on the rack.

When she returned to the family room, Brian was standing in front of the sliding glass doors with his hands in his trousers pockets, feet widespread, gazing out at the snowy yard where twilight was falling. For a long moment Theresa studied the back of his sky blue shirt where three crisp laundry creases gave him that clean-cut appearance of a model on a recruiting poster. The creases rose up out of the belted waistline of his trousers but disappeared across his shoulders where the blue fabric stretched taut as the head of a drum.

She crossed the room silently and flipped on an outside spotlight that flooded her father's bird feeder. Brian started at the snap of the light, glancing aside at her as she crossed her arms beneath the sweater and joined him at the wide window, studying the scene beyond.

"Every winter dad tries to entice cardinals, but so far this year we haven't had any. This is his favorite spot in the house. He brings his coffee down here in the mornings and sits at the table with his binoculars close at hand. He spends hours here."

"I can see why." Scanlon's eyes moved once more to the view outside where sparrows, caught in the beam of light that lit the snow to glimmering crystals, twittered and searched for fallen seed at the base of the feeder pole. The far edge of the property was delineated by a line of evergreens that appeared almost black in the waning light. Their limbs were laden with white. Suddenly a blue jay darted from them, squawking in the crass, impertinent note of superiority only a blue jay can muster, scattering the sparrows as he landed among them, then cocking his head and disdaining the seeds he jealously guarded.

"I wasn't sure if I should come with Jeff. I felt a little like I was horning in, you know?"

His hands were still buried in his trousers pockets, but she felt his eyes turn her way and hoped she wouldn't blush while attempting to lie convincingly. "Don't be silly, you're not horning in."

"Any stranger in the house at this time of the year is like a fifth wheel. I know that, but I couldn't resist Jeff's invitation when I thought about spending two weeks with nothing to do but stare at the bare walls of the quarters and talk to myself."

"I'm glad you didn't. Why, mother didn't hesitate a minute when Jeff called and suggested bringing you home. Besides, we've all heard so much about you in Jeff's letters, you hardly seem like a stranger. As a matter of fact, I believe *one* of us had a tiny bit of a crush on you even before you stepped out of the car in the driveway."

He laughed good-naturedly and shook his head at the floor as if slightly embarrassed, then rocked back on his heels. "It's a good thing she isn't six years older. She's going to be a real knockout at twenty."

"Yes, I know. Everybody says so."

Brian heard no note of rancor in Theresa's words, only a warm, sisterly pride. And he need not lower his eyes to her chest to see that as she spoke, her forearms unconsciously guarded her breasts more closely.

Thanks for warning me, Brubaker, he thought, recalling all that Jeff had told him about his sister. *But apparently Jeff told his family as much about my background as he told me about them,* he thought, as Theresa went on in a sympathetic note.

"Jeff told us about your mother. I'm sorry. It must have been terrible to get the news about the plane crash."

He studied the snow again and shrugged. "In a way it was, in a way it wasn't. We were never close after my dad died, and once she'd remarried, we didn't get along at all. Her second husband thought I was a drug addict because I played rock music, and he didn't waste any more time on me than was absolutely necessary."

She evaluated her own family, so warm, supporting, so full of love, and resisted the urge to lay a comforting hand on

Brian's arm. She felt guilty for the many times she'd wished Jeff wouldn't bring him home. It had been thoroughly selfish, she chided herself, guarding her family's Christmas from outsiders just as the jay guarded the seeds he didn't want to eat.

This time when she said the words, Theresa found they were utterly sincere. "We're glad to have you here, Brian."

Chapter Two

"They're home!" shouted Jeff overhead, then he stuck his head around the basement doorway and ordered, "Hey, you two, get up here!"

As an outside observer, Brian couldn't help envying Jeff Brubaker his family, for the greeting his friend received in the arms of his mother and father was an emotional display of honest love. Margaret Brubaker was hiking her rotund body out of the deep bucket seat of the low-slung Celica when Jeff swooped down on her. The grocery bag in her arms was unceremoniously dropped onto the snowy driveway in favor of hugs and kisses interspersed with tears, hellos and general exuberance while Willard Brubaker came around the car and took his turn—albeit with far fewer tears than his wife, but there was an undeniable glitter in his eye as he backed off and assessed Jeff.

"Good to have you home, son."

"I'll say it is," put in his mother, then the trio shared an enormous three-way hug. Margaret stepped back, crushing a loaf of bread. "Land! Would you look at what I've done with these groceries. Willard, help me pick 'em up."

Jeff waylaid them both. "Forget the groceries for now. I'll come back and get 'em in a minute. Come and meet Brian." With an arm around each of his parents' shoulders, Jeff shepherded them into the kitchen where Brian waited with the two girls. "These are the two who had the courage to have a kid like me—my mom and dad. And this is Brian Scanlon."

Willard Brubaker pumped Brian's hand. "Glad to have you with us, Brian."

Margaret's greeting was, "So this is Jeff's Brian."

"I'm afraid so, for all of two weeks. I really appreciate your invitation, Mrs. Brubaker."

"There are two things we have to get settled right now," Margaret stated without prelude, pointing an accusatory finger. "The first is that you don't call me Mrs. Brubaker, like I'm some commanding officer. Call me Margaret. And the other is...you don't smoke pot, do you?"

Amy rolled her eyeballs in undisguised chagrin, but the rest of them shared a good-natured laugh that managed to break the ice even before Brian answered frankly, "No, ma'am. Not anymore." There was a moment of surprised silence, then everyone burst into laughter again. And Theresa looked at Brian in a new light.

To Brian it seemed the Brubaker house was never quiet. Immediately after the introductions, Margaret was flinging orders for "you two boys" to pick up the groceries she'd dropped in the driveway. Supper preparations set up the next clatter as fried potatoes started splattering in a frying pan, and dishes were clinked against silverware at the table. In the living room, Jeff picked up his old guitar, but after a few minutes, shouted, "Amy, will you go shut off your damn stereo! It's thumping through the wall loud enough to drive a man crazy!" The only quiet one of the group appeared to be Willard, who calmly settled himself into a living-room chair and read the evening newspaper as if the chaos around him didn't even register. Within ten minutes it was evident to Brian who ruled the Brubaker roost. Margaret issued orders like a drill sergeant whether she wanted to be called Margaret or not. But she controlled her brood with a sharp tongue that wielded as much humor as hauteur.

"Theresa, now don't fry those potatoes till they're tougher than horsehide the way you like 'em. Don't forget your father's false teeth. Jeff, would you play something else in there? You know how I've always hated that song! What ever happened to the good old standards like 'Moonlight Bay'? Amy, get two folding chairs out of the front closet and keep your fingers off that coconut frosting till dessert time. Willard, keep that dirty newsprint off the arms of the chair!''

To Brian's surprise, Willard Brubaker peered over the top of his glasses, muttered too softly for his wife to hear, ''Yes, my little turtledove,'' then caught Jeff's eye, and the two exchanged grins of amused male tolerance. Willard's gaze caught Brian's next, and the older man gave a quick wink, then buried himself behind his paper again, resting it on the arms of the chair.

Supper was plentiful and plain: Polish sausage, fried potatoes, baked beans and toast—Jeff's favorite meal. Willard sat at the head of the table, Margaret at the foot, the two ''girls'' on one side and the two ''boys'' across from them.

While they ate, Brian observed Margaret's buxom proportions and realized from whom Theresa had inherited her shape. Throughout the pleasant meal Theresa kept her blue sweater over her shoulders, though there were times when it plainly got in her way. Occasionally, Brian glanced up to find Amy gazing at him with an expression warning of imminent puppy love, though Theresa never seemed to look at him at all.

Midway through the meal the phone rang, and Amy popped up to get it.

''Hello,'' she said, then covered the mouthpiece and looked disgusted. ''It's for you, Jeffy. It sounds like dumb old Glue Eyes.''

''Watch your mouth, little sister, or I'll wire your top braces to your bottom ones.'' Jeff took the phone and Amy returned to the table.

''Glue Eyes?'' Brian glanced at Theresa.

''Patricia Gluek,'' she answered, ''his old girlfriend. Amy

never liked the way Patricia used to put on her makeup back in high school, so she started calling her Glue Eyes."

Amy plopped into her chair with a grunt of exasperation. "Well, she plastered it on so thick it looked like her eyelashes were glued together, not to mention how thick she used to plaster Jeff with all those purrs and coos. She makes me sick."

"Amy!" snapped Margaret, and Amy had the grace to desist.

Brian curled an eyebrow at Theresa, and again she enlightened him. "Amy worships Jeff. She'd like to keep him all to herself for two solid weeks."

Just then Jeff dropped the receiver against his thigh and asked, "Hey, you two, want to pick up Patricia after supper and go to a movie or something?"

Brian craned around to look over his shoulder at Jeff.

Theresa gulped. "Who, me?"

Jeff flashed an indulgent smile. "Yeah, you and Bry."

Already Theresa could feel the color creeping up her neck. She never went on dates, and most certainly not with her brother's friends, who were all younger than herself.

Brian turned back to Theresa. "It sounds fine with me, if it's all right with Theresa."

"Whaddya say, Treat?" Jeff was jiggling the phone impatiently, and the eyes of everyone at the table turned to the blushing redhead. A bevy of excuses flashed through her mind, all of them as phony as those she'd dreamed up on the rare occasions when single male teachers from school asked her out. At her elbow she sensed Amy gaping in undisguised envy.

Brian realized the house was totally silent for the first time since he'd entered it and wished the rock music was still throbbing from Amy's room. It was obvious Theresa was caught in a sticky situation where refusal would be rude, yet he could tell she didn't want to say yes.

"Sure, that sounds fun."

She avoided Brian's eyes, but felt them hesitate on her for

a minute while Jeff finalized the plans, and she withdrew from center stage by going to get dessert plates for the German chocolate cake.

When the meal was finished and Theresa was helping with dishes, she cornered Jeff for a moment as he passed through the kitchen.

"Jeffrey Brubaker, what on earth you were thinking of, to suggest such a thing?" she whispered angrily. "I'll pick my own dates, thank you."

"Lighten up, sis. Brian's not a date."

"You bet he's not. Why, he must be four years younger than I am!"

"Two."

"Two! That's even worse! Why, it makes it look like—"

"All right, all right! What are you so upset about?"

"I'm not upset. You just put me on the spot, that's all."

"Did you have other plans for tonight?"

"On your first night home?" she asked pointedly. "Of course not."

"Great. Then the least you'll get out of the deal is a free movie."

Oh no! the peeved Theresa vowed. *I'll pay my own way!*

Getting ready to go, Theresa couldn't help but admire how carefully Brian had concealed his reluctance. After all, who'd want to be saddled with a *big* sister? And worse yet, a frecklehead like her? She scowled at the copper dots in the mirror and despised each one with renewed intensity. She tried to yank a brush through her disgusting hair, but it was like a frayed sisal rope, only not nearly as pleasing in color. *Damn you, Jeffrey Brubaker, don't you ever do this to me again.* She drew the hair to the nape of her neck, tied it with a navy blue ribbon and considered makeup. But she owned none except lipstick, which she slashed onto her surly lips as if scrawling graffiti on a rest room wall. *I'll get you for this, Jeff.* Little thought was given to the clothing she chose, beyond the certainty that she'd put on her gray coat and leave it buttoned until they got back home.

She wasn't, however, planning on running into Brian in the front hall by the coat closet. When she did, she came up short, caught without a sweater or guitar or table to hide behind. Instinctively, one hand went up to finger her blouse collar—it was the best she could do.

"Jeff went out to start the car," Brian announced.

"Oh." The word was barely out of her mouth before Theresa realized Brian had shed military attire in favor of brown tennis shoes, bone-colored corduroys and a polo-style shirt of wide horizontal stripes in red and beige. He'd been carrying a brown leather waist-length jacket, and shrugged it on while she watched, transfixed. If Brian had subjected Theresa to the blatant inspection she gave him, she'd have ended up in her room in tears. She hadn't even realized how pointedly she'd been staring until her eyes traveled back up to his. She felt utterly foolish.

But if he noticed, he gave not the slightest clue beyond the hint of a smile that disappeared as quickly as it had come. "All ready?"

"Yes." She reached for her gray coat, but he took it from her hands without asking and held it for her. Even as Theresa felt the flush coloring her cheek at the unfamiliar gesture of good manners, she could do nothing but slip her arms into the coat, exposing the front of her so there was no hiding her proportions.

They called good-night to her parents and Amy and stepped out into the biting winter night. Theresa had gone on few enough dates in her life that it was difficult not to feel seduced into believing this was one, for he held the door of the station wagon while she slid in next to Jeff, then slipped his arm across the back of the seat as he settled in, too. She caught the drift of the same scent she'd detected when he handed her his cap earlier, and since Theresa wasn't a woman given to using perfumes herself, his faint hint of...sandalwood, that was it, came through all the clearer.

Jeff had the radio on—there was always a radio on—and he turned it louder as the gravelly voice of Bob Seger came on. Jeff's own voice had the grating earthiness of Seger's, and he picked up the refrain and sang along.

"We've got to learn this one, Bry."

"Mmm...it's smooth. Nice harmony on the chorus."

When the chorus came around again, the three sang along with it, their harmony resonant and true. "Ooo, shame on the moon...." Beside her, Theresa heard Brian's voice for the first time—straightforward, mellow, the antithesis of Jeff's. It sent shivers up her arms.

When they reached Patricia Gluek's house, Jeff went inside while Theresa and Brian transferred to the back seat, leaving a respectable distance between them. The radio was still playing and the lights from the dashboard lent an ethereal glow to the space beyond the front seat.

"How long have you and Jeff been playing and singing together?"

"Over three years now. We met when we were stationed at Zweibrücken together and started up a band there, and luckily we both landed at Minot Air Force Base, so we decided to look for a new drummer and bass player and keep a good thing rolling."

"I'd love to hear the band sometime."

"Maybe you will."

"I doubt it. I don't have many chances to swing by Minot, North Dakota."

"We'd like to get a new group started when we get out next summer, and hire an agent and make it a regular thing. Hasn't Jeff mentioned it?"

"Why, no, but I think it's a great idea, at least for Jeff. He's wanted to be a musician since he spent that first fifteen dollars on his Stella and started picking up chords from anybody who'd teach him.''

"Same with me. I've been playing since I was twelve, but I want to do more than just play.''

"What else?''

"I'd like to try writing, arranging. And I've always had the urge to be a disc jockey.''

"You have the voice for it.'' He certainly did. She remembered her first appreciative surprise upon hearing it earlier. But it went on now, turning attention away from himself.

"Enough about me. I hear you're into music, too.''

"Grades one through six, Sky Oaks Elementary.''

"Do you like it?''

"I love it, with the rare exceptions like yesterday during the Christmas program when Keri Helling and Dawn Gafkjen got into a fight over who was going to be the pink ornament and who was going to be the blue one and ended up crying and getting the crepe-paper costumes all soggy.'' She chuckled. "No, seriously, I love teaching the younger kids. They're guileless, and open, and...'' *And they don't gawk.* "And accepting,'' she finished.

Just then Jeff returned with Patricia, and introductions were made as Brian and Patricia shook hands over the front seat. Theresa had known the girl for years. She was a vivacious brunette, now in her second year at Normandale Community College. She was waiting to step into her former status as Jeff's girlfriend the moment he got out of the service, though they'd agreed to date others during their four years apart. So far, though, the attraction had not faded, for each of the three times Jeff had been home, he and Patricia had been inseparable.

When the pretty brunette turned toward the front, Theresa was chagrined to see her and Jeff share a more intimate hello than they'd apparently exchanged inside the house. Jeff's arms went around Patricia, and her head drifted to his shoulder while they kissed in a way that sent the blood filling up the space between Theresa's freckles. Beside her, Brian sat unmoving, watching the kiss that was taking place in such a forthright manner it was hard to ignore.

Goodness, would they never stop? The seconds ticked away while the music from the radio didn't quite conceal the soft murmurs from the front seat. Theresa wanted to crawl into a hole and pull the earth over her head.

Brian laced his fingers over his belly, slumped low in the seat, dropped his head back lazily and politely turned to gaze out his side window.

I am twenty-five years old, thought Theresa, *and I've never known before exactly what was implied by "double date."* She, too, gazed out her dark window.

There was a faint rustle, and, thankfully, it was Jeff's arm lifting from around Patricia's shoulders. The wagon chunked into gear, and they were moving at last.

At the theater, Theresa made a move toward her purse, but Brian stepped between her and the counter, announcing unceremoniously, "I'll get it." So, rather than make an issue of the four-dollar expenditure, she politely backed off.

When he turned, she said, "Thank you."

But he made no reply, only tipped his shoulders aslant while slipping his billfold into a back pocket where the beige wales of the corduroy were slightly worn in a matching square that captured Theresa's eyes and made her mouth go dry. He turned around, caught her gaze, and she wished she'd never come.

Things got worse when they'd settled into their seats and the movie began, for it had an "R" rating, and exposed enough skin to create sympathetic sexual reactions in a sworn celibate! Halfway through the film the camera zoomed in on a bare spine, curved hips and a naked feminine back over which two masculine hands played, their long, blunt fingers feathered with traces of dark hair. A naked hirsute chest rolled into view, and the side of an apple-sized breast, then—horror of horrors!—an upthrust nipple, controlled by the broad, dark hand. A bearded jaw eased into the frame, and a mouth closed over the distended nipple.

In her seat beside Brian, Theresa wanted more than ever to simply, blessedly, *die*. His elbows rested on the armrests, and his fingers were laced together, the outer edges of his index fingers absently stroking his lips as he slumped rather low in the seat.

Why didn't I consider something like this happening? Why didn't I ask what was playing? Why didn't I wisely stay home in the first place?

Theresa tolerated the remainder of the love scene, and as it progressed a queer reaction threaded through her body. Saliva pooled beneath her tongue. She could feel her pulse throbbing in the place where her purse was pressed tightly against her lap. And a quicksilver liquid sensation trickled through her innards, setting her alive with sensations she'd never experienced before. But outwardly, she sat as if a sorcerer had cast a spell upon her. Not so much as a pale eyelash blinked. Not a muscle twitched. She stared spellbound as the climax was enacted, reflected in the facial expressions of the man and woman on the screen and the animal sounds of fulfillment.

And not until those climaxes ended did Theresa realize Brian's elbow had been skewering hers with pressure that grew, and grew, and grew....

The scene changed, and he wilted, pulling his elbow against his side as if only now realizing what he'd been doing. Her elbow actually hurt from the pressure he'd been applying. He shifted uncomfortably in his seat, crossed an ankle over a knee and negligently dropped his laced fingers over the zipper of his corduroy pants.

Considering what had happened within her own body, Theresa had little doubt the same had happened to Brian. The remainder of the film was lost on her. She was too aware of the man on her right, and she found herself wondering who he'd been thinking of while the pressure on her elbow increased.

She found herself wondering things about the male anatomy that the screen had carefully hidden. She recalled pictures she'd seen in the bolder magazines, but they seemed as flat, cold and lifeless as the paper upon which they'd been printed. For the first time in her life, she ached to know what the real thing was like.

When the film ended, she took refuge in chattering with Patricia, making certain she walked far enough ahead of Brian that their elbows didn't touch or their eyes meet.

"Anybody hungry?" Jeff inquired when they were back in the station wagon.

Theresa felt slightly queasy, sitting once again with Brian only a foot away. If she tried eating anything, she wasn't sure it would stay down.

"No!" she exclaimed, before anybody else could agree.

"Yeah, I—" Brian spoke at the same time, then politely changed course. "I've been thinking about a piece of your mother's German chocolate cake all through the movie."

In a pig's eye, thought Theresa.

Oddly enough, nobody talked about the film as they drove back to Patricia's house. Nobody said much of anything. Patricia was snuggled up with her shoulder behind Jeff's. Now and then he'd turn and smile down at her with the dash lights clearly outlining the ardent expression on his face. Patricia's shoulder moved slightly, and Theresa conjured up the possibility of where her hand might be. Theresa gazed out her window and blushed for perhaps the tenth time that day.

When they pulled up in Patricia's driveway, Jeff turned off all the lights and gathered Patricia into his arms without a moment's hesitation. Behind the couple, another man and woman sat like two bumps on a log.

Kisses, Theresa discovered, have more sound than you'd think. From the front seat came the distinct rush of hastened breathing, the faint suggestive sounds of lips parting, positions changing, the rustle of hands moving softly. The rasp of a zipper sizzled through the dark confines of the car, and Theresa jumped, but immediately wished she hadn't, for it was only Jeff's jacket.

"Come on, Theresa, what do you say we go for a little walk?" Brian suggested. The overhead light flashed on, and she hustled out his door, so relieved she wanted to throw her arms around him and kiss him out of sheer gratitude.

When the door slammed behind them, Theresa surprised herself by releasing a pent-up breath and bursting out with the last words she expected to say. *"Thank you."*

He stuck his hands into his jacket pockets and chuckled. "No need to thank me. I was getting a little uncomfortable myself."

His admission surprised her, but the frankness definitely relieved some of the tension.

"I can see I'll have to talk with my little brother about decorum. I wasn't exactly sure what to do!"

"What did you used to do when that happened on double dates?"

She was embarrassed to have to admit, "I've never been on a double date bef—" She stopped herself just in time and amended, "I've never been on one."

"Aw, think nothing of it. They're both adults. He loves her—he's told me so more than once—and he intends to marry her soon after his hitch is done."

"You amaze me. I mean, you take it all in stride." *Heavens,* thought Theresa, *do couples do things like that in the same car with as little compunction as her brother showed and think nothing of it?* She realized suddenly how very, very naive she must seem to Brian Scanlon.

"He's my friend. I don't judge my friends."

"Well, he's my brother, and I'm afraid I do."

"Why? He's twenty-one years old."

"I know, I know." Theresa threw up her hands, exasperated with herself and uncomfortable with the subject.

"How old are you, Theresa? Twenty-five, right?"

"Yes."

"And I take it you haven't done a lot of that sort of thing."

"No." *Because every time I got in a car with a boy, he went after only the most obvious two things, never caring about the person behind them.* "I was busy studying when I was in high school and college, and since then...well, I don't go out much."

They were ambling down a snowy street, feet lifting lazily as the streetlights made the surface snow glitter. Her coat was still buttoned high, and her hands were buried in its pockets. Their breaths created white clouds, and their soles pressed brittle ice that crunched with each step.

"So, what did you think of the movie?" Brian asked.

"It embarrassed me," she admitted.

"I'm sorry."

"It's not your fault, it's Jeff's. He's the one who picked it."

"Next time we'll be sure to ask before we blindly follow him, okay?"

Next time? Theresa glanced up to find Brian smiling down at her with an easy laziness that was meant to put her at ease, but that lifted her heart in a strange, weightless way. She should have answered, "There won't be a next time," but instead smiled in return and concurred. "Agreed."

They turned around and were heading toward the Gluek driveway when Jeff backed the station wagon onto the street and its lights arced around, caught them in the glare, and he pulled up beside them.

"Would you two mind if we took you home?" Jeff asked when Theresa and Brian were settled in the back seat again.

"Not at all," Brian answered for both of them.

"Thanks for understanding, Bry. And Treat, you'll take good care of him, won't you?"

She wanted to smack her brother on the side of the head. Jeffrey Brubaker certainly took a lot for granted!

"Sure." What else could she have answered?

When they pulled up at home, Brian opened his door and the light flashed on. Patricia Gluek turned around and hooked an elbow over the back of the seat.

"Listen, a group of us are getting together at the Rusty Scupper on New Year's Eve, and you're both invited to join us. We plan to have dinner there and stay for the dancing afterward. It'll be a lot of the old gang—you've met them all before, Theresa—so what do you say?"

Damn it, does the whole world think it has to line up escorts for the wimpy little Theresa Brubaker who never gets asked out on dates? But she knew in her heart that Patricia was only being cordial and thinking about Brian, too, who was Jeff's houseguest and couldn't very well be excluded. He had one foot on the driveway, but this time instead of putting Theresa on the spot, he answered, "We'll talk it over and let you know, okay?"

"Some people from school are having a party in their home, and I told them I might go." The manufactured tale came glibly to Theresa's lips while she was still puzzling out where it had come from.

"Oh." Patricia sounded genuinely disappointed. "Well, in that case, you'll come, won't you, Brian? We have to make dinner reservations in advance."

"I'll think it over."

"Fine."

Brian swiveled toward the open door, but Jeff reached out and caught his arm. "Listen, Scan, thanks. I mean, I guess I ought to come in with you and play the host, but I'll see you in the morning at breakfast."

"Go on. Have a good time and don't worry about me."

When the car pulled away, Theresa and Brian stood on the back step while she dug in her purse for the house keys. When she found them and opened the door, they stepped into a dim kitchen where only a single bulb shone down on top of the white stove. It was silent—no stereo, no guitar, no voices.

They were both excruciatingly aware of what Jeff and Patricia were probably going off to do, and it created a corresponding sexual tension between them.

Seeking a diversion, Theresa whispered, "You said you were hungry for cake. There's plenty of it left."

He wasn't, really, but Brian wasn't at all averse to spending a little more time with Theresa, and the cake offered an excuse.

"I will if you will."

"It sounds good."

She moved toward the front hall, which was in total shadow, and made no move to turn on the light while removing her coat. Again, Brian was behind her to help her out of the garment, then hang it up. She left him there with a murmured thanks and returned to the kitchen to find two plates, forks and glasses of milk, taking them to the table where the cake still sat.

He joined her, choosing a chair at a right angle to hers, and they sat for a long time eating, saying nothing. The rafters of the house creaked in the December cold, and though it was very dark with only the small hood light illuminating the blotch of stove beneath it, she sensed Brian Scanlon studying her while he downed gulps of milk that sounded clearly in the silence.

"So, you're going to a party with someone from school on New Year's Eve?"

"No, I made that up."

His chin came up in surprise. "Oh?"

"Yes. I don't like people arranging dates for me, and furthermore, you don't need to be saddled with *me* on New Year's Eve. You go with Jeff and meet his friends. He's got some really nice—"

"*Saddled* with you?" he interrupted in that smooth, deep, unnerving voice that sent shivers up her nape.

"Yes."

"Did I give you the impression tonight that I resented being with you?"

"You know what I mean. You didn't come home with Jeff to have to haul me around every place you go."

"How do you know?"

She was stunned, she could only stammer. "You...I...."

"Would it surprise you to know that you're a big part of why I wanted to meet Jeff's family?"

"I...." But once again, she was struck dumb.

"He's told me a lot about you, Theresa. A lot."

Oh, Lord, how much? How much? Jeff, who knows my innermost fears. Jeff, who understands. Jeff, who can't keep anything to himself.

"What has he told you?" She tried to control the panic, but it crept into her voice, creating a vibrato that could not be disguised.

He made himself more comfortable, stretching his long legs somewhere beneath the table to find the seat of a chair as he leaned back to study her shadowed face speculatively. His eyes held points of light as he caught an elbow on the table edge and braced one jaw on his knuckles, tipping his head.

"About how you looked out for him when he was a kid. About your music. The violin and piano. How you used to sing duets for your family reunions and pass the hat for nickels afterward, then, as soon as you had enough, go to the store to buy your favorite forty-fives." His lips lifted in a slow half smile, and his free hand moved the milk glass in circles against the tabletop.

"Oh, is that all?" Her shoulders wilted with relief, but in the dimness she had crossed her elbows on the tabletop and took refuge behind them as best she could.

"You always sounded as if you'd be someone I could get along with. And maybe I liked you even before I met you because he likes you so much, and you're his sister and I also like him very much.''

Theresa was unused to being told she was liked. In her lifetime a few of the opposite sex had overtly tried to demonstrate what they "liked" about her, in the groping, insulting way she'd come to despise. But Brian seemed to have come to admire something deeper, her little-exposed self, her musicality, her familial relations. All this before he had ever laid eyes on her.

But those eyes were on her now, and though she could not make out their color in the veiling shadows, she caught the sparkle as he continued perusing her freely, the tip of his little finger now resting in the hollow beneath his full lower lip. She seemed unable to draw her eyes away from it as he went on quietly.

"I'd love to go to that party with you on New Year's Eve.''

Their eyes met, hers wide with surprise, his carefully unflirtatious.

"But you're...you're two years younger than I am.'' Once she'd said it, she wanted to eat the words.

But he asked undauntedly, "Does that bother you?''

"Yes, I....'' She blew out a huge breath of air and leaned her forehead on the heel of one hand. "I can't believe this conversation.''

"It doesn't bother me in the least. And I sure as hell don't want to go to that kind of a thing alone. Everybody'll be paired off, and I won't have anybody to dance with.''

"I don't dance.'' *That* was the understatement of the night. Dancing was a pleasure she'd abandoned when her breasts grew too large to make fast dancing comfortable, their sway and bob not only hurting, but making Theresa feel sure they must appear obscene from the sidelines. And chest-to-chest dancing was even worse—being that close to men, she'd found, only gave them ideas.

"A musical woman like you?''

"Music and dancing are two different things. I've just never cared for—"

"There's time before New Year's Eve to learn. Maybe we can change your mind."

"Let me think about it, okay?"

"Sure." He got to his feet, and the chair scraped back, then he carried their two plates across the room and set them in the sink with a soft chink.

She opened the basement door and snapped on the light above the steps. "Well, I'm not sure if mother made your bed down here or not."

She heard his steps following her down the carpeted incline, and prayed she'd find his bed all decked out, ready for him, so she could simply wish him good-night and escape to her own room upstairs.

Unfortunately, the davenport wasn't either opened or made up, so Theresa had little choice but to cross the room and begin the chore. She tossed the cushions aside, conscious now that Brian had snapped on the lamp, and it flooded the area with mellow light that revealed her clearly while she tugged on the folded mattress and brought it springing out into the room.

"I'll get the bedding," she explained, and hustled into the laundry room to find clean sheets and blankets on a shelf there. He had turned on the television set when she came back out to the family room, and a late movie was glimmering on the screen in black and white. The volume was only a murmur as she shook out a mattress pad, concentrating fully on it when Brian stepped to the opposite side of the davenport to help her.

His long fingers smoothed the quilted surface with the expertise of a soldier who's been trained to keep his bunk in inspection-ready order. A sheet snapped and billowed in the air between them, and above it their glances met, then dropped. Images of the movie's love scene came back to titillate Theresa, while they tucked the corners of the sheets in, and Brian's hands pulled it far more expertly than hers, for hers were shaking and seemed nearly inept.

"Tight enough to bounce a coin," he approved.

She glanced up to find him looking at her instead of the sheet, and wondering what this man was doing to her. She had never in her life been as sexually aware of a male as she was of him. Men had brought her nothing but shame and intimidation, and she'd avoided them. Yet here she stood, gazing into the green eyes of Brian Scanlon over his half-prepared bed, wondering what it would be like to do with him the things she'd seen on a movie screen.

Redheads look ugly when they blush, she thought.

"The other sheet," he reminded her, and abashed, she turned to find it.

When the bed was finally done, she found her pulses leaping like Mexican jumping beans. But there still remained one duty she, as hostess, must perform.

"If you'll come upstairs, I'll give you clean towels and washcloths, and show you where the bathroom is."

"Jeff showed me after supper."

"Oh. Oh...good. Well, feel free to shower or...or whatever, anytime. You can hang your wet towels over the sink in the laundry room."

"Thank you."

They stood one on either side of the bed, and she suddenly realized she was facing him fully for the first time without shielding her breasts. Not once since she'd met him had she noticed him looking at them. His eyes were fastened on the freckled cheeks, then they moved up to her detestable red hair, and she realized she'd been standing without moving for a full thirty seconds.

"Well...good night then." Her voice was soft and shaky.

"Good night, Theresa." His was deep and quiet.

She scuttled away, racing up the stairs as if he were chasing her with ill intent. When she was settled into bed with the lights out, she heard him come upstairs and use the bathroom.

Put a pillow over your ears, Theresa Brubaker! But she listened to all the sounds coming from beyond her bedroom wall, and two closed doors, and envisioned Brian Scanlon performing his bedtime rituals and wondered for the first time in her life how a husband and wife ever made it through the intimacies of the first week of marriage.

Chapter Three

The following morning, Theresa was awakened by the thump-thump-thump of Amy's stereo reverberating through the floor. Rolling over, she squinted at the alarm clock, then shot out of bed as if it was on fire. Ten o'clock! She should have been up two hours ago to fix breakfast for Brian and Jeff!

Within minutes she was washed, combed, dressed in blue jeans and a loose white blouse with a black cardigan slung across her shoulders and buttoned beneath the blouse collar.

Her parents had gone to work long ago. Jeff's door was closed, and the sound of his snoring came from beyond. It appeared Amy was still in her room, torturing her hair with a curling iron while Theresa tried to tame her springing curls by smoothing a hand over the infamous tail that bounced on her shoulders.

She crept down the hall to the kitchen but found it empty. The basement door was open—it appeared Brian was up. She was filling the coffeepot when he slipped silently to the doorway leading directly to the kitchen from one side of the living room.

"Good morning."

She spun around, sending water flying everywhere, pressing a hand to her heart.

"Oh! I didn't know you were there! I thought you were still downstairs."

"I've been awake for a long time. Routine is hard to break."

"Have you been sitting in there all by yourself?"

"No." He grinned engagingly. "With Stella."

She grinned back. "And how did you two get along?" She put coffee in the percolator basket and set the pot on the stove burner.

"She's a brassy old girl, but I talked sweet to her and she responded like a lady."

It wasn't what he said, but how he said it that made Theresa's cheeks pink. There was an undertone of teasing, though the words were totally polite. She wasn't used to such a tone of voice when speaking with men, but it, combined with his lazy half smile while he leaned one shoulder against the doorway, gave her the feeling she imagined a cat must have when its fur was slowly stroked the wrong way.

"I didn't hear you playing."

"We were whispering to each other."

Again, she couldn't resist smiling.

"I...I'm sorry nobody was up to fix breakfast for you. It's my first day of Christmas vacation, and I guess my body decided to take advantage of it. I never even wiggled at the usual wake-up time. I heard Jeff still snoring. He must have come in late."

"It was around three."

So—he hadn't been able to sleep. Neither had she.

"Three!"

He shrugged, his shoulder still braced on the doorway. He was wearing tight, faded blue jeans and a white football jersey that hugged his ribs just enough to make them tantalizing.

She recalled how long it had taken her to get to sleep after the curious way he'd managed to stir her senses last night, and wondered what had really kept him awake. Had he lain in the dark thinking of the movie as she had? Thinking of Jeff and Patricia in the car? Himself and her having cake and milk in the dusky kitchen?

His slow perusal was beginning to make Theresa's nerves jump, so she shrugged. "Why don't you sit down, and I'll pour you a glass of juice?"

He obliged, though she still wasn't rid of his gaze, even after she gave him a glass of orange juice. His eyes followed her lazily as she turned the bacon, scrambled eggs and dropped bread into the toaster.

"What do you and Jeff have planned for today?"

"I don't know, but whatever it is, I was hoping you could come along."

Her heart skipped, and she was disappointed at what she had to reply. "Oh, no, I have too much to do to help mother for tomorrow night, and I have to get ready for the concert I'm playing in tonight."

"Oh, that's right. Jeff told me. Civic orchestra, isn't it?"

"Uh-huh. I've been in it for three years and I really enjoy—"

"Well, good morning, you two." It was Amy, barely giving her sister a glance, aiming her greeting primarily at Brian. To his credit, he didn't flinch even slightly at the sight of Amy, decked out in crisp blue jeans that fit her like a shadow, a skinny little sweater that fit nearly as close, craftily styled hair with its shoulder-length auburn feather cut blown and curled back from her face in that dewy-fresh style so stunningly right for teenage girls. Her makeup application could have taught "Glue Eyes" a thing or two several years ago.

"I thought teenagers spent their vacations flopping around in baggy overalls these days," Brian noted, managing to compliment Amy without encouraging any excess hope.

"Mmm..." Amy simpered. "That just goes to show what you know."

But Theresa was fully aware that had Brian not been under the roof, that's exactly how Amy would have spent her day, only she wouldn't have poked her nose out of her burrow until one o'clock in the afternoon.

Amy stepped delicately to the stove and lifted a piece of cooling bacon, nibbled it with a provocative daintiness that quite surprised her sister. Where in the world had Amy learned to act this way? When? Just since Brian Scanlon had walked into the house?

"Amy, if you want bacon and eggs, get yourself a plate," Theresa scolded, suddenly annoyed by her sister's flirtatiousness. Even though she realized how small it was to feel a twinge of irritation at this new side Amy was displaying, Theresa was undeniably piqued. Perhaps because the fourteen-year-old had the remarkably freckle-free skin, hair the color of most Kentucky Derby winners and a trim, tiny shape that must be the envy of half the girls in her freshman class at school. Theresa suddenly felt like a gaudy neon sign beside an engraved invitation, in spite of the fact that it was Amy who wore the makeup. Theresa held her sweater over her elbow as she reached to turn off a burner.

From the table, Brian observed it all—the quick flash of irritation the older sister hadn't quite been able to hide, the guarded movements behind the camouflaging sweater and even the guilt that flashed across her face for the twinge of envy she could not quite control in moments such as these.

He rose, moved to her side and smiled down into her startled eyes. "Here, let me pour the coffee, at least. I feel like a parasite sitting there and doing nothing while you slave over a hot stove." He reached for the pot while she shifted her eyes to the eggs she was removing from the pan.

"The cups are...." She half turned to find Amy watching them from just behind their shoulders. "Amy will show you where the cups are."

They had just begun eating when Jeff came slogging out of his room in bare feet and faded Levi's, scratching his chest and head simultaneously.

"I thought I smelled bacon."

"And I thought I smelled a rat," returned Theresa. "Jeff Brubaker, you should be ashamed of yourself. Bringing Brian here as your houseguest, then abandoning him that way."

Jeff shambled to a chair and strung himself upon it, more lying then sitting. "Aw hell, Brian didn't mind, did you, Bry?"

"Nope. Theresa and I had a nice long talk, and I got to bed early."

"What did you think of old Glue Eyes?" put in Amy.

"She's just as cute as I expected from Jeff's descriptions and the pictures I've seen," replied Brian.

"Humph!"

Jeff leaned his elbows on the table and closely scrutinized his younger sister. "Well, lookee here now," he sing-songed. "If the twerp hasn't taken a few lessons from old Glue Eyes herself."

Amy's mouth puckered up as if it was full of alum. She glared at her brother and snapped, "I'm fourteen years old, Jeffrey, in case you hadn't noticed! And I've been wearing makeup for over a year now."

"Oh." Jeff lounged back in his chair once again. "I beg your pardon, Irma la douce."

She lurched to her feet and would have stormed out of the room, but Jeff caught her by the elbow and swung her around till she landed on his lap, where she sat stiffly with her arms crossed obstinately over her ribs, an expression of strained tolerance on her face.

"Wanna come along with Brian and me to shop for mom and dad today? I'm gonna need some help deciding what to get for them."

Her irritation dissolved like a mist before a wind. "*Reeeally?* You mean it, Jeff?"

"Sure I mean it." He pushed her off his lap, swatted her on the backside and sent her on her way again. "Get your room cleaned up, and we'll go right after we eat." When she was gone he looked at the spot from which she'd disappeared around the hallway wall. "Her jeans are too tight. Mother ought to talk to her about that."

* * *

Left behind, Theresa recalled the breakfast conversation with something less than good humor. Why was it so irritating that Jeff had noticed Amy's burgeoning maturity? Why did she herself feel lonely and left out and—*oh, admit it, Brubaker!*—jealous, because her sister of fourteen was accompanying Brian Scanlon, age twenty-three, on an innocent Christmas-shopping spree?

With the house to herself, Theresa put on her classical favorites, and spent the remainder of the morning boiling potatoes and eggs for the enormous pot of potato salad they'd take to the family gathering scheduled for the following night, Christmas Eve. In the afternoon she washed her hair, took a bath, filed her nails and rummaged in Amy's room for some polish with a little more pizzazz than the colorless stuff she usually wore. She came up with something called "Mocha Magic" and grimaced as she painted the first stripe down a nail. *I'm simply not a "Mocha Magic" girl,* she thought, but completed the single nail, held it aloft and assessed it stringently. She fluttered her fingers and watched the light dance across the pearlescent surface and decided—thinking in Amy's current teenage vernacular—what the heck, go for it!

When all ten nails were finished she wasn't sure she'd done the right thing. She imagined them glistening, catching the lights while she fingered the neck of her violin. *I'm a conservative person trapped inside the body of a Kewpie doll,* she decided, and left the polish on.

She put on a beef roast for supper and pressed her long, black gabardine skirt and the collar of the basic long-sleeved white blouse that completed the orchestra "uniform" worn by its female members. The blouse was made of a slick knit jersey, and there'd be no sweaters to hide behind, no bulkiness to disguise the way the slippery fabric conformed to her frame.

She was at the piano, limbering up her fingers with chromatic scales, when the shopping trio returned.

Jeff was bellowing her name as he opened the door and

followed his ears to the living room. He reached over her shoulder and tapped out the melody line to "Jingle Bells," then sashayed on through the living room with two crackling sacks on his arm, followed by Amy, also bearing packages. By the time the pair exited to hide their booty, Brian stood in the opposite doorway, his cheeks slightly brightened by the winter air outside, jacket unzipped and pulling open as he paused with one hand in his back pocket, the other surrounding a brown paper sack. His eyes were startlingly attractive as the dark lashes dropped, and he glanced at Theresa's hands on the keyboard.

"Play something," he requested.

Immediately she folded her palms between her knees. "Oh, I was only limbering up for tonight."

He moved a step closer. "Limber up some more, then."

"I'm limbered enough."

He crossed behind her toward the davenport, and her eyes followed over her shoulder. "Good, then play a song."

"I don't know rock."

"I know. You're a classy person." He grinned, set his package down on the davenport and drew off his jacket, all the while keeping his eyes on her. She pinched her knees tighter against her palms. "I meant to say, you're a classical person," he amended with a lazy grin. "So play me a classic."

She played without sheet music, at times allowing her eyelids to drift closed while her head tipped back, and he caught glimpses of her enraptured eloquent face. When her eyelids opened she focused on nothing, letting her gaze drift with seeming unawareness. He had little doubt that while she played, Theresa forgot he stood behind her. He dropped his eyes again to her hands—fragile, long-fingered, with delicate bones at wrist and knuckle. How supplely they moved, those wrists arching gracefully, then dropping as she weaved backward, then forward. Once she smiled, and her head tipped to one side as the pianissimo chords tinkled from her fingertips while she inhabited that captivating world he knew and understood so well.

Watching the language of her hands, her body, was like having the song not only put into words but illustrated as well. He sensed that within Theresa the music acted as bellows to embers and saw what passions lay hidden within the woman whose normally shy demeanor never hinted at such smoldering fires.

By the time the song ended and Theresa's hands poised motionless above the keys, he was certain her heart must be pounding as heavily as his own.

He laid a hand on her shoulder and she jerked, as if waking up.

"That's very nice," he praised softly, and she became conscious of that warm hand resting where the strap of her bra cut a deep, painful groove into her flesh. "I seem to remember an old movie that used that as its theme song."

"*The Eddy Duchin Story.*"

The hand slipped away, making her wish it had stayed. "Yes, that was it. Tyrone Power and...." She heard his fingers fillip beside her ear and swung around on the bench to face him, again tucking her palms between her knees.

"Kim Novak."

"That's it. Kim Novak." He noted her pose, the way she rounded her shoulders to minimize the prominence of her breasts, and it took an effort for him to keep his eyes on her face.

"It's Chopin. One of my favorites."

"I'll remember that. Chopin. Do you play Chopin tonight, too?"

He stood very close to her, and Theresa raised her eyes to meet his gaze. From this angle, the shoulder-to-shoulder seam across his white jersey made his torso appear inordinately broad and tapered. His voice was honey smooth and soft. Most of the time he spoke that way, which was a balm to her ears after the affectionate grate of Jeff's clamorousness and her mother's usual bawling forte.

"No, tonight we do all Christmas music. I believe we're starting with 'Joy to the World' and then a little-known French carol. We follow that with...." She realized he probably couldn't care less what they were playing tonight, and buttoned her lip.

"With?"

"Nothing. Just the usual Christmas stuff."

She was becoming rattled by his nearness and the studied way he seemed to be itemizing her features, as if listing them selectively in credit and debit columns within his head. She suddenly wished she knew how to apply makeup as cleverly as Amy, picturing her colorless eyelashes, and her too-colorful cheeks, knowing Brian could detect her many shortcomings altogether too clearly at such close range.

"I have to peel potatoes for supper." Having dredged up that excuse, she slid off the bench and escaped to the kitchen, where she donned a cobbler's apron to protect her white blouse as she worked.

A short time later her mother and father returned from work, and in the suppertime confusion, the quiet moment with Brian slipped to the back of Theresa's mind. But as she prepared to flee the house with violin case under the arm of her gray coat, she came to a halt in the middle of the kitchen. There stood Brian with a dish towel in his hands, and Amy, with her arms buried in suds, having uttered not a word of her usual complaints at having the job foisted on her.

"I'm sorry I had to eat and run, but we have to be in our chairs ready to tune up by six forty-five."

Jeff was on the phone, talking with Patricia. "Just a minute—" He broke off, and lowered the receiver. "Hey, sis, do good, okay?"

She gave him a thumbs-up sign with one fat, red mitten as she headed toward the door, found it held open by Brian, his other hand buried inside a dish towel and glass he'd been wiping.

"Good luck," he said softly, his green eyes lingering upon her in a way that resurrected the closeness she'd shared at the piano earlier. The cold air rushed about their ankles, but neither seemed to notice as they gazed at each other, and Theresa felt as if Chopin's music was playing within her heart.

"Thanks," she said at last. "And thanks for taking over for me with the dishes."

"Anytime." He smiled, grazed her chin with a touch so light she wondered if she'd imagined it as she turned into the brisk night that cooled her heated cheeks.

The annual Christmas concert of the Burnsville Civic Orchestra was held each year at the Burnsville Senior High School auditorium. The risers were set up and the curtains left open and the musicians made their way to their places amid the metallic premusic of clanking stands and metal folding chairs. The conductor arrived and tuning began. The incessant drone of the A-note filled the vaulted space of the auditorium, and gradually, the room hummed with voices as the seats slowly filled. The footlights were still off, and from her position at first chair Theresa had a clear view of the aisles.

She was running her bow over the honey-colored chunk of resin when her hand stopped sawing, and her lips fell open in surprise. There, filing in, came her whole family, plus Patricia Gluek, and of course, Brian Scanlon. They shuffled into the fourth row center and began removing jackets and gloves while Theresa's palms went damp. She had played the violin since sixth grade and had stopped having stage fright years ago, but her stomach drew up now into an unexpected coil of apprehension. Amy waggled two fingers in a clandestine hello, and Theresa answered with a barely discernible waggle of her own. Then her eyes scanned the seat next to Amy and found Brian waggling two fingers back at her. *Oh, Lord, did he think I*

waved at him? Twenty-five years old and waving like her giggling first graders did when they spotted their mommies and
daddies in the audience.

But before she could become any further unnerved by the
thought, the footlights came up, and the conductor tapped his
baton on the edge of the music stand. She stiffened her spine
and pulled away from the backrest of the chair, snapped her
violin into place at the lift of the black-clad arms and hit the
opening note of "Joy to the World."

Midway through the song Theresa realized she had never
played the violin so well in her life, not that she could remember. She attacked the powerful notes of "Joy to the World"
with robust precision. She nursed the stunning dissonants of
"The Christmas Song" with loving care until the tension eased
from the chords with their familiar resolutions. As lead violinist, she performed a solo on the compelling "I Wonder As I
Wander," and the instrument seemed to come alive beneath
her mocha-colored fingernails.

She began by playing for him. But she ended playing for
herself, which is the true essence of the real musician. She
forgot Brian sat in the audience and lost the inhibitions that
claimed her whenever there was no instrument beneath her fingers or no children to direct.

From the darkened house, he watched her—nobody but her.
The red hair and freckles that had been so distracting in their
brilliance when he'd first met her took on an appropriateness
lent by her fiery zeal as she dissolved into the music. Again,
there were times when her eyelids drifted shut. Other times she
smiled against the chin rest, and he was somehow certain she
had no idea she was smiling. Her sleeves draped as she bowed
the instrument, her wrist arched daintily as she occasionally
plucked it, and the hem of her black skirt lifted and fell as she
tapped her toe to the sprightlier songs.

The concert ended with a reprise of "Joy to the World,"

and the final thunder of applause brought the orchestra members to their feet for a mass bow.

When the house lights came up, Theresa's eyes scanned the line of familiar faces in row four, but returned to settle and stay on Brian, who had lifted his hands to praise her in the traditional way, and was wearing a smile as proud as any on the other faces. She braved a wide smile in return and hoped he knew it was not for the others but just for him. He stopped clapping and gave her the thumbs-up signal, and she felt a holiday glow such as she'd never known as she sat to tuck her instrument back into its case.

They were waiting in the hall when she came from the music room with her coat and mitts on, her case beneath an arm.

Everybody babbled at once, but Theresa finally had a chance to croon appreciatively, "Why didn't you *tell* me you were coming?"

"We wanted to surprise you. Besides, we thought it might make you nervous."

"Well, it did! No, it didn't! Oh, I don't know what I'm saying, except it really made the concert special, knowing you were all out there listening. Thanks, all of you, for coming."

Jeff looped an elbow around Theresa's neck, faked a headlock and a punch to the jaw and grunted, "You did good, sis."

Margaret took command then. "We have a tree to decorate yet tonight, and you know how your father always has trouble with those lights. Let's get this party moving home!"

They headed toward the parking lot, and Theresa invited, "Does anybody want to ride with me?" She could sense Amy reserving her reply until she heard what Brian answered.

"I will," he said, moving to Theresa's side and taking the violin case from her hands.

"I will too—" Amy began, but Margaret cut her off in midsentence.

"Amy, you come with us. I want you to run into the store for a carton of milk on our way home."

"Jeff? Patricia?" Theresa appealed, suddenly feeling as if she'd coerced Brian into saying yes, since nobody else had.

"Patricia left her purse in the station wagon, so we might as well ride with them."

The two groups parted, and as she walked toward her little gray Toyota, Theresa suddenly suspected that Patricia had had her purse with her all along.

In the car she and Brian settled into the low bucket seats and Theresa put a tape in the deck. Rachmaninoff seemed to envelope them. "Sorry," she offered, and immediately pushed the eject button. Without hesitation, he reseated the tape against the heads and the dynamic Concerto in C-sharp Minor returned.

"I get the idea you think I'm some hard-rock freak. Music is music. If it's good, I like it."

They drove through the moonlit night with the power and might of Rachmaninoff ushering them home, followed by the much mellower poignance of Listz's "Liebestraum." As its flowing sweetness touched her ears, Theresa thought of its English translation, "Dream of Love." But she kept her eyes squarely on the road, thinking herself fanciful because of the residual ebullience of the performance and the occasional scarlet, blue and gold lights that glittered from housefronts as they passed. In living-room windows Christmas trees winked cheerfully, but it wasn't just the trees, it wasn't just the lights, it wasn't just the concert and not even Jeff's being home that made this Christmas more special than most. It was Brian Scanlon.

"I saw your foot tapping," he teased now.

"Oh?"

"Sure sign of a dancer."

"I'm still thinking about it."

"Good. Because I never get to dance much anymore. I'm always providing the music."

"Never fear. If I don't go, there'll be plenty of others."

"That's what I'm afraid of. Rhythmless clods who'll abuse my toes and talk, talk, talk in my ear."

"You don't like to talk when you dance?" Somehow she'd always imagined dancers using the close proximity to exchange intimacies.

"Not particularly."

"I've been led to believe that's when men and women whisper...well, what's known as *sweet nothings.*"

Brian turned to study her face, smiling at the old-fashioned phrase, wondering if he knew another woman who'd use it. *"Sweet nothings?"*

She heard the grin in his voice, but kept her eyes on the street. "I have no personal knowledge of them myself, you understand." She gave him a quarter glance and lifted one eyebrow.

"I understand. Neither do I."

"But I'll give it some thought."

"I already have. Sounds like not a half-bad idea."

She felt as if her face would light up the interior of the car, for it struck Theresa that while she had no knowledge of sweet nothings, she and Brian were exchanging them at that very moment.

They made it home before the others, and Theresa excused herself to go to her room and change into jeans, blouse and loose-thrown sweater again. From the living room she heard the soft, exploratory notes of the piano as a melody line from a current Air Supply hit was picked out with one finger. She came down the hall and paused in the living-room doorway. Brian stood before the piano, one thumb hooked in the back pocket of his pants while he lackadaisically pressed the keys with a single forefinger. He looked up. She crossed her arms. The piano strings vibrated into silence. She noticed things about him that she liked—the shape of his eyebrows, the way his expression said *smile* when there really was none there, his easy unhurried way of speaking, moving, shifting his eyes, that put her much more at ease the longer she was with him.

"I enjoyed the concert."

"I'm glad."

"My first live orchestra."

"It's nothing compared to the Minneapolis Orchestra. You should hear them."

"Maybe I will sometime. Do they play Chopin?"

"Oh, they play everything! And Orchestra Hall is positively sensational. The acoustics are world acclaimed. The ceiling is made of big white cubes of all sizes that look like they've been thrown up there and stuck at odd angles. The notes come bouncing off the cubes and—" She had looked up, as if expecting the living-room ceiling to be composed of the same cubes she described, not realizing that she looked very girlish and appealing in her animation, or that she had thrown her arms wide.

When her eyes drifted down, she found Brian grinning in amusement.

The kitchen door burst open and the noise began again.

When the Brubaker family decorated their Christmas tree, the scene was like a three-ring circus, with Margaret its ringmaster. She doled out commands about everything: which side of the tree should face front, who should pick up the trail of needles left scattered across the carpet, who should fill the tree stand with water. Poor Willard had trouble with the tree lights, all right, but his biggest trouble was his wife. "Willard, I want you to move that red light so it's underneath that branch instead of on top of it. There's a big hole here."

Jeff caught his mother by the waist, swung her around playfully and circled her arms so she couldn't move, then plopped a silencing kiss on her mouth. "Yes, his little turtledove. Shut up, his little turtledove," Margaret's tall son teased, gaining a smile in return.

"You're not too big to spank yet, Jeffrey. Talking to your mother like that." But her grin was as wide as a watermelon slice. "Patricia, get this boy off my back." Patricia made a lunge at Jeff and the two ended up in a heap on the sofa, teasing and tickling.

Margaret had turned on the living-room stereo, but while it played Christmas music, Amy's bedroom was thumping with rock, and though the door was closed, the sound came through to confuse the issue. Jeff sang with one or the other in his deep, gravelly voice, and before they got to the tinsel, the phone had rung no less than four times—all for Amy.

Brian might have felt out of place but for Patricia's being an outsider, too. When it was time to distribute the tinsel, she was given a handful, just as he was, and protesting that it was *their* tree would have sounded ungracious, so he found himself beside Theresa, hanging shimmering silver icicles on the high branches while she worked on the lower ones. Jeff and Patricia had taken over the other half of the tree while the two elder Brubakers sat back and watched this part of the decorations, and Amy talked on the phone, interrupting herself to offer some sage bit of direction now and then.

They ended the evening with hot apple cider and cinnamon rolls around the kitchen table. By the time they finished, it was nearing eleven o'clock. Margaret stood up and began stacking the dirty cups and saucers.

"Well, I guess it's time I get Patricia back home," Jeff announced. "Do you two want to ride along?"

Brian and Theresa both looked up and spoke simultaneously.

"No, I'll stay here and clean up the mess."

"I don't feel like going out in the cold again."

Theresa took over the task her mother had begun. "You're tired, mom. I'll do that."

Margaret desisted thankfully and went off to bed with Willard, ordering Amy to retire also. When the door closed behind Jeff and Patricia, the kitchen was left to Theresa and Brian.

She carried the dishes to the counter and filled the sink with sudsy water and began washing them.

"I'll dry them for you."

"You don't have to. There are just a few."

Overruling her protest, he found the dish towel and stood beside her at the sink. She was conscious that he was comfortable with silence, unlike most people. He could go through long stretches of it without searching for ways to fill it. The stereos were off. Jeff's teasing was gone, and Margaret's incessant orders. Only the swish of water and the clink of glassware could be heard. It took them less than five minutes to wash and dry the cups and saucers and put the room in order. But while five minutes of silence beside the wrong person can be devastating, that same five beside the right man can be totally wonderful.

When she'd hung up the wet cloths and switched out all the lights except the small one over the stove, she found a bottle of lotion beneath the sink and squirted a dollop in her palm, aware of Brian watching silently as she worked the cherry-scented cream into her hands.

"Let's sit in the living room for a while," he suggested.

She led the way and sat down on one end of the davenport while he sat at the other, leaning back and draping his palms across his abdomen, much as he had in the theater. Again silence fell. Again it was sustaining rather than draining. The tree lights made Theresa feel as if she was on the inside of a rainbow looking out.

"You have a wonderful family," he said at last.

"I know."

"But I begin to see why your dad needs to spend some quiet time with the birds."

Theresa chuckled softly. "It gets a little raucous at times. Mostly when Jeff's around."

"I like it though. I don't ever remember any happy noise around my house."

"Don't you have any brothers and sisters?"

"Yeah, one sister, but she's eight years older than me, and she lives in Jamaica. Her husband's in exporting. We were never very close."

"And what about your mom and dad? I mean, your real dad. Were you close to them?"

He stared at the tree lights and ruminated at length. She liked that. No impulsive answers to a question that was important. "A little with my dad, but never with my mother."

"Why?"

He rolled his head and studied her. "I don't know. Why are some families like yours and some like mine? If I knew the answer and could bottle it, I could stop wars."

His answer made her turn to meet his eyes directly—such stunning, spiky-lashed beauties. She was struck again by the fact that such pretty eyes somehow managed to make him even more handsome. In them the tree lights were reflected—dots of red and gold and green and blue shining from beneath chestnut eyebrows and lashes, studying her without a smile.

His steady gaze made Theresa short of breath.

There were things inside this man that spoke of a depth of character she was growing surely to admire. Though he was really Jeff's senior by only two years, he seemed much older than Jeff—much older than her, too, she thought. Perhaps losing one's family does that to a person. It suddenly struck Theresa how awesome it must be to have no place to call home. She herself had clung to home far longer than was advisable. But she was a different matter. Brian would leave the Air Force next summer, and there would be no mother waiting with pumpkin pies in the freezer. No familiar bedroom where he could lie on his back and consider what lay ahead, while the familiar lair secured him to the past. No siblings to tease or go Christmas shopping with. No old girlfriend waiting with open arms....

But how did she know? The thought was sobering. She suddenly wanted to ask if there was a woman somewhere who was special to him, but didn't want to sound forward, so she veiled the question somewhat.

"Isn't there anyone left behind in Chicago?"

The smile was absent, but why did it feel as if he was charming her with the twinkle in his eye? "Since we've already eliminated parents and sisters and brothers, you must mean girlfriends." She dropped her eyes and hoped the red tree lights camouflaged the heat she felt creeping up her neck. "No, there are no girlfriends waiting in Chicago."

"I didn't mean—"

"Whether you did or not doesn't matter. Maybe I just wanted you to know."

The silence that followed was scarcely comfortable, quite unlike that which had passed earlier. It was filled with a new, tingling two-way awareness and a thousand other unasked questions.

"I think I'll say good-night now," he announced quietly, surprising Theresa. She wasn't *totally* naive. She'd sat on living-room davenports with those of the opposite sex before, and after a lead-in like Brian's, the groping always followed.

But he rose, stretched and stood with his fingers in his hip pockets while he studied the tree a minute longer. Then he studied her an equal length of time before raising a palm and murmuring softly, "Good night, Theresa."

Chapter Four

Brian Scanlon lay in bed, thinking about Theresa Brubaker, considering what it was that attracted him to her. He'd never cared much for redheads. Yet her hair was as orange as that of a Raggedy Ann doll, and her freckles were the color of overripe fruit. When she blushed—and she blushed often—she tended to glow like the Christmas tree.

Brian had been playing in a band since high school. In every dance crowd there were women who couldn't resist a guitar man when he stepped down from the stage at break time. They flocked around like chickens to scattered corn. He'd had his share. But he'd always gone for the blondes and brunettes, the prettiest ones with artful makeup and hair down to the middle of their backs, swinging like silk—women who knew their way around men.

But Theresa Brubaker was totally different from them. Not only did she look different, she acted different. She was honest and interesting, intelligent and loving. And totally naive, Brian was sure.

Yet so much heart lay beneath that naivety. It surfaced whenever she was around her family, particularly Jeff, and whenever she was around music. Brian recalled her voice, when the three of them had been harmonizing in the car, and the verve she radiated when playing the violin and the piano. Why, she even had him listening to classical music with a new, tolerant ear. The poignant strains of the Chopin Nocturne came back to him as he crossed his wrists behind his head in the dark and thought of how she'd looked in the long black skirt and white blouse. The blouse had, for once, been covered by no sweater.

He wondered how a man ever got up the nerve to touch breasts like hers. When they were that big, they weren't really...sexy. Just intimidating. He'd been scared to death the first time he'd felt a girl's breasts, but since then he'd touched countless others, and still the idea of caressing Theresa's breasts gave him serious qualms. There'd been times when he'd managed to study them covertly, but Theresa allowed few such opportunities, covered as she usually was with her cardigans. But when she'd been playing the piano, he'd stood behind her and looked down at the mountainous orbs beneath her blouse, and his mouth had gone dry instead of watering.

Forget it, Scanlon. She's not your type.

The next morning, when Brian arose at his usual wake-up hour and crept barefoot upstairs to the bathroom, he came face to face with Theresa in the hall.

They both stopped short and stared at each other. He wore a pair of blue denim jeans, nothing else. She wore a mint green bathrobe, nothing else. There wasn't a sound in the house. Everyone else was still asleep, for it was Christmas Eve day so neither of her parents had to go to work.

"Good morning," she whispered. The bathroom door was right beside them.

"Good morning," he whispered back. Her feet were bare, and it was obvious even without a glance that her breasts were untethered beneath the velour robe, for they drooped nearly to her waist while she lifted her arms and pretended the zipper needed closing at her throat.

"You can go first," she offered, gesturing toward the doorway.

"No, no, you go ahead. I'll wait."

"No, I...really, I was just going to put on a pot of coffee first."

He was about to raise another objection when she swept past him toward the kitchen, so he hurried into the bathroom, taking care of necessities without wasting time, then heading for the kitchen to tell her the room was free. She was standing before the stove waiting for the coffee to start perking when he padded up silently beside her.

The sun wasn't up yet, but it had lightened the sky to an opalescent gray that lifted over the east windowsills of the kitchen, providing enough light for Theresa to see very clearly the dark hair springing from Brian's bare chest and diving into his waistline like an arrow. His nipples were like twin raspberries, shriveled up in the centers of squarely defined muscles. The only bare chests she'd ever seen in this house had been Jeff's and her father's. But this one was nothing like either of theirs, and the sight of him brought to mind vivid scenes from the movie they'd seen two nights ago. She dropped her eyes after the briefest glance, but down below she encountered more hair—dark wisps on his big toes. And suddenly she couldn't stand there beside him a moment longer, with him only half dressed and herself coming totally unstrung inside her mint green robe.

"Would you mind watching the coffee till it starts perking, then turn it down to low?"

In the bathroom she switched on the light above the vanity and checked her reflection in the mirror. Sure enough, beet red! That horribly unflattering red that made her look as if she was going to go off like a Fourth of July rocket. She pressed her palms to her cheeks, closed her eyes and wondered how it felt to be *normal* and come up against a half-naked man like Brian Scanlon in your kitchen.

Lordy, he flustered her so.

What do other women do? How do they handle the first attraction they feel? It must be so much easier when you're fourteen, like Amy, and you go at the natural pace: a first exchange of glances, a first touch of hands, a first kiss, then nubility taking over as boy and girl together begin exploring their awakening sexuality.

But I was thwarted at square one, Theresa thought miserably, looking at her awful freckles and hair, which by themselves would have been enough to overcome without the other even greater obstacles. *I was cheated by nature out of those first kittenish glances that might have led to all the rest, because all the first glances I ever received contained no more than shock or lasciviousness. And now here I am, midway through my twenties, and I don't know how to handle my very first sexual attraction to a man.*

She took a bath, washed her hair and didn't reenter the kitchen until she was properly dressed in a color she wore defiantly—cranberry. She loved it, but when it got anywhere near her hair, the two hues went to war and made her look like beets and carrots mixed in the same bowl. She had to keep the cranberry corduroy slacks separated from her flaming hair by a band of neutral color across her torso. When she explored her closet, she came upon a wonderful white sweat shirt Amy had given her for Christmas last year, which Theresa had never worn, no matter how many times she'd been tempted. To the average woman the sweat shirt would have been absolutely dishwater plain. It had hand-warmer pockets on the belly, zipper up the front and two sport stripes running down the sleeves: one of navy, the other of cranberry.

She took it from the hanger, slipped her arms into it and stepped before her mirror while she zipped it up. But the reflection that met her eyes made her want to cry. It looked like two dirigibles had been inflated beneath the garment. There was no power on earth that could make her wear this thing out to the kitchen and face Brian.

Angrily, she jerked it off and tossed it aside, replacing it with a prim oxford-cloth shirt in off-white with long sleeves and a button-down collar, over which she draped the everlasting, hated cardigan.

She was saved from encountering Brian's bare chest again, when she heard him take over the bathroom while she was arranging her hair in a round mound just above her collar. When it was confined, at least it didn't look as if it was going to carry her away into the wild blue yonder if a stiff wind came up.

In the bathroom, Brian, too, assessed himself in the mirror. *She's scared of you, Scanlon, so the issue is settled. You don't have to think about the possibilities of falling for her.*

But the room was scented with feminine things—the flowery essence of soap left behind in the damp air. There was a wet washcloth over the shower-curtain rod, and when he grabbed it down to close the curtains, he found himself staring at it for a long moment while he rubbed a thumb across the cold, damp terry cloth. With an effort, he put her from his mind and folded the cloth very carefully, then laid it on a corner of the tub. But while he stood beneath the hot spray, soaping his body, he thought of her again, and of the movie, and couldn't help wondering what it would be like in bed with that freckled body, the generous breasts and red hair.

Scanlon, it's Christmas, you pervert! What the hell are you doing standing here thinking about your best friend's sister like some practiced lecher?

But that's not the only reason I can't get her off my mind, his other self argued honestly. *She's a beautiful person. Inside, where it counts.*

He intentionally kept things light and breezy when he met Theresa in the kitchen again. But it was easier, for the rest of her family was beginning to rouse, and one by one they padded out to have coffee or juice. By the time they all sat down to breakfast together, the day had changed mood.

It was set aside for preparations. There was a family gathering planned at Grandma and Grandpa Deering's house, and everybody would take something for the supper buffet. Then tomorrow, the pack would descend upon the Brubaker house for Christmas dinner, so Margaret, Theresa and Amy were busy all day in the kitchen.

Margaret was at her dictatorial best, issuing orders like a drill-team sergeant again while her daughters carried them out. Willard spent part of the day watching for cardinals, while Jeff and Brian broke out their guitars at last, and from the kitchen Theresa heard her first of Brian's guitar playing. She dropped what she was doing and moved to the living-room doorway, pausing there to observe him tuning, then fingering an augmented chord of quietly vibrating quality, bending his head low over the instrument, listening intently as the six notes shimmered into silence. He sat at the piano bench, but had swung to face the davenport where Jeff sat, and didn't know Theresa stood behind him.

Jeff, too, strummed random chords, the two guitars quietly clashing in that presong dissonance that can be as musical in its own off-harmonic way as cleanly arranged songs.

Jeff played lead, Brian rhythm, and from the moment the discordant warmup crystalized into the intro to a song, Theresa recognized a marvelous communion of kindred musicians. No signal had been spoken, none exchanged by eye, hand or tongue. The inharmonious gibberish of tuning had simply resolved into the concord of one single silently agreed-upon song.

Between musicians there can be a connection, just as between friends who somehow single each other out, recognizing empathy from the moment of introduction, just as a man and woman sometimes attract each other at first glimpse. It's something that cannot be prompted or dictated. Among members of a band this connection makes the difference between simply playing notes at the same time and creating an affinity of sound.

They had it, these two. There was almost a mystical quality about it, and as Theresa looked on and listened from the kitchen doorway, shivers ran up her arms and down her legs. They had picked up on "Georgia on My Mind." Where was the clashing rock? Where were the occasional sour chords she used to hear from Jeff's guitar? When had he gotten so *good?*

Neither Brian nor Jeff looked at each other while they played. Their heads were cocked lazily, eyes blankly turned to the waists of their guitars in that indolent, concentrative pose Theresa recognized well. How many times had she stood before Jeff and asked him a question when he was in such a trance, only to be separated from him by the wall of music until the song finished and he looked startled to find her standing there?

Jeff began to sing, his softly grating voice evocative of Ray Charles's immortal rendition of this song. A lump formed in Theresa's throat. Amy had come up silently behind her, and they stood as motionless as the hands of a sundial. Jeff "took a ride" at the break, and Theresa stared at his supple fingers running along the frets with an agility she'd never seen before. Pride blossomed in her heart. *Oh, Jeff, Jeff, my little brother, who started on that fifteen-dollar Stella in the corner, just listen to you now.* He vocalized the last verse, then together he and Brian "rode it home," and as the last poignant notes ebbed to fade-out, Theresa looked back over her shoulder into Amy's wide, amazed eyes. The room was silent.

Jeff's eyes met Brian's, and they exchanged smiles before they concurred, in their two deep voices, "All ri-i-ight."

"Jeffrey," Theresa said softly at last.

He glanced up in surprise. "Hey, Treat, how long have you been standing there?"

Brian swung around on the piano seat, and she gave him a passing smile of approval but moved to her brother, bending across his guitar to give him a hug. "When did you get so good?"

"You haven't heard me for over a year, closer to a year and a half. Brian and I have been hittin' it hard."

"Obviously."

She turned back to Brian. "Don't take me wrong, but I think you two were made for each other."

They all laughed, then Brian agreed, "Yeah, we kind of thought so the first time we picked a song together. It just happened, you know?"

"I know. And it shows."

Amy, with her hands jammed in her jeans pockets, inched closer to Brian's shoulders. "Gol, wait'll the kids hear this!"

Theresa couldn't resist the temptation to tease. "Is this Amy Brubaker speaking? The same Amy Brubaker who inundates us with AC/DC and scorns anything mellower than Rod Stewart?"

Amy shrugged, showed a flash of braces behind a half-sheepish grin, and returned, "Yeah, but these guys are really *excellent,* I mean, *wow.* And anyway, Jeff promised they'd do some rock, too. Didn't you, Jeffy?"

Instead of answering, Jeff struck a straight D chord, hard and heavy, with a dramatic flourish, and after letting it sizzle for a prolonged moment he met Brian's eye, and the next chord bit the air with the brashness of unvarnished rock. How they both knew the chosen song was a mystery. But one minute only Jeff's chord hung in the air, and the next they were hammering away at the song as if by divine design. Amy stood between them, getting into the beat with her hips. "Yeah..." she half growled, and Brian gave her a nonchalant quasi smile, then turned that same smile on Theresa, who shrugged in reply, a proud smile on her face while she enjoyed every note, rock or not, and each sideward thrust of Amy's hips.

When the song ended, Margaret and Willard were standing in the doorway, applauding. Amy rushed for the telephone, undoubtedly to rave on about the good tidings to as many friends as possible, and Theresa reluctantly returned to the kitchen to listen from there while she worked.

In the late afternoon, they all went to their respective rooms to change and get ready for the trip across town to Grandpa and Grandma Deerings'. When they rendezvoused in the kitchen to load the car, it was Margaret who suggested, "Why don't you bring your guitars? We'll do some caroling. You know how your grandparents enjoy it.''

So the station wagon was packed with potato salad and cranberry Jell-O, a vintage Gibson hollow-body 335 and a classic Epiphone Riviera, a rented amp, a stack of Christmas presents and six bodies.

Willard drove. Theresa found herself in the back seat sandwiched between Jeff and Brian. His hip was warm, even through her bulky coat, and when he and Jeff exchanged comments, she was served up tantalizing whiffs of his sandalwoody after-shave, for he'd slung an arm across the back of the seat and repeatedly leaned forward to peer around her.

If Brian thought he'd feel out of place at the family gathering, the delusion was put to rout within minutes of arriving. The tiny house of mid-forties' vintage was popping at the seams with relatives of all ages and sizes. Grandpa Deering was deaf, and when Jeff took Brian over to introduce him to the shriveled little man, he shouted for his grandfather's benefit. "Grandpa, this is my friend, Brian, the one who's in the Air Force with me.''

The old man nodded.

"I brought him home to spend Christmas with us," Jeff bawled at the top of his lungs.

Mr. Deering nodded again.

"We play in a band together, and we brought our guitars along tonight to do a few carols.''

The bald head nodded still once more. Grandpa Deering raised a crooked forefinger in the air as if in approval, but said not a word until the two were turning away. Then he questioned in his reedy old quake, "This y'r friend who fiddles with you?''

It was all Brian could do to keep a straight face. Jeff turned back to his grandfather, leaning closer. "Guitar, grandpa, guitar.''

The old man nodded and said no more, replaced his arthritic

palms one on top of the other atop a black, rubber-tipped cane and seemed to drift into a reverie.

When Brian and Jeff turned away, Brian whispered in his friend's ear. "Doesn't his hearing aid work?"

"He turns it down whenever it's convenient. When the music starts he'll hear every note."

The thirty-odd aunts, uncles and cousins ate from a table containing more food than Brian had ever seen in one place, and after the buffet supper, opened gifts, having exchanged names at Thanksgiving. When it was time for the music, everyone found a spot as best he could on the floor, the kitchen cabinets, end tables, arms of furniture, and the entire group sang the old standard carols while Theresa was cajoled into playing along with the guitars on an ancient oak organ whose bellows were filled by foot pedals. She complied good-naturedly and pulled out the old stops from whose faces the mother-of-pearl inserts had long ago fallen. For the benefit of the small children in the group, Brian and Jeff were enticed into doing a run-through of "Here Comes Santa Claus," which evolved into a jazz rendition that would have shocked its composer, Gene Autry. Jeff took an impromptu ride, taking outrageous liberties with the melody line, ad-libbing arpeggios while Brian modified the chords to smooth, fluid jazz. When it was over, the house burst into whistles and clapping, and the youngsters called for "Jingle Bells." When that was finished, someone called, "Where's Margaret? Margaret, it's your turn. Get up there."

To Brian's surprise, the hefty-chested dictatorial Margaret stepped center front, and while her daughter played an accompaniment on the wheezy organ, she belted out a stunning "Oh Holy Night." When the song ended, and Theresa spun around on the seat of the claw-foot organ stool to face Brian's eyebrows raised in surprise, she leaned near his ear and whispered, "Mother was a mezzo-soprano with a touring opera company before she married daddy."

"That leaves only Amy. What about her?"

From his far side, Amy spoke up. "I only got the beat, I didn't get the voice, so I play drums in the school band."

Brian smiled. "And dance, I'll bet."

"Yeah. Just wait and see."

Theresa knew a kind of keen envy. Amy could dance the socks off any three partners who tried to keep up with her. The sample she'd given earlier today in the living room had been only a hint of the rhythm contained in her svelte, teenage limbs. Theresa had always been extremely proud of Amy's dancing ability, and more so, her sister's lack of inhibition whenever any music started. While Theresa herself had felt a lifelong urge to dance, she'd never yielded to it.

She should have grown inured to giving up enjoyments such as dancing. By now, she shouldn't miss them, but she did. She transferred all her emotions into her music and took from it the satisfaction she was denied in other modes of self-expression, as she did now on this Christmas Eve.

She shunned the petty envy that she'd come to hate in herself and lauded, "Amy is the best dancer I know. It's too bad she isn't old enough to go with you on New Year's Eve."

Brian only smiled from one sister to the other, hoping the older of the two would agree to go with him, after all.

On the way home they dropped Jeff off at Patricia's house, where another family celebration was winding down. Jeff would get in on the end of it. When the remainder of the group reached the Brubaker house, the two older ones toddled off to bed while the remaining three turned on the tree lights and sat in the cozy living room exchanging anecdotes about past Christmases, music, the Air Force, school dances, Grandpa Deering and a myriad of subjects that kept them up well past midnight. Jeff joined them then, announcing that he'd just flown in on his jet-propelled sleigh and was looking for a plate of cookies and glass of milk before he filled any stockings.

When Theresa went to sleep that night, it was not to visions of sugar plums dancing in her head, but to visions of Brian Scanlon's long, dexterous fingers moving along the fingerboard of an Epiphone Riviera, picking out the chords to a love song whose words she strove to catch.

On Christmas morning Theresa was awakened by Amy, pouncing on her bed, giggling. "Hey, come on! Let's make it to those prezzies!"

"Amy, it's blacker than the ace of spades outside."

"It's seven o'clock already!"

"Ohh!" Theresa groaned and rolled over.

"Come on, get your buns out of here and let's go get the boys and mom and dad."

From down the hall came a hoarse call. "Who's doin' all that giggling out there?" Jeff. "Come in here and try that!"

Amy sprang off Theresa's bed and went to wage an attack on her brother, and the squealing that followed told clearly of a bout of tickling which soon awakened Margaret and Willard. The thumping on the floor aroused their houseguest downstairs, and within ten minutes they had all gathered in the living room and snuggled around the Christmas tree, dressed in hastily thrown-on robes, jeans, half-buttoned shirts, bare feet and bedroom slippers, sipping juice and coffee while gifts were distributed.

Brian was sharing a Christmas unlike any he'd ever experienced. This boisterous, loving family was showing him depths he'd never known. The gifts exchanged among them underscored that love again, for they were not many but well chosen.

For Willard, his children had decided on a telescope that would take its place before the sliding glass door downstairs; for Margaret, a mother's ring that would take its place proudly on her right hand, and which prompted a listing of the three birthdays. Brian carefully marked in his memory the date of Theresa's. To Margaret and Willard together the children gave a gift certificate for a weekend at the quiet, quaint Schumaker's Country Inn in the tiny town of New Prague, an hour's ride from the Twin Cities.

From their parents, Jeff, Amy and Theresa received, respectively, a plane ticket home for Easter, a pair of tickets to an upcoming rock concert by Journey and a season ticket to Orchestra Hall.

To Brian's surprise, each of the Brubakers had bought a gift for him. From Margaret and Willard, a billfold; from Amy, blank tapes—obviously she knew he and the other band members learned new songs by taping cuts from the radio; from Jeff, a Hohner harmonica—they'd been fooling around on one at a music store, and Brian had said he'd always wanted to play one; and from Theresa, an LP of classical music, including Chopin's Nocturne in E-flat.

When he opened the last gift, he looked up in surprise. "How did you have time to find it on such short notice?"

"Secret." But her eyes danced to her father's, and Brian remembered Willard's leaving the house for "last-minute items" yesterday.

To Brian's relief, he, too, had brought gifts. For Mr. and Mrs. Brubaker, a selection of cheese and bottle of Chianti wine; for Amy, a pair of headphones, which brought a round of good-natured applause from the rest of the group; for Jeff, a wide leather guitar strap tooled with his name; and for Theresa, a tiny pewter figurine—a smiling frog on a lily pad, playing the violin.

She smiled, placed it on her palm and met Brian's irresistible green eyes across the living room.

"How did you know I collect pewter instruments?"

"Secret."

"My darling brother, who can't keep anything to himself. And for once, I'm happy he can't. Thank you, Brian."

"Thank you, too. You'll make a silk purse of this sow's ear

yet." Which was ironic, for Brian was far, far from a sow's ear.

She studied the frog with its bulging pewter eyes and self-satisfied smile and lifted a similar smile to Brian. "I'll call him 'The Maestro.'"

The fiddling frog became one of Theresa's most cherished possessions, and took his place at the forefront of the collection shelved on a wall in her bedroom. It was the first gift she'd ever received from any male other than a family member.

That Christmas Day, filled with noise, food and family, passed in a blur for both Brian and Theresa. They were more conscious of each other than of any of the others in the house. The family ate and got lazy, ate again, and eventually their numbers began thinning. That lazy wind-down prompted dozing and eventually, an evening revival of energy. As most days did in this house where music reigned supreme, this one would have seemed incomplete without it. It was eight o'clock in the evening, and the crowd had dwindled to a mere dozen or so when out came the instruments, and it became apparent the family had their favorites, which they asked Jeff and Theresa to play. Margaret and Willard were nestled like a pair of teenagers on the davenport, and applauded and chose another and another song. Eventually, Brian and Jeff branched off into a rousing medley of rock songs, during which Theresa joined in, Elton John-style, on the piano. Then Jeff had the sudden inspiration, "Hey, Theresa, go get your fiddle!"

"Fiddle!" she spouted. "Jeffrey Brubaker, how dare you call great-grandmother's expensive Storioni a *fiddle*. Why, it's probably cringing in its case!"

Jeff explained to Brian. "She inherited her fiddle from one of our more talented progenitors, who bought it in 1906. It's modeled after a Faratti, so Theresa is rather overzealous about the piece."

"Fiddle!" Theresa teased with a saucy twitch of the hip as she left the room. "I'll show you *fiddle*, Brian Scanlon!"

When the beautiful classic violin came back with Theresa, Brian was amazed to hear the sister and brother strike into an engaging, foot-stomping rendition of "Lou'siana Saturday Night," along with which he himself provided background rhythm, while he wondered in bewilderment how Theresa happened to know the song, so different from her classics. After that, the hayseed in all of them seemed to have stuck to their overalls, and Jeff tried a little flat picking on "Wildwood Flower," and by that time, the entire group had gotten rather punchy. The usually reserved Willard captured Margaret and executed an impromptu hoe-down step in the middle of the room, which brought laughter and applause, to say nothing of the sweat to Margaret's brow as she plopped into a chair, breathless and fanning her red face but totally exhilarated.

"Give us 'Turkey In The Straw'!" someone shouted.

Again Brian was shown a new facet of Theresa Brubaker, a first-chair violinist of the Burnsville Civic Orchestra, as she sawed away on her 1906 classic Storioni, scraping out a raucous version of the old barn-dance tune, in the middle of which she lowered the violin and tapped the air with the bow, the carpet with her toe and watched her mother and father circling and clapping in the small space provided, while in a voice as clear as daybreak, Theresa sang out:

Oh, I had a little chicken
And it wouldn't lay an egg
So I poured hot water up and down her leg
Then the little chicken hollered
And the little chicken begged
And the damn little chicken
Laid a hard-boiled egg.

She was joined by the entire entourage as they finished by bellowing in unison, "Boom-tee-dee-a-da...*slick chick!*"

Brian joined in the rousing round of applause and shrill whistles that followed. As he laughed with the others, he saw again the hidden Theresa who seemed able to escape only when wooed by music and those she loved most. She covered her pink-tinged cheeks with both hands, while the "fiddle" and bow still hung from her fingers and her laughter flowed, sweet and fresh as spring water.

She was unique. She was untainted. She was as refreshing as the unexpected burst of hayseed music that had just erupted from her grandmother's invaluable 1906 Storioni.

He watched Theresa bestowing hugs of goodbye on her aunts and uncles. She had forgotten herself and impulsively lifted her arms in farewell embraces. Already Brian knew how rare these moments of forgetfulness were with Theresa. Music made the difference. It took her to a plane of unselfconsciousness nothing else could quite achieve.

He turned away, wandered back to the deserted living room, wondering what it would take to make her feel such ease with him. He sat down on the piano bench and picked out a haunting melody, one of his favorites, with a single finger, then softly began adding harmony notes. Soon he was engrossed in the quiet melody as his hands moved over the keyboard.

The house quieted. Amy was in her room with the new headphones glued to her ears. Willard was downstairs setting up his new telescope. Margaret had gone to bed, exhausted.

There were only three left in the room where the tree lights glowed.

"What are you playing?" Theresa asked, pausing behind Brian's shoulder, watching his long fingers on the piano.

"An old favorite, 'Sweet Memories.'"

"I don't think I know it."

Jeff wandered in. "Play it for her." He swung the old Stella up by its neck, extending it toward Brian, who looked back

over his shoulder, with a noncommittal smile. "Do old Stella
a favor," Jeff requested whimsically.

Brian seemed to consider for a long moment, then nodded
once, turned on the bench to face the room and reached for the
scarred, old guitar. The first soft note sent a shudder up Theresa's spine.

Jeff sat on the edge of the davenport, learning forward, elbows to knees, for one of those rare times when he didn't have
a guitar in his hands. He simply sat and paid homage. To the
song. His friend. And a voice that turned Theresa's nerve-
endings to satin.

She realized she had not heard Brian sing before. Not alone.
Not... not....

It was a song whose eloquent simplicity brought tears to her
eyes and a knot to her throat, tremors to her stomach and goose
bumps to the undersides of her thighs as she sat on the floor
before him.

My world is like a river
As dark as it is deep.
Night after night the past slips in
And gathers all my sleep.
My days are just an endless string
Of emptiness to me.
Filled only by the fleeting moments
Of her memory.

Sweet memories...
Sweet memories...

He hummed a compelling melody line at the end of the
verse, and she watched his beautiful fingers, the tendons of his
left thumb grown powerful from years of barring chords, the
square-cut nails of his right hand plucking or strumming the
steel strings.

She watched his eyes, which had somehow come to rest on her own as the words of the last verse came somberly from his sensitive lips.

She slipped into the darkness
Of my dreams last night.
Wandering from room to room
She's turning on each light.
Her laughter spills like water
From the river to the sea
Lord, I'm swept away from sadness
Clinging to her memory.

The haunting notes of the chorus came again, and Theresa softly hummed in harmony.

Sweet memories...
Sweet memories...

She had crossed her calves, hooked them with her forearms and drawn her knees up, raising her eyes to his. And as he looked deeply into the brown depths, grown limpid with emotion, Brian realized she was not some soulful groupie, gazing up in adulation. She was something more, much more. And as the song quietly ended, he realized he'd found the way to break down Theresa's barriers.

The room rang with silence.

There were tears on Theresa's face.

Neither she nor Brian seemed to remember her brother was there beside them.

"Who wrote it?" she asked in a reverent whisper.

"Mickey Newbury."

She was stricken to think there existed a man named Mickey Newbury whose poignant music she had missed, whose words and melodies spoke to the soul and whispered to the heart.

Since she could not thank the composer, she thanked the performer who had gifted her with an offering superseding any that could be found wrapped in gay ribbons beneath a Christmas tree.

"Thank you, Brian."

He nodded and handed the Stella back to Jeff. But Jeff had quietly slipped from the room. Brian's gaze returned to Theresa, still curled up at his feet. Her hair picked up the holiday colors from the lights behind her, and only the rim of her lips and nose was visible in the semidarkened room.

He slipped from the piano bench onto one knee, bracing the guitar on the carpet, his hand sliding down to curl around its neck. He could not make out the expression in her eyes, though he sensed the time was right...for both of them. Her breathing was fast and shallow, and the scent he'd detected in the steamy bathroom seemed to drift from her skin and hair—a clean, fresh essence so different from the girls in smoky night spots. Bracing elbow to knee, he bent to touch her soft, unspoiled lips with his own. Her face was uplifted as their breaths mingled, then he heard her catch her own and hold it. The kiss was as innocent and uncomplicated as the Chopin Prelude, but the instant Brian withdrew, Theresa shyly inclined her head. He wanted a fuller kiss, yet this one of green, untutored innocence was oddly satisfying. And she wasn't the kind of woman a man rushed. She seemed scarcely woman at all, but girl, far less accomplished at the art of kissing than at the art of playing the violin and the piano. Her unpracticed kiss was suddenly more refreshing than any he'd ever shared.

He pushed back, straightened and intoned quietly, "Merry Christmas, Theresa."

Her eyes lifted to his face. Her voice trembled. "Merry Christmas, Brian."

Chapter Five

The week that followed was one of the happiest of Theresa's life. They had few scheduled duties, the city at their feet and money with which to enjoy it. She and Brian enjoyed being together, though they were rarely alone. Everywhere they went the group numbered four, with Jeff and Patricia along, or five, if Amy came, too, which she often did.

They spent an entire day at the new zoo, which was practically at their doorstep, located less than two miles away, on the east side of Burnsville. There they enjoyed the animals in their natural winter habitat, rode the monorail part of the time, then walked, ate hot dogs and drank hot coffee.

It was a sunless day, but bright, glittery with hoarfrost upon the surface of the snow. The world was a study in black and white. The oak branches startled the eye, so onyx-black against the backdrop of pristine landscape. The animals were sluggish, posed against the winter setting, their breaths rising in nebulous vapors, white on white. But the polar bears were up and about, looking like great shaggy pears with legs. Before their den, Theresa and Brian paused, arms on the rail, side by side. The bears lumbered about, coats pure and as colorless as the day. A giant male lifted his nose to the air, a single black blot against all that white.

"Look at him," Brian said, pointing. "The only things that are black are his eyes, lips, nose and toenails. On an arctic ice floe he becomes practically invisible. But he's smart enough to know how that nose shows. I once saw a film of a polar bear sneaking up on an unsuspecting seal with one paw over his nose and mouth.''

It was a new side of Brian Scanlon: nature lover. She was intrigued and turned to study his profile. ''Did it work?''

His eyes left the bears and settled on her. ''Of course it worked. The poor seal never knew what hit her.'' Their eyes clung. Theresa grew conscious of the contact of Brian's elbow on the rail beside hers—warm, even through their jackets. His eyes made a quick check across her shoulder where the others stood, then returned to her lips before he began to close the space between them. But Theresa was too shy to kiss in public and quickly turned to study the bears. Her cheeks felt hot against the crisp air as Brian's gaze lingered for a moment before he straightened and said softly, ''Another time.''

It happened before the habitat of another animal whose coat had turned winter white. They were watching the ermine coats of the minks when Theresa turned toward Brian saying, ''I don't think I could wear—''

He was only three inches away, encroaching, with a hand covering his nose and mouth, eyes gleaming with amused intent.

She smiled and pulled back. ''What in the world are you doing?''

From underneath his glove came a muffled voice. ''I'm trying the polar bear's sneaky tactics.''

She was laughing when his glove slipped aside and swept around her, his two hands now holding her captive against a black railing. The quick kiss fell on her open lips. It was a failure of a kiss, as far as contact goes, for two cold noses bumped, and laughter mingled between their mouths. After the brief contact, he remained as he was, arms and body forming a welcome prison while she leaned backward from the waist, the rail pressed against her back and her hands resting on the front of his jacket.

"There, you see," she claimed breathily, "it didn't work. I saw you coming anyway."

"Next time you won't," he promised.

And she hoped he was right.

Patricia took them on a guided tour of Normandale College campus, beaming with pride at its rolling, wooded acres. They were walking along a curving sidewalk between two buildings with Patricia and Jeff in the lead, when Jeff's elbow hooked Patricia's neck and he hauled her close, kissing her as they continued ambling. Brian's eyes swerved to Theresa's, questioning. But Amy walked with them, and the moment went unfulfilled.

The following night they went to St. Paul's famed Science Omnitheater and lay back in steeply tilted seats, surrounded by an entire hemisphere of projected images that took them soaring through outer space, whizzing past stars and planets with tummy-tickling reality. But the dizzying sense of vertigo caused by the 180-degree curved screen seemed nothing compared to that created by Brian when he found Theresa's hand in the dark, eased close and reached his free hand to the far side of her jaw, turning her face toward his. The angle of the seats was severe, as if they were at a carnival, riding the bullet on its ascent before the spinning downward plunge. For a moment he didn't move, but lay back against his seat with the lights from the screen lining his face in flickering silver. His eyes appeared deep black, like those of the polar bear, and Theresa was conscious of the vast force of gravity pressing her into her chair and of the fact that Brian could not lift his head without extreme effort.

His forehead touched hers. Again their noses met. But their eyes remained open as warm lips touched, brushed, then gently explored this newfound anxiety within them both. There was a queer elation to the sense of helplessness caused by their positions. She wished they were upright so she could turn fully into his arms. But instead she settled for the straining of their bodies toward each other, and again, the unfulfilled wishes that grew stronger with each foray he initiated.

The elementary kiss ended with three teasing nibbles that caught, caught, caught her mouth and tugged sensuously before he lay back in his seat again, watching her face for reaction.

"No fair making me dizzy," she whispered.

They were still holding hands. His thumb made forceful circles against her palm. "You sure it's not the movie?"

"I thought it was at first, but I'm much dizzier now."

He smiled, kept his eyes locked with hers as he lifted her hand and placed its palm against his mouth, wetting it with his tongue as he kissed it.

"Me too," he breathed, then carried the hand to his lap and held it against his stomach, folded between his palms before he began stroking its soft skin with the tips of his callused fingers while he turned his attention back to the broad screen. She tried to do likewise, but with little success. For the interstellar space flight happening on the screen was vapid when compared to the nova created by Brian Scanlon's simplest kiss.

One evening Brian and Jeff provided the music for the promised rock session, to which Amy invited a mob of her friends. The house was inundated with noisy teenagers who gave their approval by way of prompt, rapt silence the moment the music began.

Theresa was cajoled into joining the two on piano, and before ten minutes were up, the boys and girls were dancing on the hard kitchen floor, after Margaret came through the living room decreeing, "No dancing on my carpet!" She seemed to forget she and her husband had danced a hoedown on it within the past week.

Still, the evening was an unqualified success, and at its end, Amy was basking in the reflected glow of "stardom," for all her friends went away assured that Jeff and Brian would be cutting a record in Nashville soon.

The day following the party there were no plans made. All five of them were together in the living room, lounging and visiting. The stereo was tuned to a radio station, and when a familiar song come on, Brian unexpectedly lunged to his feet, announcing, "The perfect song to learn to dance to!" He exaggerated a courtly bow before Theresa and extended his hand. "We've got to teach this woman before Saturday night."

"What's Saturday night?" Amy asked.

"New Year's Eve," answered Patricia. "I've invited these two to join Jeff and me and a group of our friends."

Jeff added, "But your sister claims ignorance and has declined to go."

Theresa dropped her eyes from the hand Brian still held out in invitation. "Oh no, please. I can't...." She felt utterly foolish, not knowing how to dance at age twenty-five.

"No excuses. It's time you learned."

She replied with the most convenient red herring she could dream up on short notice. "No dancing on the carpet!"

"Oh, go ahead," Amy said, then admitted, "the girls and I dance on the carpet all the time when mother's at work. I won't tell."

"There!" Theresa looked up at Brian, feeling her face had grown red. "Dance with Amy."

To Theresa's relief, Brian willingly complied. "All right." He directed his courtly gesture to the younger girl. "Amy, may I have this dance? We'll demonstrate for your reluctant sibling."

Amy's braces caught a flash of afternoon sun from the window as she beamed in unabashed delight. "I thought you'd never ask," she replied cheekily.

Looking on, Theresa felt years younger than Amy, who, at fourteen, could bound to her feet, come back with a coquettish response, then present her slim body for leading. Theresa wished she could be as uninhibited and self-confident as her younger sister. Jeff and Patricia joined in the demonstration, Jeff holding his partner stiffly and frowning. "Watch carefully now...a-one...a-two...."

As he always could, Jeff made Theresa laugh with his proficient clowning, for he held Patricia in a prim, stiff-backed, wide-apart mime of the traditional dance position, until the girl threw up her hands and declared laughingly, "You're a hopeless case, Brubaker. Find yourself another partner."

Jeff didn't ask, he commandeered. One minute Theresa was watching from the piano bench, the next she was on her feet, being sashayed around in Jeff's arms. Askance, she saw Brian watching her progress. In all honesty, Theresa had no delusions about being able to dance and dance gracefully. Now, with her brother, her natural rhythm couldn't be denied. Theresa's feet took over where her self-consciousness left off. Within a dozen bars, she was moving smoothly to the music.

She'd been hoodwinked—she realized it later—by Jeff and Brian, who'd probably been in cahoots the entire time—for she'd been following Jeff's lead no more than a minute when her hand was captured by Brian's. "I'm cutting in, Brubaker. Snowball time."

After that there seemed no question about New Year's Eve. And when Theresa surreptitiously took Patricia aside to ask what she was wearing, the issue seemed settled.

On Friday, Theresa knocked on Amy's door, but when she got no answer, she peeped inside to find her sister lying in a trancelike state, arms thrown wide, ankle draped over updrawn knee, eyes shut, with the black vinyl headset clamped around her skull.

Theresa went in, closed the door behind herself and touched Amy's knee.

Amy's eyes came open, and she lifted one earpiece from her head. "Hmm?"

"Would you take that thing off for a minute?"

"Sure." Amy flung it aside, braced up on both elbows. "What's up?"

"Hon, I have a really big favor to ask you."

"Anything—name it."

"I need you to come shopping with me."

Amy mused for a minute, then rolled to one hip, reaching for the controls of the stereo to stop the music that was still filtering through the headphones. Then she sat up. "Shopping for what?"

Even before she asked, Theresa realized how ironic it was that she, the older, should be seeking the advice of a sister eleven years her junior. "Something to wear tomorrow night."

"You goin' to the dance?"

For a moment Theresa feared Amy might display an adolescent jealousy and wasn't sure how she'd deal with it. But when Theresa nodded, Amy bounded off the bed exuberantly. "Great! It's about time! When we goin'?"

An hour later the sisters found themselves in the Burnsville Shopping Center, scouring three levels of stores. In the first dressing room, Theresa slipped on a black crepe evening dress that gave her shivers of longing. But it was scarcely over her head before her perennial problem became all too evident: her bottom half was a size nine, but her top half would have required a size sixteen to girth her circumference.

Theresa looked up and met Amy's eyes in the mirror. They'd never before exchanged a single word about Theresa's problem. But, distraught, the older sister suddenly became glum and depressed. Her gaiety evaporated, and her expression wilted. "Oh, Amy, I'll never find a dress. Not with these damn, disgusting...*dirigibles* of mine!"

Amy's expression became sympathetic. "They make it tough, huh?"

Theresa's shoulders slumped. "Tough isn't the word. Do

you know that I haven't been able to buy one single dress without altering it since I was the age you are now?''

''Yeah, I know. I…well, I asked mom about it one time…I mean, if it's hard for you and stuff, and if…well, if I might get as big as you.''

Theresa turned and placed her hands on Amy's shoulders. ''Oh, Amy, I hope you never do. I worry about it, too. I wouldn't wish a shape like mine on a pregnant elephant. It's horrible—not being able to buy clothes and being scared to dance with a man and—''

''You mean, *that's* why you wouldn't dance with Brian?''

''That's the only reason. I just.…'' Theresa considered a moment, then went on. ''You're old enough to understand, Amy. You're fourteen. You've been growing. You know how the boys look at you funny as soon as you have a pair of goose bumps on your chest. Only when mine started growing they just kept right on until they got to the size of watermelons, and the boys were merciless. And when the boys were no longer boys, but men, well.…'' Theresa shrugged.

''I figured that was why you wear those ugly sweaters all the time.''

''Oh, Amy, are they ugly?''

Amy looked penitent. ''Gol, Theresa, I didn't mean it that way, I just meant…well, I know you never wore that neat sweat shirt I gave you last Christmas. It was way more *in* than anything you had—that's why I bought it for you.''

''I've tried it on at least a dozen times, but I'm always scared to step out of my bedroom in it.''

''Gol.…'' The word was a breathy lament as Amy stood pondering the everyday dilemmas her sister had to face. ''Well, we could pick out something nice for tomorrow night if we got separate pieces, like a skirt and sweater or something.''

''Not a sweater, Amy. I wouldn't be comfortable.''

''Well, you can't go out for New Year's Eve in corduroy

slacks and a white blouse with an old granny cardigan over your shoulders!''

"Do you think I *want* to?"

"Well...." Amy threw up her palms in the air. "*Horse poop,* there's got to be something in this entire shopping center that's better than *that.*" She cast a scathing look at the fashionless shirt Theresa had discarded.

Theresa found her sense of humor again. "Horse *poop?* I suppose mother doesn't know you say things like that, just like she doesn't suspect you dance on the living-room carpet?" Theresa knew perfectly well that at fourteen, Amy experimented with a gamut of profanity much worse than what she'd just uttered—she was at the age where such experiments were to be expected.

Suddenly the gleam in Amy's eyes duplicated the one from her dental hardware. "Listen, what about the sweater? Don't say no until you try, okay?" She splayed her fingers in the air and gazed toward heaven, theatrically. "I have *theee* perfect one. *Theee* most *excellent* sweater ever created by sheep or test tube! I've had my eye on it since before Christmas, but I was outa bucks, so I couldn't get it for myself. But if they have one left in large, you're gonna love it!"

A quarter hour later, Theresa stood before a different mirror, in a different shop, in a different garment that solved all her problems while remaining perfectly in vogue.

It was a lightweight bulky acrylic of rich, deep plum. The neckline sported a generous cowl collar that seemed to become one with wide dolman sleeves. Because it draped rather than clung, it seemed to partially conceal Theresa's overly generous silhouette.

"Oh, Amy, it's perfect!"

"I told you!"

"But what about slacks?"

Amy nabbed a pair of finely tailored gabardine trousers of indefinable color: soft, subtle, as if tinted by the smoke from burning violets. She stood back to assess her older sister and proclaimed in the most overused word of her teenage vernacular, *"Excellent."*

Theresa whirled around and grabbed her sister in a compulsive hug. "It is! It is excellent."

Amy beamed with pride, then took command again. "Shoes next. He's got a good six inches on you, so you could stand a little extra height. Some classy heels. Whaddya say?"

"Shoes…right!"

Theresa was pulling her head from beneath the sweater when she thought of the one last thing she'd need help with. "Amy, do you think I'd look too conspicuous if I tried a little bit of makeup?"

Amy's lips were covering her braces as Theresa asked, but her smile grew crooked, and wide, then winked in the glow of the dressing-room's overhead light fixture. "Well, it's about time!" she declared.

"Now, just a minute, Amy," Theresa said as she noted the gleam in her sister's eye. "I haven't decided for sure.…"

But that evening, something happened that crystallized the decision. She was in her room, the door open as she was examining the new sweater, when she felt someone's eyes on her. She looked up to find Brian in the doorway, studying her. It was the first time he'd seen her bedroom, and his eyes made a lazy circle, pausing on the shelf holding her pewter figurine collection, then dropping to the bed, neatly made, and finally returning to Theresa, who had quickly replaced the sweater in the closet.

"Have I managed to change your mind about the dance yet?" He crossed his arms and nonchalantly leaned one shoulder against the doorframe.

Theresa had never been honorably pursued before; it took some getting used to. It was disconcerting, having him peruse her bedroom, which seemed an intimate place to come face to face with a man. She'd turned toward him, and he remained very still, one hip cocked as he lounged comfortably and kept his eye on her. *Do I look him in the eye? Or in the middle of his chest? Or at some spot beyond his shoulder? Twenty-five years old and acting less self-confident than I'm sure Amy would act in this situation.* She chose the middle of his chest.

"Yes, you have, but don't expect me to dance as well as Amy."

"All I'll expect is that at some point during the evening, you'll at least look me in the eye."

Her unsettled gaze flew up to his, caught a teasing grin there and dropped again, flustered.

"So this is where you hide away." As he moved farther into the room, he nodded toward the shelf. "I see The Maestro has joined the others. I envy him his spot, looking down on your pillow." He stopped close before her.

She searched but could find not a single reply and swallowed hard, feeling the blush creep up.

"Jeff was right, you know?" Brian teased softly.

She raised questioning eyes to his teasing brown ones.

"R...right? About what?"

"The blush camouflages the freckles. But don't ever stop." With a gentle fingertip he brushed her right cheek. "It's completely irresistible." Then he turned and sauntered off down the hall, leaving Theresa with her fingertips grazing the spot of skin he'd so lightly touched. It seemed to tingle yet. The touch had been petal light, but she'd felt the calluses on his fingertips. Both the sensation and his teasing had left her with a light head and a fluttering heart.

That night, late, Theresa tapped softly at Amy's door, then went in to announce, "I'm going to need your help learning how to put on makeup, and I'll have to borrow some of yours, if you don't mind."

Amy's only answer was a beam of approval as she dragged Theresa farther into the room and shut the door with a decisive click.

They did a trial run that lasted till the wee hours. Sitting before a lighted makeup mirror in Amy's room, Theresa experienced the full range of giddy adolescent give-and-take she'd missed out on when she'd been at the age of puberty. The makeup session brought a twofold benefit: not only did it free the butterfly from the chrysalis, it also brought the two sisters closer. Given the disparity in their ages, they'd had little chance to share experiences of this kind.

Amy began by experimenting with foundation colors, trying a rainbow of skin tones on various sections of Theresa's face until the redhead declared, "I look like a Grandma Moses painting!"

Assessing, Amy corrected, "No, more like her palette, I think." They shared a laugh, then went to work finding the right hue that skillfully camouflaged the freckles and gave Theresa a new, subdued radiance.

Next came the eyes, but as Amy bent over Theresa's shoulder and peered critically in the mirror at the blue grease they'd smeared on one freckled eyelid, they burst out laughing once more.

"Yukk! Get it off! It feels like lard and looks like I took a beating."

"Agreed!"

Next they tried a green powder-base eyeshadow, but it made Theresa look like a stop-and-go light, so off it went, too. They settled on an almost translucent mauve that had so little color it couldn't clash with the skin and hair tones that needed to be catered to.

The first time Theresa tried to use the eyelash curler, she pinched her eyelid and yelped in pain.

"This is like trying to curl the hair on a caterpillar's back!" she despaired. "There's nothing there. I hate my eyelashes anyway. They have as much color as a glass of water."

"We'll fix that."

But the tears rolled from beneath her abused lids, and it took several long, painful minutes before Theresa got the hang of the curler, then learned how to brush her lashes with a mascara wand. The results, however, surprised even herself.

"Why, I never knew my lashes were so long!"

"That's 'cause you never saw the ends of 'em before."

They were a total wonder—quite spiky and alluring and made her whole face look bright and...and sexy!

The powdered blush proved an absolute disaster. They swabbed it off faster than they'd brushed it on, deciding Theresa's natural coloring couldn't compete with added highlighting, and decided to stick with the foundation hue only.

Theresa had always worn lipgloss, but now they tried several new shades, and Amy demonstrated how to skillfully blend two colors and accent the pretty bowed shape of her sister's upper lip with a highlighter stick.

With the makeup complete, Theresa appeared transformed. It was a drastic change but one that made her smile at Amy in the mirror.

Yet, Amy wasn't totally pleased. "That hair," Amy grunted in disgust.

"Well, I can't change the color, and I can't keep it from pinging all over like it was shot out of a frosting decorator."

"No, but you could go to the beauty shop and let somebody else figure out what to do with it."

"The beauty shop?"

"Why not?"

"But I'm going to look conspicuous enough with all this makeup on. What would he think if I showed up with a different hairdo, too?"

"Oh, horse poop!" Amy pronounced belligerently, jamming her hands onto her trim hips. "He'll think it's super."

"But I don't want to look like...well, it's a date."

"But it *is* a date!"

"No, it's not. He's two years younger than I am. I'm just filling in, that's all."

But in spite of her protests, Theresa recalled Brian's teasing earlier this evening and admitted he'd seemed fully amenable to being her escort.

Several minutes later, standing before the wide mirror at the bathroom vanity, she caught her glistening lower lip between her teeth in an effort to contain the smile of approval that wanted to wing across her features. Then her lip escaped her teeth, and she smiled widely at what she saw. She liked her face! For the first time in her life she genuinely liked it. It seemed a desecration to have to cleanse the skin and remove the radiance from the creature who looked so happy and pleased with herself.

As she forced herself to turn on the water and pick up the bar of soap, it seemed as if tomorrow night would never get there.

But New Year's Eve day arrived at last, and Theresa managed to get an eleventh-hour appointment on this busiest day of the year in the beauty shops. In the late afternoon, she returned home the proud possessor of a new haircut and of the simple tool required to achieve the natural bounce of ringlets on her own: a hairpick.

The beautician's suggestion had been to simply shape the hair and stop trying to subdue it but to soften it with a cream rinse and let it bounce free, with just a few flicks of the wrist and pick to guide it into a halo of color about her head. Even the redness seemed less offensive, for with the light filtering through it, it looked less brash.

While she hung up her coat in the entry closet, Brian called from the living room, "Hi."

But she avoided a direct confrontation with him and hurried down the hall to her room with no more than a "Hi" in return.

And now everyone was scuttling around, getting ready. The bathroom had a steady stream of traffic. Theresa took a quick shower, then went to her room and was applying a new after-bath talc she'd ventured to buy. It had a light, petally fragrance reminiscent of the potpourri used by women in days of old. Subtle, feminine.

She paused with the puff in her hand and cocked her head. On the other side of her bedroom wall was the bathroom, so sounds carried through. She heard a masculine cough and recognized it as Brian's. The shower ran for several minutes during which there were two thumps, like an elbow hitting the wall, while images went skittering through her mind. There followed the whine of a blow dryer, then a long silence—shaving—after which he started humming "Sweet Memories." Theresa smiled and realized she'd been standing naked for some time, dwelling on what was going on in the bathroom.

Crossing to the mirror, she assessed her devastatingly enormous breasts and wished for the thousandth time in as many days that she'd been in the other line when mammary glands were handed out. She turned away in disgust and found a clean brassiere. Donning it, she had to lean forward to let the pendulous weights drop into the cups before straightening to hook the back clasp of the hideous garment. It had all the feminine allure of a hernia truss! The wide straps had shoulder guards, meant to keep the weight from cutting into her flesh, but the deep grooves dented her shoulders just the same. The bra's utilitarian white fabric was styled for "extra support." How she hated the words! And how she hated the lingerie industry. They owed an apology to thousands of women across America for offering not a single large-size brassiere in any of the feminine pastels of orchid, peach or powder blue. Apparently women of her proportions weren't supposed to have a sense of color when it came to underwear! No wistful longing to clothe themselves in anything except antiseptic, commonsense, white!

Just once—oh, just once!—how she'd love to browse along the counters of feminine underthings with tiny bikini panties and bras to match and consider buying a foolishly extravagant teddy, only to see what it felt like to have such a piece of feminine frippery against her skin.

But she wasn't given the chance, for a teddy with size double-D cups would look as if it were two lace circus tents.

White undergarments in place, Theresa covered the full-figure white cotton bra with the new sweater and immediately felt more benevolent toward both herself and the clothing industry. The sweater was stylish and attractive and helped restore her excitement. The smoke-hued trousers fit smoothly, flatteringly, over her small hips, and the strappy high-heeled sandals she'd chosen added just the right touch of frivolity. Theresa had never been fond of jewelry, particularly earrings, for they only drew attention to a woman's face. But as she slipped a wristwatch beneath the cuff of the sweater, she decided her new mocha nail treatment deserved setting off, so clipped a delicate gold chain bracelet around her left wrist. Finally, into the draped cowl neck of the sweater, she inserted a tiny gold stick pin shaped like a treble clef.

Then she went across the hall to Amy's room to reproduce the makeup magic created in last night's secret session. But Theresa's hands were so shaky she couldn't seem to manage the applicators and wands.

Amy noticed and couldn't help teasing. "Considering this is *not* a date, you're in a pretty twittery state."

Theresa's brown eyes widened in dismay. "Oh, does it show?"

"You might want to stop wiping your palms on your thighs every thirty seconds. Pretty soon your new slacks are going to look like a plumber's coveralls."

"It's silly, I know. I wish I could be more like you, Amy. You're always bright and witty, and even around boys you always seem to know the right things to say and how to act. Oh, this must sound ridiculous coming from a woman my age."

Somehow Amy's next comment was again just the perfect

choice to calm Theresa's nerves somewhat. "He's going to love your new hairdo and your makeup and your outfit, too, so quit worrying. Here, give me that eyeshadow and shut your eyes."

But as Theresa tipped her head back and did as ordered, her sister was given the difficult job of applying makeup to trembling lids. Yet, she managed to produce the same magical effect as the night before, and when Theresa looked into Amy's lighted makeup mirror, all complete, dewy and lashy, she unconsciously pressed a palm to her chest in astonishment.

Smiling, Amy encouraged, "See? I told you."

And for that precious moment, Theresa believed it. She swung around to give Amy an impulsive hug, thinking how happy she suddenly was that none of this had ever happened before. It was wonderful experiencing these first Cinderella feelings at age twenty-five.

"Good luck, huh?" Amy's smile was sincere as she stood back and stuck her hands in the pockets of her jeans.

In answer, Theresa blew an affectionate kiss from the doorway. As she turned to leave, Amy added, "Oh, and put on some perfume, huh?"

"Oh, perfume. But I haven't got any. I got some new bath powder, but you must not be able to smell it."

"Here, try this."

They chose a subtle, understated fragrance from the bottles cluttering Amy's dresser top, leaving nothing more for Theresa to do but face Brian Scanlon. That, however, was going to be the most difficult moment of all.

Back in her room, Theresa puttered around, putting away stray pieces of clothing, checking her watch several times. She heard the voices of Jeff and Brian from the other end of the house, joined by Amy's and her parents'. Everyone was waiting for her, and she suddenly wished she'd been ready first so she wouldn't have had to make a grand entrance. But it was too late now. She didn't care if she soiled her new trousers or not, she gave one last swipe of her palms along the gabardine, took a deep breath and went out to face the music.

They were all in the kitchen. Her mother and father were sitting at the table over cups of coffee. Amy stood with her hands in her front pockets telling Jeff she was going babysitting tonight. Brian was at the sink, running himself a glass of water.

Theresa stepped into the room with her heart tripping out sixteenth notes. Jeff caught sight of her, and his smiling response was instantaneous. "Well, would you lookit here...I think I asked the wrong girl to go out with me tonight." He swooped Theresa into his arms and took her on a Ginger Rogers-Fred Astaire swirl while grinning wickedly into her eyes, then affecting a convincing Bogart drawl, "Hiya, doll, whaddya say we get it on tonight?"

Brian looked back over his shoulder, and the water glass stopped half way to his lips.

As Jeff brought his sister to a breathless halt, she was laughing, aware that Brian had spilled out the water without drinking any. He turned away from the sink and crossed to clap a hand on Jeff's shoulder.

"Just your tough luck, Brubaker. I asked her first." His approving gaze settled on Theresa, creating a glow about her heart.

"Isn't her new hairdo great?" piped up Amy. "And she bought the outfit especially for tonight."

Amy Brubaker, I could strangle you. Jeff lightened his hold and settled Theresa against his hip. "She did, huh?"

Brian's eyes made a quick trip down to her knees, then back up to her makeup and hair. To the best of Theresa's recollection, it was the first time his eyes had ever scanned anything below her neck.

Margaret spoke up then. "Jeffrey, turn your sister around. I haven't had a look at what that beauty operator did to her yet."

Does everybody in the house have to blurt out everything? Beneath her fresh, translucent makeup Theresa could feel the pink ruining the entire effect and hoped that for once it didn't show. Jeff swung her around for her mother and father's approval, but at her shoulder she felt Brian's eyes following.

To Theresa's further chagrin, her mother's verdict was, "You should have done that years ago."

"You look pretty as a picture, dear," added Willard.

Unaccustomed to being the center of attention like this, Theresa could think only of escape.

"It's time to leave."

Jeff released her to check his watch. "Yup. You can head out. Patricia should be here any minute. She's picking me up in her car."

Theresa whirled around in surprise. "Aren't we all going together?"

"No, she's afraid I might overindulge tonight, and since she claims she's always levelheaded, she thought it would be best if she drove her car and dropped me off at home instead of the other way around."

"Oh." Once she grunted the monosyllable, Theresa felt conspicuous, for nobody said anything more. She realized she sounded rather dubious and ill at ease about being left alone with Brian. But he went to get her coat from the front-hall closet, and Jeff nudged her in the back. She followed and let Brian ease the coat over her shoulders, then she found herself doing something she'd never done before: helping Brian with his. He was dressed in form-fitting designer blue jeans, and a corduroy sport coat of cocoa brown under which showed a neutral tweed rag-knit sweater with the collar of a white shirt peeking from under its crew neck. As he struggled to thread his arms into a hip-length wool coat, she reacted as politeness dictated, reaching to assist him when the shoulder of his jacket caught. Theresa experienced an unexpected thrill of pleasure, performing the insignificant service.

"Thanks." He lifted the outer garment and shrugged his shoulders in a peculiarly masculine adjustment that made her knees feel weak. He smelled good, too. And suddenly all she could think of was getting out of the house and into the car where darkness would mask the feelings she was certain were alternately making her blush and blanch.

She kissed her mother and father good-night. "Happy New Year, both of you." They were spending it at home, watching the celebration in Times Square on television. "Amy...." Theresa turned to find her sister's eyes following her wistfully. "Thanks, honey."

"Sure." Amy leaned her hips back against the edge of the kitchen counter and followed their progress as Brian opened the door for Theresa and saw her out. "Hey, you're both knockouts!" she called just before the door closed.

They smiled goodbye, and a moment later were engulfed by the cold silence outside. Theresa's car waited in the driveway where she'd left it as she'd rushed in from the hair appointment. Brian found her elbow while they crossed the icy blacktop, but she suddenly didn't want to drive. It would take some of the magic away. "Would you mind driving, Brian?"

He stopped. They were at the front of the car, heading around toward the driver's side. "Not at all." Instead of leaving her there, he guided her to the passenger side, opened her door and waited while she settled herself inside.

When his door slammed, they found themselves laughing at his knees digging into the dashboard.

"Sorry," Theresa offered, "my legs are shorter than yours."

He fumbled in the dark, found the proper lever, and the seat went sliding back while he let out a whoof of breath. "Whoo! Are they ever!"

She handed him the keys and he fumbled again, groping for the ignition. "Here." In the blackness, their knuckles brushed as she reached to point out the right spot. The brief touch set off a tingle in her hand, then the key clicked home and the engine came to life.

"Thanks for letting me drive. A person misses it." He adjusted the mirror, shifted into reverse, and they were rolling.

The quiet was disarming. The scent she remembered emanated from his hair and clothing and mingled with her own borrowed perfume. The dash lights lit his face from below, and she wanted to turn and study him, but faced front, resisting the urge.

"So that's where you went this afternoon—to the beauty shop. I wondered."

"Amy and her big mouth." But Theresa grinned in the dark.

He laughed indulgently. "I like it. It looks good on you."

She glanced left and found his eyes on her dimly lit hair and quickly looked away.

"Thank you." *What is a woman expected to reply at a time like this?* Theresa wanted to say she loved his hair, too, but she really preferred a man's hair longer than the Air Force allowed, though she loved the smell of his, and the color of it. She heartily approved of the clothing he'd chosen tonight, but before she could decide whether or not to say so, Brian suggested, "Why don't you put on something classical? We'll have our fill of rock before the night is over."

The music filled the uncomfortable transition period while they rode, with Theresa giving occasional directions. Within fifteen minutes they reached the Rusty Scupper, a night spot frequented by a young adult crowd, many of them singles. They helped each other with coats, left them at the coat check and were shown to a long table set up for a large group. Theresa recognized some of Jeff's friends and performed introductions, watching as Brian shook hands with the men and was ogled by some of the women, whose eyes lingered on him with that inquisitive approval of the single female presented with an attractive male novelty. She watched their eyes drop down his torso and realized with a start that some women checked out men in much the same way men checked out women. She was totally abashed when an attractive sable-haired beauty named

Felice returned her eyes to Brian's and smiled with a blatant glint of sexual approval. "Keep a dance free from me later, okay, Brian? And make sure it's a slow one."

"I'll do that," he replied politely, withdrawing his hand from the one that had retained his longer than was usual. He returned to Theresa's side, pulled out her chair and settled himself beside her.

In a voice low enough for only her ears, he questioned, "Who's she?"

Theresa felt dreadfully deflated that he should ask. "Felice Durand is one of the crowd. She's hung around with Jeff and his bunch since high school."

"Remind me to be monopolized by you during the slow dances," he returned wryly, filling Theresa with a soaring sense of relief. She herself had little experience on the boy-girl social scene, and Felice's bold assessment of Brian's body, followed by her forward invitation, was unnerving. But apparently not all men were hooked by bait as obvious as that dangled by Felice Durand. Theresa's respect for Brian slid up another notch.

Jeff and Patricia arrived then, and the table filled with lively chatter, laughter and orders for cocktails. Soon thereafter menus arrived, and Theresa was astounded at the inflated New Year's prices that had been substituted but told herself an evening with Brian would be worth it.

Carafes of wine were delivered, glasses filled and toasts proposed. Touching his glass to Jeff's, Brian intoned, "To old friends...." And with a touch of the rim upon Patricia's glass, and finally upon Theresa's, he added, "and to new."

His eyes held a steady green spark of approval as they sought hers and lingered after she self-consciously dropped her gaze to the ruby liquid, then drank.

Dinner was noisy and exuberant, and for the most part Theresa and Brian listened to the banter without taking part. She felt relieved that he, like her, was rather an outsider. She felt drawn to him, in a welcome semiexclusion.

Over tiny stem glasses of crème de menthe, they relaxed, sat back in their chairs and waited for the dancing to begin.

The dancing. Just the thought of it filled Theresa with a mixture of apprehension and eagerness. It hadn't been so difficult turning into Brian's arms that day in the living room. Here, the dance floor would be crowded; nobody would notice them among all the others. It should be easy to submit to the embrace of an attractive man like Brian, yet at the thought, Theresa felt a tremor tumble through her lower belly. *He's been stuck with me.*

Just then the waitress approached and spoke to the group at their general end of the table. ''As soon as the dancing starts, it's a cash bar only, so if you wouldn't mind, we'd like to get the dinner bill settled up now.''

Automatically, Theresa reached for her purse, just as Brian lifted one hip from the chair, pushed back his sport coat and sought his hip pocket. As he came up with a billfold, she produced the purse and was reaching to unzip it when his fingers closed over hers.

''You're with me,'' he ordered simply. Her eyes flew to his. They were steady, insistent. His cool fingers still rested upon her tense ones while her heart sent out a crazy stutter step.

Yes, I am, she thought. *I'm really with you.*

''Thank you, Brian.''

He squeezed her fingers, then his slipped away, and for the first time she truly felt like his date.

Chapter Six

The band had a lot of talent wrapped up in five members, plus a female singer. They played a mix of mid- to easy rock, ranging from The Eagles to Ronstadt to The Commodores to Stevie Wonder, but all their music had a hard, sure beat to encourage dancers onto the floor, then once they were warmed up, back to the tables to cool down with another round of drinks. When half the group deserted their table in favor of the dance floor, Brian and Theresa remained behind in companionable silence, watching the dancers.

The band slammed into the driving beat of a recent Journey hit, and Theresa found herself mesmerized by the back view of Felice Durand's gyrating hips. She was wearing a fire engine red dress that slithered on her derriere with so much resistance that Theresa was certain the friction would soon send up a trail of smoke. But she was good. She moved with feline seductiveness, never missing a beat, incorporating hands, arms, shoulders and pelvis in a provocative invitation to naughtiness. Watching, Theresa felt a twinge of jealousy.

Suddenly Felice spun in a half circle, her back now to her partner as she sent an open-mouthed look of innuendo over her shoulder at him. Two more shakes and her eyes spied Brian. His chair was half turned toward the dance floor while one elbow hung on the table edge. A quick glance told Theresa he'd been watching Felice for some time.

Without missing a beat, the woman somehow managed to shift all her attention to Brian. Her hips traced corkscrews, her mouth puckered in a glistening pout, and her hands with their glossy bloodred nails conveyed come-hither messages. Theresa's eyes moved back to Brian, and she saw his gaze drop from Felice's face to her breasts to her hips and stay there.

A moment later, Felice spun adroitly to face her partner, then maneuvered herself into the crowd where she couldn't be seen, as if to say, you want more, boy, come and get it.

Brian glanced at Theresa and caught her watching him. She quickly dropped her eyes to a plastic stir stick she'd been playing with. She felt herself coloring and felt suddenly very much out of place. This young, brash crowd wasn't for her. Jeff fit in here, maybe even Brian, but she didn't.

Just then the music changed. The keyboard player chimed the distinctive intro to "The Rose"—slow, moody, romantic.

From the corner of her eye, Theresa caught a flash of fire engine red zeroing in on Brian, but before it quite registered, he'd lunged to his feet, captured Theresa's hand and was towing her toward the dance floor. They'd barely left their chairs when they were intercepted by Felice and her partner returning to the table.

The sable-haired beauty looked attractively flushed and sheeny from her exertions as she stopped Brian's progress with a hand on his chest. "I thought this one might be mine."

"Sorry, Felice. This is our song, isn't it, Theresa?" Too astounded to answer, she let herself be pulled through the crowd onto the dance floor, where she was swung loosely into Brian's arms.

"Is it?" She peered up at him with a gamine grin.

"It is now." His own conspiratorial grin eased the discomfiture Theresa had been feeling while watching him observe Felice.

"It occurs to me that in less than two short weeks we've gathered enough of *our songs* to fill a concert program."

"Imagine what a mixed-up concert it would be. Chopin's Nocturne and Newbury's 'Sweet Memories.'"

"And 'The Rose,'" Theresa added.

"And don't forget 'Oh, I had a little chicken and he wouldn't lay an egg....'"

"*She* wouldn't lay an egg."

"What's the dif—"

"*He* chickens don't lay eggs, not even when you pour hot water up and down their legs."

Brian laughed, a melodic tenor sound that sent ripples of response through his dance partner. Something wonderful had happened. During their foolishness their feet had been unconsciously moving to the music. Theresa's natural musicality had taken over of its own accord. With her guard down, and distracted by both Felice and their conversation, she'd forgotten to bring her shy reservations along with her onto the dance floor. She was following Brian's graceful, expert lead with a joyous freedom. He was a superb dancer. Moving with him was effortless and fluid, though he kept a respectable distance between their bodies.

When had their laughter died? Brian's green eyes hadn't left Theresa's but gazed down into her uplifted face, while both of them fell silent.

"Brian," she said softly. "I don't care if you dance with Felice."

"I don't want to dance with Felice."

"I saw you watching her."

"It was rather unavoidable." His dark eyebrows drew together with a brief flicker of annoyance. "Listen, Felice is like the countless groupies who hang around at the foot of the stage and shake it for the guitar man, whichever one is playing that night, hoping to score after the dance. They're a dime a dozen, but that's not what I want tonight, okay? Not when I have something so much better."

At his last words his arms tightened and hauled her against him, that place she'd so often wondered about with half dread, half fascination. Her breasts were gently flattened against the corduroy panels of his sport coat, and her thighs felt the soft nudges of his steps. Upon her waist pressed a firm, secure palm, while hers found his solid shoulder muscle, his cool, extended palm. Against her temple his jaw rested.

I'm dancing. Breast to breast and thigh to thigh with a man. And it's wonderful. Theresa felt released and loose and altogether unselfconscious. Perhaps it was because, in spite of the fact that their bodies brushed, Brian retained a hold only possessive enough to guide her. His hips remained a discreet space apart while the other spots where Theresa's body touched his seemed alive and warmed.

He hummed quietly, the notes sure and true. The gentle vibrations of his voice trembled through his chest, and she felt it vaguely through her breasts. He smelled clean and slightly spicy, and she thought, *look at me, world. I'm falling in love with Brian Scanlon, and it's absolutely heavenly.*

The song ended, and he retreated but still held her lightly. His smile was as miraculous as the revelation she'd just experienced. Her own smile was timorous.

"You're a good dancer, Theresa."

"So are you."

The band eased into "Evergreen" without a pause, and as the notes began, it became understood Brian and Theresa would dance again. He took her against his body, dipping his head down a little lower this time, while she raised hers a fraction higher. And somehow it seemed portentous that the first word of the song was, "Love...."

"Theresa, you look as pretty tonight as I imagined you when Jeff first told me about you."

"Oh, Brian..." she began to protest.

"When I turned around and saw you standing in the kitchen I couldn't believe it."

"Amy helped me. I...well, I'm not too experienced at getting ready for dances."

He lifted his head, gazed into her eyes, folded her right palm against his heart and whispered, "I'm glad."

And the next thing she knew, her eyes and nose and forehead were riding within the warm, fragrant curve of his neck. Her cheek felt the textures of corduroy, wool and cotton and freshly shaved masculine skin. She drifted in his spicy scent that grew more pronounced as the heat of their joined skins released it from his jaw and neck. Somehow—some magical somehow— their hips had nestled together, and she felt for the first time the contour of his stomach against hers, of his warm flesh within the tight blue jeans, seeking to find hers as his forearm held her securely about her waist, pressing her and keeping her close.

She tried closing her eyes but found she was already dizzy from the emotions his nearness stirred in her, and the slow turns he executed increased her vertigo. She opened her eyes and saw through her own lacy lashes the outline of his Adam's apple only an inch away. She watched his thumb as it rubbed the backs of her knuckles in rhythm with the music. He had captured her hand by cupping its backside, and her palm lay flat, pressed against his chest. She felt the steady thump of his heart, then became aware of how callused his fingers were as they stroked her hand. She recalled that long-fingered left hand upon the neck of the guitar as he'd been singing to her. Her eyes drifted closed again as she basked in the new feeling of wonder at where she was, who she was with and what kind of man he was.

This time when the song ended, neither of them moved immediately. He squeezed the back of her hand harder and tightened his right arm until his elbow dug into the hollow of her spine.

Brian, she thought. *Brian.*

He eased back, never releasing her hand as he led the way to their table, and the band announced a break.

At their places, Theresa sat in a private cloud with nobody but him. Their chairs were side by side, turned slightly outward from the table, and when Brian sat, he crossed an ankle over a knee in such a way that the knee brushed the side of her thigh. He left it there intentionally, she thought, a thread of contact still bonding them together while they had to forgo dancing.

"So, tell me about what it's like to teach music to elementary-school kids."

She told him. More than she'd ever shared with any other man.

And while she talked, Brian studied her face, with its shifting expressions of laughter, thoughtfulness and something utterly pure and wholesome. *Yes, wholesome,* he thought. *This woman is wholesome in a way I've never encountered in another woman. Certainly in none of the Felices whose offers I've taken up whenever the mood struck me.*

Women like Felice, in their siren-red dresses, with their sleek hair and slithery hips—women like that are one-nighters. This woman is a lifetimer. What would she be like in bed? Naive and unsure and very likely a virgin, he thought. *Totally opposite to the practiced felines who could purr deep in their throats and press themselves against a man with skilled teasing, which somehow always managed to repel even as it allured. No, Theresa Brubaker would be as honest and fresh as...as the Chopin Nocturne,* he thought.

"So, tell me what it's like to be on a Strategic Air Command base during the day and playing at the officer's club in the evenings."

He told her.

And while he talked, Theresa pictured the Felices, the "townies" who gazed up at the guitar man from the foot of the stage, for his and Jeff's band also played gigs in the canteens where enlisted men were allowed to bring civilian dates. Theresa thought about what he'd said—something about countless groupies hanging around the stage and *shaking it* for the guitar man, hoping to score after the dance. But he'd added, that's not what he wanted tonight. *Tonight?* The implication was clear. Back at their air base there would doubtless be others who'd capture Brian's attention, others in fire engine red dresses with faces and bodies like Felice Durand's. A man like him wouldn't be content for long with a wallflower like herself.

She imagined Brian stepping off the stage, taking up the offer of some groupie, tumbling into bed with her for the night.

And if Brian had ample opportunity, she supposed her brother did, too. The thought was sobering.

She came from her musing to find Brian's eyes steady on her face as he spoke in a sober voice. "Theresa, next June, when Jeff and I get out, I'm thinking about settling around Minneapolis some place so he and I can get another band going here."

"You are?" Crazy commotion started in the vicinity of her heart. Brian, returning here to live permanently? "But what about Chicago?"

"I've got no ties there anymore. None that matter. The people I knew will practically be strangers after four years."

"Jeff has mentioned that you two talked about staying together, but what about the rest of the band?"

"We'll audition a drummer and a bass player here, and maybe a female singer, too. We'd like to get into private parties, but it'll take a couple of years of playing night spots and bars before we can manage that."

He seemed to be waiting for her approval, but she was speechless. "Well...." She gestured vaguely, smiled brightly into his eyes and tried to comprehend what this could mean to her future relationship with him.

"That's not exactly the reaction I'd hoped for." She dropped her eyes to her lap and needlessly smoothed the gabardine over her left knee as he went on. "I told you before, what I really want to be—ultimately—is a disc jockey. I want to enter Brown Institute and go to school days and play gigs nights. Jeff is all for it. What about you?"

"Me?" She lifted startled brown eyes and felt her heartbeat tripping in gay expectation. "Why do you need my approval?"

Not a muscle moved on Brian for a full fifteen seconds. He skewered Theresa with his dazzling green eyes, but they were filled with unsaid things.

"I think you know why," he told her at last, his voice coming from low in his throat.

A resounding chord announced the beginning of the next set, and Theresa was saved from replying by the booming sound that filled the house. She and Brian were still staring into each other's eyes when the undauntable Felice appeared out of nowhere and commandeered Brian's left arm, hauling him out of his chair while his eyes still lingered on Theresa.

"Come on, Brian, let's see what you've got, honey!"

He seemed to shake himself back to the present. "All right, just one."

But Theresa was subjected to the prolonged torture of watching Felice appropriate her date for three throbbing, upbeat songs. It took no more than sixty seconds of observation for Theresa's mouth to go dry. And in another sixty, wet.

Brian moved his body with the understated liquidity of a professional stage dancer. But he did it with a seemingly total lack of guile. When he rotated his hips, the movement was so subtle, so sexy, Theresa's lips unconsciously dropped open. The supple twisting of his pelvis appeared to come as naturally to Brian as walking. His face wore a pleasant expression of enjoyment as he occasionally maintained eye contact with Felice. She circumnavigated him in a sultry trip that ended when she almost touched him with her breasts, shimmying her shoulders while the suspended offerings swayed, unfettered, within the folds of her halter-style dress. Felice said something, and Brian laughed.

The song ended and he placed a hand at the small of her back as if to guide her off the floor, but she swung to face him, pressing both hands on his chest, looking up into his face. He glanced briefly toward the table, and Theresa looked quickly away. The music gushed out in another jungle rhythm, and when Theresa's eyes returned to the dance floor she was stung with jealousy. Watching the lurch and roll, the toss and pitch of Brian's lean, oscillating body set up queer yearnings in her own, and it occurred to Theresa that she was as human as some of the men who ogled her when she walked into a room.

Felice managed to link her arm with Brian's at the end of the song and introduce him to somebody on the floor, thereby commandeering him for a third dance. But as Theresa looked on, she saw him put up no resistance.

When the pair arrived at the table, Felice cooed to Theresa. "Ooo, if I were you, I'd hang on to this one. He's a live one." Then, to Brian, "Thanks for the dance, honey."

Jealousy was something new for Theresa. So was the feeling of sexual attraction. Although Theresa no longer spoke in the teenager vernacular, a phrase of Amy's came to her now: *strung out.* She suddenly knew what it meant to be strung out on a man. It had to be this hollow, gutless, wonderful awareness of his masculinity and her own femininity; this sensation that your pulses had somehow found their way to the surface of your skin and hovered there just beneath the outermost layer, as if ready to explode; this supersensitivity to each shift of muscle, each facial expression, even each movement of his clothing upon his body. She watched in a new acute fascination as Brian shrugged out of his corduroy jacket and hung it on the back of his chair. It seemed each of his motions was peculiar to him alone, as if no other man had ever performed this incidental task in as attractive a way. Was this common? Did others who found themselves falling in love feel such out-of-proportion pride and possessiveness? Did they all find their chosen one flawless, superlative and sexy while performing the most mundane movements, such as sitting on a chair and crossing his ankle over a knee?

"I'm sorry," Brian muttered, taking his full attention back to Theresa.

"You didn't look very sorry. You looked like you were enjoying every minute of it."

"She's a good dancer."

Theresa's lips thinned in disapproval.

"Listen, I said I was sorry I left you sitting here for three dances."

She glanced away, finding it difficult to deal with her newfound feelings. Brian wiped his brow on the sleeve of his sweater, reached for a glass with some partially melted ice cubes and slipped one into his mouth. Theresa watched his lips purse around it as he turned to study the dance floor. The ice cube made his cheek pop out, then she watched his attractive jaw as he chewed and swallowed it.

When his eyes roved back to hers, she quickly glanced away. Her forearm rested on the table, and his warm palm fell across the sleeve of her sweater.

Their eyes met. He squeezed her arm once, gently. Her heart lifted. Though not another word was said about Felice, the issue was set aside.

A powerful force, this jealousy, thought Theresa, loving the feel of his hand on her arm.

When the tempo of the music slowed, Brian rose without asking her and reached for her hand. On the dance floor, wrapped close to his rag-knit sweater, she could feel how the exertion had released both heat and scent from his skin. The moist warmth radiated onto her breasts. His palm, too, was warmer than before. The keen scent of his after-shave and deodorant was stronger than ever since he'd danced with Felice, and with a secret smile against his shoulder, Theresa thanked the bold temptress for warming Brian up.

Jeff and Patricia danced past, and Jeff leaned toward Brian to ask, "Hey, man, wanna change partners on the next dance?"

"No offense, Patricia, but not a chance."

He resumed his intimate hold on Theresa, who peered over Brian's shoulder at her brother to receive a lopsided smile and a broad wink.

Several times during the remainder of the evening Felice tried to snare Brian for a slow dance, but he refused to be appropriated again. He and Theresa sat out the up-tempo songs together and danced only the slow ones. She was growing increasingly aware of the approach of midnight. When they were at their table she surreptitiously checked her watch as Brian slipped his jacket back on. The discreet time check proved that she'd been consulting her watch at the rate of once every two minutes or less.

They were on the dance floor when a song ended, and Theresa turned toward their table to be waylaid by Brian's hand on her forearm. "Not so fast there, young lady." When she turned back to him, he lifted a wrist, tugged his corduroy sleeve up over his watch. "Only five minutes to go. Let's stay out here until the big moment, okay?"

A flush of sexual awareness radiated through Theresa. Without realizing where her eyes were headed, they centered on Brian's lips. His mouth was very beautiful, very sensual, the lower lip slightly fuller than the upper, those lips slightly parted now, glistening enticingly as if he'd just passed his tongue along them. She remembered the brief times they'd touched her own, and the maelstrom of emotions his fleeting kisses had created within her heart. The same reaction began again, just from her gazing at his lips.

Her eyes raised to find his upon her own mouth. The lingering gaze held sensual promise she'd never dreamed of finding in a man. She had kissed relatively few men in her life, and all of them in private. The idea of doing so in public heightened Theresa's inhibitions. She glanced around the dance floor: there was a certain amount of anonymity when so many people were pressed almost shoulder to shoulder in a throng of this size and density.

Just then someone nudged Theresa from behind. She turned to find a waitress elbowing through the dancers, passing out hats and noisemakers, confetti and streamers. Brian got a green foil top hat that would have done Fred Astaire proud. He perched it on his head, then adjusted its brim to a rakish angle and pulled it low over the left side of his forehead. He touched the brim, looking as though he wished his hands were encased in formal white gloves, and cocked an eyebrow at Theresa. "How do I look?"

"Like Abraham Lincoln gone Irish."

He laughed. "A little respectable and a little roguish?"

"Exactly." The green hat set off his dark, handsome face and hair in a way that made it difficult for Theresa to draw her eyes away.

"Aren't you going to put yours on?"

"Oh!" She lifted the tiara and turned up her nose in disgust. It was covered with horrible, shocking pink glitter that would clash abominably with her red hair. But she lifted her hands and gamely settled the circlet atop her head. As she felt with her fingertips to determine if it was on straight, Brian took over.

"Here, let me."

He brushed her fingertips aside, then adjusted the gaudy headpiece on Theresa's bouncy curls. His touch seemed to send fire straight down each hair follicle into her scalp. Just being near the man did the most devilish things to her senses.

"How do *I* look?" she asked, trying to get command of herself, keeping spirits light.

"Like the angels sprinkled you with stardust." He touched a fingertip to her left eyebrow. It felt as if she'd received a 110-volt shock. "But there's nothing wrong with a little stardust. Guess I'll put it back." Again he touched her, replacing the flake of pink glitter, this time on the crest of her left cheek, then running the finger slowly down to her chin before dropping his hand between them and capturing both of her hands without looking away from her astounded eyes. His own were penetrating, admiring and seemed to be radiating messages much like those she was unable to hide.

"You'd better close your eyes, Brian, or all this color will give you a headache," Theresa warned, realizing how garish she must look in the gaudy vermilion tiara, with hot pink glitter highlighting her freckle-splattered cheeks.

The drummer began a drum roll. It seemed to both Brian and Theresa the sound came from the opposite side of the universe, so wrapped up in each other had they become.

"Gladly," Brian agreed, "but not because anything gives me a headache." He was clutching her hands so tightly she completely forgot about everything except his eyes, reaching toward hers with a deep, probing knowledge of something she'd yearned to see in the eyes of one special man, a man just like the one before her now. Around them the crowd bellowed the countdown to midnight. "Five...four...three...two... one!" The band hit the opening chord of "Auld Lang Syne," and neither Theresa nor Brian moved for the duration of several heartbeats.

Then she was being enfolded in strong, warm arms and dragged against his hard chest, against his belly, against his hips and his warm, seeking mouth.

A coil of pink paper came flying through the air and drifted across the brim of Brian's green top hat, trailing down over his ear and jaw, but he was totally unaware of it. A shower of confetti settled onto Theresa's hair and shoulders and drifted down the bridge of Brian's nose, but they were lost in each other, aware only of the closeness they'd at last achieved. Their eyes were closed as they kissed with a full, lush introduction of tongues that sent shock waves skittering down Theresa's spine. Her arms were threaded beneath his, and her palms rested on the center of his back while one of his pressed between her shoulder blades, and the other slipped up into the warm secret place at her nape, under the cloud of soft hair.

The interior of his mouth was warm, wet and compelling.

The shifting exploration of his tongue brought hers against it in answer, as a river of longing coursed through Theresa's body.

Brian started moving as if unable to be drawn from a deep spell—slowly, seductively—carrying her with him to the nostalgic rhythm and words of the song. Their hips joined, pressed and swayed together, but their feet scarcely shuffled on the crowded floor. He moved his head in a sensuous invitation to deepen the kiss and opened his mouth wider over hers. Her response was as natural as the evocative dance movements they shared: her own mouth opened more fully. She felt the sensuous drawing of his lips and tongue, and the moist heat of his mouth seemed to burn its way down the length of her body.

In her entire life, nothing like this had ever happened to Theresa. The kisses of her past had been accompanied either by timidity or groping, and sometimes by both in rapid succession. She let Brian rub her hips with his own, lightly at first, then with growing pressure until the side-to-side motion evoked images of further intimacies. Finally, he drew her against him with a possessiveness that made her ribs ache sweetly. And still the kiss continued....

He began humming into her open mouth, and auld acquaintances were indeed forgotten by both of them while she answered by humming too. Before the song was half through, before the new year had been completely ushered in, before she could quite capture the realization that it was really happening to her, Theresa felt Brian's body go hard within the blue jeans. But she remained against him, marveling that someone at last had unlocked her to the wondrous side of physical contact.

"Auld Lang Syne" drifted to an end, and somewhere in the reaches of her consciousness Theresa knew the song had changed into another as Brian lifted his head but not his hands. He held her in a warm embrace while they rocked, remaining hip to hip, breast to chest, gazing into each other's eyes.

"Theresa." He lifted his eyes to her hair, let them skim back to her enraptured face, which reflected amazement, arousal and perhaps a touch of apprehension. "This started before I ever met you. You know that, don't you?" His voice was rich with passion. Her lips dropped open, and she found it very difficult to breathe.

"B...before you met me?"

"Jeff told me things that used to make me lie in bed at night and wonder what you'd be like when I met you. I would have been the most disappointed man in the world if you hadn't turned out to be exactly as you are."

She dropped her eyes to the dusting of confetti on his shoulders. "But, I'm—"

"You're perfect," he murmured, lowering his head until his mouth cut off further words. Then, to her astonishment, he did something utterly provocative, and distractingly sexy. He loosened his hold momentarily and opened his corduroy jacket so that its bulk no longer disguised the state of his body—not in the least. Then he took her back where she belonged, inside the open jacket, with her hands between it and her sweater while they danced the remainder of the song.

When it ended, he backed away, but kept his arms looped behind her waist as their hips rested tightly together.

"Let's get out of here," he suggested in a low, throaty voice.

"B...but it's only midnight," she stammered, awed by the suddenness of the sexual urgings she felt. He lifted his eyes to her hair. It was peppered with confetti. The glittered crown had tipped awry, and he plucked it from her hair, then smiled down at her open lips.

"Let's go home."

"What about Jeff and—"

"Are you scared, Theresa?"

She felt the press of blood staining her neck and pushing upward, but he lifted her chin and forced her to meet his eyes.

"Theresa, are you scared of me? Don't be. I want to be alone with you, just once before I leave."

But, Brian, I don't do things like that. I'm not like your groupies. The words crossed her mind, but not her lips. She'd look like a complete idiot if she said them and his intentions were honorable all along. Yet he'd opened his jacket and made his sexual state unquestionably clear! And she was a twenty-five-year-old virgin who was both tormented and compelled by the traumatic first that might very well happen if she agreed to leave early with him.

Instead of waiting for her answer, he turned her toward the edge of the dance floor, his palm riding the hollow of her spine while she led the way to the table, found her purse and couldn't quite meet Jeff's eyes as she and Brian said good-night.

He drove again, by tacit agreement. Inside her warm woolen coat, Theresa was shuddering throughout most of the ride home, even after the heater was blowing warm air. In the familiar driveway, he pulled the car to a stop, killed the engine and handed her the keys in the dark. She began pivoting toward her door when his strong grip on her wrist brought her up short.

"Come here." His command was soft-spoken, but tinged with gruff emotion. "It's been a long time since I kissed a girl in a car. I'd like to take the memory back to Minot Air Force Base with me."

It had been easier on the crowded dance floor when proximity took care of logistics. Now Theresa had to willingly lean her half of the way across the console that separated them. She hesitated, wondering how women ever learned to perform their part in these rites that seemed to inhibit her at every turn.

He exerted a light pressure on her wrist, pulling her slowly toward him, and tipped his head aside to meet her lips with a new kind of kiss that, though lacking in demand, was no less sensitizing. It was a tease of a kiss, a falling rose petal of a kiss. And it made her long for more.

"Your nose is cold. Let's go in and warm it up."

Chapter Seven

Inside, the house was quiet. The light above the stove was on again, and she hurried past its cone of brightness to the shadows of the hallway, knowing that if Brian got a look at her face, he'd see how uncertain and scared she'd suddenly become. She felt his hands taking the coat from her shoulders, though she hadn't known he'd followed her so closely. A myriad of conversational subjects jumped into her mind, but scattered into pieces like the colors in a kaleidoscope. Unable to believe she'd sound anything less than petrified if she introduced any of them, she was preparing to wish him a fast goodnight and skitter off to bed, when he turned from the closet and lazily took her hand in one of his.

"It sounds like your mom and dad are in bed already."

"Yes...yes, it's awfully quiet."

"Come downstairs with me."

Trepidation stiffened her spine. She tried to dredge up a reply, but both yes and no stuck in her throat. He threaded his fingers through hers as if they were setting out to stroll hand in hand through a meadow and turned them both toward the basement stairs.

She allowed herself to be led, for it was the only way she could approach the seduction she knew was in the offing.

At the top of the basement stairs she snapped on the light, but once downstairs, he released her hand, crossed to the ruffled lamp and substituted its mellower glow, then unconcernedly switched off the garish overhead beacon.

Theresa hovered by the sliding glass door, staring out at the black rectangle of night, while she chafed her upper arms.

Behind her, Brian noted, "It looks like your folks had a fire. The coals are still hot."

"Oh," she squeaked, knowing what he wanted, but unwilling to abet it.

"Do you mind if I add a log?"

"No."

She heard the glass doors of the fireplace being opened, then the metallic tinkle of the wire-mesh curtains being pushed aside. The charcoal broke with a crunching sound as he settled a new log, and the metal fire screen slid closed again. And still Theresa cowered by the door, hugging herself while her knees trembled.

She was staring out so intently that she jumped and spun to face Brian when he reappeared beside her and began closing the draperies. He was watching her instead of the drapery pulls while he worked the cord, hand over hand. She licked her lips and swallowed. Behind him, the fresh log flared with a *whoosh* and she jumped again as if the puff had announced the leaping arrival of Lucifer.

The draperies drew to a close. Silence bore down. Brian kept his disconcerting gaze riveted on Theresa as he came two steps closer, then extended his hand in invitation.

She stared at it but only hugged herself tighter.

The hand remained, palm up, steady. "Why are you so scared of me?" His deep, flawlessly modulated voice delivered the question in the softest of tones.

"I...I...." She felt her jaw working but seemed unable to close it, to answer, or to go to him.

He leaned forward, balancing on one foot while capturing one of her hands and tugging her along after him toward the far side of the room where the sofa faced the hearth. The fire glowed brightly now; passing the lamp he switched it off, leaving the room dressed in soft, flickering orange. He sat, gently towed her down beside him, and resolutely kept his right arm around her shoulders while he himself slunk rather low, catching the nape of her neck on the cushion, and crossing his calves on the shiny maple coffee table before them.

Beneath his arms, Brian could feel Theresa's shoulders tensed and curled. Everything had changed during their ride home. She'd had time to consider what she was getting into. Her withdrawal gave him a corresponding sense of hesitation, which he hoped he was hiding well. One skittish partner in such a situation was enough. He had misgivings about kissing her again in an effort to break down her reserve. She was pinched up as tightly as a newly wound watch, and he knew she hadn't done anything like this very often in her life. Jeff had told him she was spooked by men, that she turned down most invitations or advances that came her way. And Jeff had told Brian, too, the reason why. That knowledge hovered above him like a wall of water about to curl in upon his head. He felt as if he was savoring his last lungful of air in anticipation of being sucked under when the tidal wave hit.

Brian Scanlon was scared.

But Theresa Brubaker didn't know it.

She rested against the side of his ribs, with her head cradled on his shoulder and the crown of her hair against his cheek. But her arms remained crossed as tightly as if she wore a straitjacket.

With the hand that circled her shoulders, he gently rubbed her resilient upper arm. Her hair smelled flowery and created a warm patch of closeness where it pressed beneath his cheek. He pinched the knit sleeve of her sweater between thumb and forefinger and drew it away from her flesh.

"Is it true that you bought this whole new outfit just for tonight?"

"Amy's worse than Jeff. She can't keep *any* secrets."

His hand fell lightly upon her arm again. "I like the new clothes. The color goes great with your hair."

"Don't mention the color of my hair, please." She clasped an open hand over the top of her head, burying her face against his chest.

He smiled. "Why? What's the matter with it?"

"I hate it. I've always hated it."

The arm that had been circling her shoulders lifted, and what he'd done with the sweater, he did with her hair, lifting a single strand, rubbing, testing it between his fingers while studying it lazily. "It's the color of sunrise."

"It's the color of vegetables."

"It's the color of flowers—lots of different kinds of flowers."

"It's the color of a chicken's eye."

Beneath her cheek she felt his chest heave as he laughed silently, but when he spoke, it was seriously. "It's the color of the Grand Canyon as the sun slips down beyond the purple side of the mountains."

"It's the color of my freckles. You can hardly tell where one stops and the others start."

His index finger curled beneath her chin and forced her to lift her face. "I can." The way he lounged, his chin was tucked against his chest, and she gazed up across his corduroy lapel, feeling its raised wales digging into her cheek as she met his slumberous green eyes. "And anyway, what's wrong with freckles?" he teased, running the callused tip of his left index finger across the bridge of her nose and the crest of one cheek. "Angel kisses," he whispered, while the finger moved down the tip-tilted nose and the rim of her lips, over the pointed chin and on to her soft throat where a pulse thrummed in rapid tempo.

She tried to say, "Heat spots," but nothing came out except shaky breath and a tiny croak.

His nape came away from the back of the sofa in slow motion while his sea-green eyes locked with hers. "Angel kisses," he whispered, closing her eyes with his warm lips—first touching the left, then the right eyelid. "Have you been kissed by angels, Theresa?" he murmured. The tip of his tongue touched and wet the high curve of her left cheek, and the end of her nose, then her right cheek.

"Nobody but you, Brian."

"I know," came his final murmur before his soft mouth possessed hers. His kiss plucked at her reserve, encouraging a foray into the unknowns of sensuality, but her crossed arms still maintained a barrier between them. His tongue sought nooks and crannies of her mouth that it seemed her own tongue had never discovered before. It swept across warm, moist valleys from where tiny explosions of sensation burst upon her senses. He eased the pressure, catching her upper lip between his teeth, sucking it, releasing it, sensitizing the lower one next in the same seductive way.

Framing the contours of her open lips with his, he eased her back firmly against the sofa, twisting at the waist until his chest pressed her crossed wrists.

"Put your arms around me like you did when you were dancing."

He waited with his lips near her ear, measuring her hesitation by the number of thundering heartbeats that issued the pounding blood through her body and raised a delicate pulsepoint at her temple, just beside her hairline. Just when he thought it was hopeless, she at last moved the first hesitant hand, and he lingered above her until finally her arms curved about his shoulders.

"Theresa, don't be afraid. I'd never hurt you."

She began to say, "Brian, don't!" just as his mouth stopped the words from forming, and she felt herself flipping sideways beneath the force of his chest and hands. He shifted and adjusted her without moving his mouth from hers, until she lay beneath him, stretched out on the long sofa, with one foot clinging to the floor for security. Panic and sexuality seemed to be pulling her in opposite directions. *Let him kiss me, let him lie on me, but please, please, don't let him touch my breasts.*

His body was warm and hard, and when he'd tucked her beneath him, Brian opened his knees wide, lifting one to press it over her left thigh, while the other flanked the outside of her right leg all the way to the floor. His belt buckle and zipper pressed hard into her thigh, biting through the thin gabardine of her slacks and bringing to mind images from the movie that was her chief frame of reference to a man's physique. This was more than she had ever willingly let a man do with her. She remembered watching Brian on the dance floor, and his hips took up the same rhythmic tempo that had stirred her earlier. It worked an identical magic on her now, releasing a flood of inner enticement that answered the dance of his body on hers.

"Theresa, I've thought of you for months and months, long before I ever met you." His eyes, as he pulled away only far enough to look into hers, held neither smile nor twinkle. To Theresa's awe-struck wonder, they held what seemed to be a look of near reverence.

"But why?" she whispered.

His left hand contoured her neck underneath her hair, while his right meandered across her brow as he traced her bone structure with two fingertips. "I knew more about you than any man has a right to know about a woman he's never met. Sometimes I felt almost guilty about it, but at the same time it drew me to you as if I'd been hypnotized."

"So Jeff told you more than you let on before."

His parted lips pressed against the side of her nose, then he looked into her eyes again. "Jeff loves you as much as any brother could love a sister. He understands what makes you tick...and what doesn't. I had a picture of you as a sweet-natured little music teacher, directing freckle-faced kids for their mommies and daddies, but until I met you, I had no idea you'd look quite so much like one of them yourself."

She tried to turn aside.

"No." He captured her chin, rubbed his index finger along her jawbone. "Don't turn away from me. I told you, I like your freckles, and your hair, and...and everything about you, just because they're you."

She stiffened involuntarily as his hand left her nape and slid between her shoulder blade and the cushion of the sofa. He felt her rigidity, so instead of slipping the hand around to the front of her ribs, he moved it to her shoulder, then down the length of her arm to entwine Theresa's fingers with his. He forced their joined hands up between his chest and her breasts, his forearm now pressing against one of the warm, generous orbs.

Brian thought of the hours he and Jeff had lain in their bunks and talked about this woman. He knew about the times she'd come home in tears over the teasing of some boy, as long ago as when she was only fourteen years old. He knew about the time Jeff had beaten one of her persecutors and been kicked out of school on probation. He knew about the time she'd gone to the high-school prom but came home in tears after her date had proved he was only after two handfuls of the most obvious thing. He knew why she hid in an elementary school where she had to deal mostly with children who were too young and innocent to care about her accursed size; and why she hid inside dark, unattractive clothes; and behind sweaters; and beneath the chin rest of a violin. He knew he was in a spot where, to the best of Jeff's knowledge, no man had ever been allowed before. And he understood that by making the wrong move, he could cause her interminable hurt, and himself as well.

He sought to relax her with soothing endearments, all of them genuinely from the heart. "You smell better than any girl I've ever danced with." He nuzzled her neck, stringing kisses along her jaw like pearls upon a waxed thread. "And you dance just the way I like a girl to dance." He dropped a kiss on the corner of her mouth. "I love your music..." On her nose. "And your innocence..." On her eye. "Your Nocturnes..." On her temple. "And your long, beautiful fingers on the piano keys...." He kissed five knuckles in turn. "And being with you at midnight on New Year's Eve." At last he kissed her mouth, lingering there to dip his tongue between her soft, innocent lips, to join her in a celebration of a new year, a new discovery, a new awareness of how right they seemed for each other.

Theresa felt lifted, transported above herself, as if this must certainly be someone other than herself in Brian Scanlon's arms, hearing his murmured words of admiration. Perhaps she was an understudy having stepped in at curtain time when the star performer fell ill. Perhaps these words were meant for that other woman, the one with the silhouette of a sylph, with mink-brown hair and golden, flawless skin. That other woman had performed this part so many times she knew instinctively how to react to this man's voice and movements.

But Theresa was not that practiced artiste. She was a hesitant ingenue to whom the part did not come naturally. She wanted to lift her arms around Brian's shoulders and return the string of kisses he'd just bestowed upon her, but relinquishing the guard she'd maintained for years was no easy thing. Experience had taught her only too clearly that to believe she could attract someone because of her hidden attributes was a pipe dream. Each time she had done so, the man upon whom she'd pinned her hopes had proved himself no more honorable than the boy who'd made one blossom-kissed May prom night eight years earlier not a memorable celebration of the end of a school year but an ugly memory of shame and disgust she'd made sure had never been repeated since.

Brian's forearm rested across her right breast, depressing it in an almost lackadaisical fashion that felt natural and accept- able to Theresa, until he began moving his wrist back and forth as if something had tickled it and he was relieving the itch by rubbing the skin across her sweater. His fingers were still in- terlaced with Theresa, and he carried her own hand atop his, turning it now so that the back of only his hand came into contact with her breasts.

Don't panic. Don't resist. Let him. Let him touch you and see if it makes you react like the woman reacted in the movie. Theresa swallowed, and Brian's tongue did sensuous things to the inside of her mouth.

He pulled back, teased the rim of her mouth with a butterfly's touch of his lips. "Theresa, don't be scared." She tried not to be, telling her muscles to relax as he released her tense fingers and rested his warm palm upon the ribbed waist of her sweater. *No. Don't let him be like all the others. Don't let him want me for only that. Not Brian, who's been so careful not to even look at me there during all these wonderful days while he grew dearer.*

Beside them the fire danced, sending warmth radiating against the sides of their faces and bodies. But she pinched her eyelids shut, unaware of the troubled expression on Brian's face as he gazed down at her. She lay beneath him with the stillness of fallen snow, pale and motionless, and breathing with great difficulty. But her breath was not drawn through lips fallen open in passion, rather through nostrils distended in apprehension.

Her flesh was warm beneath the sweater, and her ribs surprisingly fine-boned, the skin over them taut and toned. Her frame, Brian now realized, was built for bearing much smaller breasts than those with which she'd been endowed. *Trust me, Theresa. It's you, your heart, your uncomplicated simple soul that I'm learning to love. But loving the soul of you means loving the body of you as well. And we must start with that. Sometime, we must start.*

He moved his hand up her ribs, his warm palm molding itself to the arch of her rib cage, finally placing four fingertips in the warm hollow just beneath one breast. Gently he brushed back and forth, giving her time to accept the idea of his imminent intrusion. Beneath the heel of his hand he felt an unnatural tremor, as if she were holding her breath to keep from crying. Against his belly her midsection was arched up off the cushions, not in enthusiastic acquiescence, but in fortification as if steeling herself to defend at a second's notice.

He covered her lips with his in forewarning, then rolled aside just enough to allow freedom of access to the warm, soft globe of flesh that brushed his fingernails and moved toward it with as much gentleness as he could muster. Seeking not to violate or to trespass, he breached the remaining space, playing her the first time with as fluttering a touch as he might have used to chime the strings of a guitar instead of strumming them. Beneath his mouth, hers quivered. *Easy, love, easy,* he thought.

His first touch brushed scarcely more than the seam of the stiff cotton garment that covered her, as he ran his fingertips along its deep curve, from the center of her chest across her breast to the warm, secret place beneath her arm.

She shuddered and tensed further.

He lightened his hold on her lips until their kiss became more of a commingling of breath than of flesh, a foretoken of the gentleness he was preparing for her. *Trust me, Theresa.* Once more he nudged her lips with a blandishment so weightless it might have been the gossamer approach of nothing more than the shadow cast by his head bending over hers.

But caution cracked through Theresa's nerves and kept her from mellowing and melting beneath him. She waited, instead, like a martyr at the stake, until at last he enfolded her breast, firmly, fully, running his thumb along the horizontal seam of her bra. She acquiesced for the moment, allowing him to discover the breadth, resilience and warmth of her breast.

As his hand caressed and explored, Theresa waited in agony, wanting so much more than what she was able to allow herself to feel in the way of response. She wanted to stretch and loll, to utter some thick sound in her throat as the woman had in the movie. She wanted to know the pleasure other women seemed to derive from having their breasts caressed and petted.

But her breasts had never been objects of pleasure, only of pain, and she found herself recalling the hurt of countless callous insults, feeling diminished by those recollections, even while Brian bestowed a touch of utmost honor and respect. But as he pushed her sweater up to her breastbone, she was like a hummingbird poised for flight.

He sensed it, yet steeled himself and moved the next step further along the road toward mutuality, inching down until his hips rested on the sofa between her open legs, and his head dipped down, his open mouth replacing his hand, kissing her through the cotton fabric that separated her flesh from his.

Brian's breath was warm, then hot, and it sent waves of sensation shimmying up her ribs and along the outer perimeter of her breasts, cresting in a tightening sensation that drew her nipples up into a pair of hard knots, shriveling them like rosebuds that refuse to open. Through her bra he gently bit, and the sweet ache it caused made her hands fly into the air behind him, palms pushing at nothing.

He lifted his head. She heard him whisper, "Shh..." but she could not open her eyes and meet his gaze, for behind her lids was the vivid image of her nipples. She saw again the tiny, demure nipples of other girls in shower scenes from years ago, envying them their delicacy, their femininity, and her terror grew. If she could be assured he'd go no further, she might have relaxed and enjoyed the shivering sensation his kiss sent through her. But she knew, as surely as she knew the shape of her own bovine proportions, that the next step was one she could not suffer. She could not bare herself to the eyes of any man. Her breasts were freckled, unattractive and when released fell aside like two obscene mounds of dough.

Oh, please, Brian, I don't want you to see me that way. You'll never want to look at me again.

The fireplay illuminated their bodies, and she knew if she opened her eyes she would see too clearly how visible she was by its light. His mouth bestowed a breath-stealing warmth to her opposite breast, and, as with the first, it was a seductive nip through stiff cotton whose very scratch seemed to beguile her flesh to succumb.

But when Brian braced himself above her and slipped his hands behind her back to free the catch of her brassiere, no power on earth could allow Theresa to let him see her naked.

"Don't!" she whispered fiercely.

"Theresa, I—"

"Don't!" She pushed against the hollows of his elbows, her eyes wide with trepidation. "I...please...."

"All I'm going to do—"

"No! You're not going to do anything!" She flattened her shoulder blades to prevent his captured hands from doing what they'd been reaching behind her to do. "Please, just get off."

"You haven't given me a ch—"

"I'm not that kind of woman, Brian!"

"What kind?" Relentlessly he held her where she was.

"Loose, and...and easy." She struggled, unable to free her writhing limbs from the weight of his.

"Do you really believe I could ever think of you that way?"

Tears of mortification stung her eyes. "Isn't that what all men think?"

She saw the hurt flash across his green eyes, the line of his jaw harden momentarily. "I'm not *all men*. I thought maybe you'd come to realize that since I've been here. I didn't start this to see how much I could get out of you."

"Oh, no? Considering where your hands are right now, I'd say I have cause to doubt that."

He closed his eyes, let his head droop forward and shook it in a slow gesture of exasperation while emitting an annoyed puff of breath. He withdrew his hands and dragged himself away, rolling to sit on the edge of the sofa. But their limbs were still half tangled, and she was caught in a vulnerable, splayed pose, with one knee hooked beneath his, the other up-drawn behind his back.

She arched up and tugged her sweater down to her waist while he heaved a frustrated sigh and ran a hand through his hair, then slouched forward, elbows to knees, letting his hands dangle limply while he stared absently into the fire, a deep frown upon his face.

"Let me up," she whispered.

He moved as if only now realizing he had her pinned in a less than modest sprawl. She disentangled herself and curled into the corner of the sofa, not quite cowering, but withdrawn behind her familiar shield of crossed arms.

"You really are an uptight woman, you know?" he said angrily. "Just what the hell did you think I was going to do?"

"Exactly what you tried!"

"So what does that make me?" He flung up both palms. "A pervert? Theresa, for God's sake, we're adults. It's hardly considered perverted to do a little petting."

She found the word distasteful. Her expression soured. "I don't want to be gawked at like some freak in a sideshow."

"Oh, come on, aren't you being a little dramatic?"

"To you it's dramatic, to me it's…it's traumatic."

"Are you saying you've never let a guy take off your bra before?"

She only puckered her mouth and refused to look at him.

He pondered her silently for several seconds before asking, "Had you considered that's not exactly normal—or healthy— for a twenty-five-year-old woman?"

Now her eyes met his, but they shot sparks. "Oh, and I suppose you're volunteering to break me in for my own good, is that it?"

"You'll have to admit, it might be good for you."

She snorted quietly and cast her eyes aside while he grew increasingly upset with her. "You know, I'm getting awfully damn tired of you crossing your arms like I'm Jack the Ripper…*and* of having my motives questioned when the way I look at it, I'm the one with the normal impulses here."

"Well, I've had plenty of lessons on the *normal impulses* of the American male!" she shot back.

They sat stonily for several long, strained minutes, staring straight ahead, disappointed that this night that had started so magically was ending this way.

Finally Brian sighed and turned to study her. "Theresa, I'm sorry, all right? But I feel something for you, and I thought you felt the same about me. Everything between us was right tonight, and I thought it led to this quite naturally."

"Not every woman in the world agrees with you!" she shot back.

"Would you look at me...please?" His voice was low, caring, hurt. She pulled her gaze away from the fire, feeling as if its hue had been drawn to the skin of her face, which was flooded with a heat of a very different kind. Theresa confronted his eyes to find a wounded expression there that disconcerted her. He rested an elbow along the back of the davenport, his fingertips very near her shoulder. "I don't have much time, Theresa. Two more days and I'll be gone. If I had weeks, or months to woo you, things would be different, but I don't have. So I used the accepted approach, because I didn't want to go back to Minot and wonder for the next six months about your feelings." His fingertips brushed the shoulder of her sweater very lightly, sending a shudder down her spine.

"I like you Theresa, do you believe that?" She bit the soft inside of her lip and stared at him, becoming undone by his words, his sincerity. "*You.* You, the person. The sister of my friend, the musician who shares a love of music with me, the girl who kept her brother straight, and who laughs while she fiddles a hayseed hoedown on her classic 1906 Faretti and understands what I feel when I play Newbury's songs. I like the you that never knew how to put on makeup before tonight and had to learn how from her fourteen-year-old sister, and the you that walked into the kitchen with the refreshing shyness of a fawn. I like the fact that you wouldn't know the first thing about dancing the way Felice does. As a matter of fact, there's not much about you I don't like. I thought you understood all that. I thought you understood the reason why I tried to express my feelings the way I just did."

Her heart felt swollen, her throat thick, and her eyes and nose stung. Words like these, she'd always thought, were always spoken only in love stories, to the other girls, the pretty ones with miniature figures and silken hair.

"I do." She wanted very much to reach out and touch his cheek, but her inhibitions were long nurtured and would take time to crumble. So she attempted to tell Brian with the wistful, downturned corners of her lips, with the aching expression in her tear-bright eyes how remorseful she was at that moment. "Oh, Brian, I'm sorry I said that. And it wasn't true. I said it because I was scared, and I...I just got panicky at the last minute. I said the first thing I could think of to stop you, but I didn't mean it. Not about you."

His fingertips still brushed her shoulder. "Did you think I didn't know you were scared?"

"I...." She swallowed and dropped her eyes.

"I've known it since before I met you. I've watched you hiding behind sweaters and purses and even your violin ever since I first got here, but I thought if I took it slow, if I showed you that other things came first with me, you'd...." He made a gesture with his palms, then his hands went limp. She felt her face heating up again, radiating with the embarrassment she felt at confronting this issue. It seemed impossible that she was actually talking about it...and with a *man*.

"Theresa, don't look away from me, damn it. I'm not some pervert who took a bead on you and came here to see if he could make another score, and you know it."

Her tears grew plump and then spilled over, and at the moment of her discomposure, she drew her knees up tightly, circled them with her arms, dropped her forehead and emitted a single sob.

"B...but you don't know wh...what's it's like."

"I understand that when you feel something as strong as I feel for you, it's natural to express it like I tried to."

"Maybe for you its n...natural, but for me it's awful."

"*Awful?* You find being touched by me *awful?*"

"No, not by *you,* just...*there.* On my breasts, I...kn...knew you were going to and I was so...so...." She couldn't finish but kept her face hidden from him.

"My God, Theresa, do you think I don't know that? The village idiot couldn't miss seeing how you hide them. So what should I have done? Bypassed them and touched you someplace else? What would you have thought of me then? I told you, I wanted—" he stopped abruptly, glowered at the fire, ran his hands down the length of his face and grunted, almost as if to himself, "Oh, damn." He seemed to gather his thoughts for a minute, then faced her again and gripped her shoulder to force her to meet his eyes. Her own were still streaming, and his were angry. Or perhaps frustrated. "Listen, I knew about your hangup before I stepped off that plane. I've been trying to come to grips with it myself ever since I've been here, but I like you, damn it! And part of it is physical, but that's how it is. Your breasts are part of you, and you like me, too, but if you're going to shy away every time I try to touch you, we've got a real problem."

She was surprised with his directness in stating the issue. Even the word *breasts* had inhibited her all her life. Now here he was, pronouncing it with the candor of a health teacher. But she could see he didn't understand how difficult it was for her to cast off her mantle of self-consciousness. It was seated in too many painful memories from her teenage years. And he, Brian Scanlon, long, lean, perfect, the target of admiration of countless enamored females, could hardly be expected to fathom what it was like to be shaped the way she was.

"You just don't understand," she said expressionlessly.

"You keep saying that. Give me a chance, will you?"

"Well, it's true. You're...you're one of the lucky ones. Look at you, all lean and trim and handsome and...well, you take for granted being...being *normal* and shaped like everyone else."

"Normal?" he frowned. "You don't think you're normal, just because you're built like you are?"

"No!" She glared at him defiantly, then dashed away a tear with an angry lash of her hand. "You couldn't possibly understand what it's like to be...to be gawked at like a...a freak in a sideshow. They started growing when I was thirteen, and at first the girls were jealous that I was the first one to need a bra. But by the time I was fourteen the girls stopped being jealous and were only...amazed."

Oddly Brian had never considered how girls had treated her. This was a secret hurt even Jeff hadn't known. He felt Theresa's remembered pain keenly as she went on.

"In school when we had to take showers the girls gaped at me as if I was the ninth wonder of the world. Gym class was one of the greatest horrors of my life." A faraway look stole over her face, and her eyes closed wearily. "Running." She laughed ruefully, the sound seeming to stick in her throat as her lids lifted again. "Running wasn't only embarrassing, it hurt. So I...I gave up running at an age when it's a natural part of a teenager's life." She blinked once, slowly, staring at a distant point while wrapping her arms around her knees. Brian gently closed a hand over her forearm, urging her to meet his gaze.

"And you resent it? You feel cheated?"

He understood! He understood! The knowledge freed her to admit it at last. "Yes! I couldn't...." She choked and tears came to her eyes. "I gave up so many th...things I wanted. Trading clothes w...with my friends. B...bathing suits. Sports. Dancing." She took a deeper gulp. "Boys," she finished softly.

He rubbed her arm. "Tell me," he encouraged.

Her gaze shifted to his face. "Boys," she repeated, and again stared at the patterns in the fire. "Boys came in two categories then. The gawkers and the gropers. The gawkers were the ones who went into a near catatonic state just being in the same room with me. The gropers were...well...." Her voice trailed away and she looked aside.

Brian understood how difficult this was for her. But it had to be said to clear the air between them. He touched her jaw. "The gropers were...."

She turned and met his eyes, then hers dropped as she went on. "The gropers were the ones who ogled and leered and liked to talk dirty."

A shaft of heat and anger speared through Brian, and he wondered guiltily if there were times in his youth when he might have tormented a girl like Theresa. Again she continued.

"I went on a couple of dates, but that was enough. Their side of the front seat hardly got warm before they were over on my side to see if they could get a feel of the...the notorious Theresa Brubaker." She turned and asked sadly, "Do you know what they called me, Brian?"

He did, but he let her admit it so the catharsis might be complete.

"Theresa Boob-Acres. Acres of boobs, that's what they said I had." She laughed ruefully, but tears like sad diamonds shot with orange from the fireglow dropped down her cheeks. She seemed unaware they had fallen. "Or sometimes they called me Tits Boobaker. Jugs. Udders—oh, there are a hundred insulting words for them and I know every one."

Brian's heart hurt for her. So much of this he'd learned from Jeff, but it was far more wrenching, hearing it from Theresa herself.

"The gropers..." she repeated, as if steeling herself to face one memory worse than the rest. Brian sat without moving, one hand along the back of the sofa, the other still lightly resting on her arm. Her voice was thick and uneven. "When I was in the ninth grade a bunch of boys caught me in the hall after school one day. I can remember exactly what I was wearing b...because I came home and b...buried it in the bottom of the g...garbage can.'' Her eyelids slid closed, and he watched her throat working. He'd heard it before and wished he could prevent her from going on, but if she shared it all it meant she trusted him, and this he wanted very badly. ''It was a white blouse with little pearl buttons down the front and a tiny round collar edged with pink lace. I'd always 1...loved it because it was a C...Christmas present from Grandma Deering.'' A tear plunged over her eyelid and she dashed it away, then gripped her own sleeves again. ''Anyway, I had an armful of books when they—they caught me. I re...remember the books skittering along the floor when they...p...pushed me back against the lockers, and how...c...cold the lockers were.'' She shivered and rubbed her arms. ''Two of the boys held my arms straight out while the other two f...felt me up.'' Her eyes closed, lips and chin quivered. Brian's hand squeezed the back of her neck, but she was lost to all but the memory and the hurt it revived. She drew a deep, shaking breath and her lips dropped open. ''I was too sc...scared to tell mother, but they'd torn the b...buttonholes of my blouse, and I d....'' She shrugged helplessly. ''I didn't know how I'd answer questions about it, so I...I threw the blouse away where I was sure she wouldn't find it.'' A sob erupted at last, but she immediately firmed her lips and lifted her chin.

He could bear it no longer and gently forced her close, circling her neck with one arm, urging her into the curve of his body until her updrawn knees pressed his chest and her feet slipped beneath his thigh. She was trembling terribly. He rested his cheek against her hair and felt a devastating sting at the back of his eyes. He closed them and uttered, ''Theresa, I'm sorry,'' and kissed her hair and made futile wishes that he could change her memories to happier ones. She remained tightly curled in the circle of his arms. Again her voice went on tremulously, and she unconsciously plucked at the fibres of his sweater.

"In eleventh grade there was a boy I liked a lot. He was nothing like those other boys. He was quiet and musical and he...he liked me a lot. I could tell. Prom time came, and I'd catch him staring at me across the orchestra room—not at my breasts, but at my face. I knew he wanted to ask me to the prom, but in the end he chickened out. I knew he was scared of my...my enormous proportions.

"But s...somebody else asked me. A boy named Greg Palovich. He seemed nice enough, and he was handsome and really polite...until...until the end of the evening when we were in the c...car." All was silent for a long, tense moment. Her voice was sorrowful as she finished. "He didn't t...tear my dress. He was very careful not to." She turned her face sharply against Brian's chest. "Oh, B...Brian, it was so humiliating, s...so degrading. I still cringe every t...time I hear the word prom."

Brian's hand found her head and smoothed her hair, holding her face protectively against the aching thud of his heart. Again he experienced the deep wish to be sixteen, to be able to invite her to the prom himself and give her a glowing memory to carry away with her. He tipped her face up and ran a thumb beneath her eye, wiping the wetness aside. "If we were in school now, I'd see to it you had some happy memories."

Her heart swelled with gratitude. She watched the fire light the planes and curves of his face. "Oh, Brian," she said softly, "I believe you would." She sat up regretfully and resumed her former pose, feeling his eyes on the side of her face as she again stared at the fire and hugged her knees. "But nobody can change what's past. And neither can you change the nature of man."

"It's still happening?" he questioned quietly. When she only gazed ahead absently without answering, he caught her chin with a finger and forced her to look at him. "Look at me

Theresa. Tell me the rest so we can put it behind us. It's still happening?''

She shifted her chin aside and dropped her eyes to her crossed arms. ''It happens each time I walk into a room where there's a strange man I've never met before. I tell myself this time it won't happen. This time it'll be different. When we're introduced, his eyes will stay on my face.'' Theresa's voice was nearly a whisper now, filled with chagrin and an edge of shame. ''But no man ever meets my eyes when he meets me. Their eyes always drop straight down to my chest.'' She fell silent, sensing his frowning scrutiny. His hand was gone from the back of her neck. Only his gaze touched her. When he spoke, his voice was firm.

''Mine didn't.''

No, his didn't. And that was why she'd begun liking him almost immediately. But she knew why.

''You were forewarned.''

He couldn't deny it, or the fact that if he hadn't been, his eyes very likely would have widened and dropped. ''Yes, I'll admit it. I was.''

She stared at a spurting blue flame that gathered a sudden surge of life, even as the fire dwindled. The shadows in the room were deep fingers of gray.

''I've never talked about this with anyone else before in my life.''

''What about your mother?''

She turned her troubled eyes to his, and each of them saw the glint of the dying flames reflected beneath unsmiling eyebrows. ''My mother?'' Theresa gave a soft, rueful chuckle deep in her throat, closed her eyes and dropped her head back against the sofa cushion. Brian watched the curved line of her throat as she spoke. ''My mother's answer to the problem was to tell me all I needed was a heavy-duty bra. Oh God, how I hate them. Wearing pretty underclothes is just another one of the things I had to give up. They don't make pretty ones for girls like me, and when you tried to...." She lifted her head but wouldn't meet his eyes. "Well, *before,* I couldn't bear the thought of you seeing me either with my bra or without it. I'm not a very pretty sight either way."

"Theresa, don't say that." He eased closer and laid a hand on the top of her head and stroked her hair, then let his palm lie lightly on her bright, airy curls.

"Well, it's true. But it was never anything I could talk about with my mother. She's generously endowed herself, and once when I was around fourteen and came to her crying over how big I was getting, she treated the problem like it was something I'd get over when I got older. After all, she said, *she did.* When I asked if I could talk to somebody else about it, like our doctor or a counselor, she said, 'Don't be foolish, Theresa. There's nothing you can do about it but accept it.' I don't think she ever realized she's got a totally different personality than mine. She's...well, brazen and domineering. A person like that *can* overcome their hangups more easily than someone like me."

They sat in silence for several long minutes. She heard Brian draw a deep breath and let it out slowly. "So how do you feel about it now, now that you've talked about it with me?"

"I...." She glanced up to find him watching her closely. His hand had fallen from her head, but those knowing eyes held her prisoner. "Surprised that I really managed to tell you everything like I did."

"I'm glad you confided in me, Theresa. Somehow I think it'll help you in more ways than just...well, letting go."

She studied him now as carefully as he studied her. "Brian, tell me something." Her forearms were crossed atop her up-drawn knees, and she picked at a thread of her knit sleeve, thoughtful for a moment, before turning to catch his eyes again. "Tonight at the dance you said that Felice reminded you of the groupies who hang around the stage and hope to...to score with the guitar man after the dance. You said...." She swallowed, amazed at her own temerity, but somehow finding herself unleashed in a new way. "Well, you said they were a dime a dozen, but that wasn't what you wanted...*tonight*." Again she swallowed, but he refused to help her along. He was going to make her voice her question if she wanted an answer. "Does that mean you've...indulged with lots of girls like this...on other nights?"

"Some." The word was quiet, truthful.

"Then why...I mean, I'm not...experienced like those girls. Why would you want to be with me instead of them?"

He moved closer, his right elbow hooked on the back of the sofa, his hand gently stroking her arm. "Because bodies are not what love is about. Souls are."

"Love?" Her eyes widened and met his in surprise.

"You don't have to look so threatened by the word."

"I'm not threatened by it."

"Yes you are."

"No I'm not."

"If you fell in love, you'd have to face the inevitable sooner or later."

"But I haven't fallen in love, so I'm not threatened." She'd had to deny it—after all, he hadn't actually said he loved her.

"Fair enough. I answered your question, now you answer one of mine. And I want an honest answer."

But she refused to agree until she knew what he was going to ask.

"Why did you go through all the trouble of buying new clothes, learning how to put on makeup and fingernail polish and going to the beauty shop before our date tonight?"

"I...I thought it was time I learned."

He smiled, a slow grin that appeared briefly, then was gone, replaced by his too-intense study. He moved nearer, until she had to lift her face to meet his eyes above her. "You're a liar, Theresa Brubaker," he stated in a disarmingly quiet tone. "And if you didn't feel threatened, we wouldn't have had the discussion we just had. But you've got nothing to fear from me.''

"Brian...." Her breath caught in her throat as he moved unhesitatingly to encircle her in his arms.

"Put your damn knees down and quit hiding from me. I'm not Greg Palovich, all right?"

But she was too stunned to move. He wouldn't! He wouldn't! Not again. Her muscles were tensing tighter, and she'd just begun to tighten her hold around her knees when with one swift sweep of his hand, Brian knocked her feet off the edge of the davenport. His strong hands closed around her shoulders, and he jerked her forward with deadly accuracy, pulling her up against his chest with their arms around each other. "I'm getting damn sick of seeing you with your arms crossed over your chest. And I'm starting back at the beginning, where you should have started when you were fourteen. Let's pretend that's how old you are, and all I want is a good-night kiss from the girl I took to the dance."

Before Theresa's astonishment could find voice, she was neatly enfolded against the strong, hard chest of the guitar man who'd had plenty of experience at seduction. His warm, moist, open mouth slanted across hers while one warm hand slipped up her neck and got lost in her hair. His tongue tutored hers in the ways of one far beyond fourteen years of age, slipping erotically to points of secrecy that started sensual urges coursing through her limbs and spearing down her belly. He lifted the pressure of his lips only enough to be heard while their tongues still touched. "I'm going to be so damn good for you, Theresa Brubaker. You'll see. Now touch me the way you've been wanting to since we left the dance floor." His tongue returned fully to her mouth, teasing, stroking hers with promises of delight. But he kept one arm around her ribs, the other hooked over the side of her neck, and his hands played only over her back, caressing it slowly but thoroughly while she let hers do the same upon him. Her hand wandered up his neck, to the soft, short hair that still retained the vestige of masculine toiletries she'd first smelled when she'd taken his cap. She thought of a line from the Newbury song: "Wandering from room to room, he's turning on each light...." And it felt as if Brian was showing her the light, one small room at a time. Their kiss grew more intimate as he murmured wordless sounds of approval, and she wanted to respond in kind, to give voice to the new explosive feelings she was experiencing. But just at that moment, he pushed her back gently.

"I'll see you tomorrow, okay, sweets? I can only be honorable up to a point."

He got to his feet and tugged her along behind him. Looping a lazy arm around her shoulders, he sauntered with her to the stairway. There he stopped her just as she'd gained the first step. He stood on the floor so their eyes were now on the same level. In the deep shadows, his palms held her hips and he turned her to face him before he enclosed her in a warm embrace once again, found her lips for a last, lingering kiss, then turned her away with a soft, "Good night."

Chapter Eight

Theresa and Brian were not alone long enough during that day to speak of anything that had happened the night before, or to exchange touches or insight as to what the other was thinking of all that had passed between them. It was a lazy day. They'd all been up late and took turns napping, sprawled in chairs, on floors before the New Year's Day football games that flickered on the television screen or tucked into their own rooms. It seemed to take until nearly suppertime for everyone to come fully alive, and even then, it was a subdued group, for with only one more day before Brian and Jeff would be gone, they all felt an impending sense of loss.

The following morning, Theresa awakened shortly after dawn and lay staring at the pewter frog Brian had given her. She recalled everything that had happened between them since the first night when they'd sat side by side with his elbow pressing hers throughout that extremely sensuous love scene.

Who was she trying to fool? It had almost been predestined, this feeling she had for Brian Scanlon. She was falling in love with him, with a man two years her junior who admitted he'd had sexual encounters with any number of admiring fans. The idea that he was fully experienced and worldly made her feel inadequate and puerile. Again she wondered why he'd want an introverted, frightened virgin like her. She was daunted by his physical beauty, for it seemed to dazzle when compared to her ordinary-to-homely features, making her believe he couldn't possibly be attracted to her, as he'd said he was. How could he possibly be? With women like Felice fawning over him, pursuing him, eager to share more than just a bump-and-grind dance with him, why would Brian Scanlon possibly pursue Theresa Brubaker?

She sighed, closed her eyes and tried to imagine lying naked with him but found it impossible to picture herself in that context. She was too inhibited, too freckled, too redheaded to fit the part. She wished she were shaped like a pencil and had russet skin and sleek, auburn hair. She wished she'd found at least one boy or man sometime during her life who'd have been able to break through the barriers of self-consciousness to give her some sense of what to expect if she allowed Brian more sexual liberties.

The pewter frog sat on the shelf, caught in a still life, fiddling his silent note and smiling. *I'm like that frog. My life is like a silent note; I play, but I haven't felt the music of the heart.*

It was seven-thirty. She heard her parents leave for work, but the rest of the house was silent. She dragged herself from bed, dressed and made coffee, and still nobody else roused. Tomorrow Brian and Jeff would leave, and the house would seem abandoned. The mere thought of it filled her with loneliness. How would she make it from day to day when Brian was gone? How unfair that he should be snatched away just when they discovered their attraction for each other. She wandered to the bathroom, collected the dirty towels from the rack, hung up fresh ones, went to her room and added her own soiled laundry to the pile. She wondered how long she should wait before starting the washing machine to launder Jeff's clothes so he could take them back clean and save a laundry bill.

They had been running free all week, the whole bunch of them, and nobody had bothered much with homemaking chores. The pile of dirty clothes at the bottom of the laundry chute would be mountainous.

She waited until ten o'clock before creeping down the basement stairs like a burglar, sneaking onto each tread, afraid the step would creak and awaken Brian, who lay on his belly with both arms flung up, his ear pressed to one biceps. She halted in her tracks, gazing across the dim room at his bare back, at the outline of his hips and legs beneath the green blanket. His right leg was extended, his left bent with the tip of its knee peeking from under the covers. The only men she'd ever seen in bed were her father and Jeff. But seeing Brian there, listening to the light snuffle of his regular breathing, had a decidedly sensual effect upon Theresa.

She clutched her armload of dirty laundry and tiptoed to the laundry-room door, turned the knob soundlessly and latched it behind her with equally little noise.

She sorted out six piles of colors, dropped the first stack into the machine and grimaced at how loud the selector dial sounded when she spun it to its starting position—the clicks erupted through the silence like a tommy gun. When she pushed the knob to start the water flowing, it sounded like Niagara Falls had just rerouted through the basement. Soap, softener, then she picked her way across the floor between hills of fabric and opened the door to the family room.

She had just managed to get it closed silently again when Brian—still on his belly—lifted his head, emitted a snort and scratched his nose with the back of one hand. She stood transfixed, watching the light from the sliding glass door find its way across the ridges of his shoulder blades and the individual ones of his spinal column to the spot where the sheet divided his body in half. He cleared his throat, lifted his head again and intuitively glanced back over his shoulder.

Theresa stood rooted to the spot, holding onto the doorknob behind her, feeling the blood raddle her cheeks at being discovered there, watching him awaken.

His hair was standing up at odd angles. His cheek and jaw wore the shadow of a night's growth. His eyes were still swollen from sleep. "Good morning," he managed in a voice raspy from disuse. The greeting was accompanied by a slow over-the-shoulder smile that drew up one side of his mouth engagingly. Lazily, he rolled over, crooking one arm behind his head, presenting an armpit shadowed by dark hair and a chest sprinkled with a liberal portion of the same.

"Good morning." Her voice came out a whisper.

"What time is it?"

"After ten." She flapped an apologetic palm at the laundry-room door. "I'm sorry I woke you up with the washer, but I wanted to get the laundry started. Jeff's clothes...are...he...." To Theresa's dismay the words chugged away into silence, and she stood staring at half of a naked man, one who made everything inside her body go as watery as the sounds emanating from the other side of the wall.

"Come here." He didn't move; nothing more than the beguiling lips formed the invitation. His right arm cradled the back of his head. His left lay flat on his belly, the thumb resting in his navel, which was exposed above the blanket. One knee was straight, the other one bent so that its outline formed a triangle beneath the blankets. "Come here, Theresa," he repeated, more softly than before, lifting a hand toward her.

Her startled expression warned him she'd dreamed up an excuse, even before she began to voice it. "I have to—"

"Come." He rolled to one hip, and for a horrifying moment she thought he was going to get up and come to get her. But he only braced up one elbow and extended a hand, palm up.

She wiped her own palms on her thighs and advanced slowly across the room but stopped two feet from the edge of his mattress. His hand remained open, waiting. Upon it she could see the calluses on each of its four fingertips from playing the guitar. He had very, very long fingers. And he slept with his watch on.

It was so still just then she thought she could hear its electronic hum.

He moved himself up just high enough and strained forward across the remaining two feet to capture her hand and drag her toward him. Her kneecaps struck the frame of the bed, and she toppled down, twisting at the last minute to land half on one hip but coming to rest at an awkward angle, half across his bare chest.

"Good morning." His smile was thorough, teasing and warming places inside Theresa that she'd never realized hadn't known complete warmth before. He slipped one arm between her and the mattress and rolled to his hip facing her, managing to maneuver her stomach flush against his. She recalled in bemused fascination that she'd read that men often wake up fully aroused, but she was too ignorant to know if it was true of Brian this morning. He brushed her cheek with the backs of his knuckles, and his voice was charmingly gruff. "I find it hard to believe there's one woman left in this world who still blushes at age twenty-five." He dipped his head to touch her lips with a nibbling kiss. "And you know what?" He ran the tip of an exploring index finger across the juncture of her lips, causing them to fall open as she caught a breath in her throat. "Some day I'm going to see you wearing only that." He dipped his head again, but when their mouths joined, he rolled her over on her back and lay half across her body. His back was warm, firm, and beneath her palm she felt each taut muscle across his shoulders, then explored his ribs, like a warm, living vibraphone upon which her fingers played.

His naked chest was pressed against her breasts, flattening them in a way that felt wholly wonderful. She was wearing a thick wool hunter's shirt of gold and black squares, buttoned up the front, its deep tails flapping loose about her hips, which were squeezed tightly into a pair of washed-out denim Levi's. The shirt left her totally accessible—she realized that just as his weight bore down on her, and he lifted one knee across her thighs, rubbing up and down repeatedly, slowly inching higher until the inner bend of knee softly chafed the feminine mound at the juncture of her legs. Still kissing her, he found the arm with which she was protecting her breast and forced it up over his shoulder. Then his hand skimmed down the scratchy wool shirt, up under its tails and onto the bare band of skin between her jeans and bra. He drew a valentine on her ribs, then cupped her breast with unyielding authority, pushing on it so hard it caused a queer but welcome ache in the hollow of her throat. She felt the nerves begin to jump deep in her stomach, but controlled the urge to fight him off. The caress was brief, almost as if he was testing her, telling her, get used to it, try it, just this much, a little at a time. But, to Theresa's surprise, when his fingers left her breast, they skimmed straight down the center of her belly, along the hard zipper of her jeans and cupped the very warm, throbbing spot at the base of the zipper. Within the constricting blue denim her flesh immediately responded with a heat so awesome it caught her by surprise. She sucked in a quick, delighted breath, and her eyelids slammed closed. Her back arched up off the mattress and fire shot from the spot he caressed down to her toes. He clutched her with a hard, forceful palm, pushing upward until she was certain he could feel the pulsebeat throbbing through the hard, flat-felled seams of the Levi's. He stroked her through the tight, binding denim—once, twice, almost as if marking her with his stamp of possession.

Before she could decide whether to fight or yield, his hand was gone. She lay looking up at his stormy green eyes while he braced on both elbows, and their labored breathing pounded out the message of mutual arousal.

"Theresa, I'm going to miss you. But six months and I'll be back. Okay?" His voice had gone even huskier with desire. What was he asking? The answer to the ambiguous question stuck in her throat.

"Brian, I...I'm not sure." She didn't think she could make such a promise, if he meant what she thought he did.

"Just think about it then, will you? And when June comes, we'll see."

"A lot can happen between now and June."

"I know. Just don't...." His troubled eyes traveled up to her hair. He soothed it back almost roughly, then returned his gaze to her amazed brown eyes, sending a message of fierce possession as absolute as that he'd delivered in his startling caress of a moment ago. "Don't find somebody else. I want to be first, Theresa, because I understand you, and I'll be good for you. That's a promise."

Just then Jeff's voice boomed from above; the washing machine had brought the house to life at last. "Hey, where is everybody? Brian, you awake?"

"Yeah, just dressing. I'll be right up."

Theresa nudged Brian aside and leaped off the bed. But before she could scamper away he captured her wrist and pulled her back down. She landed with a soft plop, sitting on the edge of the bed. He braced on one elbow, half curling his body around her to look up into her face.

"Theresa, will you kiss me just once, without looking like you're scared to death?"

"I'm not very good at any of this, Brian. I think you'd be a lot happier if you gave up on me," she whispered.

He frowned, released the hand she'd been tugging in an effort to regain her freedom. But when it was released, it lay on the mattress beside her hip with the fingers curled tightly underneath. He studied it, then with a single finger stroked the backs of the freckled knuckles. Looking up into her uncertain eyes, he said, "Never. I'll never give up on you. I'll be back in June, and we'll see if we can't get you past age fifteen."

How does a person grow to be so self-assured at twenty-three, she wondered, meeting his unsmiling gaze with her own somber eyes.

His weight shifted. He kissed her fleetingly and ordered, "You go on up first. I'll make my bed and wait a few minutes before I follow."

That night they spent quietly at home. Patricia came over to be with Jeff. Margaret and Willard sat side by side on the sofa while Jeff sat Indian fashion on the floor and Brian took the piano bench, and the two played their guitars and sang. Theresa was curled up in one armchair, Amy in another, and Patricia sat just behind Jeff, sometimes resting her forehead on his upper arm, sometimes stroking his shoulder blade, sometimes humming along. But Theresa sat wrapped up with feet beneath her, and palms tucked between her thighs, watching Brian only when his eyes dropped to the fingerboard of his guitar or veered away to some other spot in the room.

She waited for the song she was certain would come sooner or later, and when Jeff suggested it, her heartbeat quickened, and she felt hollow and hot and sad.

Brian was playing his own guitar this time, a classic Epiphone Riviera, with a smooth, mellow sound and a thin body. She stared at the guitar cradled against Brian's belly, and imagined how warm the mahogany must be from his skin.

> My world is like a river
> As dark as it is deep
> Night after night the past slips in
> And gathers all my sleep....

The poignant words affirmed the melody, speaking directly to Theresa's heart. Long before the song reached its second verse, her eyes had locked with Brian's.

> She slipped into the silence
> Of my dreams last night
> Wandering from room to room
> She's turning on each light.
> Her laughter spills like water
> From the river to the sea
> I'm swept away from sadness
> Clinging to her memory.

Theresa's eyes dropped to Brian's lips. They seemed to tremble slightly as they formed the next words.

Sweet memories…
Sweet memories…

His lips closed as he softly hummed the last eight notes of the song, and Theresa didn't realize Jeff's voice had fallen silent, leaving her to hum the harmony notes with Brian.

When the final chord diminished into silence, she became aware that everyone in the room was watching the two of them, adding up what seemed to be passing between them.

Jeff broke the spell. "Well, I've got packing to do." He began settling his guitar into its velvet-lined case. "I'd better get Patricia home. We'll have to get up and rolling by 8:30 in the morning."

The guitar cases were snapped shut. Jeff and Patricia left, and within twenty minutes the rest of the household had all retired to their respective beds.

Theresa lay in the dark, not at all sleepy. The words of the song came back to beguile with their poignant message…. "Night after night the past slips in and gathers all my sleep." She knew now what true desire felt like. It was tingling through each cell of her body, made all the more tempting by the fact that he lay in the room directly below hers, probably just as wide awake as she was, and for the same reason. But desire and abandon were two difference things, and Theresa Brubaker would no more have gone down those stairs and lain with Brian Scanlon beneath her parents' roof than she would have at age fourteen. Along with desire came an awareness of immorality, and she was a very moral woman who retained the age-old precepts taught her throughout her growing years. Knowing she would be disdained as "Victorian" in this age of promiscuity, she nevertheless had deeply ingrained feelings about right and wrong and realized she would never be able to have a sexual relationship with a man unless there was a full commitment between them first.

But the tingling, pulsing sensations still coursed through her virgin body when she thought of lying on the bed with Brian that morning, of his intimate touches. She groaned, rolled onto her belly and hugged a pillow. But it was hours before sleep overcame her.

They had a last breakfast together the next morning, then there were goodbye kisses for Margaret and Willard, who went to work with tears in their eyes, waving even as the car moved off up the street.

Theresa was driving to the airport again, but this time Amy was coming along. All the way, the car had a curious, sad feeling of loneliness, as if the plane had already departed. By unspoken agreement, Brian had taken the front seat with Theresa, and she occasionally felt his eyes resting on her. It was a sunny, snowy morning, its brightness revealing every colorful freckle, every strand of carroty hair she possessed. There was no place to hide, and she wished he wouldn't study her so carefully.

At the airport, they each carried a duffel bag or a guitar case to the baggage check, then entered the green concourse through the security check and walked four abreast down the long, slanting floor that echoed their footsteps. Their gate number loomed ahead, but just before they reached it, Brian grabbed Theresa's hand, tugged her to a halt and told the others, "You two go on ahead. We'll be right there." Without hesitation, he dragged her after him into a deserted gate area where rows of empty blue chairs faced the walls of windows. He took the guitar case from her hand and set it on the floor beside his own duffel bag, then backed her into the only private corner available: wedged beside a tall vending machine. His hands gripped her shoulders and his face looked pained. He studied her eyes as if to memorize every detail.

"I'm going to miss you, Theresa. God, you don't know how much."

"I'll miss you, too. I've loved...I...." To her chagrin, she began to cry.

The next instant she was bound against his hard chest, Brian's arms holding her with a fierce, possessive hug. "Say it, Theresa, say it, so I can remember it for six months." His voice was rough beside her ear.

"I've l-loved being w...with you...."

She clung to him. Tears were streaming everywhere, and she had started to sob. His mouth found hers. Theresa's lips were soft, parted and pliant. She lifted her face to be kissed, knowing a willingness and wonder as fresh and billowing as only first love can be—no matter at what age. She tasted salt from her own eyes and smelled again the masculine scent she'd come to recognize so well during the past two weeks. She clung harder. He rocked her, and their mouths could not end the bittersweet goodbye.

When at last he lifted his head, he circled her neck with both hands, rubbing his thumbs along the bone structure of her chin and jaws, searching her eyes. "Will you write to me?"

"Yes." She grasped one of his hands and held it fast against her face, his fingertips resting upon her closed eyelid before she pulled them down and kissed them, feeling beneath her sensitive lips the tough calluses caused by the music that bound Brian to her, made him someone so very, very right for her.

She raised her eyes at last, to find his etched with as much dread of parting as she herself felt. Oddly she had never thought men to be as affected by sentiment as women, yet Brian looked as if his very soul ached at having to leave her.

"All right. No promises. No commitments. But when June comes...." He let his eyes say the rest, then scooped her close for one last long kiss, during which their bodies knew a renewed craving such as neither had experienced before.

"Brian, I'm twenty-five years old, and I've never felt like this before in my life."

"You can stop reminding me you're two years older, because it doesn't matter in the least. And if I've made you happy, I'm happy. Keep thinking it, and don't change one thing about yourself until June. I want to come back and find you just like you are now."

She raised up on tiptoe, taking a last heart-sweeping kiss she couldn't resist. It was the first time in her life she had ever kissed a man instead of the other way around. She laid a hand on his cheek then, backing away to study him and imprint the memory of his beloved face into her mind.

"Send me your picture."

He nodded. "And you send me yours."

She nodded. "You have to go. They must be boarding by now."

They were. As Brian and Theresa rounded the wall toward their gate area, Jeff was nervously waiting by the ramp. He noted Theresa's tear-stained face and exchanged a knowing glance with Amy, but neither said anything.

Jeff hugged Theresa. And Brian hugged Amy. Then they were gone, swallowed up by the jetway. And Theresa didn't know whether to cry or rejoice. He was gone. But, oh, she had found him. At last!

At home the house seemed as haunted as an empty theater. He was there in each room. Downstairs she found the hideaway bed converted back to a davenport, and his sheets neatly folded atop a stack of blankets and pillows. She picked up the folded, wrinkled white cotton and stared at it disconsolately. She lifted it to her nose, seeking the remembered scent of him, pressing her face against the sheet while she dropped to the sofa and indulged in another bout of tears. *Brian, Brian. You're so good for me. How will I bear six months without you?* She dried her eyes on his sheet, brought his pillow into her arms and hugged it to her belly, burying her face against it, wondering how she would fill 176 days. She experienced the profound feeling that seemed to be the true measure of love—the belief that no one had ever loved so before her, and that no one would ever love in the same way after her.

So this was how it felt.

And it felt the same during the days that followed. School began and she was happy to get out of the house with its memories of him, happy to be back with the children, schedules, the familiar faces of the other faculty members she worked with. It took her mind off Brian.

But never for long. The moment she was idle, he returned. The moment she got into her car or walked into the house, he was there, beckoning. The way in which she missed him was more intense than she'd ever imagined loneliness could be. She cried in her bed that first night he was gone. She found smiling difficult during the first days back at school. Brooding came easily, and dreaminess, once so foreign to her, became constant.

On the first day after he'd left, Theresa returned home from school to find a note pinned to the back door: "Bachman's Florist delivered something to my house when they couldn't find anyone here at home. Ruth."

Ruth Reed, the next-door neighbor, answered Theresa's knock with a cheery greeting and wide smile. "Somebody loves somebody at your house. It's a huge package."

It was encased in orchid-colored paper to which was stapled a small rectangle of paper bearing the terse delivery order: "Brubaker...3234 Johnnycake Lane."

"Thank you, Ruth."

"No need for thanks. This is the kind of delivery I'm happy to take part in."

Carrying the flowers home, Theresa's heart skipped in gay anticipation. *It's from him. It's from him.* She jogged the last ten feet up the driveway and catapulted into the kitchen, not even stopping to take off her coat before ripping aside the crackling lavender paper to find a sumptuous arrangement of multicolored carnations, daisies, baby's breath and statice, interlaced with fresh ivy, all billowing from a footed green goblet. Theresa's hand shook as she reached for the tiny envelope attached to a heart-shaped card holder among the greenery.

Her smile grew, along with the giddy impatience to see his name on the gift card.

His name was there all right, but hers wasn't. The card read, "To Margaret and Willard. With many thanks for your hospitality. Brian."

Instead of being disappointed, Theresa was more delighted than ever. *So he's thoughtful, too.* She studied the handwriting, realizing it was written not by Brian but by some stranger in a florist shop someplace across town. But it didn't matter; the sentiment was his.

Brian's first letter came on the third day after he'd left. She found it in the mailbox herself, for she was always the first one home. When she flipped through the envelopes and found the one with the blue wings in the upper left-hand corner and the red and blue jets on the lower right, her heart skittered and leaped. She took the letter to her room, got the fiddling frog from his perch on the shelf and held him in her hand while she sat cross legged on the bed, reading Brian's words.

But his picture was the first thing that fell out of the envelope, and she dropped the pewter frog the moment Brian's face appeared. He was clothed in his dress blues, his tie crisply knotted, the visor of his garrison cap pulled to the proper horizontal level over his brow. He was unsmiling, but the green eyes looked directly into hers from beneath their familiar, sculptured brows. Dear face. Dear man. She turned the picture over. "Love, Brian," he'd written on the back. Theresa's heartbeat accelerated, and warmth stole over her body. She closed her eyes, took a deep breath and pressed the picture against her breast, against the crazy upbeat rhythm his image had invoked, then laid the picture face up on her knee and began reading.

Dear Theresa,
I miss you, I miss you, I miss you. Everything has suddenly changed. I used to be pretty happy here, but now it feels like prison. I used to be able to pick up my guitar and unwind at the end of a day, but now when I touch it I think of you and it makes me blue, so I haven't been playing much. What have you done to me? At night I lie awake, thinking of New Year's Eve and how you looked when you came out into the kitchen dressed in your new sweater and makeup and hairdo, all for me, and then I wish I could get the picture out of my head because it just makes me miserable. God, this is hell. Theresa, I want to apologize for what happened that morning on my bed. I shouldn't have, but I couldn't help it, and now I can't stop thinking about it. Listen, sweets, when I come home I'm not going to put the pressure on for that kind of stuff. After everything we talked about, I shouldn't have done it that day, okay? But I can't stop thinking about it, and that's mostly what makes me miserable. I wish I'd been more patient with you, but on the other hand, I wish I'd gone further. Man, do I sound mixed up. This place is driving me crazy. All I can think about is your house, and you sitting on the piano bench. Last night I put the Chopin record on but I couldn't stand it, so I shut off the stereo. When I can handle it again I'll make a tape of "Sweet Memories," and send it to you, okay, sweets? It says it all. Just how I'm feeling every minute. You, slipping into the darkness of my dreams at night, and wandering from room to room, turnin' on each light. I don't think I can make it till June without seeing you. I'll probably go AWOL and show up at your door. Do you get Easter vacation? Could you come up here then? Listen, sweets,

I gotta go. Jeff and I play a gig this Saturday night, but no girls afterward. That's a promise.

I miss you,
Brian

She read the letter nonstop for half an hour. Though each line thrilled her, Theresa returned time and again to his offhand question about Easter vacation. What would her parents say if she went? The thought rankled and made her chafe against having to tell them at all, at her age. The house seemed restrictive after that, and she felt increasingly hemmed in.

She had put off writing to Brian, feeling that to write too soon would seem...what? Brazen? Overstimulated? Yet his words were thrillingly emotional. His impatience and glumness were a surprise. She'd never dreamed men wrote such letters, holding back nothing of their feelings.

She didn't want to send her picture. But now that she knew what heart's ease there was to be found in having Brian's picture to bring him near, she realized he'd probably feel the same. She got out one of her annual elementary-school pictures, but for a moment wavered. It was a full-color shot: black and white would have pleased her more. The camera had recorded each copper-colored freckle, each terrible red uncontrollable hair and the breadth of her breasts. Yet this was just how she'd looked when he first met her, and still he'd found something that pleased him. Along with the photograph, Theresa sent the first love letter of her life.

Dear Brian,

The house is so lonely since you've been gone. School helps, but as soon as I step into the kitchen, everything sweeps back and I suddenly wish I lived somewhere else so I wouldn't have to see you in every room. The flowers you sent are just beautiful. I wish you could've seen the look on mom's face when she first saw them (and on mine when I opened the package and found they weren't for me). Naturally, mom got on the phone right away and called everyone in the family to tell them what "that thoughtful boy" had sent.

I really wasn't disappointed to find the flowers weren't for me, because what I got two days later was dearer to me than any of nature's beauties.

Thank you for your picture. It's sitting on the shelf in my room beside The Maestro, who's guarding it carefully. When your letter came I was really surprised to read how you were feeling, because everything you said was just what's happened to me. Playing the piano is just awful. My fingers want to find the notes of the Nocturne, but once I start it, I can't seem to finish. Songs on the radio we listened to together do the same thing to me. I seem to have withdrawn from mom and dad and Amy, even though I'm miserable when I sit in my room alone in the evenings. But if I can't be with you, somehow I just don't want to be with anyone.

It's really hard for me to talk about this subject, but I want to set the record straight. I know I'm really naive and inexperienced, and when I think of how uptight I get about the really quite innocent things we did together, I realize I'm paranoid about…well, you know. I really want to be different for you, so I've decided to talk to the school counselor about my "problem."

Did you really mean it about Easter? I've read that part of your letter a hundred times, and each time my heart goes all sideways and thumpy. If I came I'm afraid you'd expect things I'm not sure I'm prepared for yet. I know I sound mixed up, saying in one breath I'm going to see the counselor and in the next I'm still old-fashioned. I'm sure mother and dad would have a fit if their little Theresa announced she was going up to spend Easter with Brian. Some days mother drives me crazy as it is.

Here's my awful picture, taken in October with the rest of the Sky Oaks Elementary student body and faculty. You say it's the color of flowers. I still say vegetables, but here I am anyway. I miss you so much.

Affectionately,
Theresa

P.S. Hi to Jeff
P.P.S. I like the names "sweets."

Dear Sweets,
I can't believe you didn't say no, flat out. Now I'm living on dreams of Easter. If you come, I promise you'll set the rules. Just being with you would be enough to tide me over. You'll probably think I'm speaking out of turn, but I think somebody twenty-five years old shouldn't even be living with their parents anymore, much less having to get their okay to go off for a weekend. Maybe you're still hiding behind your mother's skirts so you won't have to face the world. God, you'll probably think I'm an opinionated sex maniac now, and that all I want is to get you up here so I can act like Greg What's-His-Name. Don't be mad, sweets, okay? Ask the counselor about it and see what she says. Your picture is getting curled at the edges from too much handling. I've been thinking, I wouldn't mind getting away from this place for a while. Instead of coming up here, maybe we could meet halfway in Fargo. Let me know what you think. Please decide to come. I miss you.

Love,
Brian

The counselor's name was Catherine McDonald. She was in her mid-thirties, always dressed in casual yet extremely up-to-date clothes and always wore a smile. Although they hadn't had many occasions to work together, Theresa and Catherine had shared many friendly visits in the teachers' lunch room, and Theresa had come to respect the woman's inherent poise, objectivity and deep understanding of the human psyche. There were school counselors whom Theresa thought more qualified to be truck drivers. But Catherine McDonald suited her role and was immensely respected by those with whom she worked.

Rather than meet in school, Theresa requested that they get together over cups of tea at the Good Earth Restaurant at four o'clock one Thursday afternoon. Potted greenery and bright carpeting gave the place a cheerful atmosphere. Theresa was led past the Danish tables and chairs on the main floor to a raised tier of booths overlooking it. Each booth was situated beside a tall window, and it was in one of these where Catherine was already waiting. The older woman immediately stood and extended a hand with a firm grip. Perhaps the thing Theresa had first admired about Catherine was the way the woman's eyes met those of the person to whom she spoke, giving an undivided attention that prompted one to confide in her and believe she cared deeply about the problems others unloaded upon her. Catherine's intelligent, wide-set blue eyes remained unwaveringly on Theresa's as the two greeted each other, settled down and ordered herbal tea and pita-bread sandwiches, then got down to the crux of the meeting.

"Catherine, thank you for taking time to meet me," Theresa opened, as soon as their waitress left them alone. Catherine waved a hand dismissively.

"I'm happy to do it. Anytime. I only hope I can help with whatever it is."

"It's personal. Nothing to do with school. That's why I asked you to meet me here instead of in the office."

"Herbal tea has a mellowing influence anyway. This is much much nicer than school. I'm glad you chose it."

Catherine stirred unrefined sugar into her tea, laid down the spoon and looked up with a laserlike attention in her blue eyes. "Shoot," she ordered tersely.

"My problem, Catherine, is sexual." Theresa had rehearsed that opening line for two weeks, thinking once the last word fell from her mouth the barriers might be broken, and it would be easier to talk about the subject that so easily made her blush and feel adolescent.

"Go ahead, tell me." Again the blue eyes held, while Catherine leaned her head with prematurely silver hair against the tall back of the booth in a relaxed attitude that somehow encouraged Theresa to relax, too.

"It has to do mostly with my breasts."

Amazingly, this woman still kept her eyes on Theresa's. "Am I correct in assuming it's because of their size?"

"Yes, they're...I've...." Theresa swallowed and was suddenly overcome by embarrassment. She braced her forehead on the heel of a hand. Catherine McDonald reached across the table and circled Theresa's wrist with cool, competent fingers, letting her thumb stroke the soft skin in reassurance before gently lowering the hand and continuing to hold it for a full thirty seconds. The contact was something strange and new to Theresa. She had not held a woman's hand before. But the firm squeeze of the counselor's fingers again inspired confidence, and soon Theresa went on speaking.

"I've been this size since I was fifteen years or so. I suffered all the usual persecution, the kind you might expect during adolescent years...the teasing from the boys, the awed stares from the girls, the labels males somehow can't help putting on that part of a woman's anatomy, and even the misplaced jealousy of certain other girls. I asked my mother at the time if I could talk to a doctor or counselor about it, but she's almost as big as I am, and her answer was that there was nothing that could be done about it, so I'd better learn to live with it...and start buying heavy-duty bras—"

Here Catherine interrupted with a single brief question. "You still live with your mother and father, don't you, Theresa?"

"Yes."

"I'm sorry. Go on."

"My normal sexual growth was…impaired by my abnormal size. Every time I found a boy I liked, he was scared by the size of them. And every time I settled for a date with somebody else, he was out for nothing but a groping session. I heard rumors at one time in high school that there was a bet among the boys that anybody who could produce my bra would win a pot worth twenty-five dollars." Theresa looked into her tea-cup, reliving the painful memory. Then she swept it from her mind and squared herself in her booth. "Well, you don't want to hear all the sordid details, and they're not really as important anymore as they once were." Theresa's eyes grew softly expressive, and she tipped her head slightly to one side. "You see, I've met a man who…who seems to…to look beyond the exterior and find something else that attracts him to me." Theresa sipped her almond tea.

"And?" Catherine encouraged quietly. This was the hard part.

"And…and.…" Theresa looked up pleadingly. "And I'm a virgin at twenty-five, and scared to death to do anything with him!"

To Theresa's amazement, Catherine's response was a softly exclaimed, "Wonderful!"

"Wonderful?"

"That you've come right out and unloaded it at last. It was hard to say, I could tell."

"Yes, it was." But already Theresa found herself smiling, loosening up and feeling more and more eager to talk.

"All right, now let's get down to specifics. Tell me why."

"Oh, Catherine, I've been living with this oversize pair of pumpkins for so many years, and they've caused me so much pain, I hate them. The last thing on earth I want to do is let a man I think I love see them naked. To me they're ugly. I thought when he…if he saw them, he'd never want to look at me without my clothes on again. So I…I.…"

"You held him off?" Catherine's eyes were steady as Theresa nodded. "And you denied your own sexuality."

"I…I hadn't thought about it that way."

"Well, start."

"Start?" Theresa was astounded by the advice.

"Exactly. Work up a good healthy anger at what you've been robbed of. It's the best way to realize what you deserve. But first, let me back up a square and ask about this man."

"Brian."

"Brian. Did his reaction to your size offend you?"

"Oh no! Just the opposite! Brian was the first man I've ever met who *didn't* stare at my breasts when we were introduced. He looked me straight in the eye, and if you knew how rare that was, you'd understand what it meant to me."

"And when he tried to make sexual contact and you put him off, was he angry?"

"No, not really. He told me he'd come to like other things about me that went deeper than superficialities."

"He sounds like a wonderful man."

"I think he is, but I have such an odd feeling about…well, he's two years younger than I am—"

"Maturity has nothing to do with chronological age."

"I know. It's silly of me to bring it up."

"Not at all. If it's a concern, you're right to introduce it. Now go on, because I interrupted again."

For the next hour and fifteen minutes Theresa expounded on all her secret hurts gathered up, stored through the years. She expressed her dismay over the things she'd had to forgo because of her problem, and the reluctance she'd always felt to discuss it with her mother, once Margaret had expressed her opinion on the subject all those years ago. She admitted she'd gone into elementary music because it allowed her to work with children who were less discerning than adults. She confessed that Brian had accused her of hiding in various ways. It all came out, and when Theresa had spilled every thought she'd harbored for so many years, Catherine pushed her teacup away, crossed her forearms on the table edge and studied Theresa intently.

"I'm going to suggest something, Theresa, but I want you to remember it's only a suggestion, and one you should think about for a while and mull over. There *is* an answer for you that you may never have considered before. I believe in time you and Brian will come to work out your self-consciousness, because he sounds like a man willing to go slowly at building your self-confidence. But even when you achieve sexual ease with this man, the other problems will not go away. You'll still feel angry about the clothes you're forced to wear, about your Rubenesque proportions, about the stares of strange men. What I'm suggesting you inquire about is a surgical procedure called mammoplasty—commonly called breast-reduction surgery.''

Theresa's eyes widened unblinkingly. Her lips fell open in surprise.

"I can see it never entered your mind.''

"No, it…breast-reduction surgery?'' The words came out on a breathy note of suspicion. "But that's *vanity* surgery.''

"Not anymore. The surgery is becoming an accepted treatment for more than just bruised egos, and the idea that it's prompted only by self-indulgence is antiquated. It's my guess that you have more physical discomfort than you even attribute to breast size, and the surgery is being used to eliminate many physical ailments.''

"I don't know. I'd have to think about it.''

"Of course you would. It's not the kind of thing you jump into on a night's consideration. And it may not be the answer for you, but dammit, Theresa! Why should you live your life with backaches and rashes and without the amenities of a woman of more modest proportions comes to take as her due? Don't you deserve them, too?''

Yes, came the immediate, silent answer. *Yes, I do. But what would people think? Mother, dad, the people I work with.*
Brian.

"The yellow pages still list the surgeons under Surgeons—Cosmetic. The term has come to have negative connotations in some circles, but don't let it deter you if you decide to look into the possibility. Better yet, I know a woman who's had the surgery, and I know she'd give you the name of her surgeon and be willing to share her feelings with you. She spent her life suffering all the same ignominies as you, and the surgery has made a profound change not only in her self-image but in her general health. Let me give you her name." Catherine extracted a note pad and pencil from her purse and wrote down the name, then reached out to touch the back of Theresa's hand. "For now, just consider it, let the idea settle in, with all its constituent possibilities. And if you're worried about facing people, don't be. It's your life, not theirs. Not your mother's or your father's or those you work with." The sharp blue eyes brightened further. "Aha! I can see I've struck a nerve already. People be damned, Theresa. This decision is one you make for yourself, not for anyone else."

As they left the restaurant, the silver-haired woman turned toward the redhead. "Whenever you want to talk again, let me know. I'm always available."

That night in bed, Theresa considered the rather stupendous possibilities of "Life After Surgery." She thought of what it would be like to walk proudly, with shoulders back, wearing a slim size-nine sundress. She considered how it would feel to lift her arms and direct the children without the drogueish weights pulling at her shoulders. She dreamed of having no more painful shoulder grooves from the slicing bra straps that marred her flesh. She thought of summer without rash beneath her breasts where the two surfaces rubbed together constantly now. She imagined the sheer joy of buying the sexiest underwear on the rack, and of having Brian see her in it, then without it.

Brian. What would he think if she did such a thing?

In the dark, beneath the covers, Theresa ran her hands over her breasts, feeling their enormity, hating them afresh, but suddenly smitten by a hundred unasked questions about what it would entail to have them reduced in size. It was heady simply knowing she had the option!

She tried to imagine the freedom of having only half as much where all this flesh was now, and it seemed almost unbelievable that it could happen for her. But it was too important a decision to make on one night's consideration, and without all the facts, as Catherine had pointed out.

And there was her mother to consider. Somehow, she knew her mother would disapprove—her fatalistic attitudes already having been voiced. And the people at work—what would they think? How many times in her life had women—ignorant of the attendant miseries of having massive breasts—told her she should be happy she was endowed as she was? Their attitude was programmed by a cultural bias toward large breast size, so she shouldn't blame them for their uninformed opinions.

But with the new seed of suggestion planted, those countless comments and hurts from the past had already ceased to hurt as much.

But what if Brian objected? Always her thoughts went back to Brian, Brian, Brian. What would it feel like to have him see her naked if she was proud of her body instead of ashamed of it?

Chapter Nine

Theresa didn't mention it in any of her letters to Brian, though their correspondence continued weekly, and more often semi-weekly. He sent the tape of "Sweet Memories," and the first time she played it Theresa knew an aching loneliness. She closed her eyes and pictured Brian playing his guitar and singing the poignant song, felt again his kisses, yearned to see him, touch him. She still hadn't given him her answer about meeting him in Fargo. She wanted to—oh, how she wanted to—but she trembled to think of telling her parents about her plan. And no matter what Brian had said in his letters, she was sure if she went he'd expect a sexual commitment before the weekend was over.

In early March, Theresa was crossing the parking lot at school, picking her way across the ice-encrusted blacktop when one of her two-inch heels went skittering sideways and dumped her flat onto her back. Books flew, scattering across the pitted ice while she lay looking at the leaden sky with the wind knocked out of her.

Joanne Kerny, a fellow teacher, saw Theresa go down and hurried to help her sit up, a worried frown on her pretty face. "Theresa, what happened? Are you hurt? Should I get help?"

"N...no." But Theresa felt shaky. "No, I think I'm all right. My heel slipped, and I went down so fast I didn't realize I was falling until my head hit the ice."

"Listen, stay right here and I'll go get somebody to help you inside, right away."

The fall had made Theresa's head hurt, but she managed to

stay on the job through the remainder of the day. She worked the following day, also, but by the third day she was forced to call for a substitute teacher: her back was in spasm. She went to the doctor, and his examination turned up no broken bones, but some very painfully bruised muscles, for which he prescribed a relaxant. But in the course of his examination and questioning, Dr. Delancy asked some questions he'd never asked before.

"Tell me, Theresa, do you have back pain regularly?"

"Not exactly regularly. Rather *ir*regularly and more so in my shoulders than my back."

He probed further. How often? Where? What seems to bring it on? Does it bother you to wear high heels? Are you on your feet all day? At what age did the back irritation start? And when he stopped at the door on his way out, his next order sounded dire enough to strike a bolt of fear through Theresa: "When you're dressed I'd like to talk to you in my office."

Five minutes later Dr. Delancy informed her without preamble, "I believe, young lady, that you're in for increasing back problems unless something is done about the cause of these aches, which, if I diagnose them correctly, are happening with increasing frequency the older you get. They can only be expected to get worse if untreated." At her startled expression he rushed on. "Oh no, this fall is only a temporary inconvenience. It'll heal and cause nothing permanent. What I'm speaking of is the strain on your back, knees and chest by the extreme weight of your breasts. The back and shoulder aches you've had, which started in your teen years, are undoubtedly being caused by a bone structure too small to support all that weight. I'm going to recommend a good specialist for you to talk to about it, because there is a solution to the problem, one that's far less critical, less risky, and less painful than the back surgery you may eventually have to undergo if you ignore the problem."

She knew what Dr. Delancy was talking about even before

she put the question to him. "Are you talking about breast-reduction surgery?"

"Oh, so someone's suggested it to you before?"

She left the doctor's office with an odd feeling of predestination, as if the fall in the parking lot had happened to lend her a further and more valid reason for considering the surgery. Certainly if she were to bring up the subject to her mother and tell Margaret what Dr. Delancy's prognosis was, her mother would accept the idea of breast reduction far more readily than if Theresa suggested having it only to relieve herself of sexual hangups, and so she could wear the clothing of her choice.

Dear Brian,
I've done the most foolish thing. I slipped and fell down in the parking lot at school. We'd had rain on top of ice and I was wearing shoes with little heels, and down I went. I'm staying home for a couple of days, on doctor's orders, but he says it's just bruised muscles and they'll fix themselves. But meanwhile, I have another vacation (sort of), but I wish you were here to spend it with me.

The pen fell still. Theresa's gaze wandered off to the dismal gray day beyond the window. The clouds scuttled low while sleet pelted down to run in rivulets along the pane.

What would he think if she wrote, I've been thinking about having my breasts made smaller?

She hadn't realized, up to that point, she *was* considering it. But there were many questions yet to be answered before she could make her decision. And somehow, it seemed too intimate a revelation to make to Brian yet.

She pulled herself from her musing and touched the pen to the paper again.

I've been thinking a lot about Easter. I want to come, but you're right. I'm afraid to tell my folks....

Two days later the phone rang at four in the afternoon.

"Hello?"

"Hello, sweets."

It seemed the winds and rain of March dissolved, and the world erupted in flowers of spring. Theresa's free hand clutched the receiver and joy spiraled up through her limbs.

"B...Brian?"

"Do any other men call you sweets?"

"Oh, Brian," she wailed, and the tears suddenly burned her eyes. Her back still hurt. She was depressed. She missed him. Hearing his voice was the sweetest medicine of all. "Oh, Brian, it's really you."

He laughed, a brief dissatisfied sound ending with a gulp. His voice sounded shaky. "How are you? How's your back?"

"Suddenly it's much better." Through her tears she smiled at the phone cord, picturing his face. "Much, much better."

"Your letter just came."

"And yours just came."

"But I didn't know about your accident when I wrote. Oh, babe, I got so worried, I—"

"I'm fine, Brian, really. All except...." All except her life was none of the things she wanted it to be. She was afraid to have the surgery. Afraid not to have it. Afraid to tell her parents about it. Afraid to meet Brian in Fargo. Afraid her parents would disapprove. Angry that she had to seek their approval at all.

"Except what?"

"Oh, I d...don't know. It's s...silly. I...I just...."

"Theresa, are you crying?"

"N...no. Yes!" She placed a hand over both eyes, squeezing. "Oh, Brian, I don't know why. What's wrong with me?" She tried to hold back the sobs so he couldn't hear.

"Sweetheart, don't cry," he pleaded. His voice sounded

muffled, as if his lips were touching the phone. But his plea brought the tears on in force.

"No one's ever c…called me sweetheart bef…before."

"You'd better get used to it."

The tender note in his voice reverberated through her pounding heart. She dashed the tears from beneath her eyes with the back of a hand and clung to the phone. So much to say, yet neither of them spoke. Their trembling feelings seemed to sing along the wire. She was unused to having emotions of this magnitude. Voicing them the first time was terrifying. Essential. She could not live with the sweet pain in her chest.

"I've m…missed you more than I ever th…thought human beings missed one another."

A throaty sound, much like a groan, touched her ear. Then his breath was indrawn with a half hiss and expelled in a way that made her picture him with eyelids clenched tightly. Silence swam between them again, rife with unsaid things. Her body was warm and liquid with sudden need of him.

When he spoke again his words sounded tortured, almost guttural. "You're all I think of." Tears were trailing freely over her cheeks, and she felt weighted and sick. Scintillating, silent moments slipped by, while the unspoken took on greater meaning than the spoken. If the house had not been totally silent she might have missed his next throaty words. "You and Easter."

Still he did not ask. Still she did not answer. Her heart trembled. "Brian, nothing like this.…" She stopped to swallow a sob that threatened.

"What? I can't hear you, Theresa." In her entire life of painful shyness, no teasing, no taunts had ever hurt like this shattering longing.

"N…nothing like this has ever hap…happened to me before."

"To me either," he said thickly. "It's awful, isn't it?"

At last she released a sniffly laugh that was much sadder

than tears, meant to allay the tension, but failing miserably. "Yes, it's awful. I don't know what to do with myself anymore. I walk around unaware."

"I forget what I'm supposed to be doing."

"I h...hate this house."

"I think about going AWOL."

"Oh, no, Brian, you mustn't."

"I know...I know." She listened to the sound of his labored breathing. Was he running a hand through his hair? Again stillness fell. "Theresa?" he said very, very softly. Her eyes slid closed. She touched the phone with parted lips. "I think I'm falling."

Her soul soared. Her body was outreaching, yearning, denied.

Again came his ragged breath, seeking control. "Listen, kiddo, I've got to go, all right?" The gaiety was decidedly forced. "Now you go rest and take care of your back for me, okay? There'll be a letter from me day after tomorrow or so. And I promise I won't go AWOL. Tell everybody there hello." At last he fell quiet. His voice dropped to a husky timbre. "I can't take this anymore. I have to go. But I won't say goodbye. Only...sweet memories."

Don't go! Don't hang up! Brian...wait! I love you! I want to meet you at Easter. We'll....

The phone clicked dead in her ear. She wilted against the wall, sobbing. *Why didn't you tell him you'd come? What are you afraid of? A man as gentle and caring as Brian? Do all who love suffer this way?*

Perhaps it was the bleakness and unhappiness that finally prompted Theresa to call the woman whose name had been given her by Catherine McDonald. She desperately needed to talk to somebody who understood what she was going through.

As she dialed the number several days later, her stomach went taut, and she wasn't sure she could voice the questions she'd rehearsed so often during the days she'd lain in bed under doctor's orders.

But from the moment Diane DeFreize answered the phone and greeted warmly, "Oh yes, Catherine told me you might call," the outlook in Theresa's life began to change. Their conversation was encouraging. Diane DeFreize radiated praise for the change wrought upon her life by the surgery she'd had. In little time at all she'd made Theresa eager to take the first step.

It was a day in the third week of March when she met Dr. Armand Schaum. He was a lean, lanky surgeon, one of the growing number of people she'd met lately who maintained eye contact on introduction. Dr. Schaum had the blackest hair she'd ever seen and a piercing look of intelligence in his nut-brown eyes. She liked him immediately. Obviously, Dr. Schaum was used to skittish women coming in with diffident attitudes and uncertain body language, as well as with the slumped shoulders caused by their condition. Theresa, like most, huddled in her chair at first, as if she'd come to his pleasant office asking him to perform some perverted act upon her.

Within five minutes, her attitude changed drastically, and she was struck by a sense of how very ignorant and misinformed she'd been all these years. She'd maintained the same outdated viewpoint as the rest of society: that breast-reduction surgery was vain and unnecessary.

Dr. Schaum explained the probable physical ailments Theresa could expect in the future if her breasts remained as they were now: not only backaches but also a bent spine; leg and knee troubles as well as varicose veins; breathing problems later in life when the chest wall responded to the excessive weight; recurrent rashes on the undersides of her breasts; an increase in breast size and its related discomforts if and when she chose the pill, pregnancy or nursing.

Vanity surgery? How few people understood.

But there were two negative factors Dr. Schaum was careful

to point out. His long, angular face took on an expression of somber, businesslike concern.

"In mammoplasty, an incision is made around the entire areola—the brightly colored circle surrounding the nipple. The past method of surgery was to remove the nipple completely before replacing it in a higher position. But with a new method we called the inferior pedicle technique, we can now perform the surgery without severing the nerve connection completely. Now, the nipple remains attached by a slender stalk of tissue called the pedicle. With this technique we aren't able to reduce the breast size quite as radically, but the chance of retaining nipple sensitivity is greatly increased. With *all* breast surgery, that sensitivity is lost at least temporarily. And though we can never guarantee it will return, if the nerve connection is preserved, it's very likely. But it's important that you understand there's always the remote possibility of losing the erogenous zone permanently."

Dr. Schaum leaned forward in his chair. "The other consideration you have to make is whether or not you ever want to breast-feed a baby. Although there have been rare cases in which the pedicle technique was used, where mothers *were* able to nurse afterward, the possibility is highly unlikely.

"So having the surgery means accepting the fact that two important things are at stake: the breast's ability to produce milk and to respond to sexual stimulation. It means that you'll almost certainly have to give up the one, and there's the remote possibility of having to give up the other."

So that was the risk. Theresa was devastated. She lay in bed that night wide-eyed, more uncertain than ever. The idea of having all sensation irreversibly numbed was terribly frightening and very disheartening. Suppose the feeling never returned? She recalled those tingles, the feminine prickles of sexuality brought to her breasts by Brian's briefest touch, by nothing more than dancing close enough to lightly rub the front of his corduroy jacket, and she wondered what he'd think if she robbed *him* of the ability to arouse her in that particular way and herself of the ability to respond.

She cupped her breasts in her palms. They remained unstimulated. She moved her pajamas flutteringly across the nipples. Little happened. She thought of Brian's mouth...and it began.

Sweet yearning filled her, made her curl, wanting, wondering. What if this powerful feminine reaction was severed before she'd ever known the sweet evocative tug of a man's lips here? He had said, "You'll set the rules." Would he think her a tease if she asked for that much and then pulled back? Could she ask for that, then pull back herself?

She only knew that once...just once she must know the wonder before she wagered it.

He answered the phone in a crisp, military fashion. "Lieutenant Scanlon here."

"Brian, it's Theresa."

All was silent while she sensed his great surprise. She wasn't sure she should have called him in the middle of the day.

"Yes, can I help you?"

His brusqueness was a dash of cold water. Then she understood—there was someone nearby.

"Yes, you can help me by telling me you haven't given up on me yet, and that it's not too late for me to say yes to your invitation."

"I...." He cleared his throat roughly. "We can proceed with those plans, as discussed."

Her heart was going wild. She imagined how difficult it was for him to remain stern and unemotional-sounding. "Good Friday?"

"Right."

"The Doublewood Inn in Fargo?"

"Affirmative. At 1200 hours."

"D...does that mean noon, Brian?"

"Yessir. Have the proper people been notified?"

"I plan to tell them tonight. Wish me luck, Brian."

"You have it."

"Whoever's with you, turn your face away from him because I think you're going to smile." She paused, taking a deep breath, picturing him as he'd been that first day, with his back to her while he looked out the sliding glass door at the snowy yard, wearing dress blues, his too-short hair showing only slightly beneath the stern visor of his garrison cap. She clearly recalled the warmth and scent lingering in that cap when he'd handed it to her. "Lieutenant Scanlon, I think I'm falling in love with you." Silence. Shocked silence. "And I think it's time I did something about it."

After a short pause, he cleared his throat. "Affirmative. Leave it all to me."

"Not quite all. It's time I took my life into my own hands. Thank you for being so patient while I grew up."

"If there's anything we can do at this end to implement matters—"

"I'll see you in two and a half weeks."

"Agreed."

"Goodbye, dear Lieutenant Scanlon."

Again he cleared his throat. But still the last word came out brokenly. "Good...goodbye."

Theresa tackled her mother and father that night, before she could lose her nerve. As it happened, Margaret provided the perfect lead-in.

"Easter dinner will be at Aunt Nora's this year," Margaret informed them at the supper table. The meal was over. Amy had zipped off to do homework with a friend. "Arthur and his family will be coming from California on vacation. Land sakes, it must be seven years since we've all been together. Grandpa Deering will be celebrating his sixty-ninth birthday that Saturday, too, so I promised I'd make the cake and you'd play the organ, Theresa, while we—"

"I won't be here at Easter," Theresa interrupted quietly.

Margaret's expression said, don't be ridiculous, dear, where else could you possibly be. "Won't be here? Why, of course you'll—"

"I'm spending Easter in Fargo...with Brian."

Margaret's mouth dropped open. Then it pursed as a chalky line appeared around it. Her eyes darted to Willard's, then snapped back to her daughter. "With Brian?" she repeated tartly. "What do you mean, *with* Brian."

"I mean exactly that. We've agreed to meet in Fargo and spend three days together."

"Oh, you have, have you?" Margaret bit out. "Just like that. Off to Fargo without benefit of a wedding license!"

Theresa felt herself blushing, and along with it rose indignation. "Mother, I'm twenty-five years old."

"And unmarried!"

"Had you stopped to think you might be assuming things?" Theresa accused angrily.

But Margaret had ruled her roost too long to be deterred by any one of them when *she knew she was right!* Her face was pink as a peony by this time, the double chin quivering as she claimed distastefully, "When a man and woman go off, *overnight,* alone, what else is to be done but *assume?*"

Theresa glanced to her father, but his face, too, was slightly red, and he was studying his knuckles. Suddenly she was angered by his spinelessness. She wished he'd say something one way or the other instead of being bulldozed by his outspoken wife all the time. Theresa faced her mother again. Though her stomach was churning, her voice remained relatively calm. "You might have asked, mother."

Margaret snorted and looked aside disdainfully.

"If you're going to assume, there's nothing I can do about

it. And at my age I don't feel I have to justify myself to you. I'm going and that's all—"

"Over my dead body, you're going!" Margaret lurched from her chair, but at that moment, unbelievably, Willard intervened.

"Sit down, Margaret," he ordered, gripping her arm. Margaret turned her fury on him.

"If she lives in our house, she lives by rules of decency!"

Tears stung Theresa's eyes. It was as she'd known it would be. With her mother there was no discussing things. There hadn't been when Theresa was fourteen and sought consolation over her changing body, and there wasn't now.

"Margaret, she's twenty-five years old," Willard reasoned, "closer to twenty-six."

Margaret pushed his hand off her arm. "And some sterling example for Amy to follow."

The words sliced deeply in their unfairness. "I've always been—"

But again, Willard interceded. "Amy's values are pretty much in place, don't you think, Margaret? Just like Theresa's were when she was that age."

Margaret's eyes were rapiers as she glared at her husband. It was the first time in Theresa's life she'd ever seen him stand up to her. And certainly, she'd never seen or heard them fight.

"Willard, how can you say such a thing? Why, when you and I were—"

"When you and I were her age it was 1955, and we'd already been married for a couple of years and had a house of our own without your mother telling you or me what to do."

Theresa could have kissed her father's flushed cheeks. It was like discovering some hidden person, much like herself, who'd been hiding inside Willard Brubaker all these years. What a revelation to see that person assert himself at last.

"Willard, how in the world can you as much as give permission to your own daughter to go off—"

"That's enough, Margaret!" He rose to his feet and turned

her quite forcefully toward the doorway. "I've let you steam-roll me for a lot of years, but now I think it's time we discussed this in the bedroom!"

"Willard, if you...she can't...."

He led her, sputtering, down the hall until the sound of his voice drifted back. "I think it's time you rememb—" Then the closing bedroom door cut off his words.

Theresa didn't know they were in the kitchen later that night when she roamed restlessly from her room thinking, she'd get something to drink, then maybe she'd be able to fall asleep.

They were standing in the shadows of the sparsely lit room when Theresa came up short in the dark entry, realizing she was intruding. She could see little of her mother, who stood in front of Willard. Their backs were to Theresa, their feet bare, and they wore tired old robes she'd seen around the house for years. But from the movement of her father's elbows, she suspected his hands were pleasantly occupied. A soft moan came from the throat of the woman who was so glib at issuing orders. "Will...oh, Will..." she whispered.

As Theresa unobtrusively dissolved into the shadow of the hall and crept back to her room, she heard the murmur of her father's very young-sounding chuckle.

In the morning the word Fargo didn't come up, nor did the name Brian Scanlon. Margaret was as mellow as a softly plucked harp, wishing Theresa good morning before humming her way toward the bathroom with a cup of coffee. The sound of Willard's shaver buzzed louder as the door opened. Then, from far way, she heard laughter.

It was Willard who sought out Theresa in her bedroom at the end of that day and questioned quietly from the doorway, "Are you planning to drive up to Fargo?"

Theresa looked up in surprise. "Yes, I am."

He scratched his chin contemplatively. "Well, then I'd better take a look at that car of yours, in case anything needs tunin' up.'' He began to turn away.

"Daddy?"

He stopped and turned. Her arms opened as she came across the soft pink carpet on bare feet. ''Oh, daddy, I love you,'' she said against his less-than-firm jowl as his arms tightened around her. A hand came up to pet her head with heavy, loving strokes. Rough, then gentling a bit. ''But I think I love him, too.''

"I know, pet. I know.''

And so it was, from Willard, the quiet one, the unassertive one, Theresa learned a lesson about the power of love.

Chapter Ten

The five-hour drive from Minneapolis to Fargo was the longest Theresa had ever made alone. She'd worried about getting drowsy while driving but found her mind too active to get sleepy behind the wheel. Pictures of Brian, memories of last Christmas and anticipation of the next three days filled her thoughts. At times she'd find herself smiling widely, realizing a rich appreciation for the rolling farmland through which she drove, as if her newly expanded emotions had opened her senses to things she'd never noticed before: how truly beautiful tilled black soil can be, how vibrant the green of new grass. She passed a pasture where newborn calves suckled their mothers, and for a moment her thoughts turned dour, but she wouldn't allow herself to think of anything except the thrill of seeing Brian again.

The sapphire lakes of the Alexandria area gave way to the undulating farmland of Fergus Falls, then the earth gradually flattened as the vast deltaland of the Red River of the North spread as far as the eye could see: wheat and potato fields stretching endlessly on either side of the highway. Moorhead, Minnesota, appeared on the horizon, and as Theresa crossed the Red River that divided it from its sister city, Fargo, on the Dakota side, her hands were clammy, clutching the wheel.

She pulled the car into the parking space before the Doublewood Inn, then sat staring at the place for a full minute. It was the first time in her life that Theresa was checking in to a motel by herself.

You're only having last-minute jitters, Theresa. Just because

*the sign says Motel doesn't mean you're doing anything pru-
rient by checking in to the place.*

The lobby was beautiful, carpeted in deep, rich green, decorated with Scandinavian furniture of butcher-block coloring
and a plethora of live green plants that seemed to bring the
golden spring day inside.

"Good morning," greeted the desk clerk.

"Good morning. I have a reservation." She felt conspicuous
and suddenly wished the clerk were a woman instead of a
man—a woman would sense her honorable intentions, she
thought irrationally. "My name is Theresa Brubaker."

"Brubaker," he repeated checking his records, handing her
a card to sign. In no time at all she had a key in her hand, and
to her surprise the clerk told her brightly, "Oh, Miss Brubaker,
your other party has already arrived. Mr. Scanlon is in Room
108, right next to yours." She glanced at her key: 106. Suddenly it was all real. She felt her face coloring and thanked the
clerk, then turned away before he could see her discomposure.

She drove around to the back of the motel, wondering if
their rooms faced this side, if Brian was watching her from one
of the windows above. She found herself unable to glance up
and peruse the spaces on which the draperies were drawn back.
If he was watching her, she didn't want to know it. Inside, she
stopped before room 108. Staring at the number on his door,
her heart thudded. The suitcases grew heavy and threatened to
slip from her sweating palms. *He's in there. I'm standing no
more than twenty feet from him right now.* It was odd, but now
that she was here she was suddenly reluctant to face him. What
if either of them had changed in some way since Christmas?
What if the attraction had somehow faded? *What will I say to
him? What if it's awkward? What if…what if….*

Her own door was only one foot away from his. She opened
it and stepped into a room carpeted in tarnished gold with a
queen-size bed, a dresser, console, mirror and television. Nothing extraordinary, but to Theresa, experiencing independence

for the first time, the room seemed sumptuous. She set her luggage down, sat on the end of the bed, bounced once, walked into the tiled bathroom, turned on the light, switched it off, crossed the long main room to open the draperies, switched on the TV, then switched it off again at the first hint of sound and color, unzipped her suitcase, hung up some garments near the door, then looked around uncertainly.

You're only delaying the inevitable, Theresa Brubaker. She stared at the wall, wondering what he was doing on the other side of it. *Just a minute more and my nerves will calm. I'd better check my makeup.* The mirror revealed everything fresh and unsmudged except her lips, which needed color. She dug out her lipstick and applied it with a shaking hand. It tasted faintly peachy and contained flecks of gold that glistened beneath the light when she moved. *You don't put on fresh lipstick when you want a man to kiss you, Brubaker, you dolt.* She jerked a white tissue from the dispenser on the wall and swiped it swiftly across her lips, removing all but a faint smudge of remaining color. The tissues was rough and left her lips looking faintly red and chapped around the edge. Nervously she uncapped the silver tube and reapplied the peachy gloss. She met her own eyes in the mirror. They were wide and bright with anticipation. But they were not smiling. She glanced at her breasts beneath the baby blue blouse she'd bought new for this occasion. She wore no sweater today, but felt naked without it, though the tiny blue heart-shaped buttons went from the waist of her white skirt up to the tight mandarin collar that was edged with a blue ruffle. The short gathered sleeves of the blouse had a matching miniature ruffle around their cuffs. Suddenly the puffy sleeves seemed to accentuate the size of her breasts but she forced herself to look instead at her very tiny waistband into which the blouse was securely tucked.

All it takes is a knock on his door, and this uncertainty will be over.

A minute later she rapped on 108 twice, but at the third flick of her wrist her knuckles struck air, for the door was already being flung open.

He stood motionless for a long moment, one hand on the doorknob. She, with her knuckles in the air, stared at him wordlessly. Theresa saw nothing but Brian's face, the searching green eyes with their dark spiky lashes, the lips open slightly, the familiar nose, short hair, cheeks shaven so recently they still shone. Then she became aware of how accentuated his breathing was. The form-fitting baby blue knit shirt fit his chest like liquid, hiding no trace of the swiftly rising and falling muscle beneath it.

Her body felt warm, thrumming, yet uncertain. She wanted to smile but stood immobile, staring at the face before her as if he were an apparition.

"Theresa," was all he said, then he reached out a hand and caught hers, drawing her into the room with firm certainty. And still he didn't smile, but only found her free hand, gripping both palms with viselike tenacity while gazing unwaveringly into her eyes. He swung her around, then turned his back to the door and closed it with his hips. "You're really here," he said hoarsely.

"I'm really here." What had happened to all the charming greetings she'd rehearsed for days? What had happened to the smooth entrance with all its urbane chic, meant to put them both on a strictly friendly basis from the first moment? Why wouldn't her lips smile? Her voice work? Her knees stop trembling?

Suddenly she was catapulted into his arms as he thrust forward, hugging her body full against his and taking her mouth with a slanting, wide, possessive kiss. Nothing gentle. Nothing hinting at easing into old familiarities, but the familiarity arising magically between them with all its stomach-lifting force. She found her arms around his trunk, hands pressed against his warm back. And, wonder of wonders, his heart was slamming against her so vibrantly she could feel the very difference between its beats. Her own heart seemed to lift each cell of her skin, sealing off her throat with its solid hammering. His hands at first forced her close, as if he couldn't get close enough, but then as their tongues joined in sleek reunion, Brian's palms roved in wide circles on her back, and as if it were the most natural thing in the world, he drew them up both her sides simultaneously, pressing her breasts, reaching inward with two long thumbs to seek her nipples briefly. His left arm returned to her back and he angled away from her slightly, cupping one breast fully, then exploring it through her blouse and brassiere while his tongue gentled within her mouth. Shudders climbed her vertebrae and raised the hairs along the back of her thighs while the pressure on her nipples continued in faint, sensuous, circular movements. It was so natural. So right. Theresa had no thoughts of stopping his explorations. They seemed as much a valid part of this reunion as the looks of reaffirmation they'd exchanged when she first stood before him.

The kiss went on unbrokenly as his hands clasped her narrow hipbones and pulled her pelvis securely against his. He rocked against her, undulating, weaving from side to side, pressing his most masculine muscles against her acquiescent stomach. Without realizing it, she found herself meeting each stroke of his hips, pressing against him, lifting up on tiptoe because he was so much taller and she yearned to feel his hardness closer to her point of desire.

Still clasping her hips, Brian ended the kiss. His warm palms pushed downward until her heels again touched the floor, then he held her firmly, so she couldn't move. He rested his forehead against hers while their strident breaths mingled, and their moist lips hovered close, swollen and still open.

Her hands were still on his back. She felt the muscles grow taut with resolution as he pressed firmly on her hipbones. It suddenly struck her how easily these things happen, how readily she had lifted against him, how opportune was the hand of

Nature in making a body thrust and ebb when the circumstances called for it.

She was chagrined to think that now he might believe she'd come here with sex in mind. She hadn't, not at all. But how fast her body had dictated its wishes.

"I was so scared to knock on that door," she admitted. He lifted his forehead from hers, bracketed her cheeks with his palms and studied her at close range.

"Why?"

"Because I thought...." His eyes were as stunning as she remembered. They wore an expression of ardency that surprised her. "I thought, what if things aren't the same between us? What if we imagined...this?"

His thumbs brushed the corners of her mouth. His lips were parted and glittered with fragments of gloss from her lipstick. "Silly girl," he whispered, before pulling her face upward to meet his descending one. Again she raised on tiptoe, but this time their bodies barely brushed. The peach-flavored kiss was bestowed by his tongue and lips in a testing circle around her mouth, tugging, wetting once again while his hands drew upon her jaws, first lifting her, then letting her recede as if she were drifting in the surf, mastered by its rush and release. "Oh, Theresa," he murmured while her eyes fell closed. "Nothing's changed for me. Nothing at all." He pressed her away only far enough to gaze into her eyes. "Has it for you?"

How incredible that he should ask. He, who emerged so flawless in her loving eyes. When she studied him again, reality seemed to buckle her lungs and knees. The expression in his eyes said he'd been as uncertain as she had. Theresa ran her hands from his elbows along his hard arms to the wrists. "Nothing," she whispered, allowing her eyelids to close once more while pulling first his left hand from her jaw to kiss its palm, then doing likewise with his right. "Nothing." She looked into his somber eyes and watched them change, grow light, relieved. Her gaze dropped to his mouth. "You have more of my lipstick on than I do."

He smiled and hauled her close, speaking against her mouth so that she could scarcely discern the words. "So clean me up." Her tongue seemed drawn to his by some magical attraction, and she learned a new delight in taking command during a kiss.

"Mmm...you taste good," she ventured, backing away only slightly. She ran her nose along his jaw. "And you smell good, just like I remember, only stronger." She backed away and ran a fingertip over his jaw. "You just shaved."

He grinned, his hands now on her back, holding her against him, but undemandingly. "Just like a teenager getting ready for his first date."

"How long have you been here?"

"Twenty minutes or so. How long have you?"

"About ten minutes. I was in my room, putting on fresh lipstick, then wiping it off, then putting it on again and wondering which was the right thing to do. I was so nervous."

Suddenly it struck them how funny it was that they'd been so apprehensive. They laughed together, then gazed into each other's eyes, and without warning simultaneously answered the compulsion to hug. Their arms went about each other—tight, tight—reaffirming. His hands roved her back. Hers touched his hair. When he backed away, he looped his hands around her hips until she rested against his again.

"What do you want to do first?" he asked.

"I don't know. Just...." Her heart pulsed crazily. "Just look at you some more." She shrugged shyly. "I don't know."

He moved not a muscle for a long, silent moment. Then he nudged her backward with his thighs, directing her shoulders with his hands. "Come here then. Let's indulge ourselves for a while." He lifted a knee to the bed, then fell, tugging her along till they lay on their sides, each with an elbow folded beneath an ear. He rested a hand on her hip. Their eyes locked, their feet trailed off the end of the mattress.

Incredible. She had been in his room less than five minutes and already she was lying on the bed with him. But she had no desire to get up or to protest at his taking her there. His head lifted slowly. His mouth covered hers, urging her lips open once again, his tongue delving into the soft recesses, tickling the skin of her inner cheeks then threading its tip along her teeth, as if counting each. Her body came alive with desire, and her breathing grew fast and harsh, as did his. But when he'd explored to his satisfaction, he lay as before, head upon elbow, his hand still resting on her hip, but undemandingly.

It seemed best to set things straight immediately. Timidity brought color rushing to Theresa's face and made her voice unnatural. "Brian, I...." His eyes were so close, so intense, burning into hers. "I didn't come here because I was ready to go all the way with you."

His hand left her hip and fell to the hollow of her waist. "I know. And I didn't come here to force you to. But I want to. You know that, don't you?"

"I'm not ready for that, Brian, no matter what I...well, I might have led you to believe something else when we first kissed."

"I think we're both in for a hell of a weekend then. It's not going to be easy. Obviously your conscience and your libido are at odds." His hands left her waist, squeezed her upper arm gently, then caressed its length until his hand rested on the back of hers. "And my libido...well, there's no hiding it, is there?" Then, unceremoniously, he carried her hand to the zipper placket of his white brushed cotton slacks. It happened so unexpectedly she had neither the time nor inclination to pull away. One moment her hand rested on his hip, the next it was flattened along his zipper, and he'd raised his upper knee as he gently forced her fingers to conform to the ridge of hot, hard flesh within. His hand disappeared from atop hers and he rolled closer, letting his eyes drift closed as he spoke gruffly against the hollow of her throat. "I'm sorry if I'm too direct, but I want you to know...whatever you choose is what we'll do, as much or as little as you want. I'd be a damned liar if I said I wasn't thinking about making love to you ever since last January when I left you crying in that airport."

While he spoke, his body undulated against her palm, then she reluctantly slipped her hand up his shirtfront and pressed it against his chest. Beneath her palm his heart thudded crazily.

"Shh...Brian, don't say that."

He backed away, pinning her with a distracting, direct gaze. "Why? Because it's true of you, too?"

"Shh." She rested an index finger on his lips. He stared at her silently until at last the fires in his eyes seemed to subside. He clasped the back of the hand at his mouth, kissed its palm, then threaded its fingers through his own. "All right. Are you hungry?"

She smiled. "Ravenous."

"Should we go and find something to eat, then hit all the highlights of Fargo, North Dakota?"

"Let's."

With one lithe motion he was at the foot of the bed, one foot on the floor, the other knee on the mattress. He hauled her up against him and she landed on her knees with her arms around his neck, and his hands on her buttocks. He kissed her fleetingly, then rubbed the end of her nose with his own. "God, it's good to be with you again. Let's get out of here before I change my mind." With a squeeze and a pat he turned her loose.

They were walking hand in hand along the Broadway Mall in downtown Fargo when they suddenly stopped and stared each other up and down, then burst out laughing.

"You're wearing—"

"Do you realize—" they said in unison, then laughed again, standing back, assessing each other's clothing. They were both wearing white slacks, and the baby blue of her ruffle-necked blouse closely matched that of his knit pullover. She wore white tennis shoes on her feet and he white leather sport shoes with a Velcro-closed strap across the arch of his foot.

"If we dressed to please each other, I think we both did a good job," he said with a smile. "I like your blouse."

"And I like your shirt." Again they laughed, then caught hands as they moved on, exploring the entire three-block length of the mall from Main to Second Avenues. At its south end they studied the Luis Jimenez sculpture depicting a prairie farmer behind a pair of oxen, breaking sod for the first time. Sauntering northward they discovered that the curving mall was designed to represent the pathway of the Red River, and that carved granite markers of red, gray and brown had been set into the concrete on either side of the street to represent the cities flanking the great river as it coursed the length of North Dakota from Wahpeton to Pembina. As they sauntered, they read the names of the towns on the North Dakota side and the dates of their founding: Hunter, 1881; Grandin, 1881; Arthur, 1880. The stones were set varying distances from the street to depict the setback between the actual towns and the great life-giving river that fed the area.

The sun was warm on their backs, the sky overhead flawless cerulean. They had a sense of calm and an even greater one of delight in being together, swinging hands, watching their white-clad legs matching strides. The mall was dotted with red-wood planters in which geraniums and petunias had been set out, and all along the mall's length ash trees were beginning to break into first leaf. At the Old Broadway Café, they peered into the twin oval windows on the front doors and decided to give the old landmark a try. Inside, the booths were the high private cubicles of another era, dark-varnished and set with stained-glass panels. The floor was ancient oiled hardwood that creaked and croaked as the waitress delivered their plate dinners of thick-slicked beef, potatoes and gravy and golden, buttered carrots.

"You haven't mentioned your mom and dad," Brian said, studying Theresa across the booth. "What did they say when you told them you were coming up here to meet me?"

She met his serious green eyes and decided to tell him the truth. "Mother assumed the worst. It wasn't a very pleasant scene." She dropped her eyes to her plate, drawing circles on it with a piece of beef.

Beneath the table his calf found hers and rubbed it reassuringly. He closed his ankles around one of hers and stopped the hand that had been pushing her fork in circles. She looked up at him.

"I'm sorry."

She laid her hand atop his. "Don't be. Something quite wonderful came about because of it." Wonder showed in her face. "Daddy. Would you believe he finally stood up to mother?"

"Willard?" Brian asked in surprise.

"Willard," she confirmed, still with the amazed expression on her face. "He shouted 'Margaret, that's enough' and... and...." Theresa had great difficulty not smirking. "And hauled her off to the bedroom, slammed the door, and the next time I saw them she was calling him Will, and the two of them were cooing like mourning doves. That was the end of Mother's resistance."

Brian dropped his fork with a clatter, threw his hands in the air and praised, "Hallelujah!"

They were still chuckling about it when they returned to the mall. They continued their stroll past The Classic Jewelers, stock-brokerage houses, Straus Drugs and so to the far north end where they discovered the Fargo Theater with its vintage art deco marquee announcing that Charlie Chaplin was playing tonight in *The Bank*.

"Do you like silent movies?" Brian asked hopefully.

"Love 'em." She grinned up at him.

"Whaddya say, should we give old Charlie a try tonight?"

"Oh, I'd love to."

"It's a date." He squeezed her hand, then led her across the street and they started back along the "Minnesota" side of the mall, reading the town names, peering in store windows. In one called Mr. T's, a bridal gown was displayed. Without realizing it, Theresa's feet stopped moving, and she stared at the mannequin. The sight of the white gown and veil, symbols of purity, brought to mind the coming night, the choice she had to make. She thought about other men she might meet in her life, the one she might possibly marry, and what he would think if she did not come to him as a virgin. But she found it impossible to imagine herself being intimate with any man but Brian.

While Theresa gazed at the bridal gown, two young men passed along the sidewalk. Brian watched their eyes assess her breasts—blatantly, neither of them trying to disguise their fascination. Their heads swiveled, gazes lingering as they drew alongside, then passed her. When they moved on, one of them must have made a lewd comment, for he did a little hip-swinging jive step while patting his thighs, then his companion laughed.

Brian was at first angry. Then he found himself assessing her breasts as a stranger would, and found, to his chagrin, that he was slightly embarrassed. Guilt followed immediately. He fought to submerge it, studying the back of Theresa's head as she gazed up innocently at the window display. But as they moved on up the mall, he was conscious of the eyes of each man they met. Without exception, they all dropped to Theresa's breasts, and Brian's discomfort grew.

Scanlon, you're a hypocrite. The thought was distinctly nettlesome, so he hooked an arm around Theresa's neck, settled her against his hip as they ambled back to the car, and when they reached it, he gave her a tender kiss of apology. Her hands rested on his chest. When she opened her eyes they held a dreamy expression, and he felt small and unworthy for a moment, realizing how hurt she'd be if she suspected he'd been embarrassed over her generous endowment. He traced the outline of her lips with a single finger and said softly, "What do you say we get away from people for a while?"

"I thought you'd never ask."

He smiled, kissed her nose, settled her inside, then started the engine. They crossed the river into Moorhead, drove out onto the blacktop highway heading east, then left it behind to wander the back roads between green woods, brown fields and blue ponds where ducks and blackbirds nested. Spring was burgeoning all around them. They felt it in the renewed warmth of the sun, smelled it in the damp earth, heard it as the sound of wildlife lifted through the air.

They discovered the lush wilds of the Buffalo River where it surged under a culvert beneath their gravel road. Brian pulled to the side, turned off the engine and invited, "Let's walk." She slipped her hand into his with a glad heart, letting him lead her down the steep bank to the dappled woods, where they picked their way aimlessly along the surging spring-swelled waters that rumbled southward. The river sang to them. The tangled roots of a long-fallen tree stood silver in their path. Brian led the way along the massive trunk to a spot where he could mount it, then reached down and helped Theresa up beside him. He walked the weathered trunk to its highest point, with her right behind him. Now the river flowed at their feet. A fish leaped. A trio of sparrows darted from the underbrush to the tangled roots of their tree. From far away a crow scolded. Everything smelled fecund, growing, renewed. From behind, Theresa lightly rested her hands on Brian's hips. He remained as before, unmoving, imbibing, gathering sweet memories. His hands covered hers, drew them firmly around his belt, and his arms covered hers while she pressed her cheek and breasts against his firm, warm back. A blue jay carped from a loblolly pine, and the sun shimmered on the forest floor through the partially sprouted leaves of the surrounding trees. Against Brian's back Theresa's heart thrummed steadily. His palms rubbed her arms, which were warm with gathered sunshine.

"Ahh..." he sighed, tilted his head back, said no more.

She kissed the center of his back. It was enough.

In time they moved on through the gold-and-green afternoon. As they ambled, they caught up on the past three months. Brian had stories about Jeff and air-force rigors, the band, the music they'd been working on. Theresa had anecdotes about life with a teenage sister, incidents from school, plans for spring concerts.

But none of it mattered. Only being together had meaning for them.

They found a nest with three speckled eggs, built in the reeds where the river backwashed and bent. They turned back as the afternoon waned and hunger imposed its demands. They kissed in a basswood grove, then climbed the pebbled bank again and settled into the car for the ride back to town. At their doors in the motel Brian said, "I'll pick you up at your place in half an hour." A quick kiss and they parted.

Chapter Eleven

The knock at her door announced a freshly showered and shaved Brian dressed in tight tan jeans, an open-collared shirt of pale tan-blue-white plaid, and a lightweight sport coat the color of an almond shell. She took one look and felt her mouth watering.

"Wow," she breathed.

He smiled guilelessly, looking down at himself and said, "Oh yeah?" Then he closed the door, eased his hips back against it, crossed his arms and grinned. "Come over here and say that, Brubaker."

She felt herself blushing, but swung away teasingly. "I'm not one of your groupies, Scanlon."

She was securing the latch of a trim gold bracelet when his strong hands closed over her wrists, dragging them around his neck. His eyes, ardent and determined, blazed into hers. "God, there are times when I wish you were." His mouth was warm, open and moist as it marauded hers. He swirled his tongue around her freshly applied lipstick, then delved brashly inside to stroke her teeth until they opened at his command. His tongue probed rhythmically in and out of her mouth, suggesting what was on his mind. He tasted of freshly brushed teeth and smelled like chrysanthemums and sage—not flowery, but spicy clean. He pulled back suddenly, leaving no question about the price he was paying for control. His stormy eyes sought and held hers. Then the storm cleared, he relaxed. His thumbs, still at her wrists, stroked lightly. Now it was his turn to declare breathily, "Wow."

Theresa's heart proved what a healthy, red-blooded twenty-five-year-old virgin she was. She was certain he could see it lifting the bodice of her blouse. She whispered thickly, "Let's go see what Charlie's up to."

At the Fargo Theater they were treated to a sensational performance by a local member of the American Theater Organ Society on an immense and wondrous pipe organ that rose out of the floor on a pneumatic lift. They sat in the balcony, because it was a dying species they'd have few more chances to experience. Theresa learned how readily Brian laughed at slapstick. While the organist tickled out an accompaniment, Charlie Chaplin duckwalked down a city street in his oversize shoes and baggy pants, went three times around a revolving door, then spent arduous moments whirling the dials of an imposing-looking vault. Brian snickered, slunk low in his seat. The vault door swung open and the lovable Charlie disappeared inside to return with his precious deposit: a scrub pail, mop and janitor's uniform. Brian rolled his head backward and hooted with full throat while Theresa's heart warmed more to the man beside her than to the one on the screen.

The organ created a musical echo of Charlie's misfortunes in leaving flowers for the black-eyed Edna Purviance, only to have the damsel believe they were a gift from the bank clerk named Charlie. When skulduggery started, the organ rumbled dramatically, creating vibrations through the theater seats. Beside her, Brian slumped low in his seat, trembling melodramatically, tossing his popcorn in the air when the heroine was tied and gagged, stamping and cheering when Chaplin came to her rescue, boo-hooing when the poor unfortunate bank custodian was left awakening from a dream, petting the rags of his floor mop instead of the waves of the damsel's head.

When the film ended and they returned to the street, Brian performed a superb imitation of Chaplin, knees crooked outward, shoulders rolling with his peculiar gait while he scratched his head with stiff fingers and made a vain attempt to open the door of the wrong car. He gave a Chaplinesque flap of the hands, looked around, dismayed, sad-eyed.

How easy it was for Theresa to gasp and clasp her hands before her, distraught at misfortune. She ran jerkily to her car, flung the door open, then stood on the pavement with eyes rolled heavenward in invitation.

Charlie Scanlon duckwalked to her, shyly studied his feet, swept into a clumsy bow, then waved her inside. She interlaced her fingers, simpered, then got in.

Brian made a swipe at the open door, missed, spun in a circle, missed again, spun another circle and finally connected with the difficult door and managed to slam it.

When he climbed in beside her and squeezed the invisible bulb of a horn and made a flatulent-sounding "T-o-o-t" out the side of his mouth, they wilted with laughter. In time they grew too weak to continue. Then they looked at each other in silent discovery.

They ate an Italian supper at a place chosen at random, reminiscing about old movies, but always thinking about the end of the evening ahead. Would it bring *good night* or *good morning*?

Laughter was gone when they walked slowly, slowly down the hall to their doors. They stopped dead center between 106 and 108.

"Can I come in?" he asked quietly at last.

She met his searching eyes, feeling the awesome tugs of carnality and denial warping her heart. She remembered her mother's words, the bridal gown in the window. She touched his chest lightly. "Will you understand how hard it is for me that I have to answer no?"

His hands hung loosely at his sides. He sucked in a huge gulp of air, dropped his head down as his eyes closed, then braced both hands tiredly on his hips and studied the toes of his brown boots.

She felt childish and unworthy. Tears began to burn her eyelids.

He saw and pulled her close, resting his chin against her hair. Though his body rested only lightly against hers, she was close enough to know that her nearness and this compulsion they both controlled so closely had aroused him. "I'm sorry, sweets," he whispered. "You're right and I'm wrong. But that doesn't make it any easier."

"Kiss me, Brian," she begged.

He took her head in both hands and tipped her face up for a deep, hungering kiss. But the pressure of his hands on her jaw and ears told of where he wanted those hands to be. And she clung to his wrists—the safest place—feeling beneath one thumb the surging rhythm of his pulse. They drew apart, troubled eyes clinging.

"Good night," he said raggedly.

"Good night," came her unsure reply.

Neither of them slept well, they confessed over breakfast. The day lolled before them; its hours would be too short, no matter how they were spent. Yet when considered in the light of their denial, those same hours seemed infinite. They browsed through West Acres Shopping Center, ate lunch in a McDonald's because their stomachs demanded filling, but neither of them cared the least about food. They roamed the green hills of Island Park and sat in its gazebo watching a group of children playing softball across the expanse of green grass. They had supper in the motel dining room, and afterward wandered into the casino where new laws allowed gambling with a two-dollar limit. But while Brian sat at a table playing blackjack, a man with sleek black hair, wearing an expensive silk suit, sidled up to Theresa, gave her a blatant visual assessment, slipped his hands to her hips and whispered in her ear, "You alone, baby?"

It happened so fast Theresa hadn't time to react until the

cloying scent of his after-shave seemed to plug her nostrils, and his wandering hands registered their insult.

Suddenly Brian interceded. "Get your hands off her, buddy," he growled, jerking the man's arm, spinning him away from Theresa, whose stunned eyes were wide and alarmed.

The man's eyes narrowed dangerously, then eased as lascivious speculation crossed his features. He pulled free of Brian's hand, shrugged his shoulder to right the expensive suit jacket, and his eyes roved once over Theresa's breasts. "Can't say I blame you, fella. If those were mine for the night, I wouldn't be too quick to share 'em either."

Theresa saw the muscles bunch in Brian's jaw. His fists clenched.

"Don't, Brian!" She stepped between the two men, facing Brian, gripping his arm in an effort to turn him away. "He's not worth it," she pleaded. His arm remained steeled. "Please!" she whispered.

But Brian's livid face scarcely registered if he'd heard. He moved with mechanical deliberation, reaching down without looking to grasp Theresa's hand and remove it from his jacket. Then slowly, menacingly he clutched the man's lapels, lifting until his toes scarcely touched the carpet.

"You will apologize to the lady right now," Brian ground out, "or your teeth will be biting your own ass, from the inside out." Brian's voice was chilling as he held the stranger aloft, nose to nose.

"Okay, okay. Sorry lady, I didn't know—"

Brian jerked him up another inch. Stitches popped on the expensive jacket. "You call that an apology, sucker? See if you can't do better."

The man's eyes were bugging. Sweat erupted on his sheeny forehead and beneath his lizardlike nose. "I...I'm really sorry, m...miss. I'd like to b...buy you both a drink if you'd let me."

Brian slammed him back down to the floor, released his lapels distastefully while shoving the unpalatable intruder back until he stumbled against a table. "Pour your goddamn drinks in your pants, buddy. Maybe it'll cool you off." He turned. "Let's get out of here, Theresa." His fingers were like brands as he led her by an arm to the casino door, then out into the carpeted hall. She felt his hand trembling on her elbow and had to run to keep up with him. Wordlessly he turned down the hall to their rooms and was fishing in his trousers pockets for the key even before they reached their destination. When he leaned to insert the key into 108, there was no question of where he expected her to go. The door swung back and he found her hand, leading her inside. There followed a solid thud, then they were ensconced in a world of unbroken black. His arms closed convulsively around her, his body pressed close, sheltering, rocking her as he spoke gruffly against her hair. "I'm sorry, sweets, God, I'm so sorry."

"Brian, it's all right." But she was still shaken and vulnerable and, now that it was over, felt like crying. But his protection eradicated the sudden need for tears. His arms had strength she'd never suspected. They clamped her so hard her back hurt as he bent it in a bow.

"God, I wanted to kill him!" Brian's fingers dug into her flesh, just below and behind her armpits, and she winced, lifting her hands instinctively to press against his chest.

"Brian, it doesn't matter...please, you're hurting me."

The pressure fell away. He jerked as if shot. "I'm sorry...I'm sorry...sorry...." The voice was pained in the darkness, then his hands were gentle on her, finding her face in the inkiness, fingertips caressing her temples, then sliding into her hair as his mouth sought hers. "Theresa...Theresa..." he muttered, then circled her again with his arms. "I'd never hurt you, but I want you, you know that. God, I'm no better than him," Brian finished miserably, then took her mouth with an abandon that sent tongues of fire licking down her stomach. His hands left her back and roamed up her sides, pressing hard, too hard, as if it were compulsion he was trying to fight. She clung, unwilling to stop him yet, blessing the darkness.

His caress trailed down over her small waist, took measure of her hipbones, then traveled with uniform pressure down her buttocks, cupping them, pulling her up and inward against his tormented body. Along her sides his warm hands moved, compressing the swelling sides of her breasts until all else ceased to matter but that she know more of the treasured warmth of his palms upon them.

In the dense blackness she felt herself swept off the floor. Her arms instinctively encircled Brian's neck. In four steps he reached the bed and set her upon it, then joined her.

"Brian, we should stop..." she whispered against his mouth.

His tongue drove deep once more, then he softly nipped her lips. "We'll stop whenever you say." His kiss made dissent impossible, and then so did his touch. He covered her breasts with both wide palms, pressing down hard and flat and firm, for she lay with her torso precisely aligned with his. He found her hand in the dark, clamped his fingers over the back of it, carried it to his mouth and bit the outer edge, then turned its palm against her own breast. "Feel," he whispered fiercely, rolling aside. The nipple was distended. Even through her bra and summer sweater she could feel it. "Let me touch it too." Again he kissed her hand, then placed it on his ribs. "Let me teach you how good it can feel."

She could see nothing in the infinite darkness, but as she was devoid of sight, her other senses sharpened. His spicy smell, his brandy taste, the slight tremor in his voice were all magnified in their appeal. But above all, her body seemed finely honed to the sense of touch. His breath was like the whisk of a feather upon her face, the dampness his kiss had left felt cool on her lips, the hard contours of his masculinity took on nearly visible form, the seeking conviction of his hands moving toward the clasp of her bra was felt as if from another supremely sensitive dimension.

She whimpered softly, lifting a shoulder. The clasp parted and her breasts were free. But Brian's elbows remained at her sides, bracing him above her. Across her face he took soft, teasing nips with his teeth: chin, cheek, nostril, lip, jaw, even eyebrow—bone and all. The bites grew more evocative, tightening the coil of tension in her stomach. His hands splayed over her bare back. "Theresa...so soft," he murmured, knowing the full length and width of that vulnerably soft skin, then kneading it gently. "So innocent." In one smooth motion his hands skimmed her circumference while his hips pinned hers securely. Sweater and bra were eased up by his hands. Then the objects of her long despair became those of her awakening sexuality as they were enveloped in his palms—skin on skin, warm on warm, man on woman.

It was so good, so right, and made her yearn for the forbidden.

The callused fingers that knew a guitar's strings so intimately now plucked upon her, as one might surround and pluck the fragile seeds of a dandelion from its stalk, the span of his fingertips widening, narrowing, drawing upward, encouraging her nipples to follow and reach when his touch disappeared. And they did. Repeatedly her shoulders strained to follow, as if to say, please don't leave me yet.

His hips lay still upon hers, but his flesh was at its fullest, thick and solid between their bodies. At the moment she scarcely gave it a thought, so taken was she by the sweet swellings of these first caresses on her breasts. He turned his head aside and gently rubbed his hair across the naked nipples. "Ohh..." she sang softly, in delight, entwining her fingers in the hair at the crest of his skull, guiding his head, experiencing the silken texture upon her aroused flesh. A turn of that head, and now it was his cheek where his hair had been. Her hands neither commanded nor discouraged, but rested idly in his hair while she waited...waited....

And then it happened, the first wonder of his mouth upon

her breast, a passing kiss of introduction—vague, soft—on her left nipple first, then upon her right. And she thought, *hello at last, my love.* Gradually, as he nuzzled, his lips parted until their sleek inner skin touched her. She felt the texture of teeth, closed yet, making her yearn for them to open, allowing entry. So still she lay, as still as a butterfly poised on a windless day— feeling, feeling, feeling. His silken tongue came to introduce her flesh into his mouth and lead her within where all was wet, warm and slippery soft.

"Ohhh...Bri...." His name drifted into silence, lost to the grander passion now building.

"Mmm..." he murmured, a sound of praise, while the warm breath from his nostrils dampened the swell of skin beyond reach of his mouth. "Mmm...." He was tugging now, sucking more powerfully until she twisted slightly in satisfaction. To each of her breasts he brought adulation, until it felt the threads of femininity seemed drawn from deeper within her...up, up, and into the man whose mouth taught her pleasure.

Combing his hair with limp fingers she charted the movements of his head. "Oh, Brian, it's so good..." she murmured. "All these years I've wasted...."

He lunged up, dragging his hips along her thighs, joining swollen lips to hers. "We'll make up for them," he promised into her open mouth. "Shh...just feel...feel...."

When his mouth took her breast again, it was with acute knowledge of her need, and just how far he could go to send her senses soaring without hurting her. He caressed with his palms while capturing a taut nipple between the sharp edges of his teeth, scissoring until a keen, welcome sting made her gasp. Then there came a point beyond which the arousal of her breasts alone would no longer suffice. It was painful in its yearning. It made her lift to him, made him press to her. He found her mouth in the dark; it had fallen slack in the throes of desire. His was hotter now, and as they kissed he undulated above her until her knees parted of their own accord, creating a lee into which his body arched, rocking against her.

No more difficult words had she ever spoken. "Brian, please...I can't do this."

"I know...I know," came his rough whisper, but his mouth covered hers as he continued the sinuous rhythm along her body, bringing desire knocking upon her heart's door, seeking entry, just as his body sought entry to hers.

"Brian, please don't...or soon I won't be able to stop you." Her hands clenched in his hair, pulling his head back. "But I must, don't you see?"

He stilled. Stiffened.

"Don't move," he ordered gruffly. "Not a muscle." They lay with their breathing falling hard against each other until with a soft curse he rolled from the bed and in the black void she heard him make his way into the bathroom. A line of light spilled, casting his shadow against the wall as he grasped the edge of the sink and leaned against it, his head hanging down.

She lay utterly still. Her pulse throbbed throughout her body. She closed her eyes until Brian returned and sank down on the foot of the bed, leaning his elbows on his knees while running both hands through his hair. Then, with a groan he fell backward, hands flopped palms up.

She laid a hand in his, and at her touch his fingers clasped hers tightly. He rolled toward her, pressing his face against her hip. When he spoke his words were muffled against her.

"I'm sorry."

"And I'm sorry if I led you on and made you expect more."

"You didn't lead me on. You told me from the start that you weren't coming here with sex on your mind. It was me who pushed the issue after promising not to. I thought I had enough control to settle for kisses." He gave a soft, rueful laugh and flung an arm over his eyes.

But she *had* come into his room with sex on her mind, with at least as much as she'd experienced. She had wanted those precious moments because if she decided to have the surgery she might forfeit them forever. She felt a pang of guilt, for it seemed she'd used Brian for her own ends, and now he lay beside her apologizing for his very natural desire. She considered explaining to him, telling him about the surgery. But now that she'd known the rapture to be found beneath his lips, she was doubly unsure about proceeding with it. And furthermore, it was difficult for her to believe that when June came and he was freed to the civilian world, there would not be countless other women he'd find more attractive than herself. June was a key word often mentioned in their letters, but Theresa realized how easy it was for a lonely man to make plans for the future, but when that future came, how easily those plans could be changed. The thought hurt, but it was best to be honest with herself.

There were no promises made between them. And until there were, she must avoid situations such as this.

"Brian, it's late. I should go back to my room."

He rolled onto his back again, but his fingers remained laced with hers. "You could stay if you want to, and all we'll do is sleep side by side."

"No, I don't think I have that much willpower." When she sat up to straighten her clothing she felt him watching and wished the bathroom light was off, dim though it was. Her hair was tousled, her hands shaky.

"Theresa...." He reached for her with the plaintive word.

Softly she begged, "Let me go now without persuasion... please. I'm only one step away from changing my mind, but if I did I think we'd both be unhappy with ourselves."

His hand fell. He eased off the bed, helped her up and they walked silently to the door. It yawned open, and they stood studying the carpet.

He looped an elbow around her neck and drew her temple to his lips. "I'm not disappointed in you." The words rattled quietly in his throat.

Relief flooded Theresa and left her weak. She sagged against him. "You're so honest, Brian. I love that in you."

His eyes met hers, earnest yet troubled, and still with a flicker of desire in their depths. "Tomorrow will be hard enough, saying goodbye after being together like this. It would only have been harder if we'd given in."

She raised up on tiptoe, brushed his lips with hers, then touched them fleetingly with her fingertips.

"I had begun to think I'd never find you in this big old world, Brian Scanlon...." But she could say no more without crying, so slipped into the loneliness of her own room and closed the door between them.

Chapter Twelve

Their last day together was bittersweet. They wasted precious hours silently pondering the lonesomeness they'd feel at parting. They suffered recriminations about the night before. They counted the weeks of separation ahead. Laughter was rare, and forced, and followed by long gazing silences that left them more unfulfilled than ever.

They checked out at eleven and drove aimlessly until 1:00 p.m. Brian was flying standby on his return flight, so she took him to the airport where they sat in the coffee shop at a table by the window, unable to be cheered or consoled.

"You have a long drive ahead of you. I think you should go."

She lifted startled eyes to his. "No. I'll wait with you."

"But I may not catch a plane until late afternoon."

"But...I...." Her lips started quivering, so she clamped them together tightly.

"I know," he said softly. "But will it be any easier if you stay to watch my plane take off?"

Dismally she shook her head and stared at her coffee cup through distorting tears. His hand covered the back of hers, squeezing it hurting-hard, his thumb stroking hers upon the handle of the cup. "I want you to go," he claimed, yet the unsteady words laced his request with depression. "And I want you to do it smiling." The tears swelled fuller. He tilted her chin up with a finger. "Promise?"

She nodded, and the motion jarred the tears loose and sent them spilling down her freckled cheeks. Frantically she wiped them away and pasted on the smile he'd requested. "You're right. It's a five-hour drive...." She reached for her purse, babbling inanities, making her hands look busy with important stuff, foolish words pouring from her lips while Brian sat across the table smiling sadly. She fell silent in midsentence, folded her lower lip between her teeth and swallowed an enormous lump in her throat.

"Walk me to the car?" she asked so low he could hardly hear.

Without a word he dropped some change on the table and rose. She moved a step ahead of him, but felt his hand at her elbow then sliding down to capture her fingers and hold them tighter. Then tighter.

At the car they stopped. Both of them stared at the metal strip around the driver's door. A truck pulled up beside them, someone got out and walked toward the terminal. Brian lifted Theresa's hand and studied its palm while scratching at it repeatedly with his thumbnail.

"Thank you for coming, Treece."

She felt as if she were suffocating. "I had a g...good...." But she couldn't finish, and when the sob broke, he jerked her roughly into his arms. A hand clamped the back of her head. Her fingers clenched the back of his shirt. His scent was thick and nostalgic where her nose was pushed flat against his chest.

"Drive safely." His voice rumbled a full octave lower than usual.

"Say h...hi to J...Jeff."

"June will be here before we know it." But she was afraid to think of June. What if he didn't come back to her after all? He was holding her so close all she could make out through her tears was the soft gray of his shirt. "Now I'm going to kiss you, then you get in that car and drive, do you understand?"

She nodded, her cheek rubbing a wide damp spot on the gray cloth.

"Don't think of today. Think of June."

"I...w...will."

He jerked her up. Their mouths joined for a salty goodbye. His hand clamped the back of her neck as he pressed his warm lips to her wet cheeks, as if to keep something of her—something—within his body.

He put her away from him with a sturdy push, opened the car door, then waited until the engine fired. Resolutely she put the car into reverse, backed from her parking spot, then hung her arm out the window as she pulled forward. Their fingertips brushed as she drove away, and a moment later a turn of the wheel whisked his reflection from her rearview mirror.

Theresa had expected her mother to be inquisitive, but oddly, Margaret only asked the most impersonal questions. How is Brian? Did he mention Jeff? Was there a lot of traffic? Both Margaret and Willard seemed to sympathize with their twenty-five-year-old daughter who mooned around the house as if she were fifteen. Even Amy, sensing Theresa's despondency, steered clear.

On her calendar, Theresa numbered the days backward from June 24 and grew more and more irritable as she remained indecisive about the surgery.

May arrived, and with it hot weather and uncontrollable children at school. The kids were so antsy they could hardly be contained in the stuffy schoolroom.

Spring was concert season, and Theresa busily prepared for the last two weeks of school, when teas were held for the mothers of the younger children and a combined evening performance of the choir, band and orchestra was scheduled. After-school meetings were necessary to coordinate the programs with the directors of the other two groups. It was a hectic time of year, but at the same time sad. She was sorry to have to say goodbye to some sixth graders as they moved into junior high and a new building and three of these managed to find out about Theresa's twenty-sixth birthday, presenting her with a birthday cake in class that day. The tenseness of the past days fled as she felt her heart brimming with special feelings for the three.

And the glow still lingered when she arrived home to find flowers and a note from Brian: ''With love, until June 24th, when I can tell you in person.'' The flowers created a stir within the family. Amy was awed and perhaps a trifle envious. Margaret insisted the flowers be left in the center of the supper table, though it was impossible to see around the enormous long-stemmed red roses. Willard smiled more than usual, and patted Theresa's shoulder every time their paths crossed. ''What's all this about June?'' he asked. She gave him a kiss on the jaw, but had no reply, for she wasn't sure herself what June would bring. Especially if she decided to have the surgery.

At nine-thirty that night the phone rang. Amy answered it, as usual. ''It's for you, Theresa!'' Amy's eyes were bright with excitement. She anxiously shoved the receiver into Theresa's hand and mouthed, ''It's him!''

Theresa's heart pattered. Only inadequate letters had passed between them since Fargo. This was the first phone call. Amy stood close, watching with keen interest while Theresa placed the phone to her ear and answered breathlessly, ''Hello?''

''Hello, sweets. Happy birthday.''

Theresa placed a hand over her heart and said not a word. It felt as if she'd been supping on sweet, sweet rose petals, and they'd all stuck in her throat.

''Are you there, Theresa?''

''Yes...yes! Oh, Brian, the flowers are just beautiful. Thank you.'' It was him! It was really him!

''God, it's good to hear your voice.''

Amy was still three feet away. ''Just a minute, Brian.'' Theresa shifted her weight to one hip, lowered the receiver and shot a piercing look of strained patience. Amy made a disgruntled face, shrugged, slipped her hands into her jeans pockets and grumbled all the way to her bedroom.

"Brian, I'm back. Had to get rid of a nuisance."

His laugh lilted across the wire, and she pictured him with chin raised, green eyes dancing in delight. "The kid, huh?"

"Exactly."

"I'm picturing you in the kitchen, standing beside the cupboard, and Amy beside you, all ears. I've been living on memories just like those ever since I left you."

Love talk was foreign to Theresa. She reacted with a blush that seemed to heat her belly and burn its way up to her breasts and neck to her temples. Her heart raced, and her palms grew damp.

"Oh, Brian..." she said softly, and closed her eyes, picturing his face again.

"I've missed you," he said quietly.

"I've missed you, too."

"I wish I could be there. I'd take you to dinner and then out dancing."

The memory of being wrapped in his arms, with her breasts crushed against his corduroy jacket came back in vivid detail and made her body ache with renewed longing to see him again.

"Brian, nobody's ever sent me flowers before."

"That just goes to show the world is filled with fools."

She smiled, closed her eyes and leaned her forehead against the cool kitchen wall. "And nobody's ever plied me with flattery before either. Don't stop now."

"Your teeth are like stars...." He paused expectantly, and her smile grew broader.

"Yes, I know—they come out every night." She could hear his humor blossoming as he went on to the next line of the time-weary joke.

"And your eyes are like limpid pools."

"Yes, I know—cesspools."

"And your hair is like moonbeams."

"Oh-oh! I never heard that one." But by this time they were both laughing. Then his voice became serious once more.

"What were you doing when I called?"

She watched her fingertips absently smoothing the kitchen wall. "I was in my bedroom, writing a thank-you letter to you for the roses."

"Were you really?"

"Yes, really."

It was quiet for a long time. His voice was gruff and slightly pained when he spoke again. "God, I miss you. I wish I was there."

"I wish you were, too, but it won't be long now."

"It seems like six years instead of six weeks."

"I know, but school will be out by then, and we'll be able to spend lots of time together...if you want."

"If I want?" After a meaningful pause, he added, sexily, "Silly girl."

She thought her heart might very well erupt, for it seemed to fill her ears and head with a wild, sweet thrumming. To her amazement, his next words made it beat even harder.

"I wish you could feel what's happening to my heart right now."

"I think I know. The same thing is going on in mine."

"Put your hand on it."

Only a faraway musical bleep sounded across the telephone line as Theresa digested his order.

"Is it there?" he asked.

"N...no."

"Put it there, for me."

Timidly, slowly, she placed her hand upon her throbbing heart.

"Is it there now?"

"Yes," she whispered.

"Tell me what you feel."

"I feel like...like I've been running as hard as I can—it's

like there's a piston driving in there. My hand seems to be lifting and falling with the force of it.''

After a long moment of silence he said rather shakily, ''That's where I want to be, in your heart.''

''Oh, Brian, you are,'' she replied breathily.

''Theresa?'' She waited, breathlessly. ''Now slide your hand down.''

Her lips dropped open. Her skin prickled.

''Slide it down,'' he repeated, more softly. The tremor was gone from his voice now. It was controlled and very certain. Her hand dropped to her breast. ''And that's where I want to kiss you...again. And do everything that follows. I'm sorry now that we didn't do it in Fargo. But when I get back, we will. I'm giving you fair warning, Theresa.''

The line went positively silent. Theresa's eyes were closed, her breathing labored. Turning, she pressed her shoulder blades and the back of her head to the wall. His face came clearly to mind. She moved her hand back to her breast and riffled her fingers softly up and down. The tiny movements sent shudders of sensation down the backs of her thighs. The thought of the surgery sizzled through her mind, and she opened her mouth to ask him what he would think if he came back and found her with beautifully average breasts, but ones that might not be able to show response.

''Theresa,'' he almost whispered, again sounding pained. ''I have to go. You finish your letter to me, and tell me all the things you're feeling right now, okay, sweets? And I'll see you in six weeks. Till then, here's a kiss. Put it wherever you want it.'' A pause followed, then his emotional, ''Goodbye, Treece.''

''Brian, wait!'' She clutched the phone almost frantically.

''I'm still here.''

''Brian, I....'' Her throat worked, but not another sound came out.

''I know, Theresa. I feel the same.''

She would have known he'd hang up without warning. He was a man who never said goodbye.

"I'm giving you fair warning, Theresa."

His words stayed with her during the following days while she continued weighing the possibility of undergoing breast surgery. She had a second talk with Dr. Schaum. He told her the time would be perfect, just when school ended for summer vacation, a time of low stress and less social contact—both desirable. She had learned that her insurance *would* cover the cost of the surgery because of the prognosis for late-life back troubles. She'd received a brochure from Dr. Schaum explaining the surgical procedure, what to expect beforehand and afterward. The discomforts could be expected to be minimal, but they were the least of Theresa's concerns. Neither was she especially bothered by the idea of giving up nursing—babies seemed so far in the future. But the possibility of losing an erogenous zone made her reluctant, and at times depressed, especially when remembering Brian's lips upon her, and the wonder of her own feminine response.

She grew short-tempered with her family and also with her students as the weather warmed. The children's temperaments grew feisty, too. Fights broke out on the playground, and tears were often in need of swabbing. While she performed the duty, Theresa often wished she had someone to swab her own tears, shed in secret at night, as the decision time came closer and closer. If she was going to have the surgery, the choice must be made and made soon. In two weeks summer vacation would start, and three weeks after that, Brian would come home.

She thought of greeting him in a cool, cotton T-shirt—green, maybe—with a new trim profile of her choosing. How amazing to think she could actually choose the contour of breast she preferred! The surgeons didn't even make both breasts the same size anymore, but made the right larger than the left if the woman was right-handed, and vice versa, just as nature would have done. When nipples were replaced, they were lifted to a new, perky, uptilted angle that would remain attractive for the rest of her life.

The idea beguiled.

The idea horrified.

I want to do it.

I can't do it. What would Brian say?

It's your body, not his.

But I want to share it with him. To the fullest.

You still can, even if the sensation doesn't come back.

I should at least discuss it with him.

On the basis of one weekend in Fargo that ended unfulfilled, a bouquet of roses and a seductive phone call?

But he said he wanted me to be exactly the same when he came back!

Supposing you're even better?

Dear God, they'd cut my nipples off.

Not totally.

I'll have scars.

That will disappear almost completely.

But I loved being kissed there—suppose I lose the feeling?

Chances are you won't.

I'm scared.

You're a woman the choice is yours.

A week before vacation she made her decision. When she told her parents, Margaret's face registered immediate shock and disapproval, her father's a gray disappointment that the body he'd bequeathed his daughter had turned out to be less than suitable.

As Theresa had expected, Margaret was the outspoken one. "I don't understand why you'd want to...to fool around with the body you've been given, as if it isn't good enough."

"Because it can be better, mother."

"But it's so *unnecessary* and such an expense!"

"Unnecessary!" These were all the arguments she'd been expecting, yet Theresa was deeply disappointed in her mother's lack of understanding. "You think it's unnecessary?"

Margaret colored and pursed her lips slightly. "I should know. I've lived with a shape like yours all my life, and I've gotten along just fine."

Theresa wondered about all the hidden slights her mother had suffered and never disclosed. She knew for a fact there were backaches and shoulder aches. Very quietly the young woman asked, "Have you, mother?"

Margaret discovered something important needing attention behind her and presented her back. "What a ridiculous question. Movie stars and playgirls tamper with their shapes, not nice girls like you." She swung around again. "What will people say?"

Theresa felt wounded that her mother, with typical lack of tact, could choose such a time to voice the fear uppermost in her mind—which was how it would affect herself. She cared so much about the opinion of outsiders that she let its importance overshadow the reason her daughter had come to this decision. With a sigh, Theresa sank to a chair. "Please, mom, dad, I want to explain...." She did. She went back to age fourteen and described all her disenchantment with her elephantine growth, and explained all that Dr. Schaum had predicted for her future. She omitted the details about her sexual hang-ups, but explained why she'd worn the sweaters, hidden beneath the violin, chosen to work with children and disliked meeting strange men.

When she finished, Margaret's eyes moved to Willard's. She mulled silently for a minute, sighed and shrugged. "I don't know," she said to the tabletop. "I don't know."

But Theresa knew. She had gained confidence by confronting her parents about the trip to Fargo, and she was very certain the surgery was the right thing for her. She sensed her mother softening and realized her own self-assurance was changing Margaret's opinion.

"There's just one more thing," Theresa went on. She met Margaret's questioning eyes directly. "Could you get the day off that Monday of the surgery and be there at the hospital, mother?"

Perhaps it was the realization that the young woman who was slowly but surely snipping the apron strings still needed Margaret's maternal understanding. Perhaps it was because there'd been times in Margaret's life when she'd wished for the courage her daughter now displayed. She squelched her misgivings, forced the squeamishness from her thoughts and answered, "If you're bound to go through with it, yes, I'll be there."

But when she was alone, Margaret leaned weakly against the bathroom door, compressing her own bulbous breasts with her palms, overcome by pangs of empathetic transference. She opened her eyes and dropped her hands, breathing deeply, admitting what courage it took for her daughter to make the decision she had.

On Memorial Day, Theresa washed her hair by herself for the last time for at least two weeks; she wouldn't be able to lift her arms for a while after the surgery. She packed a suitcase with one very generously sized nightgown, and three brand-new pairs of pajamas, size medium. She harnessed herself into her size 34DD utilitarian white bra, but packed several of size 34C—not blue, not pink, not even lacy; those would have to wait. She'd be wearing the smaller, sturdy white bra day and night for a month. She dressed in a size extralarge spring top, but packed a brand-new one, again size medium, that looked to Theresa as if it had been made for a doll instead of a woman.

The following morning, Margaret was there when they rolled Theresa into surgery on the gurney. She kissed her daughter's cheek, held her hand in both of her own, and said, "See you in a little while."

Three and a half hours later, Theresa was taken to the recovery room, and an hour after that she opened her eyes and lifted a bleary smile to Margaret, who leaned close and brushed the thick, coppery hair back from Theresa's forehead.

"Mom...." The word was an airy whisper. Theresa's eyelids fluttered open twice, but her eyes remained unfocused.

"Baby, everything went just fine. Rest now. I'll be here."

But a limp, freckled hand lifted and dreamily explored the sheets across her breast. "Mom, am...I...beautiful?" came the sleepy question.

Gently restraining Theresa's hand, Margaret felt tears sting her eyes. "Yes, baby, you're beautiful. But you've always been. Shh...." A drugged smile lifted the corner of Theresa's soft lips.

"Brian...doesn't...know...yet...." The lethargic voice hushed into silence, and Theresa drifted away into the webbed world of sleep.

Later Theresa was lucid and alone in her hospital room for the first time. She'd been warned to limit all arm movement, but could not resist gingerly exploring the mysteries sheathed beneath the white sheets and contained within the new, stiff, confining bra. She stared at the ceiling while moving her hands hesitantly upward. As they came into contact with the greatly reduced mounds of flesh, Theresa's eyelids drifted closed. She explored as a sightless person reads braille. She knew the exact pattern of the incisions and found them covered with dressing inside the bra, thus she imagined more than felt their outline. The stitches ran beneath the curves of both breasts, contouring them like the arcs of an underwire bra. That incision was bisected on each breast by another leading straight upward to encircle the nipple.

She felt no pain, for she was still under the influence of the anaesthetic. Instead, she knew only a soaring jubilation. There was so little there! She lightly grazed the upper hemispheres of both breasts, to find them unbelievably reduced in breadth. And from what she could tell, blind this way, it seemed her nipples were going to be as tip-tilted as the end of a water ski. She felt a surge of overwhelming impatience to see the revised, improved shape she'd been given.

I want to see. I want to see.

But beneath her armpits tiny tubes were inserted to drain the pleural cavity and prevent internal bleeding and pneumonia. For now, Theresa had to be content with imagination.

Amy came to that night, filled with smiles and flip teenage acceptance of the momentous move Theresa had made. She produced a letter bearing familiar handwriting, but teased her sister by holding it beyond reach. "Mmm...just a piece of junk mail, I think."

"Gimme!"

"Gimme?" Amy looked disgusted. "Is that the kind of manners you teach your students? *Gimme?*"

"Hand it over, snot. I'm incapacitated and can't indulge in mortal combat until these tubes are removed and the stitches dissolve."

Truthfully, as the day wore on, Theresa's discomfort had been growing, but the letter from Brian made her forget them temporarily.

Dear Theresa,
Less than four weeks and we're out. And guess how we'll be coming home? I bought a van! A class act, for sure. It's a Chevy, kind of the color of your eyes, not brown and not hazel, with smoked windows, white pinstriping and enough room to carry all the guitars, amps and speakers for an entire band. You're gonna love it! I'll take you

out for a spin the minute I get there, and maybe you can help me look for an apartment, huh? God, sweets, I can't wait. For any of it—civilian life, school, the new band, and you. Most of all *you.* (Theresa smiled at the three slashes underlining the last word.) Jeff and I leave here on the morning of the 24th. Should be pulling in there by suppertime. Jeff says to tell your mother he wants pigs in the blanket for supper, whatever that is. And me? I want Theresa-in-the-blankets after supper. Just teasing, dar-lin'...or am I?

Love,
Brian

Theresa refolded the letter, but instead of putting it on her bedside table, tucked it beneath the covers by her hip. She looked up to find Amy sprawled, unladylike, in the visitor's chair.

"Brian bought a van. He and Jeff are going to be driving it home."

"A van!" Amy's eyes lit up like flashing strobes, and she sat up straighter in the chair. "All ri-i-ight."

"And Jeff says to tell mom he wants pigs-in-the-blanket for supper when they get here."

"Boy, I can't wait!"

"*You* can't wait? Every day seems like an eternity to me."

"Yeah." Amy glanced at the sheet beneath which the letter was concealed. "You and Brian, well...looks like you two got a thing goin', I mean, since you went up and met him and everything, you two must really be gettin' it on."

"Not exactly. But..." Theresa mused with a winsome smile. Beneath the covers she touched the envelope hopefully.

"But you've been writing to each other for five months, and he sent you the roses and called and everything. I guess things are startin' to torque between you two, huh?"

Theresa laughed unexpectedly. It hurt terribly, and she

pressed a hand to her rib cage. "Oh, don't do that, Amy. It hurts like heck."

"Oh, gol...sorry. Didn't mean to blow your seams."

Theresa laughed again, but this time when she pressed the sheets against herself, she caught Amy's eyes assessing her new shape inquisitively.

"Have you...well, I mean...have you seen yourself yet?" Amy's eyes were wide, her voice hesitant.

"No, but I've felt."

"Well...how...." Amy shrugged, grinned sheepishly. "Oh, you know what I mean."

"They feel like I'm wearing somebody else's body. Somebody who's shaped like I always wished I could be shaped."

"They look a lot smaller, even under the blankets."

Theresa turned the top of the sheet down to her waist. "They are. I'll show you when we're both back home."

Amy jumped up suddenly, pushed her palms into her rear jeans pockets, flat against her backside. She looked ill at ease, but after taking a turn around the bed, stopped beside her older sister and asked directly, "Have you told him?"

"Brian?"

Amy nodded.

"No, I haven't."

"Gol, I probably shouldn't have asked." Amy colored to a becoming shade of pink.

"It's okay, Amy. Brian and I...really like each other, but I didn't feel our relationship had gone far enough for me to consult him about having the surgery. And I'm scared of facing him again because he doesn't know."

"Yeah...." Amy's voice trailed away uncertainly. She grew morose, then speculative and glanced at Theresa askance. "You could still tell him. I mean before he comes home."

"I know. I've been considering it, but I'm kind of dreading it. I...oh, I don't know what to do."

Amy suddenly brightened, putting on a jack-in-the-box smile

and bubbling, "Well, one thing's for sure. As soon as we spring you from this joint, you and I are going shopping for all those sexy, cute, *tiny* size nines you've been dying to shimmy into, okay?"

"Okay. You've got a date. Soon as I can put my arms up over my head to get into them."

The following day on his rounds, Dr. Schaum breezed around the corner into Theresa's room, the tails of his lab coat flaring out behind his knees. "So how is our miniaturized Theresa today? Have you seen yourself in a mirror yet?"

"No...." Theresa was taken by surprise at his abrupt, swooping entry and his first question.

"No! Well, why not? You haven't gone through all this to lie there wondering what the new Theresa Brubaker looks like. Come on, young lady, we'll change that right now."

And so Theresa saw her reshaped breasts for the first time, with Dr. Schaum holding a wide mirror against his belly, studying her over the top of it, awaiting her verdict.

The stitches were still red and raw looking, but the shape was delightful, the perky angle of the upturned nipples an utter surprise. Somehow, she was not prepared for the reality of it. She was...*normal.* And in time, when the stitches healed and the scars faded, there would undoubtedly be times when she'd wonder if she'd ever been shaped any differently.

But for now, a wide-eyed Theresa stared at herself in the mirror and beamed, speechless.

Dr. Schaum tipped his head to one side. "Do I take that charming smile to mean you approve?"

"Oh..." was all Theresa breathed while continuing to stare and beam at her reflection. But when she reached to touch, Dr. Schaum warned, "Uh-uh! Don't investigate just yet. Leave that until the tubes and sutures are removed." Only the internal stitches were the dissolving type. The external ones would be removed by Dr. Schaum within a few days.

Theresa returned home on the fourth day, the drainage tubes gone from beneath her arms, but the sutures still in place. Amy washed her sister's hair and waited on her hand and foot with a solicitude that warmed Theresa's heart. Forbidden to even reach above her to get a coffee cup from the kitchen shelf, Theresa found herself often in need of Amy's helping hand, and during the next few days the bond between the sisters grew.

They were given the go-ahead for the long-awaited shopping spree at the end of the second week, when Theresa saw Dr. Schaum for a postop checkup.

That golden day in mid-June was like a fairy tale come true for the woman who surveyed the realm of ladies' fashions with eyes as excited as those of a child who spies the lights of a carnival on the horizon. "T-shirts! T-shirts! T-shirts!" Theresa sang exuberantly. "I feel like I want to wear them for at least one solid year!"

Amy giggled and hauled Theresa to a Shirt Shack and picked out a hot pink item that boasted the words, "Knockers Up!" across the chest. They laughed exuberantly and hung the ugly garment back with its mates and went off to get serious.

Standing before the full-length mirror in the first item she tried on—a darling sleeveless V-neck knit shirt of fresh summer green, held up by ties on each shoulder—Theresa wondered if she'd ever been this happy. The sporty top was nothing extraordinary, not expensive, not even sexy really, only feminine, tiny, attractive—and utterly flattering. It was the kind of garment she'd never been able to even consider before. Theresa couldn't resist preening just a little. "Oh, Amy, look!"

Amy did, standing back, smiling at her sister's happy expression in the mirror. Suddenly Amy's shoulders straightened as she made a remarkable discovery. "Hey, Theresa, you look taller!"

"I do?" Theresa turned to the left, appraised herself. "You know, that was something Diane DeFreize told me people would say afterward. And you're the second one who has."

Theresa realized it was partly because her posture was straighter since her self-image had improved so heartily. Also, the absence of bulk up front carried the eyes upward rather than horizontally, creating the illusion of added height. She stood square to the mirror again, gave her reflection a self-satisfied look of approval and seconded, "Yes, I do."

"Wait'll Brian sees you in that."

Theresa's eyes widened and glittered at the thought. She ran a hand over her bustline, wondering what he'd say. She still hadn't told him.

"Do you think he'll like it?"

"You're a knockout in green."

"You can't see my strap marks, can you?" The wide, ugly indentations in Theresa's shoulders hadn't been erased yet, but Dr. Schaum said they would disappear in time. The shoulder ties of the top were fairly narrow, but wide enough to conceal the depressions in her skin.

"No, the ties cover them up. I think you should make it your first purchase. *And* be wearing it when Brian gets here."

The thought was so dizzying, Theresa pressed a hand to her tummy. *When Brian gets here. Only one more week.*

"I'll take it. And next I want to look for a dress—no, eight dresses! The last time I bought one that didn't need alteration was when I was younger than you are now. Dr. Schaum says I should be a perfect size nine."

And she was. A swirly-skirted summer sundress of pink was followed by another of navy, red-and-white flowers, then by a classic off-white sheath with jewelry neckline and belt of burnished brown leather. They bought tube tops and V-neck T-shirts (no crew necks for Theresa Brubaker this trip!) and even one blouse that tied just beneath the bustline and left her midriff bare. Jewelry, something Theresa had never wanted to hang around her neck before for fear it would draw attention to her breast size, was as exciting to buy as her first pair of panty hose had been, years ago. She chose a delicate gold chain with a tiny puffed heart, and it looked delectable, even against the red freckles on her chest. But somehow even those freckles seemed less brash to Theresa. Her choice of garment colors was no longer limited by available size, thus she could select hues that minimized her redness.

When the day ended, Theresa sat in her room among mountains of crackling sacks and marvelous clothes. She felt like a bride with a new trousseau. Holding up her favorite—the green shoulder-tie top—she fitted it against her front, danced a swirling pattern across the floor, then closed her eyes and breathed deeply.

Hurry, Brian, hurry. I'm ready for you at last.

Chapter Thirteen

It was a stunning June day, with the temperature in the low eighties and Minnesota's faultless sky the perfect, clear blue of the delphiniums that bloomed in gardens along Johnnycake Lane. Across the street, a group of teenagers were waxing a four-year-old Trans Am. Next door, Ruth Reed was standing beside her garden, checking to see if there were blossoms on her green beans yet. Two houses down, the neighborhood four- and five-year-olds were churning their chubby legs on the pedals of low-slung plastic motorcycles, making engine noises with their lips. Up and down the street the smell of cooking suppers drifted out to mingle with that of fresh-cut grass as men just home from work tried to get a start on the mowing before mealtime. In the Brubakers' front yard, an oscillating sprinkler swayed and sprayed, twinkling in the sun like the sequined ostrich fan of a Busby Berkeley girl.

It was a scene of everyday Americana, a slice of ordinary life, on an ordinary street, at the end of an ordinary workday.

But in the Brubaker house, excitement pulsated. Cabbage rolls stuffed with hamburger-rice filling were cooking in a roaster. The bathroom fixtures gleamed and fresh towels hung on the racks. In the freshly cleaned room a bouquet of garden flowers sat on the piano—marigolds, cosmos, zinnias and snap-dragons. The kitchen table was set for six, and centered upon it waited a slightly lopsided two-layer cake, rather ineptly decorated with some quite flat-looking pink frosting sweetpeas and the words, "Welcome home, Jeff and Brian." Amy adjusted the cake plate one more time and turned it just a little in an effort to make it appear more balanced than it was, then stood back, shrugged and muttered, "Oh, horse poop. It's good enough."

"Amy, watch your mouth!" warned Margaret, then added, "There's not a thing wrong with that cake, so I want you to stop fussing about it."

Outside, Willard had a hedge trimmer in his hands as he moved along the precision-trimmed alpine current hedge, taking a nip here, a nip there, though not a leaf was out of place. Periodically, he shaded his eyes and scanned the street to the west, gazing into the spray of diamond droplets that lifted and fell, lifted and fell across the emerald carpet of lawn—his pride and joy. The kitchen windows were cranked open above his head, and he checked his wrist, then called inside, "What time is it, Margaret? I think my watch stopped."

"It's five forty-five, and there's not a thing wrong with your watch, Willard. It was working seven minutes ago when you asked."

In her bedroom at the end of the hall, Theresa put the final touches on the makeup that by now she was adept at applying. She buckled a pair of flat, strappy white sandals onto her feet, inspecting the coral polish on her toenails—they'd never been painted before this summer. Next, she slipped into a brand-new pair of sleek white jeans, snapped and zipped them up, ran a smoothing palm down her thighs, and watched herself in the mirror as she worked the kelly green top over her head, covering her white bra. She adjusted the knot upon her left shoulder, stood back and assessed her reflection. *You don't look like a Christmas tree, Theresa, but you look like*—she searched her mind for a simile Brian had used—*like a poppy blossom.* She smiled in satisfaction and flicked the lifter through her freshly cut and styled hair, fluffing it around her temples and forehead until it suited perfectly. Around her neck she fastened the new chain with the tiny puffed heart. At her wrist went a simple gold bangle bracelet. She inserted tiny gold studs in her ears and was reaching for the perfume when she heard her father's voice calling through the screened windows at the other end of the house.

"I think it's them. It's a van, but I can't tell what color it is."

Theresa pressed a hand to her heart. The hand wasn't yet used to feeling the diminished contour it encountered in making this gesture. Her wide eyes raked down her torso in the mirror, then back up. *What will he think?*

"Yup, it's them!" she heard in her father's voice, before Amy bellowed, "Theresa, come on, they're here!"

A nerve jittered in her stomach, and the buildup of anticipation that had been expanding as each day passed, thickened the thud of her heart and made her knees quake. She turned and ran through the house and slammed out the back door, then waited behind the others as the cinnamon-colored Chevy van purred up the street, with Jeff's arm and head dangling out the window as he waved and hollered hello. But Theresa's eyes were drawn to the opposite side of the van as she tried to make out the face of the driver. But the windshield caught and reflected the bowl of blue sky, and she saw only it and the branches of the elm trees flashing across the glass as the vehicle turned and eased up the drive, then stopped.

Jeff's door flew open, and he scooped up the first body he encountered—Amy—lifting her off her feet and swirling her around before doing likewise with Margaret, who whooped and demanded to be set on her feet, but meant not a word of it. Willard got a rough hug, and Theresa was next. She found herself swept up from the ground before she could issue the warning to her brother not to suspend her. But the slight twinge of discomfort where her stitches had been was worth it.

Yet while all this happened, Theresa was primarily conscious of Brian slipping from the driver's seat, removing a pair of sunglasses, stretching with his elbows in the air and rounding the front of the van to watch the greetings, then be included in them himself. Theresa hung back, observing the faded blue jeans slung low on his lean hips, buckling at the knees from a long day of driving; the loose, off-white gauze shirt with three buttons open; the naked V of skin at his throat; his dark, military-cut hair and eyes the color of summer grasses that smiled while Amy gave him a smack on the cheek, Margaret a motherly hug and Willard a handshake and affectionate pat on the shoulder.

Then there was nobody left but Theresa.

Her heart pounded in her chest, and she felt as if her feet were not on the blacktop driveway but levitated an inch above it. The sensuous shock of recognition sent the color sweeping to her face, but she didn't care. He was here. He was as good to look at as she remembered. And his presence made her feel impatient, and nervous, and exhilarated.

They faced each other with six feet of space between them.

"Hello," he greeted simply, and it might have been a verse from the great love poets of decades ago.

"Hello." Her voice was soft and uncertain and quavery.

They were the only two who hadn't hugged or touched. Her tremulous lips were softly opened. The corners of his mouth lifted in a slow crescent of a smile. He reached his hands out to her, calluses up, and as she extended her fingertips and rested them upon his palms, she watched the summer-green eyes that last December had so assiduously avoided dropping to her breasts. Those eyes dropped now, directly, unerringly, down to the freckled throat and the V-neck of her new knit shirt, and then lower, to the two gentle rises within. Brian's mouth went slightly lax as he stared in undisguised amazement.

His puzzled gaze darted back up to her eyes, while Theresa felt her face suffuse with brighter color.

"How are you?" she managed, the question sounding foolishly mundane, even in her own ears.

"Fine." He released her fingers and stepped back, replacing

the sunglasses on his nose while she felt him studying her from behind the dark lenses. "And you?"

They were conversing like robots, both extremely self-conscious all of a sudden, both trying in vain to regain calm footing.

"Same as ever." They were scarcely out of Theresa's mouth before she regretted her choice of words. She wasn't the same at all. "How was your trip?"

"Good, but tiring. We drove straight through."

The others had preceded them up the back steps, and Theresa and Brian trailed along. Though he walked just behind her shoulder, she felt his eyes burning into her, questioning, wondering. But she couldn't tell his true reaction yet. Was he pleased? Shocked for sure, and taken aback, but beyond that, Theresa could only guess.

Inside, the Brubaker house was as noisy as ever. Jeff—exultant, roaring, fun loving—stood in the middle of the kitchen with his arms extended wide and gave a jungle call like Tarzan, while from somewhere at the far end of the house The Stray Cats sang rock, and at the near end The Gatlins crooned in three-part harmony. Margaret tended something on the stove, and Jeff surrounded her from behind with both arms, his chin digging into her shoulder, making her wriggle and giggle. "Dammit, ma, but that smells rank! Must be my pigs-in-the-blanket."

"Listen to that boy, calling my cabbage rolls rank." She lifted a lid off a steaming roaster, and Jeff snitched a pinch of something from inside. "Didn't that Air Force teach you any manners?" his mother teased happily. "Wash your hands before you come snitching."

Jeff grinned over his shoulder at Brian. "I thought we were done with C.O.'s when we got our walking papers, but it looks like I was wrong." He patted his mother's bottom. "But this one's all bluff, I think."

Margaret whirled and whacked at his hand with a spoon, but

missed. "Oh, get away with you and your teasing, you brat. You're not too old for me to take the yardstick to." But Jeff had leaped safely out of reach. He spied the cake, and gave an undulating whistle of appreciation, like that of a construction worker eyeing a passing woman in high heels. "Wow, would y' look at this, Brian. Somebody's been busy."

"Amy," put in Willard proudly.

Amy beamed, her braces flashing. "The dumb thing is listing to the starboard," Amy despaired, but Jeff wrapped an arm around her shoulders, squeezed and declared, "Well, it won't list for long cause it won't last for long. I'd say about twenty minutes at the outside." Then a thought seemed to occur to him. "Is it chocolate?"

"What else?"

"Then I'd say less than twenty minutes. Shh! Don't tell ma." He picked up a knife from one of the place settings and whacked into the high side of the cake, took a slice out and lifted it to his mouth before anybody could stop him.

Everyone in the room was laughing as Margaret swooped toward the table with the steaming roaster clutched in a pair of pot holders. "Jeffrey Brubaker," she scolded, "put that cake down this minute or you'll ruin your appetite! And for heaven's sake, everybody sit down before that child forces me to get the yardstick out after all!"

Brian took it all in with a sense of homecoming almost as familial as if he were, indeed, part of the Brubaker clan. And it was easy to see Jeff was their mood-setter, the one who stirred them all and generated both gaiety and teasing. It was so easy being with them. Brian felt like a cog slipping into the notches of a gear. Until he sat across from Theresa and was forced to consider the change in her.

"Take your old place," Willard invited Brian, pulling a chair out while they all shuffled and scraped and settled down for the meal. During the next half hour while they gobbled cabbage rolls and crusty buns and whipped potatoes oozing

with parsley butter, then during the hour following while they
ate cake and leisurely sipped glasses of iced tea and caught up
with news of each other, Brian covertly studied Theresa's
breasts as often as he could.

Once she looked up unexpectedly while passing him the
sugar bowl and caught his gaze on her green shirtfront. Their
eyes met, then abruptly shifted apart.

How? Brian wondered. *And when? And why didn't she tell
me? Did Jeff know? And if so, why didn't he warn me?*

The kitchen was hot, and Margaret suggested they all take
glasses of iced tea and sit on the small concrete patio between
the house and the garage. Immediately they all got to their feet
and did a cursory scraping of plates but left the stacked dishes
on the cupboard, then filed out to the side of the house where
webbed lawn chairs waited.

While they relaxed and visited, Theresa was ever aware of
Brian's perusal. He had slipped his sunglasses on again, even
though the patio was in full shade now as the sun dipped behind the peak of the roof. But occasionally, as he lifted his
sweating glass and drank, she felt his gaze riveted on her chest.
But when she looked up and smiled at him, she could not be
sure, for she saw only the suggestion of dark eyes behind the
tinted aviator lenses, and though his lips returned the smile, she
sensed it did not reach those inscrutable eyes.

"Oh yeah!" Amy suddenly remembered. "Glue Eyes called
and said you should be sure to call her as soon as you got
home."

Jeff pointed an accusatory finger at his playful sibling. "Listen, brat, if you don't can it with that Glue Eyes business, I'll
have ma take the yardstick to *you.*"

"Aw, Jeff, you know I don't mean it. Not anymore. She's
really okay, I guess. I got to like her a lot last Christmas. But
I've called her Glue Eyes for so long it kinda falls outa me,
ya know?"

"Well, someday it's gonna fall out when you're standing right beside her, then what will you do?"

"Apologize and explain and tell her that when I was learning to wear makeup I tried to put it on exactly like she does."

Jeff gave her a mock punch on the chin, then bounded into the house to make the phone call, and returned a few minutes later, announcing, "I'm going to run over and pick up Patricia and bring her back here. Anybody want to ride along with me?"

Theresa was torn, recalling the ardent reunion embraces she and Brian had witnessed last time, yet not wanting to stay behind if Brian said yes. He seemed to be waiting for her to answer, so she had to make a choice.

"I'll help Amy and mother with the dishes while you're gone," she decided.

"I'll drive you, Jeff," Brian offered, stretching to his feet, adjusting his glasses and turning to follow Jeff to the van. Theresa watched him walk away, studying the back of his too-short hair, the places where the gauze shirt stuck to his back in a tic-tac-toe design from the webs of the lawn chair, his hands moving to his hips to give an unconscious tug at the waistband of his jeans. His back pockets had worn white patches where he carried his billfold, and his backside was so streamlined the sight of it created a hollow longing in the pit of Theresa's stomach.

He's upset. I should have told him.

No, you had no obligation to confide in him. It was your choice.

In the van, the two men rode down the street where evening shadows stretched long tendrils across green lawns. Brian drove deliberately slow. He pondered, wondering how to introduce the subject, and finally attacked it head on.

"Okay, Brubaker, why didn't you tell me?"

Jeff gave a crooked smile. "She looks great, huh?"

"Damn right she looks great, but my eyeballs nearly

dropped onto the goddamn driveway when I saw her standing there with her...without her...aw hell, *they're gone.*''

"Yup," Jeff slouched low in the seat and grinned out the windshield. "I always knew there lurked a proud beauty inside my Treat."

"Quit beatin' around the bush, Brubaker. You knew, didn't you?"

"Yeah, I knew."

"Did she write and tell you and ask you not to tell me?"

"No, Amy did. Amy thought I should know, so I could warn you if I thought that was best."

"Well, why the hell didn't you?"

"Because I didn't think it was any of my business. Your relationship with Theresa's got nothing to do with me, beyond the fact that I'm lucky enough to be her brother. If she'd wanted you to know beforehand, she'd have told you herself. I figured, what business was it of mine to go stickin' my two cents worth in?"

"But...." Brian gripped the steering wheel. "But...*how?*"

"Breast-reduction surgery."

Brian's shaded brown lenses flashed toward Jeff. "Breast re—" He sounded flabbergasted. "I never heard of such a thing."

"To tell you the truth, neither had I, but Amy told me all about it in her letter. She had it done three weeks ago, right after school got out for summer vacation. Listen, man—" Jeff turned to watch his friend guide the van onto a broader double-lane avenue "—she's...I don't want to see her get hurt, okay?"

"Hurt?" Brian turned sharply toward Jeff, then back to his driving. "You think I'd hurt her?"

"Well, I don't know. You're kind of...well, you act kind of pissed off or something. I don't know and I'm not asking what went on between you and Theresa, but go easy on her, huh? If you're thinking she should have confided in you for some reason, just understand that she's a pretty timid creature. It'd be pretty damn hard for a girl like Theresa to even have the surgery, much less write and discuss it with a man—I don't care *how* close you'd been.''

"All right, I'll remember that. And I'll cool it around her. I guess I backed off pretty suddenlike when we said hello, but Christ, it was a shock."

"Yeah, I imagine it was." They rode in silence for some minutes, then just as they approached Patricia's house, Jeff turned to Brian and asked in a concerned voice, "Could I ask just one question, Bry?"

"Yeah, shoot."

"Just exactly what *do* you think of Theresa?"

Brian pulled the van up at the curb before Patricia's house, killed the engine, removed his sunglasses and half turned toward Jeff, draping his left elbow over the steering wheel. "I love her," he answered point-blank.

Jeff let his smile seep up the muscles of his face, made a fist and socked the air. "Hot damn!" he exclaimed, then opened his door and jumped down to cross the yard on the run.

Brian watched Jeff and Patricia meet in the center of the open stretch of lawn. Jeff flung his arms around the young woman, who lifted her arms around his shoulders, and they kissed, pressed tightly against each other. It was just the way he'd been planning to greet Theresa.

Patricia's parents stepped out the front door and called, "Hi, Jeff. Welcome home. Are you gonna stay this time?"

"Damn right, I am. And I'm gonna steal your daughter!"

"Somehow, I don't think she minds one bit," Mrs. Gluek called back.

Patricia clambered up into the high van, scooted over and gave Brian a peck on the cheek. "Hiya, bud. Long time, no see."

Jeff was right behind Patricia. "Come here, woman, and put your little butt where it belongs, right on my lap." There were only two bucket seats up front. Jeff pulled Patricia down on his lap, and she laughed happily, flung her arms around his neck and kissed him while the van started rolling.

The dishes were done when the van lumbered up the street a second time, pulled into the driveway and began disgorging its passengers. They meandered to the patio, where Margaret, Willard and Amy joined them. When Theresa came out of the kitchen onto the back step, she found Brian standing below her, waiting.

Her heart did a flip-flop, and everything inside her went warm and springing. He reached up a hand to take hers, and she felt a wash of relief that he was touching her at last.

"Come here, I want to talk to you." He pulled her down the steps to his side, and asked softly, "Do you think your folks would mind if we went for a walk?"

"Not at all."

"Tell them, then. I want to be alone with you, even if it's in the middle of a city street where people are sitting on their doorsteps watching us pass by."

Her heart swelled with joy, and she stepped to the edge of the patio, made their excuses and returned to Brian. He captured her hand, and their joined knuckles brushed between their hips as they ambled down the driveway and onto the blacktop street that was still warm beneath Theresa's sandals after the heat of the summer day. The shadows were falling as evening settled in. The sun rested on the rim of the horizon like a golden, liquid ball. They passed between yards where other sprinklers played the hushed vespers of water droplets spraying greenery.

"Is there someplace we can go?" he asked.

"There's a park about two blocks away."

"Good."

Nothing more was said as they sauntered hand in hand down the center of the street.

"Hi, Theresa," called a woman who was sitting on her front steps.

"Hi, Mrs. Anderson." Theresa raised a hand in greeting, then explained quietly, "I used to babysit for the Andersons when I was Amy's age."

Brian made no reply, lifting a hand in silent greeting, too, then continuing on at Theresa's side, stealing glances at her breasts when she dropped her chin and watched the toes of her white sandals. He wondered what secrets her clothing concealed, what she'd been through, if she hurt, if she was healed. But mostly, he wondered why she hadn't trusted him enough to tell him.

The eastern sky turned a rich periwinkle blue as the sun slipped and plunged into oblivion, leaving the western horizon a blaze of orange that faded to yellow, then violet as they approached a small neighborhood park where a silent baseball diamond was surrounded by a grove of trees. Deserted playground equipment hovered in the stillness of dusk. Great, aged oaks were scattered across the expanse of open recreation area, creating blots of darker shadows beneath their widespread arms, while picnic tables made smaller dots between the trees. Brian led the way from the street onto a crunchy gravel footpath, taking Theresa beneath the shadow of an oak before he finally stopped, squeezed her fingers almost painfully, then turned her to face him.

She looked up into the twin black dots of his sunglasses. "You've still got your glasses on."

Without a word he removed them, and slipped a bow inside the waist of his blue jeans so the glasses hung on his right hip.

"I guess you're a little upset with me, aren't you?" she ventured in a perilously shaky voice.

"Yes, I am," he admitted, "but could we deal with that later?" His long fingers closed over both of her shoulders, drawing her close to his wide-spraddled feet, close to the length of his faded Levi's, close to the naked V of skin above his shirt where dark hair sprigged. Her heart was hammering under her newly reshaped breasts. Her body moved willingly against his, then their arms sought to hold, to reaffirm, to answer the question, Is this person all that I remembered?

Brian's lips opened slightly as he lowered them to hers, which waited with warm, breathless expectancy. Tears bit the back of Theresa's eyes, and she was swept with a feeling of relief so overwhelming her body seemed to wilt as the apprehension eased away into the twilight. Then the waiting ended. They clung with the newly revived reassurance that what they'd found in each other twice before was still as appealing and had been magnified by their time apart.

His mouth was June warm. Indeed, he even seemed to taste of summer, of all things she loved—flowers, music, lazy sprinklers and somewhere, the remembered scent of something he put on his hair. But he had ridden nine hours in a warm van, had crossed miles of rolling prairie in the wrinkled clothing he wore now, and from that clothing emanated a scent she had never quite known before—the scent of Brian Scanlon, male, inviting, a little dusty, a little soiled, but all man.

The kiss was as lusty as some of the rock songs she'd heard him sing, a swift succession of strokes, tugs and head movements that seemed to elicit the threads of feelings from the very tips of her toes and send them sizzling up her body. She poured her feelings into the kiss, meeting his mouth with an equal ardor. With his feet widespread, his midsection was flush against hers, and it felt good, hard, sexy. Theresa was vaguely aware of a difference in the feeling of her breasts pressed against his chest—the smallness, the new tightness, the ability to be closer as his forearm slipped down across her spine and reeled her even more securely against his hips.

"Theresa...." His lips were at her ear, kissing her temple while his beautiful voice lost its mild note and took on a foreign huskiness. "I had to do that first. I just had to."

"First?"

He released a rather shaky breath and backed away from her, searching her upturned face in the deep shadow of the oaks. "It occurs to me we've got some talking to do, wouldn't you say?"

"Yes." She dropped her eyes, blushing already.

"Come on." Capturing her hand, he led her to the nearby area where the swings hung as still as the silence over the park that in daytime rang with children's voices. A steel slide angled down, casting its shadow on the grass as the moon slipped up into the eastern sky and the first stars came out. Brian tugged her along to the side of a large steel merry-go-round and sat down, pulling her to sit beside him, then dropping her hand.

"So..." he began, following the word with a sigh, then leaned his elbows on his thighs. "There've been some changes."

"Yes."

He pondered silently, made an impatient, breathy sound, then burst out, "God, I don't know where to begin, what to say."

"Neither do I."

"Theresa, why didn't you tell me?"

She shrugged very childishly for a twenty-six-year-old woman. "I was afraid to. And...and I didn't know what...well, I mean, we're not...."

"What you're trying to say is that you didn't know my intentions, is that it?"

"Yes, I guess so."

"After what we shared in Fargo, and our letters, you doubted my intentions?"

"No, not *doubted.* I just didn't think we'd had enough time together to get our relationship on its feet." *I wasn't even sure you would come....*

"With me, Theresa, it's not the *amount* of time, but the *quality* of it, and our weekend in Fargo was quality for me. I thought it was for you, too."

"It was, but...but, Brian, we hadn't done much more than

just...well, you know what I'm saying. What we did together didn't really mean a commitment or...." Her voice trailed away. This was the most difficult conversation she'd ever had.

Brian suddenly sprang to his feet, walked three paces away from the merry-go-around and swung to face her. "Couldn't you trust me enough to tell me, Theresa?" he accused.

"I wanted to, but I was scared."

"Of what?"

"I don't know."

"Maybe you thought I was some lecher who was only after you because you had big knockers, is that it? Did you think if you told me you didn't have them anymore, I'd brush you off? Is that what you thought?"

She was horrified. It had never entered her mind that he might consider such a thing. Tears blurred her eyes. "No, Brian, I never thought that...never!"

"Then why the hell couldn't you have trusted me enough to confide in me and tell me what you were planning, give me time to get accustomed to it before I walked into your yard totally unsuspecting? Christ, do you know what a shock it was?"

"I knew you'd be surprised, but I thought you'd be pleasantly surprised."

"I am, I was...." He threw his hands into the air exasperatedly and whirled, presenting his rigid back. "But, God, Theresa, do you know what I've been thinking about for six months? Do you know how many nights I've lain awake thinking about your...*problem* and figuring out ways to finesse you into losing your inhibitions, telling myself I had to be the world's most patient lover when I took you to bed for the first time, so I didn't put some irreversible phobia into you or make your hangup worse than it already was?" Again he spun on her. "We may not have had time to share much, but what we did share was a pretty damn intimate baring of souls, and I think it gave me the right to be in on your decision with you, to share it. But you didn't even give me the chance.''

''Now just a minute!'' She leaped to her feet and faced him in the flood of moonlight that was growing brighter by the minute. ''You've got no claim on me, no right to—''

''The hell I don't!''

''The hell you do!'' Theresa had never fought or sworn in her life and was surprised at herself.

''The hell I don't! I love you, dammit!'' he shouted.

''Well, that's some way to tell me, shouting at the top of your lungs! How was I supposed to know?''

''I signed all my letters that way, didn't I?''

''Well yes, but that's just a…a formal closing on a letter.''

''Is that all you took it for?''

''No!''

''Well, if you knew I loved you, why couldn't you trust me? Had you ever stopped to think it might have been something I'd have welcomed sharing? Something that might have brought us even closer? Something I would have felt *honored* to share? But you didn't give me a chance, going ahead without a word like you did.''

''I resent your attitude, Brian. It's…it's possessive and uninformed.''

''Uninformed?'' He stood now belligerently, his hands on his hips. ''Whose fault is that, mine or yours? If you'd bothered to *inform* me, I wouldn't be so damn mad right now.''

''I discussed it with people who didn't lose their tempers, like you're doing. A counselor at school, a woman who'd had the surgery before and a cosmetic surgeon who eventually performed the operation. I got the emotional support I needed from them.''

He felt shut out and hurt. During the past six months he'd felt a growing affinity with Theresa. He'd felt they were slowly becoming intimates, and he'd returned here thinking she was ready to pursue not only an emotional relationship but a physical one as well. He found himself intimidated by the changes in her body more than he'd been intimidated by her abundant breasts—they'd been only flesh, after all, and that he could approach and touch the same as he had other women's. The psychological preparations he'd made for approaching her again had been made at no little cost in both sleep and worry. Now that he found it all for naught, he felt cheated. Now that he knew she'd turned to others and implied they'd been more help than he could have been, he felt misunderstood. And now that he wasn't sure how long he'd have to wait to pursue her sexually, he felt angry—dammit, he'd wanted to make love to her, and soon!

"Brian," she said softly, sadly, "I didn't mean that the way it sounded. It wasn't that I didn't think you'd support my decision. But it seemed...presumptuous of me to involve you in something so personal without any commitments made between us." She touched his arm, but he remained stiff and scowling, so she returned to sit on the merry-go-round.

He was very upset. And hurt. And wondering if he had the right to be. He swung back to the merry-go-round, flopped down several feet away from her and fell back, draping his shoulders and outflung arms over the mound-shaped steel heart of the vehicle. As he flopped backward he gave a single nudge with his foot, setting the steel framework into motion. He lay brooding, looking up at the stars that circled slowly above him, getting a grip on his feelings.

Theresa sat with her shoulders slumped despondently, feeling the slight rumbling vibrations rising up through the tubular steel bars.

Oh, misery! She had thought this night of Brian's homecoming would see them close, loving, reveling in being together once again. She felt drained and depleted and unsure of how to deal with his anger. Perhaps he had a right to it; perhaps he didn't. She was no psychologist. She should have discussed it with Catherine McDonald and sought her advice regarding whether or not to tell Brian her intentions.

The merry-go-round was set off kilter, so centrifugal force kept it moving in what seemed a perpetual, lazy twirl. The tears gathered in Theresa's throat and then in her eyes. She brushed them away with the back of her wrist, turning away so he couldn't tell what she was doing.

But somehow he sensed it. A hand closed around her bare elbow and pulled her back and to one side. "Hey..." he cajoled softly. "Come here."

She draped backward across the domed center of the merry-go-round. The steel was icy beneath her bare arms as she angled toward him until only their shoulders touched, and the backs of their heads were pressed against the hard, hard metal as they studied the stars. Around and around. Dots of light on the blue-black sky twinkled like reflections of a revolving mirrored ball above a ballroom floor. Crickets had set up their endless chirping, and the night was growing damp, but it felt good against Theresa's hot face. The incandescent moon lit their draped bodies, the bars of the swing set and the crowns of the oak trees that passed slowly as Brian's foot kept nudging the beaten earth.

"I'm sorry, Theresa. I shouldn't have shouted."

"I am too." She sobbed once, and in an instant, he'd pulled her close.

"Listen, sweets, could I have a couple days to get used to it? Hell, I don't know whether I'm allowed to look at them or not. I do, and I feel guilty. I don't, and I feel guiltier. And your family, all avoiding the issue as if you'd never had any other shape. Anyway, I guess I built my hopes up too high, thinking about tonight and what it was going to be like, seeing you again."

"Me too. I certainly didn't want us to fight this way."

"Then let's not, not anymore. Let's go back and see if every-

body else is as tired as I am. I've been awake since two a.m.
I was too excited to sleep.''

"You too?'' She offered a shaky smile.

He smiled down at her in return, brushed a knuckle over the
end of her nose and kissed her lightly.

He'd meant to give her only that single light kiss, but in the
end, he couldn't let her go with just that. Slowly, deliberately,
he returned his mouth to hers, dipping his tongue into the secret
warmth of her lips, which opened in welcome. His body
spurted to life, and his shoulders quivered as he pressed his
elbows to the metal surface on either side of her head. God,
the things he wanted to do to her, to feel with her, to have her
do to him. How long would he have to wait? The kiss lingered
and lengthened, growing more dizzying than the slow circling
of their perch. The way Theresa lay, sprawled backward over
the curved metal, the outline of her breasts was lined by moonlight as they jutted forward. It was as sexy a pose as he'd ever
seen her in, and he knew it would take no more than a quick
shift of his palm, and he'd feel the relief of touching her intimately. He needn't touch her breast about which he was so
unsure—her stomach looked hollow and inviting, and her white
slacks were very taut and alluring. He thought about running
his hand down her ribs, exploring the warm inviting length of
her zipper, and the sheltered spot between her legs as he'd done
once before. But one thing might lead to another, and he had
no idea if she was allowed to move, twist, thrust, if she had
stitches, and where, and how many....

And once he started something, he had no intention of drawing back.

In the end, Brian pacified himself with the kiss alone. When
it ended, he regretfully lurched to his feet, dragging Theresa
with him, crossing the shadowy park toward the house where
they could mingle with people and wouldn't have to confront
the remaining issue...at least for a while.

Chapter Fourteen

The others had gone inside where they were visiting and having second pieces of cake when Brian and Theresa walked up the driveway. The kitchen lights slanted out across the darkened yard and back step in oblique slashes of creamy brightness. Mosquitoes hummed and buzzed against the back screen door, and a June bug threw its crusty shell at the light time and again. Frogs and crickets competed for first chair in the nighttime orchestra. The moon was a pristine ball of white.

From inside came the voice of the group Theresa and Brian could see as they walked up the driveway. They were clustered around the kitchen table, but outside it was peaceful and private. Just short of the back step, Brian stopped Theresa with a hand on her arm.

"Listen, there were a lot of things I wanted to talk about tonight but...." The thought remained unfinished.

"I know." Theresa recalled the many subjects she had stored up and was eager to share with him.

"And just because I didn't get into any of them doesn't mean I'm still mad, okay?"

She was studying the middle button on his shirt, which faced her and the moon. By its light the gauze appeared brilliant white while her own face was cast in shadow. He touched her beneath the chin with a single finger, forcing her to tilt her head up. "Okay?" he asked softly.

"Okay."

"And I probably won't see you for a while after tonight, because Jeff and I have a lot of running to do. I have to find an apartment and buy some furniture, and we want to start working on getting a band together right away. We have to renew our union cards and try to find a decent agent and audition the new drummer and bass guitarist and maybe a keyboard man, too. Anyway, I'm going to be jumping for a while. I just wanted you to know.''

"Thanks for telling me." But her heart felt heavy with disappointment. Now that he was back, she wanted to be with him as much as possible. In his letters he'd suggested she could come along with him and help pick out furniture, but now he was eliminating her from that excursion. She could understand that he had a lot of mundane arrangements to make, just to get settled into an apartment, and that she'd only be in the way when they were auditioning new players, but somehow she'd thought they'd find time each day to see each other. But she smiled and hid the fact that she was crushed by his advance warning. Was this how fellows turned girls down gently? *No, she reprimanded herself, you're being unfair to Brian. He's not like that. He's honest and honorable. That's why he's warning you in the first place.*

The finger beneath her chin curled, and he brushed her jaw with his knuckles. "I'll call as soon as I've got my feet planted."

"Fine." She began turning toward the back step, but his hand detained her a second time.

"Wait a minute. You're not getting away without one more kiss."

She was swung around and encircled in warm, hard arms and pulled against his moonlit gauze shirt. While his lips closed over hers, the picture of the naked V of skin at his neck came into Theresa's mind, and she suddenly wanted to touch it. Hesitantly, she slipped her hand to find it, resting her palm on the sleek hair and warm flesh, then sliding it upward to rest at the side of his neck while her thumb touched the hollow of his throat. The thudding of his pulse there surprised her. Lightly,

lightly, she stroked the warm, pliant depression. He made a soft, throaty sound, and his mouth moved over hers more hungrily. He clasped the back of her head and swept the interior of her mouth with lusty, intimate strokes of his tongue that sent liquid fire racing across her skin.

Some queer surge of latent feminine knowledge pulsed through Theresa. In her entire life, she'd never actively provoked a sexual response from a man. Instead, she'd always been too busy fighting off the bombardment of unwanted physical advances her partners seemed always too eager to display. Now, for the first time, *she* touched—a hesitant touch at best. But the response it kindled in Brian was at once surprising and telling. All she had done was stroke the hollow of his throat with her thumb, yet he reacted as if she'd done far more. The tenor of his kiss changed with a swift, swirling suddenness, and became totally sexual, not the insipid good-night gesture that it had begun to be.

It came as a surprise to think she, Theresa Brubaker, elementary music teacher, freckled redhead, inexperienced paramour, could generate such an immediate and passionate response by only the briefest of encouragements. Especially when she considered that he was a guitar man, a performer who had, admittedly, enjoyed all the adulation that went with his career. He must have known a great many very experienced women, far more experienced than her. Yet, he thrilled to her very inexperienced touch, and this in turn thrilled Theresa.

Realizing the power she possessed to stimulate this man, she suddenly grew impatient to test it further.

But she hadn't the chance, for as quickly as his ardor grew, he controlled it, lifting his head to suck in a great gulp of damp night air and push her gently away. "Lord, woman, do you know how good you are at that?"

"Me?" she asked, surprised.

"You."

"I'm not good at that at all. I've barely had any practice."

"Well, we'll remedy that when the time is right. But if practice makes perfect, I think you'll end up being more than I can handle."

She smiled and in the dark felt herself flush with pleasure at his words. "Hasn't anybody ever told you it's not nice to start things like that when you don't intend to finish them?" came Brian's husky teasing.

"I didn't start it. You did. I was heading into the house when you stopped me. But if you're done now, let's go in." Smiling, she turned toward the step again.

"Not so fast." Once more she was brought up short. "I can't go in just now."

"You can't?" She turned back to face him.

"Uh-uh. I'll need a couple of minutes."

"Oh!" Suddenly she understood and whirled around, presenting her shoulder blades. As she pressed her palms to embarrassed cheeks, he chuckled softly behind her shoulder, audaciously kissed the side of her neck and captured her hand. "Come on, let's go for a little walk through the backyard. That should cool me down. You can talk about school, and I'll talk about the Air Force. Those are two nice, safe, deflating subjects."

Brian treated sexuality with such frankness. Theresa wondered if she'd ever be as open about it as he was. Her body felt flushed with awareness, equally as charged as his. Thank heavens it didn't show on women!

They entered the kitchen five minutes later and pulled up chairs to join the others around the table, while Margaret sliced cake for them, and the conversation continued. When ten-thirty arrived, Jeff pushed his chair back, lifted his elbows toward the ceiling and gave a broad, shivering stretch while twisting at the waist.

"Well, I guess it's time I get Patricia home."

"Want to take the van?"

"Thanks, I'd love to."

Brian tossed Jeff the keys. "We'd better unload our suitcases first, cause I'm ready for the sack. I'll need my stuff."

While the unloading was being done, Theresa escaped to the lower level of the house to put out clean sheets and blankets for Brian's bed. She experienced a feeling of déjà vu, recalling the intimacies she and Brian had exchanged on this davenport, both on New Year's Eve and the following morning. Somehow, she realized it would be best not to have Brian encounter her here, with the mattress opened up and the bed between them, ready for use. So she left the bedding and the light on and said her good-night to him along with the rest of her family in the kitchen, before they each retired to their respective beds.

In the morning, Theresa was disappointed to discover both Brian and Jeff gone when she woke up. It was only a little before nine, so they must have been up early. The day stretched before her with an emptiness she hadn't anticipated. Many times she paused to wonder at how the absence of a single person could create a void this distracting. But it was true: knowing Brian was in town made it all the harder to be apart from him. It seemed he was never absent from her thoughts for more than an hour before his image popped up again, speaking, gesturing, sharing intimate caresses and kisses. And, too, angry.

It was the first time she'd seen his anger, and in the way of most lovers, Theresa found it now stimulating to remember how he'd looked and sounded when he was upset. Knowing this new facet of him seemed almost a relief. Everybody has his angry moments, and the way she was feeling about Brian, she thought it imperative to see both his best and worst sides, and the sooner the better. She had fallen totally in love with the man. If he asked her to make a commitment today, she'd do it without hesitation.

But the first day passed, and a second, and a third, and still she hadn't seen Brian again. Jeff reported he'd found a one-bedroom apartment in the nearby suburb of Bloomington. It was vacant, so Brian had paid his money and taken immediate occupancy. The two men had wasted no time going off to a furniture story to buy the single item that was essential: a bed. A water bed, Jeff said. The news brought Theresa's glance sharply up to her brother, but Jeff rambled on, relating the story of how the two of them had hauled the bed to Brian's apartment in the van, then borrowed a hose from the apartment caretaker to fill the thing. The heater hadn't had time to get the water warmed up the first night, so Brian had ended up spreading his new bedding on the carpeted living-room floor to sleep.

Theresa pictured him there, alone, while she lay in her bed alone, wondering if he thought of her as strongly as she thought of him each time she slipped between the sheets for the night. It was late June, the nights hot and muggy, and she blamed her restlessness on that. It seemed she never managed to sleep straight through a night anymore, but awakened several times and spent long, sleepless hours staring at the streetlight outside her window, thinking of Brian, and wondering when she'd see him again.

He called on the fourth day. Theresa could tell who it was by Amy's part of the conversation.

"Hello?... Oh, *hiiiii*...I hear you found an apartment... Must be kind of creepy without any furniture... Oh, a pool!... All riiiiight!... Can I really!... Can I bring a friend?... Sure she does... Sure she can... Yeah, she's right here, just a sec." Amy handed the receiver to Theresa who'd been listening and waiting in agony.

The smile on Theresa's face put the June sun to shame. Her heart was rapping out an I-missed-you tattoo that made her voice come out rather breathily and unnaturally high.

"Hello?"

"Hiya, sweets," he greeted, as if they'd never had a cross word between them. How absolutely absurd to blush when he was ten miles away, but the way he could pronounce that word always sent shafts of delight through her.

"Who's this?" she asked cheekily.

His laugh vibrated along the wires and made her smile all the more broadly and feel exceedingly clever for one of the first times in her life.

"This is the guitar man, you little redheaded tease. I just got my new phone installed and wanted to give you the number here."

"Oh." Disappointment deflated Theresa with a heavy *whump.* She'd thought he was calling to ask if he could see her. "Just a minute—let me get a pencil."

"It's 555-8732," he dictated. She wrote it down, then found herself tracing it repeatedly while the conversation went on. "I've got a nice apartment, but it's a little empty yet. I did get a bed though." Had he gone on, she might not have become so flustered. But he didn't. He let the silence ooze over her skin suggestively, lifting tiny goose bumps of arousal at the imagery that popped into her mind at the thought of his bed and him in it. Theresa glanced at Amy who stood by listening, and hoped she'd had the receiver plastered hard enough against her ear that Amy hadn't gotten a drift of what Brian said.

"Oh, that's nice!" Theresa replied brightly.

"Yes, it's very nice, but a little cold the first night."

Again, she came up against a blank wall. "Oh, that's too bad."

"I slept on the floor that night, but the water's all warmed up now."

Like a dolt, she went on speaking the most idiotic inanities. "Oh, that's nice."

"Very nice, indeed. Have you ever tried a water bed?"

"No," she attempted, but the word was a croak, hardly discernible. She cleared her throat and repeated, "No."

"I'll let you lie on it sometime and see how you like it."

Theresa was so red by this time that Amy's expression had

grown puzzled. Theresa covered the mouthpiece, flapped an exasperated hand at her younger sister and hissed, "Will you go find something to do?"

Amy left, throwing a last inquisitive glance over her shoulder.

"I've got a pool, too," Brian was saying.

"Oh, I love to swim." It was one of the few sports in which she'd ever been able to participate fully.

"Can you?"

For a moment she was puzzled. "Can I?"

"Yes, I mean...are you allowed to...yet?"

"Oh." The light dawned. Was she healed enough to swim. "Oh, yes, I'm back to full activities. It's been four weeks."

"Why didn't you tell me that the other night?"

His question and the tone of his voice told her the reason for his pause. He'd been waiting for the go-ahead! The idea threw her into a semipanic, yet she was anxious to pursue her relationship with him, though she knew beyond a doubt there would be few days of total innocence once they began seeing each other regularly. Considering her old-fashioned sense of propriety, it naturally put Theresa in a vulnerable position, one in which she would soon be forced to make some very critical decisions.

"I...I didn't think about it."

"I did."

She realized it now—how lightly he'd held her when they caressed, as if she were breakable. Even when they'd kissed in the driveway near the back door, he'd pulled her head hard against him, but hadn't forced her body in any way.

Neither of them said anything for a full forty-five seconds. They were coming to grips with something unspoken. During that silence he told her his intentions as clearly as if he'd illustrated them by renting a highway billboard with a two-foot-high caption. He was ready for a physical relationship. Was she?

When the silence was broken, it was Brian who spoke. His voice was slightly deeper than usual, but quiet. "Theresa, I'd like us to spend next Saturday together...here. Bring your bathing suit, and I'll pick up some corned beef at the deli, and we'll make a day of it. We'll swim and catch some sun and talk, okay?"

"Yes," she agreed quietly.

"Okay, what time should I come and get you?"

She had missed him terribly. There was only one answer she could give. "Early."

"Ten in the morning?"

No, six in the morning, she thought, but answered, "Fine. I'll be ready."

"See you then. And, honey?"

Being called *honey* by Brian was something so precious it made her chest ache.

"Yes?"

"I miss you."

"I miss you too."

It was Friday. Theresa had spent a restless night, considering the possibilities that lay ahead for her with Brian. She thought not only of the sexual tension between them, but of the responsibilities it brought. She had thought herself totally opposed to sex beyond the framework of marriage, but her brief experience in Fargo warned that when bodies are aroused, moral attitudes tend to dissolve and disappear in the expanding joy of the moment.

Would I let him? Would I let myself?

The answer to both questions, Theresa found, was an unqualified *yes.*

The following day she went to the drugstore to buy suntan lotion, knowing she'd suffer if she didn't apply an effective sunscreen to her pale, freckled skin that seemed to get hot and

prickly at the mere mention of the word *sun.* She chose the
one whose label said it had ultraguard, then ambled to a revolving rack of sunglasses and spent an enjoyable twenty
minutes trying on every pair at least twice before choosing a
rather upbeat pair with graduated shading and large round
lenses that seemed to make her mouth appear feminine and
vulnerable when the oversize frames rested on her nose.

She wandered along the shelves, picking up odd items she
needed: emery boards, deodorant, hair conditioner. Suddenly
she came up short and stared at the array of products on an
eye-level shelf. *Contraceptives.*

Brian's face seemed to emblazon itself across her subcon-
scious as if projected on a movie screen. It seemed inevitable
that he would become her lover. Yet why did it seem prurient
to consider buying a contraceptive in advance? It somehow
took the warm glow of love to a cooler temperature and made
her feel cunning and deliberate.

Without realizing she'd done it, she slipped the dark glasses
on, hiding behind them, though the price tag still dangled from
the bow.

*Theresa Brubaker, you're twenty-six years old! You're living
in twentieth-century America, where most women face this decision in their midteens. What are you so afraid of?*

Commitment? Not at all. Not commitment to Brian, only to
the undeniable tug of sexuality, for once she surrendered to it,
there was no turning back. It was such an irreversible decision.

*Don't be stupid, Theresa. He may keep you out by the pool
all afternoon and all this gnashing will have been for nothing.*

*Fat chance! With my skin! If he keeps me out there all af-
ternoon I'll look like a brick somebody forgot in the kiln. He's
already hinted he's going to take me into his bedroom to try
out his bed.*

So, buy something! At least you'll have it if you need it.

*Buy what? I've never paid any attention to the articles about
products like these.*

So, pick one up and read the label.

But she checked the aisle in both directions first. Even the label instructions made her blush. How on earth could she ever confront the fact that she'd have to use this stuff while she was with a man? She'd die of embarrassment!

It's either that or end up pregnant, her unwanted-companion voice persecuted.

But I'm not that kind of girl. I've always said so.

Everybody's that kind of girl when the right man comes along.

Yes, things have changed so much since Brian came into my life.

She studied the products and finally decided on one. But on her way to the checkout stand, she bought a *Cosmopolitan* magazine and dropped it nonchalantly over her other selections when setting them on the counter. *Cosmopolitan,* she thought, how appropriate. But Helen Gurley Brown would scold me for not placing the contraceptive on top of the magazine instead of vice versa.

On her next stop at the Burnsville Shopping Center, she found it necessary to buy a new purse, one large enough to conceal her new purchase. She chuckled inwardly that it turned out to be her first purchase of a contraceptive that should lead the way to her buying something she'd wanted all her life. a shoulder bag. Her shoulders had carried more than their share of strain in years gone by. She'd never felt willing to hang a purse on them as well, though she'd often wanted to own one. Well, she did now.

But the chief reason she'd come to the clothing store was to shop for a bathing suit, another item that was expanding her clothing horizon, for the suits she'd worn in the past had had to be one-pieces, altered to fit.

Now, however, she tried everything from string bikinis to skirted one-piece jobs in the Hedy Lamarr tradition. She chose a very middle-of-the-road two-piece design that wasn't exactly tawdry, but fell just short of being totally modest. The fabric was the color of her father's well-kept lawn and looked like shiny wet leather when the light caught and reflected from it. The bright kelly green was a hue that in days of old she'd have said contrasted with her coloring too sharply—the old stop-and-go-light look. But somehow, since her surgery, Theresa's confidence had grown. And since the advent of Brian in her sphere, she had felt far less plain than she used to. This gift he'd given her was something Theresa meant to repay in some way someday.

The following morning she awakened shortly after five o'clock. The sun was peeking over the eastern horizon, turning the sky to a lustrous, pearly coral, sending streaks of brighter melon and pink radiating above the rim of the world. Closing her eyes and stretching, Theresa felt as if those shafts of hot pink were penetrating her body. She felt giddy, elated and as if she were on the brink of the most momentous day of her life.

The Maestro grinned down at her from the shelf, and it seemed as if he fiddled a gay, lilting love song to awaken her. She smiled at him, slithered lower in the bed, raised both arms above her head and rolled to her belly, savoring the keen satisfaction a simple act like that now brought into her life. It made her feel diminutive and catlike. Beneath her, the bulk was gone, in its place a body proportioned by a hand that had, in this case, improved upon Nature.

There were times when she still had difficulty realizing the change had happened and was permanent. Sometimes she found herself affecting mannerisms no longer necessary: crossing one arm and resting the opposite elbow on it to give momentary relief by boosting up her breasts, yet at the same time hiding behind her arms. Walking. Ah, but there simply hadn't been a chance to run yet. But she would, someday soon. Just to feel the ebullience and freedom of the act.

She threw herself onto her back, studied the ceiling and checked the clock. Was it broken? Or had only five minutes passed since she'd awakened? Would the rest of the morning go this slowly until Brian came to her?

It did.

In spite of the fact that she performed every grooming ritual with the pomp and time-consuming attention of a ceremony. She shaved her legs…all the way up, for the first time in her life. She filed her toenails into delicate rounded peaks and polished them with Chocolate Mocha polish. She gave herself a careful and complete manicure, painting her fingernails with three coats. She washed her hair and arranged it with care that was positively silly, considering she was going to leap into a swimming pool within minutes after she got there. But she spared no less care on her makeup. She ironed the aqua blue collar of a white terry beach coverup with matching lounging pants whose ribbed ankles had a matching aqua stripe that continued up the outsides of the legs, and up the arms of the loose sweat-shirt style jacket. She took a bath and put an astringent after-bath splash up her legs and down her arms, and finally, when only a half hour remained, she put her bedroom in order, then hung up her housecoat and picked up the green bathing suit. She slipped into the brief panties, easing them up her legs and turning to present her derrière to the mirror, checking the reflection to find it firm, shapely and nothing she would change, even if she could. The elasticized brief rode across the crest of each hipbone, and just below her navel, exposing both it and the tender hollow of her spine.

As she turned to face the mirror again, with the strappy suit top in her hand, she assessed her reflected breasts. The crescent-shaped scars beneath each had been the fastest to heal, and the circular ones about the nipples had all but vanished. The only ones that were still highly detectable were those running vertically from the bottom up to each nipple. Dr. Schaum had told her to expect them to take a good six months to fade completely, but had assured her they would, for the newer method of surgery allowed the skin to be draped instead of stretched back into place, thus taking stress off the suturing and allowing the tissue to heal almost invisibly. They did, however, itch. Theresa opened the jar of cocoa butter and gently massaged a dollop of the soothing balm along the length of each scar. But as she finished, her fingertips remained on her left breast. But it was not the scar she saw. She saw a woman changed. A woman whose horizons had expanded in thousands of definable and indefinable ways since her surgery. She saw a woman who no longer cared that her freckles ran down her chest and up her legs, a woman who no longer considered her hair carrot-colored, but merely "bright," a woman whose medium, orange-sized breasts appeared almost beautiful to her own eyes. The nipples seemed to have shrunk from the surgery, and their perky position, pointed upward instead of down, never ceased to be a source of amazement.

She raised her arms above her head experimentally. When she did this, her breasts lifted with her arms, as they'd never done before. She pirouetted swiftly to the left, watching, to be rewarded by the sight of her breasts coming right along with her instead of swaying pendulously several inches behind the movement of her trunk.

A marvelous, appreciative smile burst across her face.

I am female. I am as beautiful as I feel. And today I feel utterly beautiful.

She hooked the bathing suit top behind her back, then lifted her arms to tie the strings behind her neck, examining the way the concealing triangles of sheeny green covered her breasts. She ran her fingertips along the deep V, down the freckled skin to the spot where the two triangles met. There was scarcely any cleavage! The wonder of it was almost enough to make her high!

She hated to slip the white terry pants and jacket on and

cover herself up. Oh, glorious, glorious liberation! How wonderful you feel!

She packed a drawstring bag with sunscreen, towels, hair lifter, makeup, cocoa butter, shampoo, a pair of jeans and a brand new bra made of scalloped blue lace. Her thirty days of wearing the firm support bra were over. This little wisp of femininity was what she'd long craved. While stuffing her belongings in the bag, she realized even this was a new experience to be savored, for she'd never gone skipping off with boys to the beach when she was a girl. There was so much catching up to do!

By the time ten o'clock arrived, Theresa was not only ready, she was a totally self-satisfied ready.

The van turned into the driveway, and she stepped out onto the back step to await him. Through the windshield she saw him smile and raise a palm, then shut off the ignition, open the door and walk toward her.

He was wearing his aviator sunglasses, white, tight swimming trunks beneath an unbuttoned navy blue shirt with three zippered patch pockets, white buttons and epaulettes. The shirt's long sleeves were rolled up, exposing his arms from the elbow down, and its tails flapped in the light breeze as he approached. He moved around the front of the van in a loose-jointed amble, keeping his eyes on her face until he stood on the apron of the step below her, looking up Lazily, he reached up to remove the glasses while every cell in her body became energized by his presence.

"Hello, sweets."

"Hello, Brian." She wanted very badly to call him an endearment, but the expressive way she spoke his name actually became an endearment in itself.

Was it she who reached first, or he? All Theresa knew later was that one moment she stood two steps above him, and the next, she was in his arms, sharing a hello kiss beneath the bright June sun at ten o'clock on a Saturday morning. She, the timid introvert who'd often wondered why some women were blessed with lives in which scenes like this were taken for granted, while others could only lie in their lonely beds at night and dream of such bliss.

It wasn't a passionate kiss. It wasn't even very intimate. But it swept her off the step and against his partially exposed chest while she circled his neck with both arms, captured in such a fashion that she was looking down at him. He lifted his lips, brushed them caressingly over hers, then dipped his head to bestow another such accolade to the triangle of freckles that showed above the zippered white terry coverup. "Mmm...you smell good." He released her enough to allow her breasts and belly to go sliding down his body until she stood before him, smiling up at his admiring, stunning, summer eyes.

"Mmm...you do too."

His hands rested on her hipbones. She was piercingly aware of it, even as they gazed, unmoving, into each other's faces and stood in broad daylight, for any of the neighbors to see.

"Are you ready?"

"I've been ready since six a.m."

He laughed, rode his hands up her ribs and turned her toward the door. "Then get your stuff and let's not waste a minute."

Chapter Fifteen

The Village Green Apartments were tudor-trimmed stucco buildings arranged in a horseshoe shape around a dazzling aqua-and-white swimming pool. The grounds were wooded with old elms whose leafy branches drooped in the still summer morning. Theresa caught a glimpse of the pool as Brian passed it, then pulled around the far side of the second building. Glancing up, she saw small decks flanking the length of the stucco walls, and an occasional splash of crimson from a potted geranium in a redwood tub.

Inside, the halls were carpeted, papered and silent. Padding along with Brian at her shoulder, Theresa found herself unable to keep from watching his bare toes curl into each step as he walked. There was something undeniably intimate about being with a barefoot man. Brian's feet were medium sized, shaded with hair on his big toes, and it struck her how much more angular a man's foot was than a woman's. His legs were muscular and sprinkled with a modicum of hair on all but the fronts and backs of his knees. He stopped before number 122, unlocked the door and stepped back.

"It's not much yet, but it will be."

She entered a living room with plush, bone-colored carpeting. Directly across from the door by which they'd entered was an eight-foot-wide sliding glass door decorated with an open-weave drapery that was drawn aside to give a view of the pool and surrounding grassy area. The room held one chocolate brown director's chair, a cork-based lamp sitting beside it on the floor and nothing else except musical equipment: guitars, amplifiers, speakers as tall as Theresa's shoulders, microphones, a reel-to-reel recorder, stereo, radio, tapes and records.

Forming an L in juxtaposition with the living room was a tiny galley kitchen with a Formica-topped peninsula counter dividing it from the rest of the open area. A short hall presumably led to the bathroom and bedroom beyond.

Theresa stopped in the middle of the carpeted expanse. It seemed very lonely and barren, and it made Theresa somehow sad to walk into the quiet emptiness and think about Brian here all alone, with no furniture, none of the comforts of home, nobody to talk to or to share music with. But she turned and smiled brightly.

"Home is where the heart is, they say."

He, too, smiled. "So I've heard. Still, you can see why I invited you over to swim. It's about all I'm equipped to offer."

Oh, I wouldn't say that, came the sudden impulsive thought. She shrugged, one thumb hooking the drawstring of the carryall bag that was slung over her shoulder. She glanced around his living room again. "Swimming is one of the few active pastimes I've enjoyed ever since I was little. I love it. Is all this equipment *yours?*" She ventured across to the impressive array of sound equipment, leaning forward to gaze into the smoked-glass doors of his component cabinet.

"Yup."

"Wow."

He watched her move from piece to piece, touching nothing until her eye was caught by a three-ring notebook lying open on the floor beside an old, beat-up-looking flat-top guitar. She knelt, examined the handwritten words, and looked up. "Your song-book?"

He nodded.

She turned the pages, riffling through them slowly, stopping here and there to hum a few bars. "It must have taken you years to collect all these."

She found herself drawn to the sheets simply because they contained his handwriting, with which she'd grown so familiar during the past half year. The songs were arranged alphabetically, so she couldn't resist turning to the *Ss*. *S-A, S-E, S-L, S-O*...and there it was: "Sweet Memories." Without realizing she'd done it, her fingers grazed the sheets feeling the slight indentation made by his ballpoint pen years ago.

Sweet memories of her own came flooding back. And for Brian, standing near, watching her, the same thing happened. He was transported back to New Year's Eve, dancing with her in his arms, then curling her against his chest before a slow, golden fire. But it was shortly after ten o'clock on a June morning, and he'd invited her here to swim. He brought himself back from his concentrated study of the woman kneeling before him to ask, "Would you like to change into your suit?"

Reluctantly she left her musings. "Oh, I have it on. All I have to do is jump out of these." She pinched the stretchy terry cloth and pulled it away from both thighs, while grinning up at him.

"Well, I'm ready if you are."

"Just a minute. I think I'll leave my sandals in here." She rolled to a sitting position with one knee updrawn and began unbuckling the ankle strap. While she tugged at it, he moved closer to stand beside her and study the top of her head. She was terribly conscious of his chestnut-colored legs, sprinkled with hair, just at her elbow, and of his bare toes close to her hip.

"I wouldn't have taken you for a woman who'd wear toenail polish." Her hands fell still for a second, then tugged again and the first sandal came free. As she reached for the second one, she raised her eyes to find him standing with arms akimbo, looking down at her, the front panels of his shirt held aside by his wrists. His bare chest drew her eyes almost magnetically.

"I'm trying a lot of new things these days that I've never had the nerve to try before. Why? Don't you like it?"

He suddenly hunkered down, captured her foot and began removing her sandal. "I love it. You have the prettiest toes of any violin player I've ever gone swimming with." The sandal dropped to the floor, and to Theresa's astonishment, he carried the bare foot to his lips and kissed the underside of her big toe, then the soft, vulnerable skin of her instep. Her eyes flew open, and the blush began creeping up. Brian grinned and unconcernedly retained possession of her foot, lazily stroking its arch with a thumb. "Well, you said you were trying new things you'd never tried before, and I thought this might be one to add to your list." This time, when his teeth gently nipped at the sensitive instep, her lips fell open and her eyes widened.

Theresa stared at him. Her throat had gone dry, and she was unable to move. When he'd lifted her foot, she'd lost her balance and teetered back, so sat now with elbows locked and both hands braced on the carpet behind her. Suddenly she realized her fingers were clutching the fibers. Though her eyes were riveted on Brian's face, she was arousingly aware of his pose. Balancing on the balls of his feet, his knees were widespread, but pointed at her so that it was all she could do to keep her eyes from dropping to the insides of his thighs. She knew by some magical telepathy, though she hadn't looked, that his inner thighs were smoothed of hair, just as his knees were. The muscles of his legs were bulged and taut, his insteps curved like those of Achilles running. His unbuttoned shirt fell loose and wide at his hips. The elasticized fabric of his white bathing trunks was molded to his thighs and conformed to the masculine rises and ridges between his legs.

Swallowing the lump in her throat, Theresa carefully withdrew her foot.

"I think we'd better go out," she advised shakily.

"Right. Grab your bag." Straightening those alarmingly close knees, he reached a hand down and tugged her to her feet. He rolled the sliding screen back and she moved out into the sun ahead of him, her senses so fully awakened by his nearness that even the sound of the vinyl rollers gliding in the track made her feel as if they'd just wheeled smoothly up her spinal column. How odd to be stepping into the intense heat of the late June sun, yet be shivering and experiencing the titillating effect of goose bumps rising up her arms and thighs.

There was nobody else in the pool area this early in the day. Yellow and white striped umbrellas were still closed, and the tubular plastic chairs and recliners were all pushed neatly under the tables. The concrete rectangle was surrounded by a broad stretch of thick green grass on all sides, and as Theresa crossed it, the cool blades tickled her bare toes.

The pool was stunningly clear, its surface shimmering slightly. In the aqua depths an automatic cleaning device snaked back and forth, back and forth, sweeping the pool floor.

Brian dipped one knee and stuck his toe in the water.

"It's warm. Should we go in right away and work off our breakfasts?"

"I was too excited to eat breakfast." Realizing what she'd said, she sucked on her lower lip and chanced a quick peek at the man beside her to find him gazing down benignly at her pink cheeks.

"Oh, really?"

"I'll never succeed as a femme fatale, will I? I don't think I was supposed to admit that."

"A femme fatale would keep a man guessing. But one of the first things I liked about you was that you didn't. I could read you as easily as you just read the words to 'Sweet Memories' in there. That *is* what you were reading, isn't it?"

"Yes."

"I wonder how many times I played it and thought of you during the past six months."

He stood so near, Theresa thought she could feel nothing more than the auburn hairs on his arms entwined with the strawberry blond ones on her own. His eyes held a sincerity mixed with controlled desire, and she met it with an expression much the same. On the cool ceramic coping upon which they stood, his right foot eased over an inch until his toes covered hers, and Theresa wondered if a touch that innocent could release such a wellspring of response within her body, what must the carnal act inspire? His voice was deep and held a note of self-teasing. "There. Now we're even. Whatever the male equivalent of the femme fatale is, I'm not it. I don't want to hold any of my feelings back from you. I never wanted to, not since the first day I met you."

"Brian, let's go swimming. I'm dying of the heat... whatever's causing it."

"Good idea. Especially since we have the place to ourselves for now."

He moved to the end of the pool and cranked open one of the umbrellas, then angled its top toward the sun. She flung her tote bag on the tabletop, then unzipped her coverup, shrugged it off and tossed it over the back of a patio chair. With her back to Brian she shimmied the elastic waist of the matching terry pants down past her hips, then flung them, too, onto the chair.

She heard the buttons and zippers of his shirt hit the metal tabletop with a ping, and assumed he was standing behind her, studying her back. This was the moment about which she'd dreamed and fantasized for years. She, Theresa Brubaker, clad in a bathing suit that left just enough to the imagination, was about to turn and face the man she loved. And she didn't have to cross her arms over her chest, nor keep her towel draped around her neck, or hunch her shoulders to disguise the thrust of her feminine attributes.

She turned to find him staring, as she'd known he'd be. Neither of them moved for a long, silent stretch of time. His chest was bare, and the white trunks dipped just below his navel, leaving it surrounded by a thin line of hair leading from the wider dark mat above. His nipples looked like copper pennies in the shade of the umbrella. His ribs were lean. His lips were partially open. His eyes unabashedly scanned her from face to knees, then lingeringly moved back up again with the slow deliberation of an art critic.

"Wow," Brian breathed. And incredible as it seemed, even to herself, Theresa believed him. The airy word was all she needed to reaffirm her desirability. But she could imagine her damn freckles zinging to life on her blushing neck and cheeks, so she turned to open her bag and rummage through it for the sunscreen.

"You'll probably eat your word within an hour. You've never seen what happens to me when the sun hits my skin. I'm a living demonstration of why physicians refer to freckles as heat spots. And I burn to a brilliant neon pink." From the depths of her bag she retrieved the lotion and uncapped it, then squirted a generous curl into her palm. "Want some?"

"Thanks." He took the bottle, and they busied themselves applying the sweet-scented lotion to their arms, necks, faces and legs. When Theresa rubbed it along the edge of the V-neck on her suit, she felt his eyes following the movements of her palm and glanced up to find him putting lotion on his chest. Her eyes dropped to his long fingers that massaged the firm musculature, delving through crisp hair, leaving it glistening with oils. He took another squirt, handed the bottle to her, and they stared at each other's hands—his running across his hard belly and along the elastic waist of his trunks; hers traversing delicate ribs, and the horizontal line along the bottom of her bikini top before curving into the depression of her navel, then around her exposed hipbones.

The lotion was slick and fragrant. It smelled of coconut, citrus and a hint of berry, filling the air around them like ambrosia. Watching his hands gliding over his skin, Theresa conjured up the thought of them gliding over hers. She dropped to the chair and began doing her legs, stretching first one, then the other out before her, sensing his eyes following again as she stroked the tender flesh of her inner thighs. She kept her eyes averted but saw peripherally how he lifted one leg to hook his toes over the edge of a lawn chair and massage fruit-scented magic along the length of his leg. He'd turned to the side, and she had a chance to study him without being studied herself.

Her eyes traversed his curving back, the buttock, the raised thigh and the junction of his legs where secrets waited. It suddenly flashed across Theresa's mind why in Victorian times men and women were never allowed to go ocean bathing together. It was a decidedly sensual thing, studying a man in swim trunks.

She dragged her eyes away, wondering if she was supposed to feel guilty at this new and unexpected curiosity she harbored. She didn't. Not at all. She was twenty-six years old—it occurred to her it was high time this curiosity surfaced and was appeased.

"Will you put some on my back?" he asked.

"Sure, turn around," she answered jauntily. But when she was squeezing the bottle, her outstretched palm trembled. His back was smooth and had several brown moles. He had wide shoulders that tapered to trim hips, the skin taut and healthy. When her hand touched his shoulder he twitched, as if he, too, were keyed up with awareness, and had been awaiting that first touch with as great a sense of anticipation as she. When her fingers curved around his ribs to his sides, he lifted his arms slightly away from his body to allow her access. For a moment, she was tempted to run both hands all the way around his trunks and press her face to the hollow between his shoulder blades. Instead she squirted a coil of white into her palm and worked both hands unilaterally across the crests of his hard shoulders and up the sides and back of his neck, even into the hair at its nape. Already the hair was longer, which pleased her. She had never been crazy about his Air Force haircuts, for she'd imagined that if allowed to grow to collar length, his would curve gently in thick, free swoops. As her fingers massaged his neck, he tipped his head backward and a guttural sound escaped his throat. Her palms, as well as the nerve endings along the rest of her body, felt as if they were instantly on fire.

It grew worse—or better—when he turned and took the bottle from her slippery fingers, ordering quietly, "Turn around."

She spun from the ardor in his eyes, then felt his long palms pressing a cold mound of lotion against her bare flesh, then begin turning it warm with the friction and contact of skin upon skin. His touch made it extremely difficult to breathe, and impossible to control the tempo of her heart, which seemed to rise up and search out the spots his hand grazed, pounding right through the walls of her back. His fingers curved over her shoulder, up beneath her hair, forcing her chin to drop forward, spreading the essence of wondrous exotic delicacies all about her. He massaged the breadth of her shoulder blades, skipped over the elasticized back strip of her suit, and after taking another liberal amount of sunscreen, his fingertips eased up beneath the strap, running left to right beneath it, from just beneath her left armpit to the same spot under her right. Lower they went, down the delicate hollow of her back, and along the elastic of her emerald green briefs, curving upon the sculptured hipbone, teasing at the taut rubberized waistband that cinched tightly against her flesh. The oils made his hands glide sensuously across her skin, and she shuddered beneath them.

His touch disappeared. She heard the faint sound of the cap being replaced on the bottle, then of the bottle meeting the aluminum tabletop. But she didn't move. She couldn't. She felt as if she'd never move again as long as she lived, not unless this fire in her veins was cooled and put out. If it wasn't, she'd stand there and burn into a cinder.

"Last one in's a moldy worm," came the heavy, aroused voice from behind her. Then she was sprinting to the end of the pool—running at last!—hitting the water stretched out full length, just at the instant Brian hit it. The shock was breathtaking. From the heat of a second ago her body dropped what seemed a full fifty degrees. She swam furiously, a powerful, controlled crawl to the far end of the pool, her body temperature stabilizing by the time she reached her goal.

Side by side they swam eight laps, and in the middle of the ninth, Theresa spluttered, waved limply and declared, "Goodbye, I think I'm drowning," then went under. When her head surfaced, he was treading water, waiting.

"Woman, I'm not through with you yet. Sorry, no drowning till I am." And unceremoniously he disappeared, came up in the perfect position to command her body in an exemplary demonstration of a Senior Lifesaving hold, with his left arm angled across her chest while he hauled her to the far end of the pool beneath the overhanging diving board.

She let herself go limp and he pulled along in an unresisting state of breathlessness and sensuality. His elbow clamped down on her left breast, and it felt wonderful.

At the pool wall he released her, and they both crossed their arms on the sleek concrete, resting their cheeks on their wrists while facing each other, both panting, feet flapping lazily on the surface of the blue water behind them.

"You're melting," he announced with a grin, reaching out a fingertip and running it beneath her right eye.

"Oh, my makeup!" She slipped under the water again and

scrubbed at her eyelids before emerging sparkly lashed, and asking if she was still discolored.

"Yes, but leave it. It's very Greta Garbo."

"You're a very good swimmer."

"So are you."

"As I said before, it was about the only physical exercise that was easy for me when I was growing up. But I kind of gave it up too, when I was in my late teens, because I was afraid it would...well, build up the muscles all the more, if you know what I mean."

He was studying her wet face carefully. "It seems like there are a lot of things you had to give up that I'd never have suspected."

"Yes, well that's all over now. I'm a new person."

"Theresa, is it...well, are you sure you aren't overdoing it, swimming so hard? It worries me, even though you said you're a hundred percent again."

As if to reaffirm her full recovery, she caught the edge of the pool and boosted herself up, twisting to a sitting position above him with her feet dangling in the water. "One hundred percent, Brian."

He joined her on the edge of the pool. She flung her hair back, feeling his eyes following each movement as she wrung her hair out and sent rivulets running down her back and over her shoulder. Beneath them the concrete was sun-warmed, and the water soon joined their flesh to the sleek surface with a tepid slipperiness.

He ran his hands over his cheeks to clear them of excess water, then wove his fingers through his hair, running them toward the back of his head, and studying the umbrella at the far end of the pool as he asked quietly, "Theresa, would you feel self-conscious answering some questions about your operation?"

"Probably. But ask them anyway. I've been working very

hard on my self-image and on trying to overcome self-consciousness. But if you don't mind, I'd better have a little lotion on my face and back. I feel like most of it washed off.''

They got to their feet, leaving dark gray footprints along the concrete as they made their way toward the opposite end of the pool. Theresa dried her hair, then spread her towel out on the soft grass and sat down on it while applying lotion to her face once more. When she was done, she flipped over and stretched out full length on her stomach, thinking it would be infinitely easier to answer his questions if she wasn't looking at him.

His hands eased over her skin, spreading it with lotion once more while he asked quietly, ''When did you decide to have it done?''

''Remember when I wrote and told you I slipped in the parking lot and fell down?''

''I remember.''

''It was right after that. When the doctor examined my back he told me I should look into having the problem solved permanently.''

''Your back?''

''There's a lot of back and shoulder discomfort that goes along with it. People don't know that. The shoulders are especially vulnerable. I thought probably you'd noticed the grooves—they still show a little bit.''

''These?'' His fingertips massaged one of her shoulders, and she felt a heavenly thrill ripple through her body before he went on, ''I wasn't exactly looking at your shoulders before, but I see the marks now. What else? Tell me everything about it. Was it hard for you, psychologically, I mean?''

Belly down, on a beach towel, with her cheek on the back of her hand, with her eyes closed, she told Brian everything. All about her misgivings, her mother's and father's initial reactions to her decision, her fears and uncertainties, omitting the fact that the feeling had not yet returned to her nipples. She couldn't force herself to share that intimacy with him yet. If and when the time came, she'd be honest, but for now she glossed over that and the part about being unable to nurse a baby.

When her recital was finished, he was still sitting beside her with his arm circling one updrawn knee. His voice was soft and disarming.

"Theresa, I'm sorry for getting mad at you my first night back. I never understood about a lot of it."

"I know. And I'm sorry I didn't at least write and tell Jeff, and let him tell you what my plans were."

"No, you were right. You didn't owe me anything. That first night when we went for a walk, I'll admit part of my problem was I was scared. I thought maybe now that you'd taken the big step you'd be out for bigger fish than this underage guitar man whose past isn't quite as pure as you deserve."

His words brought her head up. Bracing on one elbow she twisted to look back over her shoulder at him. "I long ago stopped placing any importance on the differences in our ages. You're more mature than most of the thirty-year-old men I work with at school. Maybe that's why you were so...I don't know. Understanding, I guess. Right from the first, I sensed that you were different from all the others I'd ever met, that you really did look into me, the person, and judge me by my inner qualities or shortcomings."

"Shortcomings?" He flopped down on his back almost underneath her partially lifted chest and touched the tangled locks above her left ear. "You don't have any shortcomings, sweets."

"Oh, yes I do. Everybody does."

"Where they been hidin'?"

She smiled at his playfulness, glanced down at her forearm, and answered, "Several thousand of them have been lurking just below the surface of my skin and are just now coming out to introduce themselves.''

Indeed, her ''heat spots'' were heating up. The freckles on her arms had already grown so fat their perimeters were dissolving into one another.

He rolled his cheek against the towel, pulled her soft inner arm to his lips, and declared quietly, ''Angel kisses.'' He kissed her again, higher, almost at the bend of elbow. ''Have you been kissing any angels lately, Miss Brubaker?''

She studied his green eyes, and let her feelings show in her own. ''Not as often as I want to.'' She smiled and added impulsively, ''Gabriel.''

''Then what do you say we remedy that?'' With a swift flexing of muscle, he was on his feet, reaching out a hand to tug her up. He gathered towels, togs and lotion and handed her the bag. She followed willingly, walking at his side while one light hand guided her shoulders as she crossed the grass toward the sliding door of his apartment.

She stepped inside where it was cool and shaded. She heard him snap the lock on the screen door, then step to the drapery cord and draw the curtain closed until the midday light was even more subdued through the open weave of the fabric. It threw gentle checkers across the thick carpet and her bare toes. She had the fleeting thought that her hair was probably plastered to her head in some places and flying at odd angles in others, and that her makeup was all washed away. Behind her she heard a metallic click, then the soft *shhh* of a needle settling onto a disc. She was frantically scrambling to find her comb in the bottom of the tote bag when a guitar introduction softly filled the room, and an insistent hand captured the drawstring bag and pulled it from her nervous fingers, as if Brian would brook no delays, no repairs, no excuses.

My world is like a river
As dark as it is deep....

As the poignant words met her ears, she was turned around by lean, hard fingers that closed over the sensitive spot where her neck met her shoulders. When his eyes delved into hers, he wordlessly searched out her palms and carried them up around his neck. His body was moving in rhythm to the music but so very slightly she scarcely felt the evocative sway of his shoulders beneath the soft flesh of her inner arms. But some magical force made her body answer the almost imperceptible beckoning as he swayed, drawing nearer and nearer until the fabric of her suit brushed the hair upon his chest. The invitation was wordless at first, as his warm palms found her naked back and pressed her lightly against him. Then he began humming softly, drawing away only far enough to continue searching her uplifted face while his palm gently caressed the hollow between her shoulder blades, then traced the depression down her spine. With only the slightest force he urged her hips closer, closer, until her bare stomach touched his—sleek to rough. He undulated slowly as if bidding her to join him. She responded with a first hesitant movement until she felt his hips and loins, confined by the taut piece of clothing that covered him, pressed firmly against her.

His breath was warm upon her mouth as he touched it first with the tip of his tongue, then lightly with the outermost surfaces of his lips. He was still humming. As her lips dropped open she felt the soft intonation tickling the crests of them. The sound, the feeling and his careful doling out of contact served only to tantalize, then he lifted his head and began singing the refrain that had been in her heart since she'd heard him sing the words with the battered old fifteen-dollar Stella in his lap.

Sweet memories,
Sweet memories....

When the voice on the record hummed the final notes and took the song home, she was settled securely against the full, hard length of Brian's body, feeling all its surfaces, ridges and textures as if she were on an elevated plane of sensory awareness.

In the thundering silence between songs, his hard body and soft voice combined in a message of latent passion. "Theresa, I love you, girl...so much...so much." It seemed too sweeping to take in. Their bodies no longer moved, but were pressed together until the naked skin of his thighs and belly seemed bonded to hers by the slightly oily, very fragrant suntan lotion whose aroma evoked images of tropical islands, warm sunlit shores and the calls of cockatoos. Her senses were filled with the smell of him, his warmth and firmness, but mostly with the sleek texture of his skin.

"Brian...my guitar man, I think I started loving you when you stepped off that plane and looked me square in the eye."

Another song had begun, but its rhythm went unheeded, for they were entwined in each other's arms, hearing only the beats of their hearts pressed together with nothing but two triangles of thin green material between them. The kiss lost all tentativeness and blossomed into a full complementary exchange of sleek tongues and throaty murmurs. His head moved sensuously above hers, wooing and winning her slow, sure acquiescences. Her inhibitions began dissolving until he felt her hips reaching toward a closer communion with his as she raised up on tiptoe to mold her curves more securely against his, all the while clinging to his sleek shoulders.

His palms moved down to learn the shape of her firm hipbones once more, then the solid flesh of her rounded buttocks, cupping them in both hands as he drew close.

He tore his mouth from hers, his eyes glowing with the fire of a passion too long denied. "Sweets, I promised I wouldn't

come back here and force this issue. I said I'd take it slow,
and give you time to—"

"I've had twenty-six years, Brian. That's long enough."

When he lifted his head she felt deprived at the loss of his
warm lips and reached with her own, as if she suddenly
couldn't get her fill of these long-delayed joys.

"Do you mean it, Theresa? Are you sure?"

"I'm sure. Oh, Brian, I'm so sure it hurts...right here." She
took her palm and pressed it against her heart. "I thought I'd
be afraid and uncertain when this moment came, but I'm not.
Not at all. Somehow, when you love, you know." She gazed
up at him in wonder, touching his lips with her fingertips.
"You just know," she breathed.

"Yes, you know, darling."

Slowly he covered her shoulders with his hands and pressed
her away from him to gaze into her ardent eyes while he spoke.
"I want you to look around at this room." She felt herself
turned until her bare back was pressed against his rough-
textured chest. From behind he circled her ribs, his forearms
resting just below her breasts, touching their undersides. "This
room has no furniture because I wanted us to pick it out together. I thought about waiting to ask you until afterward, but
I find I want to know first. Will you marry me, Theresa? Just
as soon as it can be arranged? And we can fill this place with
furniture and your piano and music and maybe a couple of
kids, and make sweet memories for the rest of—"

"Yes!" She spun and looped her arms around his neck, cutting off his words with the kiss and muffled word before lifting
her mouth from his and singing, "Yes, yes, yes! I didn't know
whether I wanted you to ask me before or after but it's probably
best before, 'cause I probably won't do so well...." His eyebrows drew into a puzzled frown. "I'm not experienced at this
part," she explained diffidently.

The next minute she was scooped up into his arms and felt

his hard belly against her hip while he carried her down the hall to his bedroom.

"Trust me. You will be, as soon as it can be arranged."

From the bedroom doorway where he paused, she saw her marriage bed for the first time. It looked like any other bed, covered with a quilted spread of brown-and-blue geometric design that matched the two sheets haphazardly thrown over the curtain rods to lend the room privacy.

"I never thought to ask you before I bought a waterbed if you like them or not."

"Can a person get seasick on it?"

"I hope not."

With her arms looped around his neck she drew his head down until his mouth joined hers. Muffled against his lips she muttered, "Well, I brought plenty of dramamine pills along, just in case."

Chapter Sixteen

The trip to the bed in Brian's arms was like crossing the bridge of a rainbow connecting the earth to heaven. When she was a girl, Theresa had wondered, as all girls do from the time they feel the first stirrings of maturity, what the man would be like when the moment came? And the setting—would it be dark? Winter or summer? Day or night? Inside or outside? And our first intimate encounter—would it be rushed or slow? Silent or vocal? Reckless or poignant? Would it leave me feeling more—or less?

The sheets rippled at the windows. The sun brought the blue-and-brown pattern alive, backlighting it until the entwined diamonds and parallellograms danced upon the shimmering fabric, while from outside came the faraway voices of children who clanged the gate to the pool area, then whooped gleefully as they took their first plunge.

From the living room came the strains of love songs, distant now, unintrusive, but mellow and wooing. Brian's bare feet moved soundlessly across the cocoa-colored carpet. His lips wore a faint smile, and his steady eyes rested upon Theresa's while he sat on the edge of the bed with her legs across his lap. She felt a faint surge of liquid motion lift them momentarily, then subside. Twisting at the hip he placed her the wrong way across the bed, across its width, lying on his side next to her with his knees slightly updrawn.

He braced up on one elbow, smiling down into her face, running the tip of an index finger along the rim of her lower lip. The smile had drifted from her face, and her lingering apprehensions were reflected in the wide brown eyes and the slightly parted lips.

"Are you scared?" he asked softly.

She swallowed and nodded. "A little."

"About anything in particular?"

"My lack of experience, among other things."

"Experience will take care of itself. What are the other things?" His fingers trailed along her jaw and began gently freeing the strands of hair from about her temples, absently arranging them in a bright corona about her head.

Already she felt the telltale blush climbing her chest. "I...." The words stuck, creating a tight knot in the center of her chest. "I don't...." His eyes left the hair he'd been toying with and met hers, but his fingers were still threaded through the red strands, resting upon the warm skull just above the left ear. "Oh, Brian." She covered her face with both hands. "This is so hard, and I know I'm blushing terribly, and there's nothing less becoming to a redhead than blushing, and I've never—"

"Theresa!" His gentle reprimand cut her off as he circled her wrists and forced her hands away from her face. She stared up at him in silence. The reprimand left his voice, and it became compelling. "I love you. Did you forget that? There's nothing you can't tell me. Whatever it is, we'll work it out together, all right? And, just to set the record straight, redheads look darling when they blush. Now, would you like to start again?"

The muscles in her stomach were jumping. Her fists were clenched, the tendons tight beneath his grasp. She sucked in a huge, fortifying gulp of air and ran the words out so fast she wouldn't have a chance to change her mind. "I - don't - want - to - get - pregnant - and - I - went - to - the - drugstore - yesterday - and - bought - something - to - make - sure - I -

wouldn't - but - the - instructions - said - I - had - to - use - it - half - an - hour - before - and - I - don't - know - before - *what* - or - how - long - anything - takes - because - I've - never - done - this - before - and - oh - please - Brian - let - my - hands - go - so - I - can - hide - behind - them!''

To Theresa's amazement, he laughed lovingly and wrapped her in both of his arms, falling to his side and taking her along until they lay almost nose to nose. ''Is that all? Ah, sweet Theresa, what a joy you are.'' He kissed the tip of her very red nose, then lay back, running a finger along the crest of her cheek. His voice was quiet and calm. ''I had the same thought myself, so I came prepared, too. That means you have a choice, sweetheart. You or me.''

She tried to say me, but the word refused to come out, so she only nodded.

''Well, now's the time.'' He sat up and tugged her along after him, and she padded to the living room for her purse, then back down the hall toward the bathroom.

When she returned to the bedroom he was lying on his back across the bed, still in his swimtrunks, with his arm folded behind his head.

Through the open doorway he had watched the green bathing suit appear as she opened the bathroom door, crossed the hall and approached the bed. Long before she reached it, he'd extended a palm in invitation.

''Come here, little one.''

She lifted one knee to the edge of the bed, placing her palm in his, and let him tug her down until she fell into the hollow of his arm, partially across his chest. The water stirred beneath them, then went still. His right arm remained beneath his head, but even one-handed he eased her closer, tighter, until she hovered above him, and his eyes conveyed the remainder of the message. She bent her head to touch his lips with her own, and the kiss began with a meeting no heavier than the morning mist settling upon a lily. It expanded into the first brief touch of tongue tips—tentative, introductory, promising. He tasted slightly sweet, as if some of the tropical sunscreen still lingered on his lips. His tongue sought the deeper secrets of her mouth, and hers his. Seek, touch, stroke, chase, devour—they shared each advancing step of the intimate kiss. Longing sang through her veins, enlivening each of her senses until she perceived each touch, sound, taste, sight and smell with that new, exultant keenness she'd discovered for the first time today. His relaxed pose lifted the firm muscles of his chest and exposed them in a way that invited exploration.

She let her hand seek out his neck first, recalling the throaty sound he'd uttered when she'd stroked that soft hollow once before. She allowed her thumb to explore the hard knot of his Adam's apple, and beneath the soft pad, the masculine point jumped as he swallowed. When her thumb slid down to the shallow well at its base, she felt his pulse racing there, pressing against her finger like a knocking engine.

It had happened again, that response she could kindle so effortlessly in this man. She sensed it and experimented, a little bit more. Her hand left his neck and flattened upon the firm rise of his chest, experiencing the rough texture of hair, then the tiny point of his nipple, which she first fanned, then scissored between her fingers, while bracing over him, moving her lips downward to touch the warm skin on his chest. She tasted him. Sweet oil and salt and sun and chlorine and coconut and papaya. She had not dreamed he would have taste, yet he did, and it was heady and sensual. Beneath her tongue the rough hairs of his body felt magnified, yet silky. Upon her lips she felt the faint oily residue left behind by the sunscreen. He was warm and resilient and utterly male.

Lifting her head, she felt drugged by senses that had sprung to life from the shield behind which they'd been protected for so many years. Suddenly she was eager to know all, feel all, to glut herself on every texture, hue and scent his body possessed. Her eyes met his, then dropped to travel across the shadowed throat, his ear, his nipples, his jaw where a tiny, tiny scab remained from some incidental nick of razor, perhaps. She touched it with a single fingertip, then pressed the length of her palm along the underside of the biceps of the arm bent beneath his head. She ran the hand down to his armpit, awed that even the wiry hair there could be something she craved to know, simply because it was part of his physical makeup.

"Brian," she breathed, looking into his eyes. "I'm like a child tasting candy for the first time. I never knew all these things before. I have so much to catch up on!"

"Catch then. We have a good seventy years."

A flickering smile passed her features, but was gone again, wiped away by this new rapt interest in his body. He closed his eyes, and like an eager child she twisted onto one hip, bracing a palm on the bed to get a better overview of this delicacy called Brian Scanlon. Still it wasn't enough. Finally, she pulled both legs up beneath her and sat on her haunches at his hip—looking, touching, familiarizing.

"You're...exquisite!" she marveled. "I never thought a man could be exquisite, but you are." His belly was hard, his ribs tapering to the indentation of his waist, just above the spot where his trunks sliced his abdomen. Within the white trunks she saw the mysterious raised contours of his arousal and wondered if it hurt him to be bound up so tightly.

She lifted her eyes to his and found he'd been watching her. A charming, lopsided grin bent the corner of his mouth.

"Darling girl." He lazily lifted his hand and ran a finger along the path of one string of her tie top, starting at the side of her neck, traveling beside it to the point where it met the band beneath her breasts. She shuddered with delight. "I don't think I'm the one who's exquisite." The finger idled up the opposite strap. Her eyelids felt weighted and a coil of anticipation wound through her stomach. His four fingertips traced the line of her collarbone, then moved downward, drawing a quartet of invisible Ss along the freckled mound of her breast. The faint tickle lifted the fine hairs on her bare stomach. He gave the other breast equal attention, fingering her skin with the brush of a dragonfly's wings. Her eyelids slid closed, and her head drooped slightly backward, listing to one side while his callused fingertips followed the first strap again, but this time also moved over the shimmery green triangle of fabric to graze the hidden, uptilted nipple that gave an unexpected spurt of sensation down her arms, stomach and straight to the seat of her femininity.

Her eyelids flew open. "Brian!"

A troubled look crossed his features as he misread her exclamation and withdrew his hand.

"Brian! There's feeling there!"

"What?" His fingers poised in midair.

"There's feeling there! It happened, when you touched me just then, something slithery and fiery went...went whooshing down my body, and...oh, Brian, don't you see? The doctor said sometimes the sensation never returns, and I've been scared to death thinking it hadn't come back to me."

He braced up on one elbow and cupped her jaw. "You never told me before."

"I am now, but oh Brian, it doesn't matter anymore, oh please, do it again!" she begged excitedly. "I want to make sure I wasn't just imagining it."

He toppled her over beside him, his lips joining hers to press her onto her back as his hand roamed across her ribs, and up, but stopped just short of her breast.

He lifted his head and she opened her eyes to find him gazing down intently into her eyes, his brows lowered in concern. "I won't hurt you, will I?"

"No," she whispered.

His mouth and hand moved simultaneously, the one to bestow a kiss, the other a caress. He contoured the warm globe of flesh with his palm, gently at first, then with growing pressure, squeezing, fondling, finally seeking out the nipple, which he tenderly explored through the slip of sheeny, damp material.

Her lips went slack and she dropped her shoulders flat to the bed, lolling in the new feelings of arousal. It was slighter than before, but there just the same. She concentrated hard on grasping it, blindly guiding his hand to the exact spot she thought would revive the strong spurt of sensation as before.

Braced above her, he watched the feelings parade across her face, and at last he reached for the bow at the nape of her neck. Her eyes opened as she felt it slipping free, but just before he could lower the green triangle, she stopped his hand.

"Brian, I have scars, but please don't let them stop you. They'll be there for several months yet, but then they'll fade. And they don't hurt, they only itch sometimes."

Some softening expression around his eyes told her he understood, and accepted. Then he peeled the first green tidbit of fabric down and laid it over her ribs, while she watched his eyes. They dropped to the vertical red scar, then flew back to her brown gaze. Wordlessly he stripped down the other half of the bathing suit top.

Where was the shame she had once known? Absent. Evaporated beneath the far greater impact of the loving concern that emanated from Brian's face.

He slipped his hands behind her back and came away with the suit top, then tossed it onto the pillows and rolled to give her his full attention again.

"How can it not hurt?" Gently he cupped her right breast, riding his thumb up the scar, then lightly, lightly circling the nipple. "Did they make an incision here?"

"Yes, but that scar is all healed."

"And here, too." He traced the faded crescent beneath, to

its inception just below her armpit. "Oh God, it hurts me to think of them doing that to you." He lowered his head, trailing his lips along the lower contour scar.

"Brian, it's all over, and it wasn't nearly as bad as you'd think. If I hadn't done it, I might not have been able to overcome all my hangups and be here with you. I feel so different. So...."

He lifted his head and searched her with tortured eyes. "What do you feel? So...what?"

"Beautiful," she admitted, with a lingering note of shyness. "Feature that, would you?" She smiled and her voice became soft and accepting. "Theresa Brubaker with her red hair and freckles, feeling beautiful. But it's partly because of you. Because of how you treated me last Christmas. You made me believe I had the right to feel this way. You were all the things I'd ever hoped to find in a man."

"I love you." His voice was strange, throaty and deep, and not wholly steady. He dipped his head and touched his lips to the cinnamon-colored dots between her breasts. "Every freckle of you." He moved his mouth to the gentle swelling mound. "Every red hair of you." And finally to the crest. "Every square inch of you."

He adored her with the gentle strokes of his tongue, and she lay in a blaze of emotions that sprang more from her consummate love for him than from the part of her he tenderly kissed.

"What's happening?" he queried, running his tongue down along the underside of her breast.

She sucked in a breath as a sensual response shuddered down her backbone. "I'm falling in love with my body, and your body, and what they can do to each other. I'm plunging through space...freefalling. Only it's so strange...I'm falling up."

He ran his tongue up to her nipple again, and closed his lips and tongue around it, murmuring some wordless accolade deep in his throat, while both of his arms reached behind her and his hands slid down to cup her buttocks and roll her firmly against him, both of them now on their sides.

"Mmm...you taste like summer...."

"Tell me," she whispered, threading her fingers through his hair, knowing an insatiable appetite for his words, as well as for his arousing touches.

"Sandy beaches and suntan oil that tastes like Popsicles and the sweetest fruit in the jungle...." He lightly nipped the top of a breast with his teeth. "Berries and coconut..." He slipped lower, licking the sensitive skin on the rib. "Mangos and kiwi... Mmm...." His mouth pressed moistly upon the softest part of her abdomen, just above the navel. "There's something else here...wait, let me see...." He dipped his tongue into her navel and made several seductive circles around and within it. "Mmm...I think it's passion fruit."

She felt him smile against her belly and smiled in return.

His mouth was arousingly warm, and his breath heated the silky triangle of fabric still covering her. His chest weighted her legs, then he lightly bit her through the bathing suit—fabric, hair and a little skin. Her ribs lifted off the bedspread, and she gasped while desire welled and bubbled over in her feminine depths. His fingers found the sensitive skin at the back of her knee, then his mouth warmed the flesh that she'd thought could not possibly know a heat any greater than it had already experienced. She trembled and lifted her hips from the bed, offering herself as fully as he cared to partake. He kissed her through the silky bikini and worked his chin firmly against the throbbing flesh within until she found herself moving against the hardness, seeking something...something....

And when her desire had grown to its fullest, he moved back up to join his mouth to hers, running his palms along the elastic waist of her briefs, then down inside to cup her firm backside while rolling his weight fully on top of hers, his hips undulating

against hers while their mouths locked in a bond of mutual
desire.

His weight lifted. She felt the wisp of fabric leave the juncture of her legs and inch downward along her thighs, then pass
lower still until his mouth was forced to leave hers, and he
eased the garment down and off, then tossed it over his shoulder to join its mate on the pillows.

He pressed her back, back, against the bed and caressed her
bare stomach with his musician's fingers that were capable, she
learned, of much more than adroitly strumming love songs.
They raised a kind of music in her flesh as he explored the soft
skin of her inner thighs, then the most intimate part of her
body.

She was eager, and open, and not in the least abashed by his
touch that sought and entered her virgin flesh. Love, that gift
of the gods, took away all insecurities, all timidity, all shame,
and allowed her the freedom to express her newfound femininity in the way she had so long dreamed.

A soft, passionate sound issued from her throat. She
stretched and allowed him total access to explore her as he
would, trembling at times, smiling at others, her heart a wild
thing in her breast.

But just short of taking her over the edge of bliss, he lay
back. And then it was her turn to explore. "Experience will
take care of itself," Brian had said. And she believed it as she
embarked upon her half of this maiden voyage toward mutuality.

She found the tight waist of his trunks and slipped her palms
inside, against the skin of his lower spine, finding it cool from
the slightly damp fabric.

Her caresses were restricted by the taut garment, yet she
thrilled at the firmness beneath her palms and the inviting
rhythm her touch had set off in his hips. He reached behind
his back, found her arm and carried it up out of the elastic and

around to his front, pressing it against the flattened, hidden hills between his legs, moving against her palm to initiate it into the ways of sexual contact.

To Theresa's amazement, her own voice begged throatily, "Take it off, Brian, please."

The words were partially muffled by his lips, but when the request had been made, he lifted his head and smiled into her beseeching eyes, his breath beating warmly upon her face.

"Anything you say, love."

He slipped to the edge of the bed, and she rolled onto her side and curled her body up like a lazy caterpillar, watching as he reached inside the garment and found a hidden string against his belly, tugged it, then stood and skinned the trunks down, down, down, before dropping to sit on the edge of the bed again and kicking the suit away across the carpet as he rolled toward her, reaching.

He was beautiful, and somehow it seemed the most natural thing in the world to reach out and caress him.

"Oh, Brian, you're silky...and so hot."

"So are you. But I think that's how we're supposed to be." He reached again for the entrance to her womanhood, touching it with a sleek, knowing rhythm until sensation dazzled her nerve endings. She closed her eyes and undulated with the protracted and relentless stroking.

"Brian, something's happening!"

"Let it. Shh...."

"But...but...." It was too late to wonder if it was torture or treasure, for in the next instant the question was answered for Theresa. A burst of sensation lifted her limbs and sent liquid explosions rocketing outward. Then she was shuddering, feeling spasms from the deepest reaches of her body, until she fell back sated, exhausted, gasping.

"Oh, sweet, sweet woman. The first time," he said against

her neck after a minute, still holding her tightly. "Do you know how rare that is?"

"No...I thought from the movies that it happens to everyone."

"Not women, not all the time. Usually just men. You must have been storing it all these years, waiting for the right one to come along and set it free."

"And he did."

He smiled lovingly into her eyes, then kissed each lid, then her nose, then her swollen lips. And while he strung the kisses upon her face, he raised his body over hers and pressed it firmly to her entire length.

"I love you, darling—keep remembering that in case it hurts."

"I love you, Br—"

She never finished the word, for in that instant he entered her and she knew the sleek ligature of their two joined bodies, but no pain, only texture and heightened sensations building once again as his hips moved above hers. She felt only pleasure as he began moving, reaching back to teach her how to lift her knees and create a nesting place of warm, firm flesh that buttressed his hips as he shared the consummation of their love.

When he clenched his fists and quivered, she opened her eyes to find his closed in ecstasy. He rode the crest of his climax while she watched the reaction expressed on his beloved features—the closed, trembling eyelids, the flaring nostrils and the lips that pulled back in a near grimace as sweat broke out on his back and the muscles rippled for an exhausted moment. Then he shivered a last interminable time, called out at the final peak, and relaxed.

So this is why I was born a woman and Brian Scanlon was born a man, why we were meant to seek and find each other in this world of strangers. She caressed his shoulder blades, coveting the dead weight of him pressing her into the resilient water-filled baffles beneath her.

"Oh, Brian it was so good...so good."

He rolled to his side and opened his eyes, lifting one hand that appeared too tired to quite succeed in the effort of caressing her face. It fell upon her cheek.

He chuckled—a rich, resonant sound from deep in his chest and closed his eyes and sighed, then lay unmoving.

She studied him in repose, smoothed the tousled hair above his temple. His eyes didn't open, and his palm didn't move. She knew an abiding sense of completion.

The noon sun lit the ceiling of the room by some magical twist of physics. The sheets at the window riffled lightly, and the sounds of the pool activity were constant now. From the living room came the repeated songs of the same record—she smiled, wondering how many times it had played.

"Do you know when I first became intrigued with you?"

She turned to find his eyes open, watching her. "When?"

They were still entwined, and he pulled her closer to keep possession of her while he went on. "It started when Jeff let me read a letter from you. In it you said you'd gone out on a date with somebody named Lyle, and he turned out to be Jack the Gripper."

She chuckled, recalling both the letter and the disastrous date.

"That long ago?"

"Uh-huh. Two years or more. Anyway, after we laughed about it, and I wondered what kind of woman had written it, I began asking questions about you. Little by little I learned everything. About your red hair." He threaded his fingers into it just where her widow's peak would have been, had she one. "And your freckles." He trailed a finger down her nose. "And your endowment." He passed a palm down her breast. "And about the time Jeff defended you and punched out that kid, and about how you taught music in an elementary school and played violin, and how Jeff thought the sun rose and set in you, and how much he wanted you to be happy, to find some man who'd treat you honorably and wouldn't ogle and grope and grip.''

"Two years ago?" she repeated, stunned.

"Longer than that. Closer to three now. Since Jeff and I were in Germany together. Anyway, when I saw your picture. It was one of your school pictures, and you were wearing a gray sweater buttoned around your shoulders, with a little white blouse collar showing from beneath. I asked Jeff a lot of questions then, and pieced together a picture of you and your hang-up even before I knew you. There have been times when I even suspected that Jeff filled me in on all the details about you in hopes that when I met you I'd be the first man to treat you right, and end up doing exactly what I just did.''

"Jeff?" she exclaimed, surprised.

"Jeff. Didn't you ever suspect that he engineered this whole thing from the start, feeding me tidbits about his marvelous, straight sister, who'd never had boyfriends, but who had so much to offer a man—the right man.''

She braced up on one elbow and looked thoughtful. "Jeff! You really think so?"

"Yes, I do. As a matter of fact, he all but admitted it when we were on the plane back after Christmas. He suspected things had fired up between us and came right out and said it'd been on his mind a while that he wouldn't mind me as a brother-in-law.''

She smirked and lifted a delicate jaw. "Remind me to give old Jeff a gigantic thank-you kiss next time I see him, huh?"

"And what about you? When did you start thinking of me as a potential lover?"

"The truth?" She peered up at him coquettishly.

"The truth."

"That night in the theater, when the love scene was on the screen. Your elbow was sharing the armrest with mine, and when the woman climaxed, your bones were almost cutting off my blood supply. Then when the man's face came on, showing him in the throes of rapture, your elbow nearly broke mine, and when it was over, *you* wilted."

"Me?" he yelped disbelievingly. "I did not!"

"You did too. I was practically dying of embarrassment, and then you dropped your hands down to cover your lap, and I wanted to crawl underneath the seats."

"Are you serious? Did I really do that?"

"Of course I'm serious. Would I lie about a thing like that? I was so turned on myself I hardly knew what to do about it. Part of it was the movie, but part of it was you and your arm. After that I couldn't help wondering what it would be like with you. Somehow I knew you'd be good...and gentle...and just what a freckled redhead needed to make her feel like Cinderella."

"Do I make you feel like Cinderella?"

She studied him for a long moment, traced his lips with an index finger and nodded.

He captured the finger, bit it, then as his eyes closed, he lay very still, pressing her four fingertips against his lips.

"What are you thinking?" she whispered.

His eyes opened, but for a moment he didn't answer. Instead he pressed his palm to hers and threaded their fingers together with slow deliberation. His fingers squeezed possessively. Hers answered. "About tomorrow. And the day after that and the day after that, and how we'll never have to be alone again. There'll always be each other...and babies." His fingers gripped more tightly. His eyes probed hers. "Do you want babies, Theresa?"

He felt her grip relax, then tug away. His stomach went light with warning, and he gripped her hand to keep it from escaping. "Theresa?"

She gazed at his face, wide-eyed, and when he saw the color begin to heighten between her freckles, he leaned above her on an elbow, frowning. "Theresa, what is it?"

She brushed his chest with her fingertips, dropping her eyes to follow the movement instead of meeting his frown. "Brian, there's something I haven't told you about my surgery."

In a split second a dozen fledgling fears spiraled through him, all dire: the surgery had somehow taken away more than met the eye, and they'd never have the babies he was dreaming of.

"Oh no, Brian, not that." She read his trepidation, soothingly bracketed his jaws. "I can have babies—all I want. And I *do* want them. But...." Again she dropped her eyes while her fingers rested against his chest. "But I'll never be able to nurse them. Not after the surgery."

For a moment he was still, waiting for the worst. Suddenly he crushed her tightly. "Is that all?" he sighed, relieved. She hadn't known he was holding his breath until it rushed out heavily upon her temple. Her lips were on his warm collarbone as he secured her fast and rocked her in his arms.

"It doesn't matter to me, but I thought you should know. I thought in case you had any feelings about it we should talk about it now. Some men might consider me only...well, half a woman or something."

He pulled back sharply. "Half a woman?" He sounded gruff as he squeezed her shoulders. "Never think it." Their eyes locked, and she read in his total love and approval. "Think about this." He drew her into the warm curve of his body as he rolled aside and snuggled her so near, his heartbeat was like a drum beneath her ear. "Think about everything we'll have some day—a house where there'll always be music and a gang of little redheaded rascals whose—"

"Brown-haired," she interrupted, smiling against his chest.

He went on with scarcely a missed beat. "Redheaded rascals whose freckles dance when—"

"Oh no! No freckles! If you give me freckled, redheaded babies, Brian Scanlon, I'll—"

The rest was smothered by his kiss before he grinned at her, continuing. "Redheaded rascals whose freckles dance when they play their violins—"

"Guitars. I won't have anybody hiding under any violins!"

"Mrs. Scanlon, will you kindly stop complaining about this family of ours? I said they'll be redheads and I meant it. And they'll play violin in the orchestra and—"

"Guitars," she insisted. "In a band. And their hair will be deep brown like their daddy's."

She threaded her fingers through it and their eyes met, heavy-lidded again with resurgent desire. Their bodies stirred against each other, their lips met, tongues sipped, and hearts clamored.

"Let's compromise," she suggested, scarcely aware of what she was saying, for already his hips were moving against hers.

He began speaking, but his voice was gruff and distracted. "Some redheads, some brown, some with freckles, some with guitars, some with vio—"

Her sweet seeking mouth interrupted. "Mmm-hmm..." she murmured against his lips. "But it'll take lots of practice to make all those babies." Her breasts pressed provocatively against his chest. She writhed once, experimentally, glorying in her newly discovered freedom. "Show me how we'll do it."

Their open mouths clung. His strong arm curved beneath her and rolled her atop him, then he settled her hips upon his, found the soft hollows behind her knees and drew them down until she straddled him in soft, feminine flesh. He pressed her hips away, and ordered thickly against her forehead, "Love me."

Her heart surged with shyness. Then love moved her hand. Hesitantly she reached, found, then surrounded.

Their smiles met, faltered, dissolved. Eyelids lowered as she settled firmly upon him. A guttural sound of satisfaction rumbled from his throat, answered by her softer, wordless reply. Experimentally she lifted, dropped, warming to his encouraging hands on her hips.

Drawing back, she found his eyes still shuttered, the lids trembling.

"Oh, Brian…Brian…I love you so much," she vowed with tears beginning to sting.

His eyes opened. For a moment his hands calmed the movement of her hips, then they reached to draw her face down as he kissed the outer corner of each eye. "And I love you, sweets…always," he whispered, drawing her mouth to his to complete the promise within it. "Always…always."

In the living room a forgotten record circled, circled, sending soft music down the hall. To its lazy rhythm their bodies moved. At the windows, sheets rippled, and beneath two lovers the soft swell of confined water rose up as an afterbeat to their rhythmic union. They would build a repertoire of sweet memories throughout their years as man and wife, but as they moved now, reaffirming their love, it seemed none would be so sweet as this moment that bound them in promise.

When their bodies were gifted with the manifest of that promise, when the sweet swelling peaked and the shudders ceased, they reaffirmed it once again.

"I love you," spoke the man.

"I love you," answered the woman.

It was enough. Together, they moved on toward forever.

One Tough Texan
Jan Freed

To LaVyrle Spencer,
for the joy, for the tears and, most of all,
for the inspiration.

And to West Houston RWA Chapter members,
for the friendship, guidance and support.

PROLOGUE

MATT GRANGER SQUINTED toward the corral fifty yards away and focused on his next ranch mortgage payment. An ugly son of a bitch.

Lug-headed. Sway-backed. Stupid, too. But pure TNT under a saddle. And from the look of the pickup truck cresting the hill, it appeared Matt would have to be the one to light the fuse.

Good thing he was already numb.

Shoving aside thoughts of the phone call he'd received thirty minutes ago, he crossed the porch to the west railing. Evening sun toasted the approaching beige truck golden brown. Gravel crunched and clunked beneath the Ford's underbelly.

A bucking horse decal on the door confirmed the driver's identity. Larry Crane, one of the top rodeo stock contractors in the Southwest.

Piss-poor timing, showing up late, now that Matt's future plans were shot to hell. Then again, what did one more bullet matter?

Don't think about the phone call. Just make the sale.

The truck veered toward the barn and skidded to a stop, spraying dust and shards of quartz. Larry's scouting trips to Texas were erratic, his time in short supply, his cash plentiful. He paid top dollar for good rodeo broncs when he found them. But he never stayed for long.

Sighing, Matt wished his thirty-two-year-old bones could afford to wait for his wrangler's younger and less brittle butt to get back from the Campbell ranch. No such luck.

He walked to the porch steps, clomped down two and stumbled against a knee-high shaggy wall. "Damn it, Pitiful, what is *wrong* with you?"

The huge mongrel lowered his head and blinked, his eyes contrite. But he didn't budge. Behind Matt, the front door rattled open.

Perfect.

"Tell me you ain't thinkin' of ridin' that bronc," a tobacco-roughened voice nagged.

Rolling his eyes heavenward, Matt turned to the grizzled cook who was more father than hired help. "You gonna ride him for me, Hal?"

"I didn't get this old by bein' stupid. You of

all people know better 'n to ride when you ain't thinkin' straight.''

Don't think about the phone call. Just make the sale.

"I'm fine," Matt lied.

"Hell, son, even Pitiful knows you're hurtin'—don't pretend you ain't! Before you rush out 'n' break your fool neck, remember there's a sweet little gal dependin' on you, now.''

Panic swirled up from deep within Matt, stirring the silt of old memories and murky emotions.

"I've got a horse to sell,'' he said flatly, turning to sidestep the dog and continue down the stairs. He hit the overgrown yard at a near jog.

"Family's more important than sellin' a danged horse,'' Hal called out, his raspy voice edged in pain.

Matt angled toward the barn, his clenched teeth blocking the denial climbing up his throat. *Nothing* was more important than making payments on the land he'd financed two years ago. Nothing.

This five-hundred-acre parcel of central Texas Hill Country was something Matt could count on. Something that wouldn't disappoint him. Something he couldn't disappoint in return. It

was a place where he could establish his reputation as a cutting horse trainer and put down
roots.

If he never saw another suitcase in his life,
he'd be happy.

He knew his priorities. And right now the
lanky rodeo stock contractor standing beside the
truck ahead was high on his list.

Slowing, Matt touched the battered brim of
his cowboy hat. "Larry. Good to see you
again."

The older man smiled and tipped his 20X
Black Gold Resistol. Business was obviously
booming.

"Hello, Matt. The place has really come along
since you sold me that dun mare. New round
pen. Fresh paint on the stable—" his roving
gaze stopped on the strawberry roan and twinkled "—new horse in training. He giving Doc
Holiday some competition?"

Matt snorted. Doc's lineage included more
NCHA champions than the roan had teeth. "He
might—if he wouldn't unload his back inside of
five seconds."

"You don't say?" Larry sniffed and hitched
up his pants. "That young wrangler from last

summer around anywhere?'' he asked casually. ''I'd like to see what the roan's got.''

Negotiations were on.

''Casey went to pick up some hay from Ben Campbell and hasn't made it back.'' Matt caught the other man's quick glance at the sinking sun. ''You have any problem with me saddling up, instead?''

Larry did a double take, then broke into a gaptoothed grin. ''Hell, no. I'd be privileged to watch! I thought you'd retired for good when you bought this place.''

Don't think about the phone call. Keep your mind on the ride. Just make the sale.

''Makes sense, though,'' Larry mused before Matt could reply, ''that you'd miss the old days. Training those fancy cutting horses must seem kinda boring.''

Matt could've argued that just the opposite was true, but the light was fading fast. ''Lemme grab some tack out of the barn and I'll show you what a crowd-pleaser you're about to buy.''

''Need some help holding him?''

''Nah. He's a pussycat until weight hits the saddle.''

That's what had fooled so many amateur riders. Matt had been lucky to hear about the roan's bucking talent before the animal had wound up in a tin can.

Five minutes later he jabbed his knee in the bronc's belly, deflating the air the gelding had sucked in to insure a loose cinch. Maybe he wasn't so stupid after all. Yanking the cinch two notches tighter, Matt rechecked the rest of his tack carefully.

One of the keys to his success on the rodeo circuit had been his ability to block out all distractions. To focus totally on his ride. How in hell could he manage that level of concentration after getting today's telephone call?

Mary, Mary, quite contrary...I'm sorry. So sorry.

Exhaling, he slumped against the roan. Like the bronc, he didn't want to be saddled with extra weight, only *he* didn't have the option of bucking. Not this time.

His sister had conceived and raised a child out of wedlock, and never told him. Never told the biological father, either, from the sound of a birth certificate marked "father unknown." Unbelievable. But the document, as well as Matt's name and phone number, had been found in a box of mementos under Mary's bed.

The fact was, he had a five-year-old niece

named Mattie...*Mattie,* for cripe's sake. Mary had named her daughter after him.

The kid was staying with Mary's roommate in California until he could arrive to claim full custody. Of all the reckless, selfish stunts his sister had ever pulled—he'd lost count and patience six years ago—this latest won the championship buckle.

A title Mary would never defend, since she'd gone and gotten herself killed. Matt dragged in a ragged breath.

"Um, you okay there, son?" Larry called from the corral rail.

No. But damned if the world would ever know. Slowly straightening his shoulders, Matt lifted one hand in a reassuring wave, then raised his boot to the stirrup.

Don't think about the phone call. Just cowboy-up and make the sale.

CHAPTER ONE

ABBEY PARKER WATCHED her customer clip on sparkling earrings, lift an oval mirror from the table and coo at his reflection. She had to agree he looked stunning.

Hundreds of Austrian rhinestones flashed and winked in the March sunshine, a dazzling contrast to the five-o'clock shadow beneath his liquid foundation. The glittering yellow and green parrot earrings matched his sarong and tank top beautifully.

Still…

"You know, Edwina," Abbey said from inside her open-air market stall, "I designed those earrings with formal evening occasions in mind. They might be a little inappropriate for the beach."

"Inappropriate?" Frowning in the mirror, he angled his head this way and that.

Just then, three tanned blondes wearing thong bikinis roller-skated through the strolling crowd.

Edwina stared admiringly after the buns of steel until all three men disappeared.

Turning back to Abbey, he arched a plucked brow. "You were saying?"

Good point. This wasn't Baker's Landing, Nebraska, with its stifling restrictions on how to dress, act and believe. On the concrete "boardwalk" of Venice Beach, California, *anything* was appropriate.

Even a drag queen from the Bronx wearing rhinestone earrings at two in the afternoon.

"You're right," Abbey declared. "You look fantastic. And the parrots are perfect with your skirt. There's a bracelet somewhere on this table that I want you to see." She rose halfway from her lawn chair and scanned the display of jewelry. "Ah, here it is."

Snatching up the unhinged bangle, she slapped it over Edwina's wrist and locked the sparkling cuff in place. *Gotcha.*

He sucked in a breath, let it out on a sustained "O-o-oh my gawd. Arrest me now and tell me where to spread." His glance held sincere respect. "This is gorgeous, Abbey!"

She couldn't help her flush of pride and victory. Gluing on all those rhinestones in her poorly lit kitchen had severely strained her eyes.

Validation of her work was sweet. But the prospect of being able to buy new glasses was sweeter.

Edwina rotated the bracelet and peered closer. "What are these little teeny...o-o-oh my gawd, they're parrots! To match the earrings! This is not just jewelry, Abbey. It's art. Mary always said you had real talent..."

He bit his lip, his false eyelashes blinking rapidly. Crimson-tipped fingers patted spectacular fake bosoms, his pectoral cleavage completing the illusion of a well-endowed babe.

"Poor Mary. I still can't believe what happened."

Abbey didn't know why not. It was exactly the sort of recklessness she'd come to expect from her roommate.

"How's my little princess doing?" Edwina asked huskily.

Abbey softened. "I don't think she fully understands that Mary isn't coming home this time." Glancing over her shoulder, she melted further. No need to guard her voice.

Mattie was absorbed in the play world that made her oblivious to conversation and activity outside her imagination. Sprawled on her stomach in a back corner of the canvas-shaded stall, busy with crayons and a coloring book, she escaped the notice of most customers. Safer than being left alone in the apartment. But a crummy place to spend a beautiful Saturday, just the same. Poor thing.

Edwina sniffed twice, then briskly raised the mirror and patted his wig, jiggling a cascade of red curls. "Kids are tougher than you think. You'll see. She'll be fine with Mary's brother."

Abbey wished she felt as confident. *Don't think about the phone call. Just take care of business.*

She pulled her receipt pad into writing position, anxious to compensate for her earlier stupidity. She'd almost talked him out of a sale when every blasted nickel counted.

"You've been admiring those earrings for ten minutes, Edwina. Ready to admit you can't live without 'em?"

He scowled at his reflection. "I really shouldn't spend the money."

"Tell you what. I'll give you a discount if you buy the earrings and bracelet as a set."

He lowered the mirror and leaned into the awning's shade. "How much of a discount?"

"Ten percent."

"Twenty-five."

"Ten." He'd bragged many times to Mary about the money he pulled down performing at The Glass Slipper.

Edwina's blue eyes hardened. Straightening to at least six feet in yellow mule sandals, he made an imposing picture of outrage.

"That's a fair offer," Abbey insisted.

"I can't justify paying so much for costume jewelry."

"I know." Abbey held his narrowed gaze. "That's why I'm so pleased you realize my jewelry is art."

Calypso music bobbed gently on the ocean breeze. Blocks away, an unseen street performer drew scattered applause.

"Will you be paying for that with cash, check or credit card?" she prodded sweetly.

His features slowly relaxed. One corner of his coral-red mouth tipped up. "Why do all the good men pee sitting down these days?"

Abbey chuckled, more flattered than offended. "I take it we have a deal?"

"Yes, you shameless piranha. But hold off on closing out the receipt. I'm not quite finished looking."

He handed over the jewelry with a resigned sigh, then began sorting through an array of brooches on the table. "You could sell these on Abbot Kinney for twice what you get here," he murmured, as if to himself.

She could, if only she could afford to rent space on the historic shopping boulevard. The boutiques and jewelry stores she'd approached wouldn't buy her designs outright. A few had agreed to display Free Bird Jewelry for an exorbitant commission, should it sell. But her profits were greater at the flea market.

Depressing thought. Although things could be worse. She mustn't ever forget that.

Boxing up Edwina's purchases, Abbey let her thoughts drift to the past.

Eight years ago, she might have caved in to Edwina and lowered her price to match her self-esteem. Eternal Light Church of the Lord and Shepherd valued obedience and docility, not self-confidence. Community, not the individual.

Life outside the church was evil. Those who coveted its attractions were sinful. Period. She'd been raised to view the world in black and white.

No tropical-parrot yellow and green allowed.

Abbey's father had doused every spark of creativity or independence in her as it appeared. Her mother, Carla, had watched with sad, defeated eyes and remained passive—except for one time.

The night her frightened nineteen-year-old daughter, betrayed by a handsome face and dazzling smile, had fled Baker's Landing and headed for freedom.

Sweet freedom!

Abbey had not only survived her exposure to the evils of society, she'd resisted them without making judgments, accepted glorious rainbow hues into her life. Three years ago she'd even launched a small business—Free Bird Jewelry— that completed the healing of her spirit in a way that therapy alone hadn't accomplished.

Unfortunately, the income from her custom-designed jewelry was still barely enough to cover basic necessities. Her apartment rent was due next week. Without Mary to kick in her share—

Abbey stopped the thought before it escalated into panic and anger. Yes, Mary's death had created a huge financial and moral dilemma for Abbey. And no, they hadn't exactly been friends.

But the woman hadn't *meant* to slam into a tree trunk beyond the clearly marked boundary of a groomed ski slope. She'd loved her child too much, or as much as Mary was capable of loving anyone. Behind her bold-as-brass facade Abbey had sensed shadows of pain.

"O-o-oh my *gawd,*" Edwina said, drawing Abbey's startled attention.

His hands hovered motionless over a tray of rings. He seemed transfixed by something in the distance.

"What is it?" She sat straight in her chair and tried to follow his gaze. The usual L.A. residents, beach exhibitionists and gawking tourists milled about, as they did every Saturday.

"Major hard-on walking our way at three o'clock."

Abbey blew out a peeved breath and slumped. Beefcakes lumbering stiffly through the crowd from nearby Muscle Beach were *his* fantasy, not hers. She focused on her receipt pad and began writing up Edwina's purchase.

"Would you look at those shoulders? Mmm—mmm—mmm."

Abbey continued writing. "Forgive me for not reacting, but I pee sitting down."

"You don't know what you're missing. I'll bet this cowboy writes his name in the snow a lo-ong way from his boots."

Cowboy? Abbey's pen jerked. A ribbon of dread unfurled in her stomach.

Mercy, it couldn't be! She wasn't ready, hadn't fully prepared Mattie for the uncle who'd

sounded unaffected by Mary's death and dis-
pleased at Mattie's existence. He wasn't due until the funeral on Monday, according to his terse
follow-up phone call.

Leaning forward, Abbey peered cautiously toward three o'clock.

"O-o-oh my god," she breathed.

"Amen, girl," Edwina seconded.

In a place where near-nudity, wild tropical
clothing and weird costumes didn't cause a second glance, this man stood out—or up, depend-
ing on where you started looking.

Abbey started with his black cowboy hat,
which bobbed well above the half-dozen men in
his vicinity, and curved down low on his forehead. He was about thirty feet away, heading in
their direction, studying each vendor stall he
passed.

A bad sign, she acknowledged sickly, looking
down at the pen gouge in her receipt pad.

Her mind scrambled for reassurance. He was
probably a drugstore cowboy strutting his stuff
for the crowd. Yeah, that was it.

Tearing off the ruined receipt, Abbey looked
back at the man in question for substantiating
clues.

His shaded eyes were a mystery, his lips determined above a chin that shouted "Out of my way." Her gaze lowered to a black western-yoked shirt emphasizing wide shoulders and his trim waist. An oval buckle flashed golden sparks to the rhythm of his athletic loose-hipped walk. Boot-cut Wranglers ended in black Ropers eating up the distance to her stall.

Abbey's heartbeat sped up—and not totally from anxiety. Section by section he was beautifully made. But the entire package was beautifully *male*.

This was no pretty-boy model playing cowboy for the tourists. Abbey had a feeling he was the genuine article. Marlboro Man without the advertising contract. She closed her eyes, pictured him on a horse...and knew she was right.

This was Mary's brother. Mattie's uncle.

And Abbey's time had just run out.

"O-o-oh my gawd, he's coming over here," Edwina whispered, sounding slightly breathless.

Abbey sensed the shadow creeping over her glasses. Her eyelids popped open level with a huge oval buckle detailing a bucking horse and rider. Exquisite workmanship, she noted absently before tilting her head back. Way back.

His eyes were a piercing light gray.

"I'm looking for Abbey Parker. I was told she'd be here."

She remembered that distinctive drawl. Lazier than strictly business and Texas deep. The kind of rich masculine timbre that caused a woman to vibrate inside and out.

Shocked at her thrum of pleasure, she could only blink stupidly at the source.

"I'll be Abbey Parker." *Big boy,* Edwina's coy glance added silently. "I can be whoever you want."

The odd stranglehold on Abbey's larynx loosened. She cleared her throat. "I'm Abbey Parker. And Mae West over there is my next-door neighbor, Edwina Drake."

The cowboy's bemused stare moved from Edwina to Abbey. He lifted his hat briefly. "Pleased to meet you."

His hair was as black as onyx.

"I guess you both knew Mary," he continued. "I'm Matt Granger, her brother."

"O-o-oh my gawd." Edwina grabbed his arm and clung. "You're Mary's brother? You don't look anything like her. I mean, she was blond, and such a tiny little thing. And you're so dark and...big. I just adore tall men."

"And I like tall *women,*" Marlboro Man

stated firmly but not unkindly. Removing the scarlet-tipped fingers curled over his biceps, he turned to Abbey and looked her over. "Petite ones, too," he added, smiling.

The deep masculine dimple in his left cheek destroyed any doubt left about his kinship to Mattie. Abbey met indulgent gray eyes and knew they'd seen a lot of women make fools of themselves over that dimple.

The knowledge rankled.

"Edwina's right. You don't look like Mary. How do I know you're her brother? I wasn't expecting him until Monday, and he would've let me know if his plans had changed. Basic common courtesy would've demanded it."

His surprise was comical. "I took advantage of a discount airfare at the last minute."

"Could I see some I.D., please?"

His brows slammed together, then relaxed. "Sure, darlin'. I've got it right here." He framed his belt buckle with both hands and tilted his pelvis.

Through the loud rush of blood to her head, Abbey vaguely heard, "O-oh my gawd." She dragged her attention to the name engraved beneath the title World Champion Saddle Bronc Rider.

His fingers lifted, one hand rising to knuckle up his hat brim a notch. Knowing amusement glimmered in his pale gray eyes. "Is that acceptable, Miz Parker?"

Abbey pushed up her glasses. Two could play at this game. "It's less than ideal, Mr. Granger, but I suppose it will suffice in lieu of more—" she paused delicately "—substantial proof."

Edwina sputtered a laugh.

Watching smugness sharpen to alertness, Abbey wondered if she shouldn't have left well enough alone. "How did you find my booth, Mr. Granger?"

"Call me Matt."

"All right...Matt. I only gave—"

"May I call you Abbey? Seems only fair, now that we're better acquainted, and all."

"Of course." She would *not* let him fluster her. "As I was saying, I only gave you my street address over the phone. How'd you know where to find me?"

"When you didn't answer my knock at your apartment, I went door-to-door asking questions. A woman named Cherry said you rent this flea market booth on weekends. She gave me directions...." He trailed off, his gaze riveted on something beyond Abbey's shoulder.

Mattie!

Twisting around in her chair, Abbey experienced a swell of emotion so conflicted it hurt to breathe. On the one hand, she loved this child with a depth she wouldn't have thought possible a year ago. On the other, she resented the tethers of responsibility attached to loving Mattie.

Her uncle had arrived none too soon, for Abbey and Mattie both. The little girl deserved to be safe and cherished. To be raised in a more stable environment than free-spirited, funky Venice Beach. A ranch in Texas with plenty of space and fresh air would fulfill the latter requirement. In no time Matt would love her as much as Abbey did.

He *would,* she assured herself. How could he not?

Oblivious to the adults, Mattie crouched beside an open tackle box, pawing carelessly through the delicate contents. The Trying On Of Completed Jewelry was a treasured ritual for woman and child whenever Abbey finished a piece. However, market days were not the time or place. That morning when they'd set up the stall, Abbey had expressly forbidden her charge to touch the inventory.

But the child was only five.

And she'd entertained herself for hours with crayons and coloring books in a back corner.

Besides, she'd only learned two days ago that her mother wasn't ever coming home, though understanding had yet to sink in.

Abbey waited until she could trust her voice before speaking. "Mattie?"

She spun around, her blond pigtails bouncing, her blue eyes wide and guilty. One ear wore a whimsical onyx cloud outlined in hammered silver, the other a tiny brass picture frame enclosing a silver cat. Her small clenched fists sprouted odd fingers of colored stone, silver and brass.

"I didn't break the doggie's tail," she assured Abbey solemnly.

So much for my matched pair of silver and onyx Dalmatians. "Put the jewelry back, sweetie, then come here."

Off the hook, Mattie flashed her biggest smile—the one that deepened the single dimple in her left cheek. She tossed painstakingly crafted pieces into the tackle box as if they were plastic fishing corks, then scampered to the table. Her gaze soon locked on the new treasures only inches away.

"Look, Mattie," Abbey said, stopping grubby

fingers as they crept forward. "We have a visitor."

The child glanced up and turned from the stranger to her familiar neighbor. "Weena!" she squealed. "You look *pretty*."

Edwina's angular face softened, making the statement true. "Hi, princess. So do you. I like your Cinderella dress. Is it new?"

Mattie thrust out her chest and smoothed both palms over a pumpkin coach. "Uh-huh. Me and Abbey went—"

"Abbey and *I* went," Abbey corrected.

"Yeah, we went to Kmart and found a *big* sale. I gots new underwear, too. See?" She flipped up the hem of her dress to chin level. "Saturday is pink," she stated the obvious. "Abbey says tomorrow I can wear blue. That's my favorite—"

"What have I told you about lifting up your dress?" Abbey asked, gently disengaging the hem from small fingers.

Mattie cast down long burnished-gold lashes. "A lady never shows her panties in public," she said in a singsong voice. Her lashes came up slyly. "Weena shows her panties in that dress with all the holes, and she's a lady. Aren't you, Weena?"

Cringing mentally, Abbey glanced at her neighbor, who was not only blushing, but also speechless—both firsts in Abbey's experience.

Matt looked stern and disapproving. Mattie still waited righteously for an answer.

Abbey tugged a curly blond pigtail for attention. "I wasn't talking to Edwina, now, was I? I was talking to you."

She encircled the little girl's waist and hugged tightly, for her own comfort as much as the child's.

"Honey, you remember me saying your mommy has a brother? And how he wants you to live with him on a ranch with lots of animals?"

Mattie's stiffening body said she did.

"Well, that man standing next to Edwina is your Uncle Matt. He's come all the way from Texas to see you."

Blue eyes turned to the looming stranger, grew round with wonder and a hint of fear. Obviously overwhelmed, Mattie turned her face into Abbey's chest.

Say something, you stupid cowboy. "Mattie, say hello to your uncle."

The little girl burrowed her face deeper, her

thin arms clutching Abbey as if afraid of being pulled away.

The stupid cowboy stayed stupid, his expression pained and increasingly grim.

"Come on, honey, show him that pretty face of yours." *The face I'll never see again after Monday.*

"I want my mommy," the child mumbled against Abbey's breaking heart.

She rubbed circles on a small back and met Edwina's gaze. Compassionate but uncertain. No help there.

Abbey tried again. "You know Mommy's in heaven with God and the angels. But your uncle is here now. He loved your mommy, and he loves you. Don't you, Uncle Matt?"

Abbey sent the cowboy an imploring look. *Tell her it's true. Lie if you have to. She needs the reassurance. You need her trust.*

I need my freedom.

He narrowed turbulent eyes and looked down. "Maybe I should come back when you're ready to close for the day," he told his boots.

You miserable coward.

His head came up as if she'd spoken aloud. Their gazes locked.

Abbey let all the outrage churning inside her

heart show hot and fierce in her eyes. "I close at six, Mr. Granger. Can we expect you then...or is that another obligation you can't handle?"

A killing freeze glazed his eyes. "I think I can manage to find my way back."

"Good." She bared her teeth in a mockery of a smile. "I'll look forward to having a nice little chat with you then. Oh, Edwina? Did you try on those jetbead earrings?"

Edwina flicked an uneasy glance at the man Abbey studiously ignored. "Not yet."

"Check them out, why don't you? They'd look great against your hair." *Don't think about the cowboy. Just make the sale.*

CHAPTER TWO

AT FOUR O'CLOCK that afternoon, Matt entered a back room of Atkins Funeral Home and faced his sister for the first time in six years.

He wasn't prepared.

No amount of rationalization *could* have prepared him for the squat black urn occupying an alcove in the wall. Recessed lighting emphasized its ugly shape and dull surface. Matt struggled to connect the graceless thing to his beautiful baby sister, and wrenched his gaze to the side.

No sir! That wasn't Mary in any way, shape or form.

Mary was the angelic blond-haired toddler he'd steered away from iron-shod hooves and their daddy's temper. She was the rowdy tomboy dogging his boot heels, mimicking his adolescent swagger and I-don't-give-a-damn attitude.

Mary was the fifteen-year-old innocent who'd run off with a bull rider from Wyoming. The sixteen-year-old Lolita who'd run off with a point judge three times her age. The seventeen-year-old stranger he'd never followed the third time or dragged back to the ramshackle trailer Charlie had called home.

She'd lived in a lot of crappy places since then, and deserved a decent final resting place.

Matt returned his shamed gaze to the shrine-like alcove. His championship buckle would've paid for a satin-lined casket *and* a cemetery plot. He should've sold it and done for his sister what he'd done for their father.

He'd handled all funeral arrangements then, too, since Charlie Granger had died the same way he'd lived: with no thought for his future— or his children. If he'd had any savings, his current girlfriend had kept the money as payment for putting up with a tomcatting drunk.

Matt hadn't pushed the issue. At least she, unlike his sister, had gone to the funeral.

He'd left three messages on Mary's answering machine in San Francisco, the last a raw plea. When Mary hadn't responded or shown up at the funeral, he'd buried his guilt and told himself it was probably best she hadn't made the trip. He wouldn't have had a clue what say.

From that point on, he gave her the space he

figured she needed, and finally lost track of her whereabouts altogether.

But damn her irresponsible hide, he hadn't known she'd had a child to support! He himself had sworn not to have kids unless he acquired a decent permanent home and the respect of his neighbors. So much for planning. Mattie would depend on him now.

The pressure in his chest started small, gathered momentum and grew quickly to burning discomfort. A pain even worse than the residual aches from his five-second ride on a tornado the day before.

Planning. Ha! He'd sold the damn horse to Larry for a hefty profit. Little good that would do in the grand scheme of things. A choked sound escaped Matt's throat. Pitiful. Glancing at the empty doorway, he hauled his emotions under control.

Better. At least he could breathe now, and see something besides that god-awful urn. Not that there was much else to look at in the room.

Two of those easel flower things and a basket, to be exact. It appeared his sister had three whole friends in the world.

Cursing softly, he walked forward to read the

card on a lavish arrangement of red and white roses.

It was a wild ride while it lasted, babe. Johnny.

Anger, hot and cleansing, rushed through Matt, ridding him of maudlin sentimentality. Johnny was the jerk who'd invited Mary skiing, who'd lured her into virgin snow off the main slopes. Matt had read the full cover-our-asses documentation from the ski resort's lawyers. He didn't doubt Mary had crossed marked boundaries at her own risk. The problem was, she'd also risked her child's well-being.

Like father, like daughter.

Frowning, he moved on to the next easel. Birds of paradise, palm fronds and some white flowers with red centers. Very flashy.

He plucked the florist's card from its little plastic pitchfork.

"Proud Mary" is my new finale. Dedicated in loving memory, Edwina.

Snorting, Matt slipped the card back in place. Edwina—the tall flamboyant redhead from the flea market. He could just imagine what kind of ''finale'' Edwina put on. To his credit, the cross-dresser did seem fond of Mattie. And Abbey wouldn't let a true pervert near the child she protected like a mama bear.

As if pulled by gravity, his gaze lowered to a huge basket of daisies on the floor. The simple, commonplace blossoms made the more exotic flowers seem gaudy and overblown.

That's why, next to Edwina's wild red wig, Abbey's long brunette braid had seemed anything but ordinary. Why the touch of huskiness in her voice had given Matt pause, and the intelligent brown eyes behind wire-rimmed glasses had interested him keenly.

Reassured, he noticed a large object...some sort of figurine...partially hidden among the potted daisies. He leaned down and lifted a ceramic angel for closer inspection.

She was about the size of a cookie jar, her flowing white robes hiding her body shape. One wing was higher than the other; her golden hair, green eyes and adoring smile were imperfectly painted.

Despite the flaws, he'd seen that smile too many times not to recognize it instantly. Or to forget the joy—and the burden—of being its recipient.

"Mary?" he said wonderingly.

She had made this. Abbey Parker. He didn't

know how he knew it, he just did. Crouching beside the basket, he tossed his hat onto the floor, set the angel down carefully, then searched for a card. Where the hell was it?

By the time he found a small envelope in the bottom of the basket, he was almost growling with impatience. His name, not Mary's, was penned in a flowing script on the outside.

He ripped open the seal and pulled out a folded note.

Dear Mr. Granger,
Mattie has been told that her mommy is in heaven with the angels. But children are usually more comforted by the tangible than the abstract. Although I couldn't re-create Mary's beauty as I'd wanted, I believe her love for Mattie is captured credibly.

I'm sure you've acquired something much finer for Mary's ashes, but I also took the liberty of leaving the angel hollow. I'll trust you to use her however she can best ease Mattie's pain. Warmly,
Abbey Parker

P.S. Please let me know if I can do anything to help.

Matt lowered the note and looked from the black urn to the ceramic angel's loving smile. For the first time in two days, his heavy heart experienced a lift of gladness. He couldn't think of a more decent final resting place for Mary.

His gaze moved to the note's "P.S.," his mind turning over an idea and inspecting it from several angles. Not perfect, by any means. But he was desperate enough to appreciate the good points and worry about the rest later.

He glanced at his watch. Still enough time to take care of his bill and get back by six to the three-ring circus called Venice Beach. Abbey wanted "a nice little chat," did she?

Well, by damn, so did he.

BESS CAMPBELL GLANCED at the kitchen clock and squeaked in alarm. She'd have to hustle to get supper ready by six. Ben Campbell would return from branding spring calves tired and hungry. A dangerous combination sure to get ugly if food wasn't steaming on the table when he walked in.

She shook off the last of her daydream, sprang up from the table and rushed to the refrigerator. Thank heavens she'd remembered to thaw the chicken. Frying would be fastest, and would please her daddy, too.

Pulling out eggs for the batter and ingredients for salad, she eyed the peas she hadn't shelled and bit her lip. Canned would have to do tonight. Maybe he wouldn't notice.

Yeah, dream on.

Bess slammed the refrigerator door hard enough to rattle the jars inside. Daydreaming was what got her into trouble most of the time lately. She'd been wondering how Matt Granger was faring in California when the kitchen clock had caught her attention.

Sympathy and nervous excitement hummed beneath her skin now. Her handsome neighbor was bringing home a motherless child to raise. Imagine that!

She carried her load to the counter and began preparing the meal, her movements quick and practiced. She'd been mistress of this kitchen since she was fourteen. Now twenty-two, she could cook in her sleep.

False modesty aside, she could bake any woman in Cottonwood under the table, and the whole town knew it. There wasn't a convalescing patient or grieving family in the past five years who hadn't received a comforting taste of heaven to ease the pain.

Why, Casey Tannen would break a leg tomorrow if he thought she'd take him a sympathy German Chocolate cake. He'd want a kiss, too, of course. One like those they'd shared her last semester in high school. One he wouldn't get. She'd stopped dating him after graduation. A girl who'd been voted Cottonwood Festival Queen two years straight had to have standards, after all.

But sometimes in the dead of night, she remembered those kisses....

Sighing, Bess wrapped the bowl of tossed salad in cellophane, stored it in the refrigerator and put a skillet of oil on the stove to heat. Her daddy was right. She deserved better than a cowhand could provide.

At one time Burt Dawson, the town's eligible young pharmacist, had gotten a peach pie from her every other week. People had started winking and asking Bess when they could expect a wedding invitation.

Now the citizens of Cottonwood winked at Emily Johnson instead. Burt had stopped asking Bess to church socials and picture shows a year ago.

Right about the same time she'd started delivering pies to Matt.

The day before, it had been cherry, with a lattice top crust browned just so. She'd arrived as Hal and Matt were leaving for the San Antonio airport. Both men had looked furious. They'd obviously been arguing.

Hal had revealed the reason for Matt's trip. And the ex rodeo-champion was far from happy about fetching his niece, she'd gathered from the look on his face.

That strong handsome face.

She intended to wake up to it every morning for the rest of her life, once Matt came to his senses.

Too bad he couldn't taste her fried chicken to speed things along. But shoot, that old geezer of a cook barely tolerated her bringing over pie. Jealous, that's what he was, because her flaky crust crumbled at the touch of a fork and his didn't.

Bess plunged a drumstick in beaten egg, rolled it in seasoned flour, snatched up a thigh and repeated the process.

Lately she'd felt time ticking away, and thought maybe she should let Matt sample a few other things she would bring to the marriage.

She was almost a virgin. Enough to be convincing, anyway. If she cried afterward, and her daddy "accidentally" found out, there'd be a shotgun wedding lickety-split. Or not.

Matt wasn't afraid of her daddy. That's why she loved him, and had from that first time he'd come to look over some quarter horses for sale. When he'd actually criticized the scars marking each hide and hadn't backed down an inch from Ben Campbell's glare, she'd nearly stepped on her jaw! A mistake that had gotten her sent back inside.

Eventually, according to her gleeful daddy, their new neighbor had bought the worst cutter in the lot. But Matt had gotten the last laugh. He'd turned the soured cutter around, and *now* who looked the fool?

Bess dipped and rolled the last chicken breast, then headed for the sink to rinse her hands. You could've knocked everybody in these parts over with a hummingbird feather when the World Champion Saddle Bronc Rider had settled not far from town.

Why on earth, folks had wondered, would he come back to a place that had once called him "trouble," his sister a "slut" and his father a "no-good drunk"?

Some thought, bein' as this was quarter horse country and all, it made sense to locate a cutter training stable here. But Bess knew they were wrong.

Matt was here because God had sent him. Just like He'd made her turn down two offers of marriage after high school, offers that would've gotten her out from under her daddy's thumb and into her own kitchen.

Destiny, that's what it was. She was meant to stay free and become Matt's wife. To teach his poor little niece how to cook and keep a nice home. To have children of her own to love, who would love her right back. The notion warmed her heart, it purely did.

She turned off the tap, walked to the stove and flicked a few drops of water into the deep cast-iron skillet. The oil inside popped and sizzled. Perfect. Fetching the plate of battered chicken, she smiled.

Let people wink at Emily and talk about wedding bells. Let Tammy Sue show off her new baby in church. Bess's patience and faith would soon be rewarded. God was sending her aid in the form of a little girl Matt hadn't expected.

A bachelor didn't necessarily want a wife. But

a substitute father would sure enough welcome a substitute mother into his home.

ABBEY STRETCHED OVER her cleared table and searched both directions in front of her stall. No sign of a lean rugged Texan whose walk was pure sin.

He was late, the miserable coward! Forty minutes late and counting. Strike two against the man who couldn't muster a few measly words of comfort for his grieving niece.

More than half of her neighboring vendors had already shut down. The rest would hope to lure after-dark strollers mellowed by dinner at The Sidewalk Café or another local restaurant.

She usually considered the profits of staying open late worth suffering Paul Frazer's escort home. Not that she didn't welcome the body-builder's self-appointed protection. It was his increasing pressure for an intimate relationship she resisted. Her unattainability was the attraction, not her. He hardly knew *her*. And darned if she'd let another man know her body before learning what was in her heart and mind. She'd told him not to stop by her stall tonight, since she'd planned to leave early in deference to Mattie. Now, all coloring books and snacks were stowed neatly in the child's backpack. All jewelry and money was packed efficiently inside two pieces of carry-on wheeled luggage.

When potential customers approached, Abbey could only watch them veer off toward Terry's Tie-Dyed Tees four stalls away. That, and watch the sun sink lower...along with her bravado.

The underbelly of Venice Beach culture rolled over to scratch its itch at night.

Two sharp tugs on the back of her calf-length flowered skirt demanded attention. Abbey turned and looked down at the source. Uh-oh.

"I'm hungry. I wanna go home," Mattie whined the refrain of a five-year-old pushed past the limits of patience.

"I know, honey. But let's give your uncle another few minutes, okay?" Abbey glanced at the two juice boxes pierced with tiny straws sitting on one corner of the table. "I have a little fruit punch left. Do you want it?"

"No-o-o. I wanna go home. He's not coming, Abbey. He doesn't like me."

Strike three, cowboy. You're out.

"Sure he does, pun'kin." Abbey dropped a kiss on the petulant mouth. "How could he not love a sweetheart like you? It's just that boys don't talk about how they feel the way girls do."

"How come?"

"Because it makes them uncomfortable."

"How come?"

Because they know we might not like hearing what they say. "Because if they talk, they don't know how girls will react. Remember how you hid your face when you met your uncle this afternoon?"

Mattie toed one purple jelly sandal into the asphalt and nodded.

"Well, *I* know you felt shy, but *he* might have thought you didn't like him. Just the way you thought he didn't like you. Isn't that silly?"

Hopefulness lurked behind Mattie's second nod.

"So next time you see your Uncle Matt, give him a great big smile and hug, so he knows you're glad to see him."

Any man who could resist that double whammy was made of tin and needed more than a wizard to make him whole.

"Will you do that for me, honey?"

But Mattie's gaze and thoughts had already shifted. "Can I play on the beach, now, Abbey? The peoples are gone, and I'll stay *right there.*" Standing on tiptoe, she pointed across Ocean Front Walk.

Devoid of umbrellas, towels and oiled bodies, the pockmarked sand resembled a moonscape ripe for exploration. Farther back, a glorious sunset tinged Pacific waves rosy gold. The Santa Monica Mountains loomed dark on the northern horizon. Along the foamy shoreline, a man and woman strolled hand in hand.

An idyllic scene. Peaceful and lovely.

"Ple-e-ease?" Mattie persisted.

A bearded man in filthy jeans and ragged T-shirt entered Abbey's line of vision. Walking stooped over, he searched the sand closely. Designer sunglasses, Walkman radios, jewelry, even wallets were often left behind or dropped unnoticed on the trek back to cars.

Lost items found tonight would fund tomorrow's drug of choice.

Abbey made her decision. "You know what, Mattie? You had the right idea before. I'm starving! Let's go home and cook some dinner, what do you say?"

What Mattie said was, "No."

"But you told me you were hungry. Doesn't a hamburger sound good?"

"No. I wanna play in the sand."

"We can make french fries," Abbey wheedled, shamelessly dangling a carrot with no nutritional value.

"I wanna play in the sand."

"Or wait!" She was out of tomato sauce, but she'd worry about that later. "How about...*nah*. You don't want to eat that."

Mutiny struggled with curiosity in expressive blue eyes. "Eat what?"

Abbey hid a smile. "No, really, Mattie, we'd better not make spaghetti. You might eat three bowls again and get sick."

Mattie's scowl cleared. "P'sketti! P'sketti!" She clapped her hands and jumped in a circle. The beach forgotten, she stopped and looked up earnestly. "I'll only eat *two* bowls tonight. I promise."

A hot blast of love caught Abbey full force. She jerked up her emotional shields too late. Her marshmallow heart melted, gooey sweet and sticky with complications.

She hadn't wanted to learn this child could eat her own weight in spaghetti. She hadn't wished to notice the lack of structure or security in Mattie's life. Abbey hadn't planned to take on the role of surrogate mother, especially after spending the past eight years avoiding emotional attachments that might tie her down.

So strong was her fear of ensnarement, she only rented furnished apartments and kept a large suitcase perpetually packed should she need to leave at a moment's notice. She should have grabbed it and escaped Mattie's growing dependency months ago.

Fate was now accomplishing the separation Abbey hadn't managed. She'd been foolish and selfish to stay. The only purpose procrastination had served was to double the pain...for them both.

"Abbey?" Mattie whispered tentatively.

"Hmm?"

"I'll only eat *one* bowl. Don't be mad."

Abbey's focus cleared. The wariness pinching Mattie's expression was reminiscent of earlier days.

"Oh, sweet pea, I'm not mad at you. I'm only cranky because I'm so hungry. In fa-a-act, I'm so hungry I could eat a little girl just your size."

Lifting curled fingers, Abbey assumed her best wicked-witch voice. "What a tasty-looking neck you have, my pretty. Mind if I have a bite?"

Her eyes widening, Mattie shrieked and whirled around.

Abbey was faster. Snatching the child close,

she nuzzle-munched the tender skin below Mattie's ear.

Forty pounds of squealing energy sprouted ten elbows and jabbed them all directions. A direct hit in Abbey's midriff dropped her flat on her rump with a lap full of flushed little girl. A round tummy beckoned and Abbey's fingers followed, tickling mercilessly, prompting infectious belly-deep giggles cute enough to soften a stone-faced cowboy.

When the joyful sound turned into groans, Abbey replaced tickles with noisy raspberries. A terribly undignified skill she'd first seen Mary demonstrate and had determined to learn immediately.

"Stop," Mattie finally gasped, scrambling upright to fling small arms around her tormentor's neck.

She hiccuped loudly, which made her giggle, which made her hiccup. A vicious cycle.

Recognizing the signs of overstimulation, Abbey patted the child's back. "Settle down now, Mattie. It's getting dark. Go put on your backpack and we'll head home."

"Okay."

But Mattie's cheek found Abbey's shoulder, and neither one of them moved.

Their breathing slowed. Ocean waves crashed and receded in the distance, the sound lulling, the rhythm hypnotic. Inhaling the scent of baby shampoo, fruit punch and wax crayons, Abbey tightened her arms.

In two days, she'd be free to live her own schedule, to forget all rules. She'd be free to go across the street—or across the country—whenever she pleased in search of the next new experience. It was the life she'd dreamed of behind locked doors. The phoenix she'd created from ashes of fear and shame.

But how in God's name could she leave Mattie in the hands of a stranger she knew nothing about?

"Abbey?"

"What, pun'kin?"

"Can we ask Uncle Matt to eat p'sketti with us?"

Whoa, speak of the devil! Pulling back, Abbey smoothed baby-fine wisps of hair from a small damp face. "We could, honey, but I think he must have made other plans for tonight." *The miserable coward.* "Besides, I don't think cowboys like spaghetti."

"How come?"

"Yeah, how come?" a baritone voice rumbled above their heads.

Abbey twisted around so fast she spilled Mattie from her lap.

The miserable coward himself, a mountainous Stetson-peaked silhouette, loomed in front of the stall table.

CHAPTER THREE

HER HEART HAMMERING, Abbey straightened her glasses, tugged down her skirt, recentered the point of her V-neck cotton sweater. Mercy, her braid no doubt looked as messy as Mattie's pigtails—without the adorable effect, of course.

Not that Abbey cared. Vanity was one subject on which she agreed with her father. Too much of it could, and often did, lead to sin.

Rising as gracefully as possible, she motioned to Mattie. "C'mere, sugar. You didn't skin your knees, did you?"

Mattie moved close. "My elbow hurts."

"Lift it up and let me see."

Abbey took her sweet time fussing over the nonexistent wound. Only a dimwit could've missed her deliberate rudeness to their onlooker. And Matt Granger appeared to have something under that Stetson besides great hair. With a last promise to bandage Mattie's elbow when they got home, Abbey turned to the girl's uncle.

"You're late," she said primly. "We've been waiting almost an hour."

"Sorry. I had a blowout on the freeway."

Her righteousness wilted. "How awful."

"Yeah, it was pretty rough out of the chute there for a while. Changin' the tire was a thrill, too."

"I can imagine." She proceeded to do just that, and suppressed a shudder.

"By the way, I don't have plans for dinner, and I happen to love spaghetti."

Abbey blinked.

"You said you thought I'd made other plans, and that you didn't think cowboys liked spaghetti, remember?" His features were hard to see in the twilight, but his voice sounded amused.

"Well, excuse me for not knowing any cowboys personally, but I've seen every John Wayne western at least twice. And *he* never hunkered down in front of the campfire with a big ol' plate of Italian food."

"No?" A chuckle hovered in his voice.

"Not hardly. The Duke ate beef jerky and cold beans. A raw steak in town after his Saturday bath. You know, manly cowboy grub."

Quelling her grin, she walked to her rolling luggage and pulled up the handles. "No offense."

"None taken. 'Course, any guy whose real name was Marion might figure he needed to compensate by eatin' raw steak. Now me..." The outdoor spotlights picked that moment to switch on, revealing his slow, cocky grin. "Hell, I eat quiche, darlin'."

A queer little flutter winged through her heart. The man was arrogant but definitely no fool. And she couldn't deny the charm of that one dimple so like Mattie's.

But he hadn't even looked at his niece, who'd slipped on her G.I. Joe backpack over her Cinderella dress, and now stood waiting for a crumb of greeting.

The miserable coward.

Abbey's heartbeat stabilized. She pushed open the stall's rickety side exit gate. "C'mon, pun'kin, let's go home."

Minutes later, with the feel of Matt's baffled gaze tickling a spot between her shoulder blades, she headed north along the boardwalk as briskly as possible. A sluggish lurching pace, as it turned out. Towing heavy wheeled suitcases was awkward. She could've really used some of Paul's muscle right now.

The sound of purposeful boot steps close behind sped up her heartbeat. She felt the heat from Matt's big body an instant before her left hand was wrested from a suitcase.

"I'll take this one," he said, his tone brooking no argument. "My rental car is about ten blocks from here. Where are you parked?"

"I don't have a car. We walked. My apartment's not that far—no, this way, Mattie." Taking the child's hand, Abbey veered sharply and headed down Breeze Avenue.

A second later, Matt fell into step beside her, a tall powerful presence. "I *know* where you live. I was there this afternoon, remember? And I can't believe you'd walk there at night alone, much less with a kid."

Abbey bristled. "It wasn't night an hour ago when we expected you. And as for walking with *your niece,* I'm surprised you even noticed."

He slanted down a brooding look. "What's that supposed to mean?"

"It means you haven't—" She broke off, conscious of the little ears tuned into their conversation. "We'll talk at the apartment. Unless you're too scared to walk us home." Mercy, she hoped not!

"You've got scared and smart mixed up," Matt said grimly.

Tightening her grip on Mattie's hand, Abbey admitted his point. She didn't do well at all in dark, closely confined spaces. And the streets surrounding her apartment were narrow and poorly lit, the buildings decorated with burglary bars or abandoned altogether.

"Anybody could've cased you out earlier and followed you from the market," Matt continued. "You might as well have a sign on your back sayin' 'Mug Me.' The miracle is you haven't been robbed yet."

Abbey stopped. "I haven't been robbed because Paul Frazer always walks me home, and the sign on *his* back says, 'Mess With Me And You Die.' Now, if you'll kindly hand over my luggage, you can take off anytime."

Though not without a loss to his masculine pride...

Frowning, Matt stared at a fixed point somewhere up the street. "Does this Paul character pack a gun or somethin'? Is he a cop?"

Gotcha.

She mustered a casual tone. "No. He works for the L.A. Parks and Recreation Department at

Muscle Beach, training kickboxers and weight lifters.''

''He's re-e-al strong,'' Mattie piped up, drawing both adults' attention. ''He doesn't need wheels.''

Matt raised a questioning brow at Abbey. ''I thought everyone in L.A. drove a car.''

''She means Paul *carries* my luggage,'' Abbey explained. ''Speaking of luggage, could I have mine, please?'' Oh, his expression was priceless! She could've kissed Mattie.

Expelling a disgusted breath, he resettled his hat. ''No, you can't have your luggage. But damned if I'll carry the one you're pullin', too. C'mon, let's hurry and get this over with.''

''Thank you.''

''I like my spaghetti spicy,'' he muttered in lieu of ''you're welcome.''

Her grin broke free and lasted all the way to the next block, where she turned left. Almost instantly the surroundings changed. Sobering, she drew reassurance from Matt's tall, solid presence.

Reconstructive surgery had bypassed this pocket of seedy businesses and apartment buildings. Like cellulite, it was an unsightly embarrassment to the rejuvenated community as a whole.

But Abbey had lived in worse conditions. The affordable rent and walking distance to the outdoor market made up for a lot of flaws, she reminded herself now.

Ten feet ahead, two young men appeared out of nowhere and turned to block the sidewalk.

Okay.

No need to panic.

A lot of teens these days adopted the gangbanger look. It didn't mean they were violent. It didn't mean they were muggers—serious residential flaws, right up there with shag carpeting and faulty plumbing.

When the taller youth whipped out a gun, Abbey's first thought was that Matt would never let her live this down. Her second slammed the air from her lungs.

If we live.

AMBUSH! AND HE'D WALKED right into it.

As Abbey thrust his niece behind her back, Matt scanned the empty street. They were sandwiched between a stretch of boarded-up buildings. A liquor store glowed one block ahead.

No cars out front. No witnesses dialing 911.

He calculated the distance and risk between him and the kid's gun.

"Hands up, *pendejo,* or the *puta* gets it!" The revolver swung to Abbey and stopped.

Matt stiffened. So much for his flying tackle idea.

Slowly raising his palms, he sized up the young Hispanics. Baggy jeans; cloth headbands with long, dangling ends; badass attitudes to match their weapons.

The second *cholo* held a switchblade and knew how to use it, Matt didn't doubt. L.A. didn't own the market on barrio gang violence. San Antonio newscasts were filled with images of pooled blood and body bags.

He assumed his gentlest horse-trainer voice. "Take it easy, buddy—"

"No chinges con migo!" the gunman shouted, his eyes as wild as any bronc's. The tendons on his tattooed forearm flexed once, twice, as if he toyed with the trigger. "I'm not your buddy, cowboy. All of you—*vengan aquí.*"

He moved off the sidewalk into the deeper shadow of a three-story building.

Matt's night vision rivaled a cat's. He spotted the nearby alleyway, their open grave if he didn't act soon.

"Andale!"

Mattie flinched and pressed closer to Abbey.

"Do what he says," Matt murmured, his gaze fixed on the pistol. The instant it wavered he'd make his move.

When he stood tamely with Abbey and Mattie on a patch of dirt fronting the building, the leader flashed a smug smile.

That's right, you bastard, Matt thought. *Relax.*

The second punk, stationed near the sidewalk, kept a wary watch on the street.

"You," the gunman addressed Matt. "Give the woman your wallet, and that hubcap on your belt. You," he spoke to Abbey. "Bring me the bags. No tricks, or maybe I shoot the little girl first and ask questions later, *comprende?*"

Abbey nodded, her face a pale oval in the dark. She twisted around, her loose hip-length sweater molding a narrow waist and unexpectedly full breasts. Matt hoped like hell the punks didn't have his view.

"Mattie, honey, don't be scared. Let go of my legs now."

The child clung tighter, pulling flower-sprigged cotton taut against Abbey's thighs.

"E-e-eh, *Mamacita,*" the gunman called.

"You been saving all that for me? Come get what you need—" he leered and made a lewd gesture "—and bring the *chica,* too."

Meeting Matt's murderous gaze, he cackled.

"What's the matter, chicken-shit?" Matt challenged, digging out his wallet and unbuckling his belt. "You afraid to get near me? You gotta hide behind a woman's skirt to get the job done?"

C'mon, c'mon, point the gun at me.

The revolver shifted away from Abbey, then jerked back. "You wanna die, *amigo? Muy bien.* But first you *watch* me get the job done."

Matt gathered himself to spring.

"Wait!" Abbey ordered. She'd managed to disengage small arms from around her legs. Now she turned her back on the gunman and nudged Mattie aside. "Stay here with your uncle and be a big girl."

"No-o-o," Mattie wailed.

"I'll be right back, honey, I promise." Abbey lifted her gaze to Matt. "Just let me give these boys what they've been asking for."

Although her tone was mild, Matt saw the iron resolve in her eyes and broke into a cold sweat. "Abbey—"

"I know what I'm doing. Hand over your

wallet and buckle like they said.'' *Be ready,* she told him silently.

With no other option, he did as she asked. Her obvious approval did little to ease his conscience while she tucked the items into her skirt pocket.

''Don't worry, they won't hurt me—'' she faced the punks again and offered a dazzling smile ''—will you, boys? I'll cooperate, and you can be on your way.''

Matt stared incredulously at the sudden stranger sashaying forward, pulling her luggage behind.

''I'm sure you two have a good reason for what you're doing. No hard feelings. 'Men do not despise a thief if he steals to satisfy his hunger when he is starving.' Proverbs 6:30,'' Abbey cited, her voice a blend of whiskey and honey.

She stopped three feet in front of the revolver. ''Is that why you're stealing my rent money, boys? Are you hungry?''

The ''boys'' appeared as stupefied as drunken bees.

Matt eased closer...closer.

''No?'' Abbey sighed. ''Somehow I didn't think so.''

Simultaneously Matt lunged forward as she whirled around, her skirt billowing, her braid whipping, her foot connecting with the gun. It catapulted into the dark. The *cholo* flung up his opposite arm, landed a backhanded smack that sent Abbey reeling.

Matt saw red. He closed the last few inches, drew back his fist and rammed gutless stomach into spine. Too soft. He punched again. Too damn easy. He punched a third time, driving the punk to his knees. Some badass. Like hitting a pillow.

Or a woman...

Hoisting up the near-puking *cholo,* he landed a crunching blow to the cheek. The bully staggered back and crumpled to the ground.

"Behind you!"

Matt spun around and ducked a knife swipe at his throat, sidestepped another at his ribs. The second punk was small but as fast as a jackrabbit.

Dodging a third near miss, Matt stumbled a halfstep, then raised his fists and slowly circled the glinting blade. No worse than a broken beer bottle. Plus, he was sober. This could be fun. He started to grin.

A thin sound penetrated his adrenaline high. A child crying?

Well, *hell,* he'd forgotten about his niece.

At the next charging pass the *cholo* made, Matt caught a bony wrist above the switchblade. Years of reining, roping and riding went into his steady, ruthless squeeze. The kid yowled, dropped the knife and sank onto his knees.

Too soft. Too easy. No challenge, after all. Time to end this thing fast.

Forcing the punk to eat dirt, Matt planted a knee on backbone, snatched off the teen's headband and untied the knot. A longer pigging string worked better, but this would do in a pinch. Grabbing two wrists and a sneaker, he wrapped them once, finished with a half hitch, then flung up his arms.

Not bad, considering calf roping wasn't his event.

A gunshot cracked.

He twisted, followed the two-handed marksman's aim of the revolver Abbey now held. Somehow she'd located the gun and fired a warning shot.

Frozen in a half crouch, a switchblade held at the ready, the first punk hovered about five feet to Matt's left.

"I wouldn't do that," Abbey advised the leader evenly. "The next shot won't miss. And *amigo?*" She held his hate-filled gaze a long moment. "*Mamacita*'s not aiming for your heart."

Stud boy got the message and dropped his knife. The one that might've been buried in Matt's back but for her quick action.

He rose slowly.

The *cholo* backed away.

But Matt's practice run had brushed up his technique. The fact he didn't have to worry about roughing up a calf shaved more seconds off his time. In short order he'd flanked and tied the bully alongside his younger pal.

They twisted like dug-up worms, loosing a filthy stream of Spanish and English curse words the entire time. "Boys, boys," Matt said, shaking his head and tsk-tsking. "Where're your manners? There's a lady present. And remember, she's got the gun."

They shut up so fast he chuckled. Amazing. Of course, the "lady" had earned his healthy respect, too. Sensing her move up beside him, he looked down.

His niece stared up at him from her perch on a sweetly curved hip, her worshipful expression eerily like Mary's at the same age. The child extended his hat, which had fallen sometime during his scuffle, and broke into a shy, dimpled smile.

His fierce surge of emotion was relief, he assured himself. A natural response to the fact they were all safe.

"Thanks," Matt said gruffly, taking the hat and jamming it low. Lifting his gaze above the child's head, he met dark eyes softer than he'd ever seen them.

"You're pretty handy with a headband, cowboy," Abbey complimented.

His heart did a funny hop-skip—unnatural as hell.

Frowning, he turned to study his handiwork. "I can't be sure how strong that cloth is. Better give me the gun, now."

A beat of silence. "Oh, *may* I?"

Matt checked her expression. Good, the softness was gone. "Yeah, sure. Then take Mattie to the liquor store and call the police." He held out his hand for the revolver and waited. "Please," he finally added.

Abbey slapped the gun into his palm. "C'mon, pun'kin," she grumbled, heading off at a brisk walk. "I suppose your uncle is safe enough without us, since the little woman *did* manage to disarm the bad guys for him."

Over Abbey's shoulder, Mattie's eyes were sympathetic. "You fight almost as good as her," she called out consolingly.

Staring after the woman and child, Matt rode out a dark wave of foreboding. The kid was right. Abbey was tough. John Wayne in a flowered skirt and wire-rim glasses.

She had one weakness, though. His niece.

Once they were finished with the cops, he would use that knowledge to his advantage and pour on the charm. He had a proposition to make. She was, after all, still a woman.

How could she possibly refuse him?

"I'M SORRY, THAT'S IMPOSSIBLE." Abbey rose from the dinette table and headed for the tiny kitchen.

Mercy, what a close call! She couldn't think straight facing that smile, a combination of "the better to eat you with" white teeth and deep dimple slashing sun-bronzed skin. She couldn't think straight meeting those eyes, their silver-gray intensity rimmed in sooty lashes. Beneath his low black hat brim, they were o-oh my gawd gorgeous.

They were also untouched by his smile. Been there, done that, no thank you.

"Would you like more coffee?" she asked from the kitchen, her back turned as she refilled her mug.

"I don't understand."

"Cof-fee," Abbey repeated, enunciating clearly. "I asked if you'd like some."

"I heard what you asked, damn it! I just don't under—"

"Shh!" Holding up a warning finger, Abbey cocked her head toward the closed bedroom door.

No sound of movement, no plea for more water. Two bowls of bad spaghetti, a hot bath and exhaustion had finally kicked in.

She reached for a spoon. "Okay, go on."

"I don't understand," Matt continued in a strained voice, "why your coming to Texas until I can hire someone to take care of Mattie is impossible."

Abbey poured in a packet of sweetener, added a dash of nondairy creamer, glad he couldn't see her trembling fingers. True, Matt's offer of room, board and a small salary would solve her financial problems temporarily. But her bond with his niece was too strong already.

"I've established a business here," she hedged. "I can't just pack up and leave."

"C'mon, Abbey. After tonight it's obvious this is no safe place for a woman living alone. Besides, you're movin' from Venice Beach, anyway. I heard what you told that cop."

The Jeweler's Warehouse logo on her mug blurred as images sifted through her mind. Red and blue strobe lights glinting off badges, skittering across flesh, reflecting in sober eyes. The past few hours seemed almost surreal.

She continued stirring. "I gave statements to several officers tonight. Which 'cop' do you mean?"

"The one foamin' at the bit for more than your statement."

"Excuse me?"

Waves of irritation bombarded her from behind.

"Spare me your coyness, darlin'. Hendricks was hittin' on you so hard *he* should be charged with assault and battery. I'll bet that understanding-cop routine of his scores big with a lot of victimized women."

Stiffening, Abbey carefully laid down her spoon, picked up her coffee and turned. "You seem to have forgotten who took that gangbanger's gun away tonight. I'm *nobody's* victim, Matt."

He watched her warily. "I never said you were."

She walked to the table and clunked down her mug. "No, you only assumed I was. Which is much more insulting." Warming to her subject, Abbey pulled out a chair and made herself comfortable "You have some nerve accusing Detective Hendricks of assault and battery when you're obviously used to getting away with murder. Don't lay your M.O. at his door."

"Huh?"

"At least *he* wasn't trying to manipulate me into moving to Texas under the pretense of caring about my safety." She arched a brow at his startled expression. "Charisma isn't the same as character, Matt. I learned the difference a long time ago."

He studied her thoughtfully, as if she were a pile of beads he didn't quite know how to string. "Seems to me like what you learned is how to hang a man without a fair trial."

She opened her mouth, but nothing came out. Had she judged him unfairly?

"Just out of curiosity, Abbey, what makes you think I'm a bastard?"

Flustered, she cupped her mug with both

hands and stared at the curling steam. "I never said you were a—well, you know."

"No, you only assumed I was a—well, you know. Which is much more insulting." He mimicked the last in a tight, prissy falsetto.

Her lips twitched. "Do I really sound so...so..."

"Constipated?"

Appalled, she met his lively gaze. "That's awful."

He flashed his dimple like a wink. "That's nothin'. I could *get* awful, but I wouldn't want to forget my manners."

"Hmm. You'd have to learn them, first." She gestured to his dusty Stetson. "Didn't your mama teach you not to wear that thing inside the house?"

Matt glanced up as if startled to see a brim. "If she did, I don't remember. She died when I was six—" he whipped off the hat and dropped it onto an empty chair "—and Mary was two. Dad never remarried."

Abbey swallowed her apology with a sip of coffee. For all she knew, this was simply another manipulative tactic. Steven had once used sympathy to turn her "no" into "yes."

"We grew up on rodeo grounds, mostly,"

Matt continued. ''The women hangin' around my dad weren't interested in teachin' manners to a scrawny little steer rider, any more than I was interested in learnin' 'em. 'Course, by age fourteen I was over six feet tall, ridin' bulls alongside my dad. A gen-u-ine cowboy. And cowboys don't take off their hats for anything but funerals and...''

Easing into a grin, he locked hands behind his rumpled black hair, propped a tooled leather ankle on his opposite knee. ''Come to think of it, I guess some of those buckle bunnies *did* ask me to take off my hat.''

Oh, brother. ''I can see why.''

His chest expanded.

''Otherwise your head would've split like an overripe pumpkin from that swollen ego of yours.''

He chuckled softly, an intimate raspy sound reminiscent of wind stirring a moonlit field of wheat.

In the space of a shiver she was back in Baker's Landing, walking off her sleepless yearning. Longing for some wonderful unidentifiable something on the horizon, her restlessness both soothed and agitated by the whispering grain.

Lowering his arms, Matt pulled his coffee mug close. "Before I forget my manners again, thanks for the spaghetti. It was...different."

Without tomato sauce in the house, she'd improvised, using ketchup and every seasoning in her cabinet. Not one of her more successful experiments.

"Hey, you wanted spicy," Abbey reminded him. "If you can't take the heat, stay out of the quiche, Marion."

He shook his head and grinned. "I may have a swollen ego. But that's one sassy mouth you've got."

"I know." She sighed sincerely. "My father always said it's one of my biggest faults."

"Oh, I wouldn't call it a fault." He focused thoughtfully on her lips. "Provocative, maybe. Some might even say sinful. But definitely not a fault." When Matt looked up, his eyes held an edgy gleam.

Her heartbeat tripled, but she played dumb. "M-my temper is definitely a fault."

"Is that a fact?"

She nodded, distracted by the thumb moving back and forth over the rim of his mug. A gentle, caressing movement at odds with the strength she'd witnessed earlier. His fingers were long, the knuckles large, the nails clean and trimmed. Several scars slashed through a faint dusting of black hair. A workman's hand.

"Sometimes temper can be a good thing," he said, recapturing her attention.

He was staring at her mouth again.

"Mercy—" Abbey said on a sigh, then recovered her wits "—is wiser than anger. 'Do not be quickly provoked in your spirit, for anger resides in the lap of fools.' Ecclesiastes 7:9," she quoted, relieved when his gaze lifted, this time filled with curiosity.

"You sure do quote scripture a lot. You a preacher's daughter or somethin'?"

CHAPTER FOUR

"Do I *ACT* like a preacher's daughter?" Abbey finally managed to say, her heart making up for lost beats.

One corner of Matt's mouth lifted. "Good point. You're too damn mean. Hell, that *cholo* tonight put his bucket down the well and brought up a rattler. Where'd you learn to kick a gun away like that?"

Abbey brushed garlic bread crumbs from the wood laminate dinette. "You think I'm mean?"

His boot slipped slowly from his knee to the floor.

Stupid, stupid, stupid. "Paul teaches kickboxing," she blurted, redirecting the conversation back where it belonged. "He's very skilled. I learned a few basic self-defense moves from him."

Matt's fingers drummed his ceramic mug. "What about the gun? You handled it like a pro, too."

She could shoot the heart out of a paper target at thirty yards, but no point inviting more analysis. He was surprisingly perceptive. ''I've seen all of John Wayne's movies, remember? Attitude is everything.''

He snorted. ''You've got plenty of that.''

Time to steer the conversation again. ''Tomorrow, it would be nice if you could spend the day with Mattie. Get to know her better, tell her about the ranch.''

His fingers stilled.

Gotcha.

''I'm not very good with kids,'' he said cautiously.

''She's not just any kid. You two share the same blood, the same dimple. You probably have a lot of the same personality traits in common. You'll do fine. And you can't forget the bond of Mary.''

Looking unconvinced, he lifted his mug, took a sip and shuddered. ''Blech! Cold.''

Abbey laughed. Big tough cowboy. ''You look exactly like Mattie does when she eats spinach.''

He grimaced again.

''See?'' she gloated. ''You don't like spinach,

either. There's another thing you have in common."

"Oh, well, hell, why was I worried? We'll do lunch, catch up on gossip, get in a little shopping. It'll be goddamn great."

Maybe it was his disgruntled pout so different from calculated charm or electrifying sexual awareness. Maybe it was the thought of Mary. Or of his loss. But Abbey suddenly empathized with this cowboy wrenched from home on the range and planted in unfamiliar territory, both physically and emotionally.

"Look, I suppose for the sake of Mattie I can take the day off tomorrow and spend it with you both. I've told her I can't go with her to Texas, but I'm not sure if she really understands. Maybe I can help get her ready for the memorial service. Ease her into the reality of leaving, talk up the plane ride and stuff. That is, if you'd like me to."

He perked up. "If I'd like you to? Does a horse shit in a parade?"

Abbey frowned and pushed up her glasses. "You'll have to watch that potty mouth of yours around Mattie. She mimics everything she hears."

"All the more reason for you to come back—"

"*No.*" She drew a deep breath. "No," she repeated quietly, then lifted the white flag again. "There's more coffee on the warmer, if you're ready for that refill now."

His glance seemed to gauge her sincerity. "Yeah, that'd be great—" he scooted his mug in her direction "—thanks."

She looked from the mug to his expectant gaze, then took a deliberate sip of her own coffee.

Three heartbeats later, he slapped his curved denim thighs. "Right. I'll just get myself a cup, why don't I?" Rising, he shrank her apartment to dollhouse proportions and looked down. "Would you like me to top yours off for you?"

"Two cups is my limit. I'm fine, thanks."

But she wasn't, or she would have been able to look away from his back pockets as he walked into the kitchen. She wasn't fine, or she wouldn't have been fascinated by the ripple and flex beneath black cotton when he poured his coffee. She wasn't close to fine, or she wouldn't have studied his shaggy raven hair and wanted to touch it.

To touch *him.*

Abbey dragged her gaze to the hands nursing her mug. They delighted in learning new textures and shapes, exploring objects in nature wherever she relocated. Many of her best jewelry designs were an extension of these tactile forays.

But she hadn't explored a man's texture and shape since Steven. Had rarely desired to, frankly. And then, only after months of acquaintanceship.

Never this fast. Never this...powerfully.

Never again, her instincts warned.

She shoved back from the table and stood, desperate for space, more thankful than ever she'd had the strength to resist his request for help with his niece.

"I'm going to check on Mattie," Abbey mumbled.

Without waiting for a response, she moved swiftly to her bedroom, then slipped inside.

She'd allowed the little girl to sleep in here last night. Their mugging warranted a second night of the debatable privilege. Abbey suspected it comforted her more than the child.

A luminous glow beneath the closet door provided comforting twilight in the small room. No one knew the potential terror of absolute darkness better than she. The rocking chair and stacked craft supplies wouldn't shape-shift into monsters for this child. Not as long as Abbey could screw in a bulb, no sir.

She tiptoed closer to the double bed and stared down.

Mattie lay sprawled on her stomach, one knee drawn up, her nose buried deep in a pillow. The covers were twisted below her pink-painted toe-nails, her nightgown bunched above blue cotton panties. Her tiny tush announced ''Sunday'' to the calendar deprived.

Abbey's throat thickened. Could she make it through Monday without falling apart?

Somehow she would have to manage. Some-how she would smile and wave as Mattie got on that plane. Because as much as Abbey hated adding to the little girl's distress, she loved her hard-won independence more. The nagging itch to move on had become a full-fledged allergic reaction tonight. Her indisputable attraction to Matt made the combination of uncle and niece lethally dangerous. Leaving for a healthier en-vironment was the only certain cure.

She'd heard great things about the Santa Fe arts and crafts scene. Maybe Paul would loan her bus fare to check out the city, visit the shop owners and gallery dealers. And Mattie...

Abbey's heart contracted painfully. Well, Mattie had a child's natural resiliency on her side. By this time next year, she would barely remember the woman who made the "bestest p'sketti in the world."

The sound of a quiet click behind her flagged Abbey's attention.

Even without the warning, she would've known. Matt's aura of command and strength preceded him like a tangible thing. Threatened to envelop her as it did everything and everyone in its path.

Near the dresser, his toe hit and knocked her suitcase over. He swore softly, righted the heavy luggage, then continued on to stop inches shy of her left hip. Without looking up, she was acutely conscious of his imposing height, his preoccupation, his morning aftershave muted by the scent of man. A foreign, beguiling contrast to the dish of potpourri on her dresser.

She drew in an appreciative breath, peeked up as he gazed down at his niece.

The hard planes of his face had softened, though his eyes gave away no tender emotion. "She's gonna miss you somethin' fierce," he said in a low, hushed tone. "Sure you won't reconsider comin' to Texas?"

Live on an isolated ranch? With him? Without easy access to train, plane or bus?

Impossible! Even temporarily. Even for Mattie.

Abbey gathered her scattered wits. "I told you, I can't simply pack up and leave. I have too many obligations here."

"Is that so?"

Yes. No. "Yes," she said weakly.

Mercy, she couldn't think straight close to this man!

"Then tell me somethin', Abbey." He folded his arms and nodded coolly toward the dresser. "Why is your suitcase loaded and ready to go?"

AT NINE THE NEXT MORNING, Matt cut the engine of his rental car and psyched himself for the day ahead. Abbey had frozen up on him last night after he'd asked about her packed suitcase.

He'd meant to point out her obvious availability and restate his offer of employment. Instead, she'd hustled him politely and efficiently out the front door.

The way his gut was knotted now, you'd think he was about to slide onto a bronc for the finals go-around instead of climb the stairs to Abbey's apartment. The comparison wasn't so far-fetched, really. The stakes were different but just as important.

If he didn't make the points he needed to today, he'd get on that plane tomorrow with a little girl he wasn't equipped to take care of in any way.

Jerking the keys from the ignition, he stuffed them irritably into his pocket. Why *shouldn't* he be upset? The NCHA Futurity was in four short weeks, and Doc Holiday was still having problems with his turns. Three owners expected to pick up "finished" two year-olds before Matt left with the stallion for the competition. The calves would start dropping soon...the list of ranch chores went on and on....

The plain fact was, he didn't have the time or know-how to deal with a five-year-old girl. Hal would do it in a New York minute, but his arthritis was so bad he could barely get around the kitchen, much less keep up with a child. And Casey had his hands full with outside chores.

No, Abbey was his best child-care option at the moment. He needed to change her mind about going to Texas, that's all there was to it.

Resolve in place, Matt slid out of the car,

headed for the apartment stairs and took them two at a time to the second floor. The wood railing on his right looked rickety, the apartment numbers on his left badly tarnished. Abbey lived in the last unit at the end of a long walkway.

A creeping sunbeam hit the door as he approached, highlighting curls of yellow paint. He raised his knuckles and paused, reminding himself that women never looked as good the next morning as they had the night before.

Knock-knock-knock!

Hollow and flimsy, he noted, his frown deepening. Not much protection in this rough neighborhood.

He listened to a rush of light-running footsteps, the click of a dead bolt lock turning, the rattle of a chain. More rattles, increasingly violent, then, "Abbe-e-e! My arm's not tall enough."

Matt's lips twitched in spite of his soured mood.

"Mattie Granger, don't open that door! Did you even look through the peephole?"

Several bumps and thuds followed as Mattie obviously tried to jump high enough to get a peek outside.

"Wait a second and let me attach this last

bead.'' Abbey's exasperation came through the cheap door loud and clear.

Matt nudged up his hat, set his hands at his waist, shook his head and glared at the peephole. Hadn't last night scared any sense into the woman? With the dead bolt unlocked, one hard slam of his shoulder could rip the flimsy chain lock right out of the wall.

Metal finally rattled. The door swung open.

''Good morning,'' Abbey said, smiling. ''I'm sorry you had to wait so long.''

His lecture got sucked in on a quick breath.

Drenched in sunshine, Abbey's thick mahogany braid sparked red embers, her deep brown eyes golden flecks. Silver wire-rimmed lenses couldn't hide the long lashes touching her brows or the elegance of her slim, straight nose.

Disapproval wasn't thinning that centerfold mouth now. Naked of lipstick, the plump flesh was a succulent vivid pink—

''Do I have jelly on my mouth?'' Abbey asked self-consciously, lifting a graceful hand. She explored for stickiness with finger dabs and dainty licks of her tongue.

Matt grimly faced the truth.

The glasses, the braid, the loose denim jumper dress she wore, her strong chin and assertive directness...all were decoys. A thin disguise, not for classical beauty, but for bone-deep femininity. The *cholos* had responded to it last night as she'd sashayed forward with her luggage.

It pulled Matt now like a rope to the snubbing post.

Moving closer, he licked his thumb pad, cupped her chin, then slowly rubbed a trace of purple jelly from her cheek. As soft as a calf's ear, he marveled, watching a flush spread beneath his touch.

"Abbey doesn't like spit," a childish voice informed him from somewhere below.

Matt captured and held Abbey's wide-eyed gaze. "She doesn't, huh?"

"Nuh-uh. Spit's got lotsa germs. 'Specially if you're sick. She wouldn't hug me or kiss me or nothin' when she had a fever."

"She wouldn't, huh? I can see where that would be a real hardship."

Abbey's eyes darkened. She wasn't indifferent, not by a long shot. And suddenly it was imperative she admit as much. He slid his thumb and middle fingers down to wrap her throat lightly.

"Now I think on it, I guess some kisses are clean and pure, and some are downright dirty.

Isn't that right, Abbey?'' For her ears alone, he
added, ''Sexy prude.''

She compressed her lips in a tight virginal
seal. But the pulse beneath his fingertips hammered a different truth.

''No comment? Now me, I don't mind swap-
pin' spit with a woman…on one condition.''

Her nostrils narrowed. ''That she's breathing?''

Matt had to grin. ''Okay, two conditions. She
can't be dead, and she can't be a hypocrite and
blame me later for somethin' we both wanted.''

Abbey made a wordless sound and turned her
head.

He sobered instantly. He'd thrown out the remark as a teasing gauntlet, but the bleak pain in
her eyes said he'd struck a tender nerve.

Had someone—some *man*—forced himself on
her in the past? She sure as hell knew more
about self-defense than the average woman.

He hooked her chin with two fingers and
steered her face forward. Her gaze was steady,
but wary. If ever a woman needed to be kissed
dirty the *right* way, it was this one.

Too bad he wasn't the right man.

He settled for giving her chin a little shake.
''You've got that noose around my neck again,

Abbey. Don't judge all kisses by the ones you've had. Some are pretty damn nice. Definitely worth pickin' up a few germs.''

Her lingering vulnerability vanished. She lifted a dark brow. ''Yes, I'm sure you and your buckle bunnies have had *many* penicillin shots. You'll have to excuse me if I'm a little more discriminating.''

He released her chin. She was the *prickliest* woman—

''You got bunnies, Uncle Matt?''

For the first time, Matt looked down at the child clutching Abbey's billowy denim dress. He didn't know whether it was the awed blue eyes, or the ''Uncle Matt'' part, or the fact he'd forgotten the squirt's presence altogether that flustered him more.

Abbey saved him from answering by moving back into the apartment and pulling the little girl with her. ''How about we let him come inside?''

Shooting her a grateful look, Matt followed them into the boxy living room, swept off his hat and turned to close the door.

''Now, then, pun'kin, why don't you ask your uncle *all* about his bunnies while I finish my earring?''

His hand froze in the process of locking the door.

"How many bunnies do you gots? If I help take care of 'em, can I play with 'em, too? I help clean Hairball's litter box, and it has lots of yucky poop in the bottom, doesn't it, Abbey?"

"Yes, I believe it does," the traitor answered, her voice rich with suppressed laughter.

Matt threw the dead bolt home and turned around. His niece stared up at him expectantly from about belt level.

Abbey sat surrounded by assorted jars and mysterious tools at the dinette table near the kitchen. When he met her gaze, she returned hastily to some task with needle-nose pliers and a small glittering object. The blasted earring, he presumed.

He looked back at the squirt.

Damn, but she was a pretty little thing. No bigger than a minute from her head full of springy blond curls to her red leather...shoes. He couldn't call those jokes on her feet cowboy boots. Wearing blue shorts and a white T-shirt splotched with grape jelly stains, she looked fragile. And needy.

His palms started to sweat.

"So can I, Uncle Matt?" Her bluebonnet eyes were Mary's all over.

"Can you what?"

"Can I play with your bunnies?"

So hopeful. So trusting. So easy for him to disappoint...like Mary.

"I don't have any bunnies, kid," he said gruffly.

Mattie's face fell.

"But I have four horses, a dog, a few barn cats and a lot of cows," he heard himself add. "If you don't mind cleaning yucky poop, you're gonna love it on the ranch."

She lit up like a full moon and shook her curls vigorously. "I don't mind. Weena said I'm the best helper he ever had."

She obviously spent more time with "Weena" than he'd thought. Dismissing a tickle of concern, Matt hula-hooped his hat on an index finger.

"Sounds like Edwina's a pretty good friend of yours. Is that right?"

"Uh-huh. He shows me how to do stuff—can I try that?" Mattie pointed eagerly to his Stetson.

Matt stopped the hat's twirl. "What kind of stuff?"

Pressing forward, she splayed a teensie hand on his thigh, lifted her opposite weensie index finger for the hat. "Can I try it now?"

"Mattie, what does he show you how to do?"

"I'm not supposed to tell on accounta it's a secret."

His stomach rolled. *"Mattie."*

Her covetous gaze jerked up from his hat and widened.

"Tell me."

Apparently something in his expression told her to cooperate. "He shows me how to put on makeup, fix hair...you know, trade secrets."

"Oh."

"Weena's got lotsa different hair, not just red."

"Is that a fact?" His knees were rubbery.

"Uh-huh. Sometimes he wears yellow hair, like Cinderella at the ball. An' sometimes he's in a Jasmine kinda mood...you know, dark and romantic?"

Matt headed for the worn brown sofa.

"But Ariel's red hair is hot and brings out the blue in his eyes, so it's Weena's favorite—"

He sat gratefully.

"—even if it is a bitch to comb out," Mattie finished in a philosphical tone.

"Mattie!" Abbey scolded, ruining the effect by laughing.

She caught Matt's accusing gaze and shrugged. "Edwina shares Mattie's love for animated Disney heroines. On the days I showed my jewelry at craft fairs, he was a godsend, baby-sitting for me at no charge. He wouldn't harm a hair on her head, and Mattie adores staying with him."

"Weena's fun," the child confirmed, clomping carefully to the couch as if her boots were too big. "He plays dress-up with me, too."

"I'll bet." There was something seriously wrong here, beyond Edwina, who was as wrong as a sidesaddle on a bronc. Matt looked at Abbey. "You told me Mary bartended at night."

"That's right. Down at The Marina. It's a nice place," she added hastily, as if that were his concern.

"Yeah, I'm sure it is." Mary had always liked nice things. And the men who provided them. "If she had a night job, then she was here in the daytime, right?"

Abbey blinked and pushed up her glasses.

Not a good sign. "So what was the problem with her baby-sitting? Why didn't *Mary* watch Mattie during the day?"

"Mommy works real late," Mattie piped up beside his knee. "She doesn't like to 'sturb us, so she sleeps at work a lot and comes home to watch Oprah. That's our special time together. Can I have your hat now, please?"

He snatched up the Stetson beside him, dropped it over her uplifted index finger and watched her arm disappear to the elbow. As she wobbled the brim around and around, he met Abbey's eyes.

She looked down quickly. But not fast enough.

Her embarrassment on his behalf shamed and angered him. Motherhood hadn't changed Mary a bit! She'd obviously gone home with different bozos from the bar and left her roommate to take care of her child. If Abbey hadn't been such a responsible person, no telling what might've happened to his niece.

A dank memory sprouted roots and mush-roomed poisonously in his mind. *He was seventeen. High on beer, a five-hundred-dollar prize check in his pocket and the pretty blonde from Houston who'd just given him an eighty-five point ride. Fumbling to open the front door to Charlie's trailer, he jumped as a bright-haired shadow slipped from the night to join him. Thirteen-year-old Mary "couldn't sleep" and had gone for a walk in the seedy trailer park. He hustled her inside and laid into her good over the sound of their father's drunken snores.*

Only the next morning did he wonder why a girl being lectured should look so relieved. But the question rolled off his cocky shoulders to make room for more pressing thoughts of his next rodeo, his next blonde...

Matt's focus cleared now on the hat turning around and around on his niece's arm.

"Your head's too big," Mattie said, tiring of her game and tossing the large Stetson onto the couch. Looking down at her feet, she draped an arm companionably over his knee.

The weight was sweet and impossibly heavy. He wanted no part of her trust.

"I got boots, too," she said, nudging her left one against his right. "See?"

He leaned over into the scent of grape jelly and something flowery. His black Ropers looked as big as water tubs next to her pointy-toed red boots.

"They're pretty," he lied without hesitation. A female was a female.

"Thank you." A telling moment passed. "Yours are, too."

His unwilling heart tugged. No one had tried to spare his feelings in a hell of a long time. He could guess where she'd learned that kind of politeness, and it wasn't from his sister.

"Did Abbey buy your boots, like she did your Cinderella dress and underwear?"

"Nuh-uh, Mommy did. After I saw your pictures."

He straightened up slowly. "Pictures?"

"Uh-huh. She keeps 'em in a big book. Your arm's kinda flappin' in front of your face, but Mommy said it's you." Mattie eyed him solemnly. "You're a ro-dee-oh star."

He could only gape.

"Were you scared?" she asked.

"Huh?"

"Were you scared riding those mean horses?" Her delicate blond brows met in an anxious line.

Scared? Nervous, maybe. But once the gate clanged open, exhilaration took over.

"Nah. I'm too tough to be scared," Matt drawled, his sarcastic tone clearly wasted on his niece.

Mattie flashed the Granger dimple, legacy

from a grandfather she'd never met. "Mommy said you're one tough oam-bray. The best rider in Texas—which means the world," she parroted, her chest puffed out.

Mary Quite Contrary had said that?

"She got me boots like yours, so if I ever get scared I can put 'em on and be tough. Like you, Uncle Matt."

His thoughts unrolled and tangled together, a barbed-wire mess of sharp guilt and shiny amazement. The sister he'd just mentally cursed, the one he'd abandoned six years ago when she'd needed him most, had not only named her baby after him, she'd also kept a scrapbook of his rodeo career. Fed who-knew-what kind of fairy tales to her daughter.

A daughter who watched him now as if he were some kind of damn hero, when he was anything but.

Snatching his hat, he thrust up from the couch, the movement flinging Mattie's small arm off his thigh, and strode to the door.

"Look," he said, unbolting the lock, "I didn't eat breakfast—" he glanced at Abbey's startled face "—and it's obvious you're not ready to leave. I'll just grab a bite to eat and come back in an hour. Lock this behind me."

Not bothering to wait for a response, he jerked open the door and stepped through, slammed it behind him and paused. When the snick of a dead bolt sounded he started for the stairs.

Up ahead, the next apartment door squeaked open. Edwina slipped outside, a startling vision in a filmy pink harem outfit and long black wig. *Dark and romantic,* Matt remembered his niece's description.

It was obviously a Jasmine kinda day.

Edwina splayed a hand on one hip. "You look a little upset, there, cowboy. Are Abbey and Mattie okay?"

"They're fine." Matt touched his hat brim and moved forward. "Excuse me."

Edwina sidled to block Matt's path.

"That's good, because I wouldn't want anything to hurt them. They're very special, you know."

Matt's focus sharpened. Behind the heavy eyeliner and false eyelashes, a steely warning flashed strong and true. Edwina took a mountainous leap up in Matt's estimation.

He nodded. "I do know. Thanks for watchin' over Mattie these last months. And don't worry. She'll be well taken care of from now on."

After a few more seconds of intense scrutiny, Edwina smiled in approval and stepped aside.

Matt continued toward the stairway, ignoring the appreciative "Mmm-mmm-mmm" murmured to his back.

He didn't deserve any admiration from Edwina *or* the squirt. The fact was, he had no idea if Mattie would be well taken care of or not. His jaw tensed.

It all depended on Abbey.

CHAPTER FIVE

SAND SHIFTING BENEATH her feet, Abbey trudged the last few steps into the unpopular shade of a lifeguard tower and turned. "There was an ozone warning this morning. I'd rather stay out of direct sun. Is this spot okay with you, Matt?"

"Yeah, sure." Braced like an immovable lighthouse in the stiff sea breeze, he looked positively miserable.

Turning around quickly, she rummaged in her purse to cover a choked laugh. He'd learned his first valuable lesson in guardianship. *Never promise Mattie she could do whatever she wanted without including a fine-print disclaimer at the end.*

Abbey pulled a tube from her purse, squeezed sunscreen onto her fingertips and gestured to the girl. "C'mere, Rudolf, and let me put more of this on your nose."

Giggling, Mattie moved close and lifted her face.

Anointing the button nose, sun-kissed cheeks and thin arms with white cream, Abbey noted the pleasure shining in the child's eyes. Matt had put it there by trying to make up to her for rushing off earlier. Despite his misgivings, uncle and niece would get along fine on their own. Just as Abbey would. In time.

Mustering a smile, she tweaked a tiny nose. "Okay, you're all set. There's a box of juice in my purse you can have if you're thirsty. I'll be with you in a minute."

"'Kay."

Abbey squeezed out more sunscreen and rubbed her arms absently, but with the same appreciation for texture she devoted to anything she touched. Mattie had found the juice box but was struggling to pierce the top.

"Turn the straw around and use the slanted end," Abbey instructed. "That's right. Careful!"

The deep red fruit punch erupted through the straw to stain the small T-shirt...next to the grape jelly stain, next to the cola stain.

Mattie raised stricken eyes. "It burped."

Abbey laughed. "So I saw. Terry's Tie-Dyed Tees, eat your heart out."

Finished applying sunscreen, she made a face at the excess lotion in her palm and turned to Matt. "Want me to rub this somewhere?"

His heavy-lidded gaze rose slowly from her palm, and he smiled lazily.

Powerful waves crashed rhythmically against the shoreline. The cry of gulls lent percussion to a pop song drifting from a nearby radio. The sounds amplified then faded beneath the louder roar of blood in her ears.

Whirling around, she rubbed lotion over skin already lubricated. Trust Matt not to pass up a sexual innuendo, however innocently served. She was beginning to think he did it on purpose, to keep her off-kilter. If so, the ploy worked far too well.

Thank heavens her life, and her pulse, would return to normal tomorrow!

A tug on her dress captured Abbey's attention. She looked down. *But, oh, how I'll miss this child.*

"Can I play in the sand, now?" Mattie asked.

"Absolutely." Abbey reached for her purse, fumbled in the depths and pulled out a plastic shovel. "Here you go. Let's find you a good spot to make a castle."

By the time she left the little girl happily stabbing sand in a far corner of the shade, Abbey had recovered her composure. She sank down beside Matt's boots and looked up.

"Aren't you going to sit?"

His brooding sensuality vanished. He eyed the sand in distaste, then lowered himself by degrees, his joints protesting like ice cubes cracking free of the tray. Wrists draped over the jutting knees of his crossed legs, he rocked side to side, grew still, rocked some more, expelled a peeved breath.

When he'd left that morning to eat breakfast, Abbey had sneaked a peek at Mary's scrapbook. The man was, indeed, a ro-dee-oh star, with an appalling number of injuries over the course of his career.

"I wasn't thinking," Abbey admitted now. "Would you rather stand?"

He eyed her askance. "Anybody ever tell you your timing really stinks?" He anchored his hat more firmly. "God, I hate the beach."

"Well, you made big points today with Mattie. She adores the beach. But then, I guess that's natural, since Mary loved it, too. Whenever I needed to find her, this is the first place I'd look. She spent as much time here as she could.''

Matt's mouth twisted. ''Yeah, I can picture her struttin' her stuff for attention, maybe riding the waves for a thrill. She take up surfing?''

''No, she wasn't even a sunbather. Her skin tended to burn, like mine. She told me once that the sound of ocean waves made her feel peaceful.''

''Peaceful!'' Matt harrumphed. ''Doesn't sound like my sister. The Mary I knew spent as much time in detention hall growing up as she did in the classroom. She kicked up a hornet's nest of trouble every time she got bored.''

Abbey could well imagine. ''Your poor father.''

''*Charlie?* Hell, our dad got into too much trouble himself to worry about gettin' Mary out.'' His bitter tone spoke of heartache, and hours of worry.

''So you took on the job?''

His expression shuttered.

Her intuitive guess had been right. Intrigued, she pressed for more information. ''What was Mary like as a child?''

''Does it matter?''

"Remembering might help you deal with Mattie."

He shot the child an indecipherable look, brushed the sand from one boot, scanned the beach speckled with colorful towels and toasting bodies. "Mary was a tough little thing," he began hesitantly. "A real tomboy. After I started ridin' steers in rodeos around age eleven? Well, she finally got so jealous, she climbed the stock pen fence and jumped on a steer's back. Rode it long enough to prove she could. That was her first broken arm." His mouth curved up as if in spite of himself.

"Her *first*. Mercy, she was only...what? Eight?"

"Seven. At eight she broke her wrist ropin' a calf and not lettin' go. She just *had* to do whatever I did. Believe it or not, for all the times she got hurt, I must've saved her ass—" he flicked another glance at Mattie "—sorry, her rear, at least a dozen times."

The exasperated love in his voice summoned a fierce wistfulness in Abbey ten times more frightening than sexual attraction. Anger followed swiftly. She didn't need anyone's smothering protection!

Even so, some platitude was appropriate.

"Mary was lucky to have a big brother like you to look out for her."

He squared his jaw and squinted toward distant whitecaps. "I'm no hero, Abbey. I was a lousy brother. A cocky teenager way too big for my chaps. I didn't want a little sister doggin' my heels, holdin' me back from doin' things with my buddies. Things with *girls*," he added, casting her a meaningful glance in case there was any rose tint still coloring her glasses.

Disconcerted, Abbey adjusted the folds of her dress. She knew all about feeling restricted. "Sounds to me like you were a normal teenager, not a lousy brother."

"Speakin' of normal," Matt said, clearly wanting to change the subject. "There are a lot of other beach communities in California, probably any one of 'em a better place to raise a kid than Venice. You were Mary's friend. Why do you think she picked a three-ring circus to live in?"

Abbey stiffened. "We were roommates, not really close friends. But I assume Mary was attracted to exactly what turns you off about Venice. It's a cross-cultural paradise."

"You mean a cross-dresser's paradise."

"I rest my case. Mary might have been a little

reckless, but she was never judgmental. She didn't think her way was the *only* way to think.''

''And I do? You're being a little judgmental, don't you think?''

She took a slow, calming breath of salty air. ''What I think is that you could never appreciate Venice's unconventional life-style.''

''C'mon Abbey. This place is full of weirdos.''

''According to whose standards?''

''Texan standards. God-fearing moral standards.''

Oooh, he sounded just like her father! ''If I had a nickel for every intolerent opinion passed off as high morals, I could rent space on Abbot Kinney Boulevard. You leave God out of this discussion. She doesn't share your prejudices.''

''She?'' Matt winked his dimple. ''Well, that explains a global oops like El Niño.''

''Don't change the subject,'' she ordered, the unholy mischief in his eyes goading her on. ''The people here have developed an alternative economy to mainstream America, true. But they're happy. They're productive. They're—''

''Weird,'' he interrupted. ''Admit it, Abbey.''

''I'll do no such thing! I loathe labels, and the communities that foster finger-pointing and superior attitudes. Venice is enlightened. Everyone is welcome here, regardless of race, sexual orientation, religion—'' she glanced scathingly at his hat ''—or bad manners.''

Matt whipped off his Stetson, clapped it over his heart and quoted solemnly, '' 'One nation, under God, indivisible, with liberty and justice for all.' ''

''*Yes,* you ignorant cowboy, 'with liberty and justice for all'! Do you have any idea what that means to someone who hasn't had it?''

''Who're you callin' ignorant? I knew the words.''

She shoved up her glasses. ''Are you so afraid to deal with real emotion you have to hide behind innuendo or jokes? Can that peanut brain of yours comprehend the privilege of being able to say what you think, create what inspires you, do exactly what you want *when* and *where* you want to, without fear of ridicule or punishment? How *dare* you mock something so precious.''

Abbey blinked rapidly while his expression shifted from amused to stunned.

''How dare you,'' she repeated brokenly, and scrambled to her feet in a billow of denim.

She turned her back and slapped the sand out of her dress, knowing he must think her certifiable, not blaming him at all, since she thought the same thing. Her anger and hurt had spewed up from somewhere so deep she hadn't realized it still existed. Had all those hours of therapy merely buried the emotions rather than eliminated them?

Shaken, she walked to Mattie and praised the lopsided sand castle, conscious all the while of Matt clamoring to his feet.

"Hey, Abbey!" A shout from the beach captured her attention.

Spotting the source, she suppressed a groan.

WATCHING ABBEY TRY and pull herself together, Matt cursed his ignorant peanut brain. In his effort to change a subject painful for him, he'd obviously opened a distressing can of worms for her. He'd almost made her cry, damn his hide. Then, in typical Abbey fashion, she'd lifted her chin, shown him her back and beaten the hell out of her dress long after every speck of sand had cried uncle.

His apology would have to wait, though. Right now they had company. Matt turned and sized up the man heading for Abbey.

Five foot eleven, give or take an inch. Shoulder-length blond hair flapping in the breeze.

Khaki shorts and a navy "L.A. Parks & Recreation" T-shirt. Pumped-up muscles giving him that restricted gait peculiar to bodybuilders and people wearing a neck brace. The clues added up to Paul, who, according to Abbey, wore a sign on his back that said "Mess With Me And You Die."

Hell, put a sword in his hand and he'd look like a damn romance-cover model. 'Course, some women went for that type....

He slanted a glance at Abbey through his lashes. She didn't seem all that thrilled. His niece looked up, rolled her eyes at the approaching man, then continued gouging her shallow moat deeper.

"Hello, Paul," Abbey said after the guy stopped. "What are you doing out here?"

His gaze was both accusing and possessive. "Detective Hendricks is a regular at the gym. He told me about some trouble on his beat last night."

Abbey let the silence stretch.

He ran an agitated hand through his sun-streaked hair. "Jeez, Abbey, I've been looking all over for you. Are you all right?"

"That's really sweet, Paul, but as you can see, I'm fine. We're all fine."

"But you could've been hurt." He reached for Abbey's hand and swallowed it with a meaty paw.

"Can we talk about this later, please?" She glanced down at Mattie, who seemed preoccupied with her digging.

"You always want to talk later. But, honey, *now's* the perfect time for you to let that apartment go. There's no reason for you to have to search for a new roommate. I can help you move into my place tomorrow after the funer—" He broke off and glanced at Mattie for the first time, his expression dutifully solemn.

"When you can," he amended.

"We've already had this discussion, Paul. I haven't changed my mind."

"But, honey, that neighborhood isn't safe, especially walking there alone after dark. Look what happened last night."

Her expression hardened. "If you talked to Detective Hendricks, then you know I wasn't walking alone."

Paul flicked a dismissive glance at Matt. "You might as well have been."

Bristling, Matt stepped forward, only to draw up short at Abbey's warning look.

Facing Paul again, she wrenched her hand

free. "Don't be rude. Mattie and I probably owe
our lives to her uncle. I really doubt you
could've protected us better. You're a tournament kickboxer, yes, but a judged round is a
very controlled situation. Matt kept a cool head
in a street fight with no rules, and if you care
about me at all, you would *thank* him—not insult him.''

When Paul's surly gaze moved past Abbey
this time, Matt was waiting with an egg-sucking
grin.

Eyes bulging, Paul puffed up like one of the
toads Pitiful sometimes substituted for a ball. "If
I'd walked Abbey home like usual, she wouldn't
have been mugged in the first place.''

"The *hell* you say,'' Matt muttered, stalking
forward to stand beside Abbey. It gave him immense satisfaction to look down on the other
man.

"That's what I say, cowboy. I've been walking her home for five months now, and she
hasn't been bothered or hurt in all that time.''

"I dunno, pal, walking with you has got to be
a huge pain in the ass.''

"Matt!'' Abbey said sharply.

"You re-e-eally don't want to piss me off,''

Paul warned in an ugly tone. "I was Division I Kickboxing Champion."

"I was World Champion Saddle Bronc Rider."

"I don't believe this," Abbey said, shaking her head and crouching beside Mattie. "C'mon sweetie, stand up and let's get you brushed off."

"Do we hafta leave *now?* I'm not sunburned."

"The ozone level is fine. But the testosterone's thick enough to choke an elephant." Abbey grabbed Mattie's hand and rose.

The child scrambled up wearing a pleading expression. "Can we stay, Abbey? I won't choke. Please, Abbey? I wanna watch Uncle Matt kick butt."

"Stick around, brat," Paul ordered in a snarling voice. "We'll see whose butt gets kicked all the way to Texas."

Matt grew deadly still. "Don't call her 'brat.'"

Glancing up at his expression, Abbey shivered.

Paul took a half step back, reddened, then firmed his stance and looked at Abbey. "What's going on here? I thought we had an understanding."

Her emotions were too frazzled for diplomacy. "That's the problem, Paul. You've never understood me. Never even tried."

"But..." Hostility clearly battled with hurt. "Mattie's leaving tomorrow without you, right?"

"Yes."

"And you'll need—"

"No-o!" The thin anguished cry raised several heads from surrounding beach towels.

Mattie stood quivering, a mixture of outrage and panic swirling in her blue eyes. She thrust out her jaw at Paul. "Go away and leave us alone, you...you *poopoohead!* Abbey's coming to Texas with me and Uncle Matt."

Abbey had explained otherwise, Matt knew. But obviously his niece was in denial.

Paul scowled. "Look, Mattie, I know you'll miss Abbey, but she has a life here—"

"No! Abbey's coming to Texas with me and Uncle Matt, and Mommy's gonna watch over us all from heaven. Isn't that right, Abbey?" Spinning around, the child clutched folds of denim dress and threw back her head.

Matt had seen that same wild desperation in newly weaned foals. If not kept in special pens,

they would literally batter themselves to death
trying to get back to their mothers.

"Right, Abbey? You're coming with us,
right? Tell him."

Abbey laid a trembling hand on Mattie's
cheek. "Oh, honey…"

"Tell him!" The child jerked hard on Abbey's dress, as if she could yank out the answer
she needed to hear. "I promise I'll be good. I
won't open your jars of beads, honest."

"Mattie—"

"I'll brush my teeth. I'll eat spinach, and I
won't spit it out when you're not looking, either."

"Mattie—"

"You got to come, Abbey. You just *got* to. If
you don't, who'll model your jewelry when it's
finished?"

Abbey laughed, a heart-wrenching choked little sound.

"I love you, Abbey," Mattie whispered.

"Oh, pun'kin, I love you, too." Abbey intercepted a crystalline tear with her thumb, ignoring the one dripping from her own chin.

The emotion shining between them was so
pure and bright it was like staring directly into

the sun. Wincing, Matt sought comfort in the cool blue Pacific horizon.

His plan to cajole or badger Abbey into traveling to Texas shamed him now. As much as she loved his niece, if she'd decided not to go, then it was in everyone's best interest.

"All right, Mattie, you win. I'll come with you. But only for a little while."

Matt turned his head in time to see stark relief flooding his niece's face. She threw her arms around Abbey and hugged fiercely, pulled back and looked up with intent eyes.

"Tell him," she ordered.

Abbey turned her gaze to Paul. "I'm sorry if you misunderstood my intentions, Paul, but I'm going with Mattie to Texas tomorrow. That is, if her uncle still wants my help."

Matt took the full impact of Abbey's soft brown eyes straight in his gut. He dragged in a breath and nodded. Even added, "Glad you changed your mind."

Only he wasn't glad. He was too damn scared to be glad. Because for a second there he'd wanted more than Abbey's help. Or her kiss. Or even her sweetly curved body in his arms.

For a second there he'd wanted her to look at him as she had Mattie.

And love wasn't in his best interest at all.

CHAPTER SIX

THE GAL HAD SNAP in her garters, he'd say that
for Abbey Parker.

Hal Bonner added eggs, milk and seasoning
to the corn bread mix already in the bowl, his
mind churning faster than his slow-stirring
spoon. You could've knocked him over with a
tumbleweed five days ago when Matt had gotten
off that plane with, not one, but two passengers—one of them a woman!

Not a "mature 45+, child-care experience
necessary" type of woman, neither, like Matt's
want ad in the San Antonio newspaper spelled
out. But a young *marriageable* filly. One who
had Charlie's boy purely bumfuzzled.

If that didn't beat all!

Pouring batter into greased muffin tins, Hal
checked the yellowed wall clock shaped like an
apple. Four-fifteen. Abbey was in her room
working on that fancy necklace she'd sketched

the day before. Mattie would be up from her late nap any minute.

A little cranky, a little hungry. Nothin' that a corn muffin wouldn't take care of till supper.

He slid the tins inside an ancient gas range, washed his gnarled hands at the chipped enamel sink. A glance out the window showed Matt working Doc in the round pen.

The man was always working. Sunup to sundown outside, then on his fancy computer at night.

That was one tough Texan, all right. Hal had seen Matt go hungry to pay entry fees, tape up cracked ribs and sprained shoulders to make his rides. He'd overcome hardships that would've stopped a weaker man and risen in the PRCA standings till he reached the top.

Then he'd come back to where it all began. Invested his winnings in the old Warner ranch. Hung up his shingle as a cutting horse trainer and started over at the bottom.

And danged if he wasn't on the rise again.

The stallion Doc Holiday would give Matt what he wanted. Respect from the folks who'd felt sorry for him as a boy. It wouldn't be enough, any more than winning a gold buckle had warmed his heart permanent.

But some things a man flat had to learn for hisself.

Hal blew out a breath, tested the potatoes boiling on the stove for tenderness, then started snapping fresh green beans for supper. Arthritis made his movements slow and deliberate.

When he'd still been living in a sorry roach motel of an apartment after retiring, there'd been some days he hadn't bothered to roll out of bed, the pain was so bad. Then Matt had bought this place and offered Hal a job as cook, complete with a trailer house behind the stable to call his own.

He'd jumped at the chance like a duck on a— well, more like a turtle on a June bug. But he'd snapped it up without thinking twice.

Hal scanned the ranch house kitchen possessively. It was old but built solid, with plenty of good years left to give a family. Kinda like him, only he creaked worse. Chuckling, he realized his spirits were lighter than they'd been in a good long time.

Despite Mary's death.

Maybe even because of it.

God had closed one door and opened another.

If she hadn't died, her daughter and Abbey wouldn't be here now. After twenty years of watching Matt scramble women's brains, Hal had about given up hope one would return the favor, maybe stir Matt's heart, too.

The little neighbor gal, Bess, had her sights set on bein' the one. She was a pretty thing, sure enough, but she had a lotta growin' up left to do. Couldn't see the man behind Matt's good looks and gold buckle, much less appreciate 'im proper, love 'im like he deserved.

But this Abbey...well, she was different. Didn't know a rodeo from a quilting bee, so Matt's fame didn't hold much weight.

She didn't wear tight jeans or paint her face or stick out her bosoms to get his attention. When he smiled, she didn't turn giggly or flirty or dumb enough for twins, like some Hal had seen.

Abbey didn't sulk when Matt ignored her, or get upset when he teased her for not knowin' country ways. But let him do either to his niece...whooee!

She'd light into him with both barrels loaded.

Four women had already phoned about the want ad in the paper, then decided not to interview after Matt told 'em the salary and location. Setting the beans aside now, Hal thought maybe the man upstairs might've had a hand in that, too.

He drained the potatoes to cool before mashing, then began flouring up pounded meat. Neither one of them California gals had ever tasted chicken-fried steak, he'd learned that morning. He couldn't let another day go by with that on his conscience.

Cooking was a pleasure these days. Abbey and Mattie loved everything he put on the table. Until recently, he'd forgotten how nice a compliment filled the silence at meals. He'd been feeding Matt now for two years with only a mumbled thanks in return, if that.

Most times Hal didn't mind. He was busy and needed, for which he humbly thanked God and Matt, not necessarily in that order. One of them *did* pay Hal's salary, after all.

And as hard as Matt worked to do that, he couldn't be faulted for not having pretty manners. He'd grown up without a mama's love and teachings.

Or, for that matter, a daddy's.

Sighing, Hal let his thoughts travel back in time while his hands kept busy in the present.

He'd been chute boss at the Cottonwood, Texas, rodeo when widower Charlie Granger had settled in town. Every weekend, April through September, Charlie had shown up at the arena, his two kids in tow.

That first year, Matt had been about ten, his sister six, and Hal hadn't paid them much mind. His job was too critical: making sure the rough stock got lined up in the right order, watching for distractions that might spook 'em in the chute, seeing the cowboys settled down tight and watching for their nod of readiness before clanging open the chute gate.

Charlie had been a damned good bull rider. One of the best Hal had seen, and he'd seen his share of pro title contenders. As a PRCA sanctioned rodeo, Cottonwood drew cowboys of all skill levels.

During the timed events when Hal could relax his guard, he'd watched those kids trail Charlie like pups. The boy copying the man's every action, the girl imitating the boy's. Cute, he'd thought. But kinda sad for Charlie, 'cause he might've been a champion given the chance to travel the Professional Rodeo Cowboy Association circuit.

The next season, Matt started riding steers, and Hal started noticing Matt. And boy howdy, could that boy ride! A natural right from the start. Still, Hal might not've taken a personal interest if Mary hadn't decided she could ride a steer, too.

He'd caught a flash of blond hair just as she'd leaped into the steer pen—

"Mercy, did you cut yourself?"

Hal jerked into awareness. Abbey stood in the kitchen doorway, staring at him in alarm.

He looked down into the bowl of potatoes he'd been mashing to kingdom come, checked his swollen knuckles. "No, 'less you see blood I don't."

She walked closer, wearing another one of them long flower-sprigged dresses that kicked up around her pretty feet. After looking at boots for so many years, sandals and painted pink toenails were a pure pleasure to watch.

Her face was no hardship to eyeball, neither.

"You turned so pale," she said, stopping beside him. "Are you sure you're okay?"

Embarrassed now, he reached for the salt. "Yep. Just rememberin' the day Mary jumped onto a steer after her brother finished his ride."

"The day she broke her arm the first time?"

Hal's hand paused mid-shake. "Mary tell you about that?"

"No. Matt did." Abbey handed him the pepper, leaned a hip against the counter and smiled curiously. "Were you there that day?"

Matt had talked to this woman about his sister? Hot damn! Maybe she really was The One.

"Yep. I was busy workin' the chutes and saw her outta the corner of my eye, but it was too late. She'd jumped down into a pen full of steers, every one of 'em spooked and goin' crazy. Miracle she wasn't killed."

Abbey looked shaken. "Mercy, I had no idea! I mean, I knew she broke her arm, but Matt left out the details."

"Sounds like he did, at that," Hal said wryly.

"What happened then?"

"Well, after I finished swallowin' my heart, I ran like the dickens and climbed the pen. Hand me that stick of butter, please."

She did, but looked distracted. "And?"

"The can of evaporated milk, too. That's the secret of good mashed potatoes, ya know. Fresh milk just don't whip up as nice—"

"*Hal,* what happened in that pen?"

He lopped off a big cube of butter, took the can she passed him and poured in a generous amount, then continued the story, his voice subdued.

"When I jumped in, I couldn't see nothin' but

hides. A cowboy told me later Mary stuck to one of them steers like a flea on a waggin' tail 'fore she got throwed. I started yellin' like a wild man, flappin my hat—and then they scattered.''

The horror of that moment came back full force. He'd seen cowboys get busted up, sure. But kids...they weren't supposed to get hurt, that's all.

''My gosh, Hal, you're pale again. Mary only broke her arm, right?''

Hal blinked into focus. ''Yeah, that's right. Her left arm.'' He held Abbey's gaze. ''Matt's body covered up everythin' else.''

She lifted a trembling hand to her throat, her expression stricken.

Left out that little detail, did he? Hal thought, unsurprised. ''Matt jumped in while I was runnin' to get there. By the time the dust cleared, he was a mess. Busted an arm, two ribs and an ankle. His poor skinny back needed thirty-six stitches. The medic said the only thing savin' him from a concussion was his daddy's hand-me-down Stetson. It was too big, and covered most of his head.''

''But, why would Matt mention Mary's arm and not his own injuries? What he did was remarkably brave for anyone to do, much less an eleven-year-old child.''

''Yes'm, it was at that.'' Hal slowly mashed the contents in his bowl.

There was a fine line between trying to help a man and trying to mind that man's business instead of his own. Still, this woman could be the one.

''I remember all the time the medic was workin' on him and Mary, he kept mumblin' he was sorry. See, his dad always put Matt in charge of lookin' out for his sister, and he'd got caught up watchin' the bull riders. Took his eyes off Mary, and next he knew she was climbin' the pen.''

''He blamed *himself?*'' She looked all mother hen ruffled, like she did sometimes takin' up for Mattie.

Hal grunted in satisfaction. ''Matt blames hisself for a lotta things he shouldn't. His daddy was a weak man. Couldn't stay away from booze or women. Saw the strength in his son and milked it but good. Least, till Matt got old enough and fed up enough to kick free of the traces. Now, well, the boy has regrets.''

''About Mary?''

Hal had said enough. At least, he hoped so. ''I reckon you'd have to ask Matt.''

A movement in the doorway caught his attention.

Mattie shuffled barefoot into the kitchen, her golden curls flattened, her yellow shorts and shirt wrinkled. She lowered a fist from her sleep-swollen eyes and frowned.

"Hi pun'kin, did you have a nice nap?" Abbey crooned, leaning down and opening her arms.

Mattie walked straight into them and buried her face grumpily in the woman's shoulder.

"Where's Pitiful?" she asked in a muffled voice.

Hal and Abbey exchanged a grin. It had been love at first sight between the child and huge shaggy mutt.

"He's probably outside with your uncle. You can play with him in a minute."

"I'm hungry," were Mattie's next words.

"Well, I'll bet I know who can take care of that."

"Who?"

Abbey rose and swiped a playful finger down the little girl's nose. "Who's the best cooker in the whole world?"

Mattie looked directly at Hal, and his heart swelled big and hurtful.

Setting down the potatoes, he cleared the gruffness from his throat. "Ever had a hot corn bread muffin with butter and honey?" he asked the little girl.

She shook her head and smiled shyly.

"Best thing you ever slapped a lip over. They should be about ready now, too."

The phone rang shrilly. He cast the thing an irritated glance.

"Go on and answer it, Hal. I'll check the muffins," Abbey offered, already tugging on oven mitts.

Hal hobbled to the wall phone and snatched up the receiver. "Hello," he barked.

There was a slight pause. "Um, hello. I'm calling about your want ad in the newspaper? I taught kindergarten for twenty-seven years, and believe I'm well qualified for the job. Could you tell me, is the position still open?"

Hal watched Abbey pull out the muffins, sniff blissfully, then warn Mattie not to touch the hot metal. The picture was so right he didn't have to think long.

"No, ma'am, it's not. Sorry."

"Oh. Well, thank you."

"No problem." Hanging up, he caught Abbey's curious glance and shrugged. "Wrong number," he lied without a blink.

A door had been opened, no doubt about it. But Hal figured even the man upstairs could use a little help now and then.

TEN MINUTES LATER, Abbey opened the back kitchen door intending to slip out. Instead, a black rubbery nose poked in, followed by a massive head and pleading eyes—one brown, one blue.

Pitiful was truly the strangest-looking dog Abbey had ever seen. He combined the size and general shape of a mastiff with an Australian shepherd's coat and markings. The color breeders called blue merle: fur with a mixture of white, black and gray hairs in varying densities.

According to Hal, three years ago at a rodeo in Oklahoma, Matt had surprised a half-grown pup tearing into a bag of groceries in the back of his pickup. Emaciated, clearly abandoned, he'd looked pitifully grateful for the can of tuna Matt opened and fed him. When nearby truck owners discovered they'd been "hit" and called authorities, Matt had driven home with a friend for life in his cab.

The look Pitiful gave Abbey now matched his

name. When she didn't open the door wider, he added a whine for good measure.

She laughed but didn't budge. "You know you're not allowed in the kitchen. Shame on you."

He lowered his head and averted his gaze.

"Hal would kill me if I let you in," she murmured.

The dog's gaze snapped to hers hopefully.

Uh-oh. She must've sounded as regretful as she felt.

"Pitiful!" Mattie cried from the kitchen table.

His head shot up, his furry face alight. He barked twice, a joyous frenzied sound that made Abbey grin. She didn't have to see the rest of his body to know his long shaggy tail was sweeping the stoop.

"Can he come inside, Hal?" Mattie asked the grizzle-haired man serving her a second corn bread muffin.

Abbey watched Hal's exasperation for the dog wage war against wide blue eyes, a milk mustache and yellow crumb goatee. *No contest.*

To Hal's credit, he tried. "He'll track in dirt and shed hair all over my clean floor."

"No, he won't. Will you, Pitiful?"

The dog woofed right on cue.

Pitiful he might look, but the animal was obviously no dummy. Neither was Mattie.

Abbey waited for the little girl to close the sale.

"I promise if he makes a mess, I'll clean it up. Please, can he come inside?"

"Well..."

She's gotcha.

"Please, please, pretty puh-leeez?"

"Oh, all right."

Mattie was up before he'd finished the sentence, her arms hugging his slight paunch tightly. "*Thank* you!"

The crevices in his weathered face softened. His rheumy blue eyes misted. He patted Mattie's head awkwardly, his Adam's apple bobbing along with his hand.

Swallowing hard herself, Abbey looked back at the dog. "Come on in, you ham, and take a bow."

She widened the door. Pitiful galloped straight toward Mattie while Abbey stepped outside onto the small concrete stoop. Whew! After California, this heat took some getting used to.

Fanning herself, she reached for the knob. Her last glimpse before shutting the door showed Pitiful cleaning Mattie's giggling face with adoring licks, and Hal protecting her milk glass from a swishing tail.

Smiling, Abbey turned and faced the working pens and stable. Two males conquered, two to go.

It was only a matter of time with Casey, the friendly hired hand she'd only talked to twice but had liked immediately. She sensed he would've fallen under Mattie's spell long before now if he'd had a spare minute to spend with the girl. Matt worked the young man almost as hard as he did himself.

And therein lay her biggest challenge.

Upon returning to Texas, Matt had given his niece and Abbey a token tour of the ranch. Unfortunately, it had been long enough to make Mattie hunger to be near the horses or small herd of cattle. Then the child's miserable coward of a guardian had asked Abbey to keep his niece away from the stable area "for her own safety."

So far, Abbey had accomplished the feat with Pitiful's help. But the dog's newness was wearing off. Mattie naturally itched to explore beyond the house. Her distant glimpses of the horses were cruel teases for a child enchanted with all animals.

Abbey knew the lure of forbidden territory

firsthand. Better to let Mattie satisfy her curiosity than let the child's yearning build until she sneaked into the stable first chance she got.

In the past five days, Matt had only seen his niece at meals or on his way to some new task. Despite several…spirited confrontations, Abbey hadn't managed to slow down the man enough to take an interest in Mattie.

His indifference was unacceptable. He had to change. And he had to do so before Abbey's replacement was hired, or she couldn't leave with a clear conscience.

Sighing, Abbey ignored the guilt that was her constant companion these days and scanned the postcard view from the back porch stoop.

Mercy, springtime in central Texas was magnificent!

Large fields of bluebonnets patched the elbows and knees of rolling hills. Closer to the house, other wildflowers sprinkled the grass. Coral red Indian paintbrush. Yellow and white daisies. Something purple she didn't recognize. Something pink she did, but couldn't name. A glorious palette she'd touched and smelled and arranged in different bouquets since she'd arrived, in an effort to brighten up the house.

To her left, Hal's vegetable garden boasted neat rows of lush greenery.

To her right, a tall cottonwood's papery leaves rustled and shimmered against an azure sky.

Ahead, the stable's whitewashed plank boards warmed in the slanting late afternoon rays.

Cows lowed. A dove cooed. The warm breeze mingled scents of clover, tilled earth, and fresh-baked corn bread into a heady perfume.

When a new burst of giggles seeped through the kitchen door behind Abbey, the sights, sounds and smells coalesced into a pain so unexpected she swayed on impact, her lids drifting shut.

With her eyes closed, she could almost make believe the charming old house was her home. That the child inside was her own precious daughter and Hal her trusted friend. She could almost pretend the beauty before her was a gift she could unwrap leisurely over the seasons. That she needn't rip it open and move on, as she'd done in seven cities over the past eight years.

If she squeezed her eyes shut *really* hard, she could almost imagine serving a man coffee day after day. Not begrudgingly, but gladly, hoping to ease the lines of strain etching his weary face.

From what she'd gathered, Matt worked harder than any two men combined.

Abbey's eyelids fluttered, then lifted. Dear Lord, what was she *thinking?* Her gaze moved to the left of the stable, to the spot she'd avoided staring at but had seen with the sixth sense she'd discovered only last week.

He was there in the largest pen, riding one of his horses. The top of his hat was barely visible over the high fence.

The leap of her heart triggered confusion and panic. Not for her, living at a man's beck and call, her own needs and dreams unimportant. Not for Mattie, either. That is, not if Abbey had anything to say about the child's future. Which she did.

Only first, she needed time to regroup her defenses against a masculine dimple and nodding wildflowers that tempted her to stay.

Spinning around, Abbey grasped the doorknob as if it were a life jacket in a stormy sea. She plunged into the warm dry safety of the kitchen, her conscience jeering, *Who's the miserable coward, now?*

CHAPTER SEVEN

THE NEXT MORNING, Abbey awakened at dawn curled on her side facing the window. As usual. No matter where she was, her slumbering body reached toward the first available light and jerked her mind awake. Even if it wasn't ready.

When she'd agreed to stay here temporarily, she hadn't realized the conditions would be so...cozy. Not that she didn't love the three-bedroom house with hardwood floors, high ceilings and wonderful old-fashioned furniture purchased from the previous owner. But listening to creaking bedsprings in the next room was a little disconcerting to say the least. It kept her aware of the man turning restlessly in bed. It made her wonder why he did.

Sleep hadn't claimed her until the wee hours.

Arching now into a joint-popping stretch, she held it a second, then collapsed in pleasant lethargy. With a start of surprise, she realized it had been months since she'd lazed alone with her thoughts.

Before moving to Venice, she'd spent hours on end by herself, absorbed in designing and crafting her jewelry. Emerging from seclusion only to work her eight-to-five jewelry store sales job in whatever city she called home at the moment. Occasionally she would rent a stall at weekend craft fairs, or show samples to retailers in hopes of finding new outlets.

She'd thought solitude a necessity for creativity. But the necklace she was working on now had been sketched with one eye on Mattie and her ears tuned to constant chatter. Lorna would've agreed it was Abbey's best design yet.

Smiling nostalgically, Abbey thought back to her first job in the evil world outside Baker's Landing, Nebraska. "A lady's companion," the ad in the *Chicago Tribune* had described the available position.

Intimidated by the worldliness surrounding her, Abbey had found the old-fashioned wording reassuring. Lorna Meyer had found Abbey's respect for her elders equally comforting.

The wealthy upper-class matron had spent the energy other women devoted to jobs or charity on her hobby: crafting jewelry. Abbey became a fascinated and apt pupil, studying the works of famous painters and sculptors, as well as jewelry designers in books her mentor supplied. She'd been encouraged to develop her talent for professional purposes, as Lorna had not been "allowed" to do.

It was Lorna who'd also ferreted out Abbey's full life story, then paid for weekly visits to a therapist. For that, Abbey would be eternally grateful. She shuddered now to think where she might've ended up otherwise.

When Lorna had died two years after hiring her young companion, she'd left her money to an absent son. But her jeweler's tools and a lifetime collection of beads, component "findings," semiprecious stones, buttons and fabric scraps had gone to Abbey.

Armed with basic knowledge, eclectic materials for fashioning jewelry, and a passion surpassing her mentor's, Abbey had developed a unique mixed-media style. Unlimited by convention. Truly free in spirit. By the time she arrived in Venice, she'd designed and crafted an impressive variety of inventory. Inspired by the risk-takers all around her, she'd attempted to live solely on the proceeds of Free Bird Jewelry.

She'd barely squeaked by.

For the moment, a free room and great meals were nothing to complain about, despite her original protests. Abbey threw back the covers and sat up. Maybe she'd give Hal a break, put some coffee on and start a simple breakfast. He'd been an angel about helping out with Mattie.

Abbey had braided her hair and just pulled on a tie-dyed T-shirt in muted blues and greens when she heard Mattie's bedroom door squeak open. Moments passed.

Uh-oh. Not coming straight to Abbey's room only meant one thing. Trouble. She slipped on the long gauzy skirt matching her tee and hurried out in search of her charge. She wouldn't at all put it past the scamp to sneak Pitiful inside. Since her arrival, Mattie had begged for the dog to be allowed to sleep with her. Wait—what was that?

Abbey headed for the quaint parlor to check out the small noise she'd heard. At the doorway, she paused.

Wearing a long white ruffled nightgown, Mattie sat on the hardwood floor in front of the fireplace, gazing up at the mantel. Her tousled curls shimmered pale gold in a beam of sunlight from the east window. With her legs tucked beneath

her gown, she looked remarkably like the ceramic angel she studied.

Entranced, Abbey wondered how to proceed.
The little girl had cried at the memorial service,
but Abbey had gotten the impression it was due
more to the strange surroundings and sadness
picked up from adults than a true understanding
of Mary's death. After they'd unpacked at the
ranch, Abbey had insisted Matt include his niece
in finding just the right spot for the angel.

When Mattie had suggested the kitchen
counter, he'd gruffly wondered if people might
mistake the angel for a cookie jar. When she'd
slapped a decisive palm on the reachable marble-
topped table next to the claw-footed blue sofa,
he'd said Pitiful might accidentally break the ceramic, "him being so clumsy and all." After
several more impractical suggestions from the
earnest little girl, Matt had finally proposed the
mantel as "someplace high, so we can remember your mama's spirit is in heaven and she's
happy."

His sensitivity had touched Abbey and given
her false hope he would continue in the same
vein.

She signed now, then softly said, "Honey?"
The child spun around on her bottom like a

human top, her eyes wide and guilty. "I didn't touch Mommy, honest."

"I know you didn't, sweetie." She moved into the room, sat on the floor and crossed her legs yoga-style. "Is everything okay?"

Mattie shrugged uncertainly.

"Were you maybe missing Mommy a little?"

She hesitated, then nodded, crystalline tears welling in her big baby blues.

"I miss her, too," Abbey said, startled to realize it was true. Mary'd had a childlike ability to discover the fun in life that was charming, unless one depended on her for half the rent. "Since I'm feeling sad, Mattie, would you mind sitting in my lap and cheering me up?"

In answer, she scrambled quickly into the nest formed by crossed legs and settled back as if she were in a comfy armchair. Contentment warmed Abbey along with the fragile little body in her arms.

She snuggled the child closer and planted her chin on a blond head. Together, they stared up at the angel. Now, if she could only get a feel for how Mattie was settling into her new life.

"Your mommy is so proud of you now, Mattie," Abbey began carefully. "You've come to a new place and you're being so brave. But you know, sometimes it's okay not to try and be grown-up. Sometimes even grown-ups get scared and need to talk about how they feel.''

"They do?"

"Oh, yes," Abbey said fervently. "They do. For instance, it took me awhile to get used to sleeping in a different place. What about you? Are you happy in your bedroom?"

"The bed's too high."

Abbey digested the implications regarding the old-fashioned four-poster bed. She didn't want to give the child ideas. "Why is it too high? Is it too hard for you to climb into?"

"Nuh-uh. I'm a *good* climber."

"Hey, you're right. You're a terrific climber! That was a silly question. Let's see, is there too much space under the bed?"

Mattie nodded so vigorously Abbey bit her tongue.

She was definitely getting out of her depth, but she waded forward. "My bed's high off the ground, too. My first night here, I wondered if there was something under there. You know, something scary?"

"Like a mean old ugly monster."

Gotcha. "Right. But then I remembered that my guardian angel watches over me and would never let a mean old ugly monster anywhere near my bed.''

"You mean like Mommy watches over me?"

Sticky territory, but certainly more healthy than tales of a tooth fairy or easter bunny sneaking into the house while one was asleep.

"That's right. Your mommy still loves you from heaven and wants to keep you safe. Plus, she's a Granger. What do you think she'd do if a mean old ugly monster tried to get under your bed?"

"Kick his goddamn butt?"

"Mattie!"

"She wouldn't?"

"Yes, she would. But don't use rude language, please."

"Okay. I mean...thank you?"

Abbey couldn't help laughing. "Don't use *bad words,*" she emphasized. "You know that god—well, what you said before, is a bad word. Why did you say it?"

"Uncle Matt says it all the time."

Abbey sniffed. "Yes, well, that doesn't mean *you* should."

"How come?"

"Because ladies don't use rude words. Neither do gentlemen."

"Oh." She scratched her chin. "So what's Uncle Matt?"

Abbey blinked.

"Don't answer that," Matt drawled from the doorway.

Woman and child whirled around.

Matt stood with arms folded, one brawny shoulder against the doorjamb, one bare foot crossed over the other. His blue-black hair wasn't combed, he needed a shave, his slate-blue western shirt hung untucked over boot-cut Wranglers that overlapped his heels.

Mercy, how long had he been there?

"How come you're not a gentleman, Uncle Matt?"

Amusement gleamed in his sleepy gray eyes. "I guess 'cause nobody taught me manners, squirt."

"How come?"

"'Cause my mama died when I was about your age and I didn't have anybody to teach me."

"Your mommy died like mine?"

"Yep."

"Oh." She heaved a gusty sigh. "Do you miss her?"

Matt looked startled, then thoughtful. "I guess I do at that, squirt."

"Did your daddy die like mine, too?"

His gaze jumped to Abbey's for help, but this was news to her. She smoothed back gossamer curls from the child's forehead. "Is that what your mommy said, honey? That your daddy died?"

"She said he left us t'go someplace better and wasn't never comin' back. So he's in heaven, right?"

Any man who abandoned his child deserved to go to a very different place, in Abbey's opinion. From Matt's expression, he'd like a chance to send the father there via his bare hands.

"That sounds logical to me," Abbey hedged.

"So did your daddy die, Uncle Matt?"

"Huh? Oh. Yea, squirt, he did. But not till I was already grown."

"So how come *he* didn't teach you manners?"

Matt's eyebrows lowered like incoming thunderheads. "He didn't have any manners himself to pass on, I guess."

"How come?"

The depth of contempt in Matt's eyes shocked Abbey. She hurried to divert the subject. "Did you know your grandfather was a rodeo cowboy like Uncle Matt?''

Mattie twisted and looked up, clearly puzzled. ''My grandfather?''

The child was as sharp as a jeweler's saw, but woefully ignorant of basic things most five-year-olds had been taught by involved parents. Abbey mentally added family structure to a tutorial list that included counting to fifty and reciting the alphabet.

''Your mommy's and Uncle Matt's father was your grandfather. His name was Charlie Granger, and he rode bulls in rodeos.''

''He did?'' Fascinated eyes hungered for more.

''That's what Hal said. I'm sure your Uncle Matt could tell you more.''

Mattie's head snapped around hopefully.

Matt unfolded his arms and straightened from the doorjamb, his gaze on Abbey. ''I've got horses to feed before Casey gets here. Tell Hal I'd appreciate it if he'd put a breakfast plate in the warmer for me, and if he'd kindly mind his own goddamn business from now on.'' He turned and managed a credible job of stomping off, considering he was barefoot.

Mattie recovered first. ''That was very rude.''

Yes. And interesting. "He isn't mad at you, sweetie."

"I know."

"Good." Abbey pulled back and to the side, the better to see a delicate angel face. "How come you know?"

"'Cause he isn't mad at anybody. He's sad."

Abbey stared thoughtfully at the empty doorway, then hugged Mattie hard.

Out of the mouths of babes.

ABBEY FLIPPED BACK her braid, moved down the porch steps and hit the grass at a brisk walk. This was ridiculous. Matt had skilfully avoided her since yesterday morning in the parlor. He'd continued his Artful Dodger role today, failing to show up for lunch. It was past time she had another "little chat" with Mattie's uncle.

The large round pen ahead was fenced with treated plank lumber, each board standing perpendicular to the ground about eight feet high. No gaps between the planks to distract a horse in training. By the same token, Abbey couldn't see inside.

It had to be stifling in there with no cooling breeze passing through. She walked around the pen until she reached the only opening: a steel-pipe gate about five feet high.

Casey stood behind it, his arms draped over the top pipe, one boot propped on the lowest. Tall and rangy, dressed in jeans, beige shirt and matching felt hat, he watched his employer with rapt attention.

There was certainly something about a cowboy that made a woman appreciate the way a man was built.

Yet when he turned and saw her, his boyishly handsome face breaking into a smile, her heart didn't jump out of her chest. She didn't forget where she was. Or what she was doing.

Relaxing, she moved up beside him. "Hi, Casey."

He tipped his hat, pleasure lighting his hazel eyes. "Ma'am. Is there somethin' I can do for you?"

"First of all, don't call me ma'am. It makes me feel like your mother." She smiled to soften her words. "Do you have any idea when Matt will be finished?"

"Another ten minutes, maybe. Unless you want me to stop the lesson?"

"Mercy, no!" She wasn't a wimp, but neither

was she incredibly stupid. "I'll just stand here and watch with you. That is, if you don't mind."

"No, ma'am." An endearing flush rose up his neck. "I mean, no, I'd be glad to have company that smells and looks pretty for a change."

She laughed, unable to help her spurt of pleasure at his appreciative stare. She'd almost forgotten how flattering a man's simple admiration could be.

What about Matt's admiration? her honesty prodded.

To cover her confusion, Abbey crouched to refasten her sandal strap unnecessarily. There was nothing simple about Matt—or the mixed emotions he inspired.

She was angry at his aloofness toward Mattie, charmed by his aw-shucks smile. Exasperated at his macho posturing, touched by his kindness toward homeless dogs and old men. At age eleven he'd displayed the heart and courage of the champion he would become: larger than life, his personality overshadowing all others.

A man who attracted and threatened her for the same reasons.

Rising, she turned and gripped the top of the gate. Inside the pen, a small group of cattle huddled against the fence to her left. Matt rode his quarter horse at a slow walk beside and slightly behind a cow hugging the right fence. All three headed her way. All three had worked up a sweat.

Suddenly Matt raised his head, his focus zooming in on her beneath his chocolate-brown hat. He wore matching leather chaps and a black T-shirt that clung damply to his torso. His attention returned instantly to the cow, but Mattie wasn't fooled.

He was aware she watched him. He knew she'd forgotten where she was and what she was doing.

She dragged in a much-needed gulp of air. There was something about this particular cowboy that made a woman forget to *breathe*.

"What they're doing now is called 'tracking,'" Casey explained in the quiet voice of a golf tournament moderator. "See how Doc speeds up or slows down to stay even, and be ready for any move?"

What she saw were chiseled arms sheening with sweat, a muscular chest and flat abdomen Matt's usual western shirts didn't do justice.

Out of nowhere, the cow made a dash for the herd. The stallion rocked back on his powerful hindquarters, then lifted his forelegs and pivoted, landing at an angle blocking the cow. The cow spun around and broke for the opposite direction. Doc rose, pivoted and blocked.

"That's called 'stepping across the cow,'" Casey continued. "Matt's taught Doc to lift his front end nice and clean for a smooth fluid movement. And look—damned if he's not 'drawing' better than last week." Excitement underlined his voice.

"Drawing?" Abbey croaked.

"It's something the best cutters develop. A kind of intensity that fascinates the cow and draws her to the horse. See how Doc almost squats? How low to the ground he gets? How they never take their eyes off each other?"

What she saw was Matt's easy balance, his uncanny oneness with a thirteen-hundred-pound horse who moved like a cat.

The cow burst into a run. The stallion exploded after her, past her, then sank onto his haunches in a stop that also halted the cow in her tracks. Holding the reins taut, his arm muscles defined and powerful, his chaps nearly invisible against the sleek brown coat of the stallion, Matt looked like a mythical centaur.

"Beautiful," Casey murmured.

Abbey couldn't agree more.

"Judges love that kind of command and presence in front of a cow."

A quick glance at Casey confirmed he meant the horse. She removed her glasses, pulled up a bit of cotton dress and cleaned the lenses. They seemed to have fogged.

"So Doc's a pretty good cutting horse, huh?" Abbey asked.

"He is now. Oh, he had the bloodlines from the beginning," Casey said, answering her curious glance. "But he never won. Ben Campbell, Doc's first owner, went through three trainers fast. Doc wouldn't give his head to any of 'em."

"Give his head?" She slipped on her glasses.

"Wouldn't do what was asked without resisting. Matt bought him cheap, then turned him around with this new 'touching' therapy he learned at a clinic. Won't let anyone else ride Doc, now. Nobody in these parts thought Matt knew much about riding cutters, much less training them."

Abbey experienced an inexplicable surge of pride on his behalf. "And now?"

Casey met her eyes and grinned. "Now everybody claims they knew he was the best all-around horseman this county ever raised.

They're bettin' he and Doc win the NCHA Futurity.''

''Casey!'' Matt bellowed.

The way the younger man snapped to attention, Abbey almost expected him to salute.

''Yeah, boss?'' he said, instead.

''I'm comin' out. Quit jawin' and open the gate, then get those cattle into the square pen.''

As Casey unlatched the spring lock and pushed the gate forward, Abbey backed up hastily. Just in time, too.

Doc Holiday breezed through at a fast trot, his saddle creaking, his tail rippling, his rider's gaze fixed on some point in the distance. She caught a whiff of leather, heated horse and sweaty man that should've been unpleasant, but went straight to her head, making her dizzy. Seconds later, she realized they'd already passed.

The flutter she felt came from deep inside, not a wake of rushing air.

Abbey turned in time to see horse and rider disappear into the stable. After that one instant of eye contact when she'd first walked up, Matt had ignored her completely. He hadn't even so much as nodded a goodbye.

How rude.

How…interesting.

She spent the next ten minutes contemplating the implications, deciding at last on a theory that suited her mood. He'd obviously sensed she wanted to talk about Mattie and had made good his escape. He therefore must find her "little chats" more threatening than she'd realized.

Experiencing a rush of confidence, Abbey swished aside the dropped skirt of her dress and marched to battle.

He hadn't seen nothin', yet.

CHAPTER EIGHT

ABBEY ENTERED THE STABLE at a full stride, only to stop short in alarm. She didn't remember it being this dark. Why weren't the overhead lights turned on?

Focusing on a large bright square at the far end of the building, she drew several deep breaths. Better. Double doors matching the ones she'd just entered were open. Two routes of escape.

Her fingers uncurled.

A muffled bump from the tack and feed room up ahead was followed by a curse. Matt, stowing away Doc's saddle, probably scooping up grain.

Vague shapes solidified as her eyes adjusted to the dim interior. The stallion was one of four horses looking toward the noise from above half doors. Ears pricked, expressions alert, they reminded her of children waiting for supper plates.

Doc snorted explosively, then curled his upper lip and whinnied.

"I'm comin', you big pig," Matt yelled, gruff affection in his voice.

Abbey grinned, relaxing further.

The scent of hay and straw mingled with inevitable horsey odors. Earthy, but not offensive. Matt was obviously a stickler for cleanliness. She studied the stable approvingly.

The packed dirt corridor appeared freshly raked, the stall doors on each side recently painted. Hardware seemed new, the entire structure in neat repair. Unlike the house.

More evidence of Matt's priorities.

Priorities that had to change, Abbey reminded herself.

Just then Matt entered the corridor and paused, a dark silhouette blocking the distant square of light. Long legs, lean hips, broad shoulders. Mmm-mmm-mmm. He seemed taller than the back doors, an optical illusion enhanced by his forceful presence.

The jittery tension tugging at Abbey now had nothing to do with escape, and everything to do with capture. She watched Matt walk forward carrying two buckets of grain, the lower portion of his chaps flapping. When Doc whinnied, shook his head and banged his front hoof against the stall door, Abbey seconded the motion.

Thank God, the man didn't wear damp T-shirts every day.

Then again, maybe she'd thanked Her too soon. Abbey did have to face Matt now, when he looked tall and powerful and hot and irritated. Street tough and wrangler rough.

At Doc's stall, Matt nodded his Stetson curtly in her direction before setting down one bucket, then shoving aside the stallion's head.

"Quit pushin'," he mumbled, stretching over the half door toward a corner-mounted feed bin. "Damn it, would you just *wait?*"

His brown chaps were tied in back at the waist, thigh and calf, leaving his blue denim rear exposed. Edwina would've swooned. Abbey merely gawked.

The schuss of pouring grain mimicked the rush of blood in Abbey's ears. This was all her own fault. She saw that now. She'd denied her healthy body's needs for too many years, and this was the result. If she'd moved in with Paul when he'd first asked, she would've been safe.

Instead she was here.

Giving the bucket one last shake, Matt straightened, turned around and picked up the second pail, ignoring Abbey. He moved to the next occupied stall and gently brushed a blond forelock out of luminous dark eyes.

"Hi ya, Marilyn. Hungry?"

The deeper, gentler tone obviously pleased Marilyn as much as it did Abbey. The palomino mare nibbled Matt's neck rather than the pouring grain.

Chuckling, he turned and caught Abbey watching. His smile vanished. "I'm kinda busy, here. Is this important?"

Important?

The word kicked Abbey's priorities into place. She walked forward and stopped close enough to read the wariness in his eyes.

"I can't think of anything more important than Mattie. And you're *always* busy. That's the problem. You haven't spent any time with her to speak of since she arrived."

His expression hardened. "Another lecture? Tell me somethin' I don't know or can do somethin' about."

"There are a lot of things—little things—you can do to help Mattie feel welcome. You saw her at the funeral, crying for her mommy. She's very fragile."

"I don't need this," he muttered.

"Well, too bad, Uncle Matt. Because your niece needs *you*."

Blowing out a breath, Matt snatched up the empty buckets and headed for the tack room in ground-eating strides.

Abbey hop-skipped to keep up. "Right now she's clinging to me because I'm the only familiar thing left in her life. But what about when I leave?"

No response.

She tried again. "She'll be devastated, unless she can turn to you."

His granite profile never twitched.

Abbey dogged his heels into the tack room and watched him yank the lid off a huge plastic trash can. As he stored one bucket, then scooped grain into the other, she scanned her surroundings.

The plank wood floor looked scuffed and worn but recently swept. Western saddles gleamed astride sawhorses. Bridles and ropes hung neatly on pegs. Shelves held bottles, jars and unidentified tools in perfect alignment. Only constant maintenance could account for the lack of dust and rust.

"Ignoring me is childish," Abbey persisted. "It won't make the situation disappear."

Matt slammed down the trash can lid, picked up the bucket and turned. "I was hopin' it might make *you* go away. Time is money, Abbey. I don't have enough of either right now to stand here arguing."

"Oh, please. You can afford six saddles and the time to keep them polished and clean, but you can't spare five minutes for a grieving little girl? I can't be with her every minute, you know. I have work of my own. Designing sometimes takes solitude."

"So ask Hal to spell you now and then." Matt brushed past her as if she were a pesky gnat.

Maybe a wasp would get his attention. "I'm not comfortable with that. *You* should understand," she lashed out at his back, "considering how worried you were about Edwina."

Matt stopped in his tracks.

Her heart pounded in time to her mental refrain, *uh-oh, uh-oh, uh-oh.*

He set the bucket on the floor and turned around, his eyes glacial chips of gray. When he stalked forward, she'd never been more aware of his looming height and superior strength. She reviewed and chose her best self-defense maneuver, tensing as he halted at the farthest saddle.

"I'll pretend you didn't say that. Hal's the most decent man I know. He's *nothing* like my fa—" Matt broke off. A nerve ticked in his jaw once. Twice. He turned his narrowed gaze on the row of sawhorses. "As for me owning six saddles...that's a necessity, not a luxury. I need them for different kinds of training."

"I didn't say Hal was like your father," Abbey pointed out quietly.

His head snapped front and center. His eyelids flickered, then lowered, then rose. Just that fast, the atmosphere changed, became heavy with simmering awareness and sexual undercurrents. He hooked a thumb through his belt loop, the action drawing her gaze to biceps that, even relaxed, appeared carved from oak.

"Never interrupt a man when he's braggin' about his equipment, darlin'." Laying his opposite palm on the nearest saddle, he caressed the swells and valleys of leather as appreciatively as he might a woman's body. "This baby here is made for ropin'. Got a big sturdy horn to dally a lariat on and hold a calf, high pommel, shallow seat so I can get out fast."

Abbey remembered the feel of those callused fingertips. Warm. Slightly scratchy. Amazingly gentle on her throat.

He moved up to the next sawhorse. "This sweetheart is a cutting saddle, built on a sixteen-inch Buster Welch tree. The seat bottom is flatter, the cantle higher, so I have mobility. But I can plant myself deep and stay there as long as I want." His unwavering gaze said it wasn't an idle boast. "There's as little skirt as possible between my knees and what I'm ridin'. I like a close feel for better performance...what about you, Abbey?"

She suppressed a scandalized thrill. "Must you be so crass?"

He offered the smile of a sinner with no plans to repent. "Must you be such a prude? Even if you are a sexy one."

Abbey refused to be distracted. "I'll tell you what I like. Honest emotions, not 'performances.' Although yours was award winning, I have to admit. Almost as good as that day on the beach when you ridiculed everything about Venice."

The lazy smile slipped from his face, the caressing hand from his saddle. He hooked that thumb loosely in a second belt loop, but the effect was anything but casual.

"Okay, I'll bite. Explain."

"You're an expert at diverting the subject

when it suits you, Matt. In California, you teased me about weirdos so I dropped our discussion of Mary. Just now, you pulled out your macho pig script to throw the scent off your father. Next time you don't want to talk about something, why don't you try telling me outright instead of playing ignorant cowboy or studly jerk?''

The muscles in his forearms corded. His features tightened into a grim mask. ''All right. I don't want to talk about Mary or Charlie.''

She cocked her head. He was screaming behind that mask, but she couldn't hear the words. ''Why not?''

With an incredulous growl, Matt turned on his heel and strode off, scooping up the bucket on his way out the door.

Lifting her dress, she ran after him, catching up as he reached the last horse waiting to be fed. She stopped an arm's length behind Matt as he poured grain.

''Guardianship is more than providing food and shelter for Mattie's body. It's providing guidance for her character and a sense of who she is. Talking to her about Charlie and Mary will help her know what it means to be a Granger. You can always edit out the more unfavorable parts.''

"Then there'd be nothing left to say." Matt shook the bucket with sharp, angry movements.

"You're being purposefully ignorant again. She's only five years old. She likes 'Sesame Street,' not the History Channel. Tell her simple things. How she has her grandfather's eyes, or how she shares his love of animals, or whatever might make her feel connected to him in some—"

Matt spun around and hurled the plastic pail with shocking violence. Before the hollow bounce had dribbled to a stop, he'd put his face nose to nose with hers.

"I don't *want* her to feel connected to him! Do I have to spell out the ugly truth? Do I have to tell you why Mary split home for good when she was seventeen? Why she went through men faster than a pack of gum? Why each one of 'em was a drunkard or a womanizer or both? Are you *that* naive, Abbey?"

No. But she suddenly wished she were. "Are you...absolutely certain of your facts?"

Matt straightened, his eyes bleak. "As sure as Charlie's deathbed confession can make me. I...didn't read the signs as a teenager. Or if I did, they were too much for me to deal with. I had other things on my mind. Like I told you before, I was a lousy big brother.'' He squinted at the open doors, his throat working.

A wrenching sight on such a big tough cowboy.

''Charlie begged me to apologize to Mary for him,'' Matt said thickly. ''I didn't even do that much.''

''Oh, Matt.'' A trickle of anger entered the compassion flooding her heart. ''It was unconscionable of your father to burden you with that task. I'm so sorry.''

Matt met her eyes, his jaw set. ''Yeah, me, too. For not helpin' Mary when it counted. But I swear to God I'll do right by Mattie. *My* way. Not by tellin' her fairy tales. By changin' what it means to be a Granger in these parts.''

Abbey was only beginning to understand the extent of the layers Matt hid from the world. But she did know Mary wasn't the only sibling who'd been scarred in childhood. Just as she knew that sympathy, however much warranted, wouldn't prod him into taking the next healing step.

''Would you consider seeing a therapist, Matt?''

He flinched as if she'd slapped him.

Flipping back her braid, she hardened her

heart. "Well, at least I wiped that martyred self-recrimination off your face." Good. Indignation had chased the last trace of desolation from his eyes.

He shouldered past her and walked to the bucket lying fifteen feet down the corridor.

She pushed up her glasses and followed. "As a veteran of therapy myself, I'll do you another favor and paraphrase hundreds of dollars and hours," she offered. "According to experts, children often take responsibility for the sins of their parents. And that's not only illogical, it's also self-destructive. Even self-indulgent."

Grasping the bucket handle, he straightened and turned. "Self-indulgent?"

She moved closer and flung back her head. "Name me *one* good thing that can come from blaming yourself now for what happened to Mary when you were only a kid yourself."

His face darkened. His mouth opened and closed.

"See? Kicking yourself won't help, even if it was justified, which it's not. Forgive yourself and move on. The best way to 'do right' by Mattie isn't to prove the rest of the world wrong about Grangers. It's to spend more time with her. Be a role model. She needs stability in her life right now. A sense of security. Surely you can understand that?''

''Yes, Sigmund, I can understand that.'' He bumped up his hat and glared. ''Can you understand Mattie won't feel secure if I lose everything?''

Abbey's momentum screeched to a stop. ''What do you mean, everything?''

''I mean losin' the house, the land, the cattle, the bed she's sleepin' in—*everything*. Because that's gonna happen if I don't make the bank payments. Which I can't make if I don't board and train these two-year-olds, and fatten up healthy calves to sell in September, and try to fill these twelve empty stalls with new boarders. Which is more work than Casey and I can manage in daylight hours as it is.

''Not to *mention* the time I need to train Doc for the Futurity. That's not an ego thing, ya know. Winnin' a title will let me put him into syndication so I can make some real money, so I can own this place outright, so Mattie can have real stability in her life, not a false sense of security.''

He flipped off his Stetson, wiped his sweat-beaded brow with one shoulder, looked into his hat crown as if a rabbit might appear. ''It's a house of cards, Abbey. Let one fall, and the whole thing tumbles down. Can you understand that I have more important things on my mind right now than spendin' time with Mattie?''

Behind him, equine molars crunched grain in a steady rhythm. A tail swished. A hoof stamped.

She studied the faint blue shadows beneath Matt's eyes, the lines of weariness bracketing his mouth. No charm. No sexual innuendo. No arrogance. Simply a strong man doing the best he could.

His brief display of vulnerability had slipped through her defenses and touched her heart as nothing else could.

Without thinking, she reached up and tenderly brushed a lock of hair from his forehead. Coarser than Mattie's, but soft, with that blue-black gleam referred to as raven. His brows were thick but not brutish. Silky to the touch and no-nonsense straight.

Her fingertips explored the supple texture of a high cheekbone, more like fine kid leather than the tough cowhide his deep tan would've suggested. She'd expected to find roughness. Ahh— there it was.

The tickle beneath her finger pads produced a

delighted lift of her lips. His beard and mustache would grow thick and heavy if he let it. She was glad he didn't. Covering up that stubborn jawline would be criminal, camouflaging that beautifully defined mouth obscene.

Halfway through the swipe of her thumb on his chin, Matt's utter stillness registered. Abbey froze. Her fog of sensual pleasure iced and shattered.

Mercy, what was she *doing!*

She jerked back her hand. Gasped when he caught her wrist. Flushed as he held her still with humiliating ease. For about twenty accelerated heartbeats, she stared at the strong tanned fingers overlapping her pale skin. Arresting. A little frightening. Strangely erotic.

Her breathing grew choppy.

Summoning all her wits, she dredged up a bitter image of Steven, her slender golden-haired angel. The man who'd chosen her alone among a flock of mortals to fulfill his spiritual and earthly needs.

But the vision wavered. Melted beside the stoked furnace of Matt's body, irrefutably powerful, incontestably masculine, radiating formidable will as much as heat.

Fear and excitement and a slow, insidious

warmth now held her immobile as much as Matt's gentled grip. Abbey slowly met his eyes.

Between narrow gray slits, the predictable heat lightning flickered and flared. A mesmerizing strobe of sexual hunger and...something elusive but stark. A hunger of the soul she'd never seen in his eyes. There it was again!

But, no, that couldn't be right. This local celebrity, this cowboy who attracted buckle bunnies like a giant carrot couldn't possibly be *lonely,* could he?

The phantom emotion vanished, leaving his intention unmistakably clear. As he tossed the bucket and his hat to the ground, Abbey experienced a terrible, wondrous sense of destiny.

"Mercy," she whispered.

"Too late for that, darlin'." He clamped an arm around her waist and yanked her close. "No mercy."

Abbey had loved Steven once with all her zealous young heart. The touch of his lips had filled her with sweet yearning. In the eight years since, no other kiss had evoked a fraction of the same ardor.

She tensed now as Matt's mouth swooped down to settle firmly over hers.

Within eight seconds, she forgot Steven's existence.

Matt's kiss wasn't sweet. It wasn't spiritual.

He drew on her mouth as if he would swallow it whole. His kiss claimed possession, commanded her to open, demanded she soften, controlled her response. His tongue swept her mouth rapaciously, tasted her greedily. Danced in hot little swirls that made her twinge and tingle. Thrust in swift, sure strokes that told her what he wanted to do, made her swell in private places and mindlessly climb his boots. Made her rub against muscles, press into hardness, moisten on contact, make noises in her throat.

Sounds she'd never made before and that would embarrass her later.

Now she only wanted more.

Please, please, more.

He touched her as if he were molding clay. His hands contoured, cupped and reshaped her flesh. Pressed and melded her curves to his angles and planes, made her smooth where she'd been jagged, whole where she'd been half. Made her crave big warm hands the size of plates, callused and scratchy. Comforting and arousing. So good she nearly whimpered. Did whimper.

It wasn't enough.

She needed more.

Matt opened his stance and adjusted her position. Yes, better! No, worse! She moved her hands restlessly over rough denim, steamy cotton, silky hair. So many textures, so many muscles, so much heat redolent of leather and musk. Eight years of deprivation fueled her frenzy. Her senses gorged on the masculine buffet. Yet she was starving and sated. Drowning and parched. Exultant and agonized.

She needed more.

She wanted to feel his naked skin against hers. She wanted to crawl inside him and breathe with the same lungs. She wanted mercy from this torture that only he could provide.

She was dying.

He was, too. The noises coming from his throat were feral, like an animal in pain. He tore his mouth from hers and looked around wildly, his chest heaving.

Then she was being dragged by the wrist into an empty stall filled with fragrant straw. A door slammed her into darkness, jolted her into remembered hell.

She blinked in shock. *Oh, God, no.*

The walls closed in.

Focusing on the light rimming the edges of

the door, she drew in a labored breath, ragged not from passion but from sharp, slicing fear. She needed to get out!

Extending her hands blindly, she encountered a rock-hard chest.

"Abbey," Matt whispered hoarsely, crowding her back against the wall and recapturing her mouth.

The body she'd craved moments before was a smothering obstacle now. She shoved ineffectually and tried to yell, the sound thick and close to the passionate noises she'd made earlier. His kiss deepened.

She twisted and squirmed fractiously, one thought, one need, one goal in mind: *escape.* Ripping her mouth from his at last, she rammed the heel of her palm into his nose.

He lurched backward with a bellow of pain.

She launched forward toward the door, scrabbled at the latch until she accidentally sprang the mechanism, yanked and watched the top half of the door open onto blessed light and space. Hitching herself up and over tangled her long dress in the latch.

Working to loosen the material from the other side, Abbey glimpsed Matt's accusing glare above cupped hands.

She grabbed the flower-sprigged cotton, gave it a savage yank to the sound of ripping fabric, then stumbled down the corridor toward the waning sunlight. Toward the beautiful evening.

Toward lovely and precious freedom.

HIS NOSE WAS BLEEDING! Might even be broken. It hurt like a son of a bitch, that was for sure.

Her jab had sent a red-hot poker of pain straight through his cranium. Neat trick, if you weren't on the receiving end.

Matt lifted his probing fingers from tender cartilage, pulled out his shirttail and dabbed at the blood. Unbelievable! What was her problem? He'd kissed a lot of women over the years, and no one had ever complained.

Shoot, most of 'em had wanted more where that came from. He always tried to give as much or more than he received. He'd never been slapped—okay, slugged—for his trouble.

Then again, Abbey wasn't like any woman he'd known.

Her tongue was sharper than spur rowels on a man's ego. From the first, she'd seemed indifferent to the smile that, in Matt's experience, made women agree to most anything. Hell, for a man who'd been asked to take off his hat at age fourteen, rejection at this late date was damn hard to take.

He sniffed once. Twitched his nostrils. Gave the bridge of his nose an experimental squeeze. Well, it wasn't broken. But if he didn't ice it down soon, his schnoz would swell as big as another appendage throbbing like hell right now.

Walking slowly to the stall's half door, he opened the latch that had snagged Abbey's dress. She'd been so crazy to get away from him, she'd ripped the fabric in her frenzy. When only minutes earlier, she'd been crazy *for* him. He was sure of that.

Almost sure.

Well, hell.

Leaning his forearms at waist level on top of the door, he reviewed the past scene for clues as to what went wrong. Why he'd gone after Abbey's mouth like Doc attacked his grain. Greedily. Possessively. God help anyone trying to pull him away until after he'd finished.

Her fault, Matt decided. She'd started it, after all.

He could've resisted those full rosy lips, as pink as the flowers on her dress, if she hadn't reached up and brushed back his hair, done it again to finger the strands, moved from there to touch his face the way he'd noticed her touch a hundred other things. Slowly. Appreciatively. Almost like she was reading braille.

As if surfaces, be it coffee mug, beaded earrings or his niece, had a story to tell. As if she savored every single word of the tale.

He'd imagined those long, graceful fingers on him too often not to damn near pass out from pleasure at her touch. Watching tender concern and then delight two-step across her expressive face, he'd known he had to find out the truth.

Was the attraction between them real, or the product of unfulfilled fantasy?

Propping his elbows, Matt lowered weary eyes into the waiting heels of his palms and laughed, a short harsh sound that ended on a groan.

Real? Hell, she should be packaged with a surgeon general's warning. "Kissing me can be hazardous to your health." The sexiest fantasy in all his experience had nothing on Abbey Parker.

His blood started bubbling just thinking about her taste, her shape, those little noises she'd made in her throat. He'd meant to stop at a single kiss, but her meltdown response had driven him over the edge. And she *had* been turned on, damn it! She'd practically climbed into his skin trying to get closer. He hadn't misread her signals. She'd been hot, willing and ready for no mercy.

So what had changed when he'd pulled her into this stall for privacy? What had turned her back into an outraged prude? She'd struggled like a woman who was...

His head came up. The word he muttered was crass and succinct.

She'd struggled like a woman who was scared. Like a woman who'd been frightened, maybe even abused, by a man in her past.

He'd sensed in California that Abbey had some personal demons making her skittish around men. But he'd hauled her caveman-style into a dark lair anyway, triggering who knew what kind of memories?

You are one ignorant pea brain cowboy, Granger.

Matt straightened and pushed through the stall door. His hat lay upside down, the empty bucket on its side in the dirt corridor ahead. Disgust and shame weighed heavy on his shoulders as he walked to pick them up.

What now? he wondered, dusting off the Stetson. He jammed it low and looked out the stable toward the house.

He'd be lucky if she stayed the night, much less until his want ad panned out. He couldn't really blame her. He'd been a first-class jerk. Maybe letting her leave was the smartest thing he could do.

In spite of what he'd sensed or guessed about Abbey, there was one thing he did know for sure.

After kissing her once, he would use every ounce of his willpower to keep from kissing her again. But he was his father's son. He could weaken and fail.

Then God help anyone—*including* Abbey—who tried to pull him away before he was finished.

CHAPTER NINE

"I'M BORED," Mattie announced petulantly, sitting across from Abbey at the kitchen table. "I wanna see the new horse. How come Uncle Matt gets to have all the fun and we're stuck inside?"

Suppressing a sigh, Abbey looked up from her jeweler's saw. In the two days since that disastrous kiss in the stable, Matt had been more withdrawn than ever.

"He's working, honey, not having fun. I'll bet he wishes he could be coloring with you instead of driving on a highway," Abbey lied.

Adding a new stable boarder had elated Matt. At lunch, she'd overheard him tell Hal he would pick up the new horse that afternoon from Guadalupe Ranch, somewhere outside San Antonio, from what Abbey gathered. Which is how she received most of her information about Matt these days. Through overheard conversations to Hal. Much to her relief, Matt hadn't spoken to or looked at her directly since their kiss.

Mattie straightened eagerly from her slump atop three stacked phone books. "Can I ask him to color with me when he gets back? I got lots of crayons. We can *share.*"

Abbey's heart twisted. Apparently not all her lectures went through one ear and out the other. "That is so-o-o generous, Mattie. I'm really proud of you. But your uncle will have to do his chores when he gets back. Why don't you wait and ask him to color when he comes in tonight?"

Mattie's expression darkened. "Never mind. He doesn't like me."

"Oh, honey, that's not true." Darn Matt's mangy hide for making this necessary! Abbey laid down her saw and arranged her thoughts. "Sometimes grown-ups have a lot on their minds, things that have nothing to do with you, and it makes them seem—"

"No!" Paper and crayons flew off the table, launched by a small thin arm. "I don't wanna color with him, anyway. Coloring's for babies."

Mattie scrambled down from the chair, ran toward the hallway entrance and barreled straight into Hal's stomach. Stumbling backward a step, he dropped a full laundry basket, then clutched her shoulders for balance.

"Whoa, whoa, slow down there, sunshine. Where's the fire?"

When she stared mutinously at the scuffed gray linoleum, he took in the scattered mess on the floor near Mattie's chair and raised a quizzical gaze to Abbey.

"She's a little tired of coloring, Hal. Let me finish cutting around this template and I'll get my things off the table, then take her for a walk."

Shrewd blue eyes seemed to read Abbey's frustration, weariness and taut nerves. Sleepless nights were taking their toll.

"You know what, Mattie?" Hal said conspiratorially. "I'm a little tired of washin' clothes right now, myself. I got the makin's for a big gooey batch of chocolate brownies over at my trailer house that's callin' my name. I sure could use some help mixin' it up, if you're interested."

Her gaze had lifted at the first mention of brownies. "I'm a good helper," she told him.

He's gotcha, Abbey thought gratefully.

"Yer dang tootin' you're a good helper. Besides, you've never seen my place, have you? What say you and me walk over and let Abbey work while we have some fun?"

"Okay. Is it pretty?"

"My place?" He scratched his gray stubbled chin as if thinking.

Hal shaved according to his own schedule, Abbey had noticed.

"Well, the walls look kinda blank and lonely. I know you're tired of colorin' and all," the wily devil continued, "but while the brownies are bakin', maybe you could draw me a pretty picture or two. Would ya mind that too much?"

"Nuh-uh! I'm a good drawer, aren't I, Abbey?"

"You're wonderful," Abbey agreed, meeting Hal's eyes and making it clear she included him in her assessment.

He reddened and busied himself helping Mattie gather up her crayons and paper.

Although Abbey had never suspected he could harm a child when she'd questioned his character in front of Matt, the younger man's outrage had cemented her own trust in Hal. Matt would never allow tragic history to repeat itself with his niece.

"You're sure you two won't get into trouble?" Abbey teased when they stood poised to leave.

He pulled open the back door and winked. "Can't promise that, now, can we, Mattie?"

"Nope! See ya, Abbey." With a flash of the Granger dimple, Mattie skipped out onto the stoop.

Abbey mouthed a silent thank-you. Hal made a shooing motion and followed the little girl outside. The door closed.

And silence settled over the kitchen.

Abbey took a moment to simply enjoy the peaceful moment. Her gaze wandered. Hal kept things spotless, but there were some things a man simply didn't care about. The milk pitcher of fresh wildflowers on the counter was the only splash of color in the room.

The window above the sink had no blinds, no curtains, no potted plants perched on the sill. The whole kitchen begged for fresh paint. Buttery yellow for the walls, maybe eggshell white for the cabinets. A stenciled border of variegated green ivy next to the ceiling would be nice. The pattern could be repeated on the door panels of the cabinets. Just a touch. Any more would overpower, not enhance.

And what she could do with this scarred wooden table and ladder-back chairs! Painted yellow—no, white—to match the cabinets, then stenciled with colorful fruit, the set would be an asset instead of an eyesore. Tie-back seat cushions would add warmth as well as comfort. A cheery cookie jar on the counter to pick up bright colors in the fruit stencil...

Abbey stiffened.

Oh, God. She was doing it again.

Weaving herself into a homey needlepoint picture that would hang on the wall forever. Her breathing quickened. Conversely her chest constricted. The familiar squeeze of her lungs was more powerful than ever before.

She would *not* surrender her own identity to support a man's personal agenda, as her mother had done for Abbey's domineering father. As Lorna had done for her forceful husband.

Conjuring an image of the packed suitcase waiting in her bedroom, Abbey focused on the symbol like a Lamaze-trained mother in labor. Gradually, with the help of her mental crutch, her anxiety subsided. Her lungs filled easily and her vision cleared.

She picked up her jeweler's saw, repositioned the fine blade where she'd left off and continued cutting an intricate winged angel out of a thin copper sheet. When riveted to a varnished teakwood square, it would make an attractive brooch to add to her collection.

Her inventory was in decent shape. Too bad

she couldn't say the same for her cash flow. If she weren't so broke, she would've left the ranch two days ago, after Matt's kiss in the stall.

Mercy, she'd been mortified. She'd almost broken the poor man's nose! After giving him every reason to believe her eager for more than his kisses, too. She'd been a brazen hussy of the worst kind, the type of woman that men referred to as a tease. He had every right to be furious, to give her the silent treatment now.

Sighing, Abbey became aware of the distant crunch of gravel. Someone was coming. She cocked an ear. The engine wasn't loud enough for Matt's pickup.

Her heartbeat slowed, and she set the delicate copper angel down on the table as the motor cut off. A car door slammed. No others followed. A single visitor, then.

Abbey was on her way to the front door when a light knock sounded on the back. Whoever it was had been here before.

Seconds later she opened the kitchen door to a startlingly lovely young woman. Wide eyes the color of bluebonnets, thick shoulder-length hair the color of corn silk. Put her in a pinafore instead of jeans and she'd be a dead ringer for Alice in the Looking Glass.

Recovering from her surprise, Abbey smiled toward the pie plate the woman held aloft. "I hope you're not at the wrong house and that *is* for us."

"Us?" There was no mistaking the alarm and trace of hostility in Alice's eyes. "It's for Matt and his niece. Who are you?"

Interesting. "Forgive me, I'm Abbey Parker. Matt needed help with his niece until he can hire a caretaker, so I agreed to act as a temporary nanny. I was his sister's roommate in California." She backed up. "Please come in."

The woman swept into the kitchen, trailing a scent that would've brought Pitiful running had he not accompanied Matt to San Antonio.

"Mmm, that smells wonderful," Abbey said, reaching for the plate. "Let me take that for you. Mercy, it looks like a photograph out of *Good Housekeeping*. Did you bake this?"

"Yes, I did. Matt loves my apple pie."

Abbey squelched a stab of ugly emotion. She had no claim on Matt, nor any desire for a romantic relationship. If this woman wanted to feed his stomach and ego, who was Abbey to stand in the way? She set the pie on the counter and turned.

"Matt's not here, but I'm sure he'd want me to thank you, Ms...?"

"When will he be back?" Alice demanded rudely.

Abbey leveled a cool look. "Who wants to know?"

At least the woman had the grace to blush.

"I'm Bess Campbell. My father and I live east of here on the neighboring ranch. I was hoping to bring Matt a pie last week and offer condolences about Mary, but Daddy was—" She stopped, a shadow clouding her eyes. "Well, March is a busy time on a ranch, what with all the new calves and foals. I'm bottle-feeding a filly right now whose dam has mastitis."

Abbey softened. "Matt should be back in two, maybe three, hours. He left thirty minutes ago to pick up a new horse in San Antonio."

"San Antonio?" The news appeared to excite Bess. "From Guadalupe Ranch?"

"I think that's what he said, yes."

"Oh, wow. Matt's been trying to work out a deal with them for months. He must've finally gotten the chance to train one of Sam West's cutters."

For a casual neighbor, the woman certainly knew a lot about Matt's business. "That's nice."

"Nice? That's great! Sam's one of the most respected quarter horse breeders in the country. But..." Bess's brow furrowed. "He wouldn't hand over a proven winner to an unproven trainer. He'll want to see if the talk about Doc is true. He's probably given Matt a horse that's leaking, or falling on his head, or too flat, or something even worse."

Abbey pushed up her glasses. "Sounds like the poor animal needs a vet, not a trainer."

After an instant of puzzled silence, Bess laughed, then explained in the voice one used with a toddler. "A horse that's 'leaking' drives the cow when he shouldn't, usually because he hasn't completed his stop before the turn. 'Falling on his head' means a horse loses his balance turning and puts all his weight on the front end. A cutter that's 'too flat' moves in a straight line next to the cow, instead of at an angle. It makes turning around in one smooth motion almost impossible."

The jargon triggered Abbey's memory of her conversation with Casey at the round pen. "Your father must be Ben Campbell, right? The man who sold Doc to Matt?"

"That's right."

Watching the me-against-the-world lift of

Bess's chin, the protective crossing of her arms, Abbey suspected that few people were fond of Ben Campbell, and that his daughter suffered a lot of secondary rejection.

"Listen, Bess, would you like to join me for a piece of that luscious pie you brought and a cup of coffee? I made a fresh pot not too long ago. Oh, and there's pecan pie here, too, if you prefer."

Suspicion sharpened Bess's gaze.

Abbey purposely misread the younger woman. "Don't worry, I didn't bake it, Hal did. I wouldn't offer otherwise."

"Why ever not?"

"Because the only one who likes my cooking is Mattie, bless her tasteless buds."

Bess relaxed enough to flap a hand. "Oh, I'm sure you're exaggerating."

"Nope. If you don't believe me, just say the words 'spaghetti sauce' to Matt. I made a batch in California that I doubt even Pitiful would've eaten."

Enduring an amazed head-to-toe inspection, Abbey saw the exact second she was dismissed as a threat. She didn't know whether to feel relieved or insulted.

"All right," Bess relented. "I'll have the pe-

can pie, if you're sure I won't be imposing..."
Her curious gaze slid from the cluttered kitchen
table to the door leading into the rest of the
house. "Is Matt's niece in her room or something?"

"Hal and Mattie are in his trailer house baking brownies. Hey, I *told* you I was a terrible
cook." Smiling ruefully, Abbey turned and
reached for the foil-wrapped pecan pie sitting
beside the coffeemaker.

To her surprise, Bess bustled forward to help,
unerringly opening correct drawers and cabinets,
obviously as familiar with this kitchen as her
own. Working in tandem, they were seated before cleared spots at the table in no time.

"Mercy!" Abbey exclaimed at her first bite.
"I thought Hal's pecan pie couldn't be topped,
but this is manna from heaven. What's your secret?"

Bess planted a forearm on the table, glanced
left and right, then leaned forward. "I could tell
you...but then I'd have to kill you."

Abbey blinked, then caught the impish gleam
beneath long golden lashes. The two women exchanged appreciative grins, and a tentative bond
of friendship was formed.

Fascinated with the materials and tools on the

table, Bess insisted on seeing samples of Free Bird Jewelry. She praised it lavishly, then asked a zillion questions, revealing a sharp and inquisitive mind. After ten minutes, she knew more about Abbey's apprenticeship and vagabond past than Matt had bothered to learn in eleven days.

Of course, Abbey had drastically edited her history, saying simply that her parents had been very strict, and she'd left home at age nineteen and hadn't looked back.

"Wow," Bess finally marveled. "You've lived in all those cities, and the farthest I've been from Cottonwood is Oklahoma City." Holding her fork limply, she scooted uneaten pecans around her plate. "Didn't you miss your parents at first? I mean, weren't you scared being totally on your own?"

"At first I was terrified," Abbey admitted, ignoring the first question. "But living alone forced me to learn self-reliance. Now, I can't imagine answering to anyone else. Well, I *can,* actually. It's all coming back to me after being around Matt. He's pretty domineering."

Bess's eyes rounded. "Matt?"

"I didn't say he *did* dominate me. He can't do that unless I let him. I mean, we can't control how other people act, but we can control how we *react* to their treatment of us, you know?''

From Bess's expression, the concept was new. ''I guess. But I wouldn't call Matt domineering. Strong willed, yes. But that's a lot different.'' She put down her fork. ''Believe me, I know.''

Don't get involved, Abbey cautioned herself. ''So let's talk about you now, Bess. What's it like living on a cattle ranch?''

The picture Bess proceeded to paint was like a Seurat canvas. One by one, the details Bess described were unrelated dots of color. But when Abbey mentally stepped back, they fused together to form a powerful impression as a whole.

Bess had been born and raised to be a rancher's helpmate and wife. She seemed quite content with her destiny, but considerably less so with her existing life-style. Having striven unsuccessfully to please her dictator ''daddy'' since age fourteen, she chafed at his treatment, yet yearned for his love and approval. Something he wasn't likely to give as long as she remained his doormat. Something he might never give, no matter what Bess did.

Collecting her thoughts, Abbey picked up her cup and stood. ''Would you like more coffee?''

Bess glanced at the kitchen wall clock, gasped

and scraped back her chair. "I had no idea it was so late! I'd better get home and start supper." She rose and smiled. "Thanks for the pie and...everything. I've missed talking to another woman."

"Me, too." With a start of surprise, Abbey realized she meant it. "You know, Bess, the world won't stop turning if you don't have supper waiting for your father. He's a grown man capable of feeding himself. Are you sure you don't want to stay a little longer?"

The idea seemed to intrigue and frighten Bess equally. Years of habit won out. "No, I'd better not." She walked to the door, opened it halfway and stopped. "Would you tell Matt I'll come by again soon to meet his niece and see his new horse?"

Abbey shoved the green-eyed monster off her shoulder. "Sure thing," she said with forced cheer.

Bess looked outside and focused on something in the distance with odd intensity.

"Is something wrong?" Abbey asked.

"Hmm?" Bess dragged her gaze into the kitchen and blushed. "No, nothing's wrong. Hey, do you think maybe we could talk again?

I mean, if you're still here when I come back to visit?''

"That would be nice." Abbey managed a weak smile.

"Great. Bye now." Bess's fingers waggled. The door closed.

Quiet settled over the kitchen, a silence far different from that following Mattie and Hal's departure.

Abbey sank back down in her chair. The sound of Bess's car faded, then disappeared.

The solution to Abbey's guilt in leaving Mattie had just driven away. Bess was beautiful. Bess could bake a pie with one hand and bottle-feed a filly with the other. Bess knew all about cutting horses and obviously worshiped Matt as he required, would undoubtedly nurture Mattie as she deserved. Bess appeared eager to love and be loved.

It was only a matter of time before Matt saw the light.

"Santa Fe, here I come," Abbey said aloud, appalled at her dull, lifeless tone.

A desolation unlike any Abbey had experienced weighed heavy on her heart. Her spine slumped. With no distractions save for the ticking clock, she examined her emotions and admitted the unthinkable.

I'm falling in love with Matt.

Abbey released her pent up breath on a moan.

Shaking her head, she collected the dishes and carried them to the sink. While scrubbing them frantically, she reviewed her options.

There was no time to waste.

She would gather her courage and apologize to Matt, something she should have done immediately after hitting his nose. She would speed up the hiring process for a nanny by every means possible. Most of all, she would forget that kiss and the vibrant heart-pounding splendor of passion.

When mixed with love, the price of succumbing was far too high to pay.

CHAPTER TEN

THE TWO LOVEBIRDS had flown in opposite directions for days, dang it. Hal didn't know how much longer he could protect the nest. Every female within a hundred-mile radius seemed to want to get her beak on a piece of it.

Dipping his mop into a bucket of ammonia water, he glared at the apple pie sitting next to his brownies on the kitchen counter. Humph. The little Campbell gal was gettin' on his nerves. It was one thing to play dueling kitchens with him, but flauntin' her flaky piecrust at Abbey the day before was downright dirty fightin'.

Hal slapped the mop onto linoleum and began his usual two-o'clock cleaning. With Mattie down for her nap and Abbey working in her room, he used this time every day to plot strategy and disinfect from Pitiful's morning romp. Matt deserved a fine woman.

Hal would do his level best to see that the boy got one.

He'd had such high hopes the afternoon Abbey'd come tearin' into the house like a prairie fire with a tailwind. When her flaming cheeks had cooled, he'd been hard-pressed not to notice the whisker burns and swollen lips of a woman kissed by someone who meant business.

He'd whistled to himself till supper, when Matt had dragged in with a nose swollen worse than Abbey's lips. The two had barely looked at each other across the table or ever since. But Hal hadn't given up hope. No sirree Bob. He'd nipped three more want-ad phone responses in the bud and told the Widow Blanton, who lived ten miles east of the Campbells, that Matt was happier 'n a hog in slop with his pretty new "nanny."

Judith Blanton had been testing air freshener at the Shop 'N Save at the time, and had dang near squirted herself in the eye. Hal had played dumb. Like he didn't know she'd pulled down the covers for Matt his first week on the ranch and kept hopin' he would crawl in permanent ever since. Humph. Over Hal's dead body.

Slap! Swish-swish-swish-swish.

When he and Mattie had returned from his trailer house with a plate of brownies the day before, Abbey had looked so sad he'd wondered

who'd up and died. Turned out Bess Campbell
had paid a little social visit. For the next hour
Hal got his fill of her virtues. Wasn't she pretty?
Wasn't she sweet? Didn't she bake the best apple pie on God's green earth? Since Abbey
hadn't tasted his yet, he forgave her the insult.
Wasn't Bess a help to her father, keeping his
house and helping with chores? Didn't she know
a lot about cutting horses? Wouldn't she and
Matt be a natural and perfect match?

Hal attacked the last dry corner of the floor in
disgust. Matt would be happy with Bess about
as long as you could hold a bull's tail. He didn't
need a cook or maid. Shoot, he had Hal, didn't
he? What Matt needed was someone who kept
him on his mental toes, someone who didn't flirt
or flatter, so her praise—when it came—would
make him stand tall. There was a light in Matt's
eyes when he looked at Abbey that Hal had
never seen before. He was almost convinced she
was The One.

Preoccupied, Hal carried the dirty water to be
emptied and pulled open the kitchen door, then
rocked back the bucket and swung it forward.
Too late, he saw the streak of mottled blue-gray
fur heading for the open door. The slush of water
caught Pitiful full in the chest. He yelped, shook

vigorously all over Hal, then slipped past his knees through the door.

Blinded by ammonia, Hal turned and danced a furious jig. "Come back here, you sorry skillet licker! Get your muddy paws off my clean floor."

Pitiful was halfway to Mattie's room by now and would nose in and jump on her bed any second. Hal had a much better chance of stopping Abbey's "competitors."

And danged if he wouldn't give it his best shot.

TWO DAYS LATER, Matt pushed through the kitchen door and stopped short at the sight of Abbey. The safest thing would be to turn around and walk back out.

But hell, this was his house. He had a right to get a drink of water out of his own kitchen instead of a horse trough!

What was she doing in here now, anyway? She was supposed to be in her bedroom working while Mattie went to the grocery store with Hal. That's what the old coot had said on his way out when he'd stopped at the county road and talked to Matt, who was stringing new fence.

Realizing he still stood frowning at Abbey, he ripped off his hat and shut the door.

Did she have to get all pale and look away like he'd burst in with a stocking over his head? *What do you expect, Granger? "Hi, darling, can I get you a cold beer?"*

His gaze returned sheepishly to the woman he'd dragged into a dark stall.

Eyes cast down, her chestnut hair neatly braided and draped over one shoulder, she looked fresh and feminine. As pretty as a morning rose in a pale pink dress that swept the floor.

He'd just dug ten postholes by hand under a broiling sun.

He moved quickly to the sink, tossed his hat onto the counter and scrubbed the worst of the grime from his face, grimacing at the stubble he wished he'd shaved that morning. Not that he cared what he looked like, mind you. But whiskers itched in the hot sun, and he still had fence to string.

Dish towel draped over his neck, Matt walked to the refrigerator, ignoring Miss Manners as if he couldn't feel her disapproving stare. A beer sounded pretty damn good, come to think of it. He yanked open the door and reached for a Lone Star tucked behind the milk.

Abbey could look down her prissy nose all she wanted. He'd earned a reward.

Slamming the refrigerator door with a hip, he twisted off the cap, swigged three quick gulps, then a long deep fourth of the ice-cold beer. Ahh. Good idea.

In the middle of a backhanded swipe of his mouth, he glanced at Abbey.

She wasn't looking down her nose, but rather, up and down his body.

And she liked what she saw. Liked it a lot, if he was any judge of women, which he was—or at least, he used to be. His pulse quickened. He lowered his arm and caught her gaze.

Blushing furiously, she picked up a hammer and started banging away at some piece of metal on the table.

Her mixed signals were driving him friggin' crazy! Avoiding her like some scared little boy wasn't the answer. Since it appeared she'd decided to stay until he found a replacement to take care of Mattie, they needed to discuss how to stay clear of trouble until then.

Now was as good a time as any.

He reached the table in three strides, the chair opposite Abbey in four. Hooking his boot on a wooden leg, he slung it around, then straddled the seat.

She stopped hammering, then started back up. All without looking him in the eye or saying a word.

Stacking his forearms on the ladder-back at chest level, his long-neck beer dangling from the fingers of one hand, he eyed the focus of Abbey's pounding.

It was a horse.

Not just any horse, but a bucking bronco. About twice the size of a silver dollar and amazingly lifelike, down to intricately cut strands of whipping mane and tail.

He'd known she sold handmade jewelry in a flea market. He'd had no idea she was an artist. A talented one. Even he could see that.

With a deliberate movement, Abbey lay down her hammer, heaved a put-upon sigh, then met his eyes.

"I'm kind of busy, Matt. Is this important?"

The woman had a memory like a damned elephant.

Ignoring the question he'd asked her two days ago in the stable, he tipped his beer bottle toward her work. "That's really good. What are you making."

She looked startled, then pleased. "A necklace."

He cocked his head at the copper horse. "You gonna put a hook on his butt and run a chain through it?"

Her laugh was like her mouth. Soft, full and womanly, triggering immense pleasure and a stirring of heat.

"Not exactly," she answered. "It's part of a larger design. This is only one piece."

He found himself wanting to prolong the smile in her eyes. "Can I see the whole thing?"

Her expression grew suspicious.

"I'd like to. Really," he persisted. "I've seen a lot of western jewelry booths at rodeo exhibition halls. Maybe I can give you some feedback."

Keen interest sparked to life in her eyes. She nodded slowly. "Okay. But it's not glued or strung together, yet. I'll have to lay it out piece by piece."

"I've got half a beer. I'm in no hurry."

He'd expected her to shove aside her tools on the table and slap the pieces down. But he'd underestimated both her presentation skills and respect for her craft.

She cleared the table completely, pulled a

large square of bleached canvas from one of three tackle boxes on the floor, then smoothed the material over the scarred wood surface. A second box produced a stack of tissue-wrapped necklace elements.

With single-minded concentration, she began carefully constructing her design. With the same intensity, Matt sipped his beer and enjoyed the beauty unfolding little by little in front of his eyes.

And it was Abbey—not the canvas—that he watched.

Absorbed in her task, her movements pulling her dress taut and loose in a mesmerizing display, she forgot his presence, shed her wary formality and became the woman whose kiss had blown off his boots.

There were the small graceful hands that had wonderingly mapped his features. There were the high breasts that had generously cushioned his chest. There was the willowy curve of her waist into hip, the shiny hair that had smelled so sweet. A fragrance he'd pinpointed during long sleepless hours as a mixture of wildflowers and new-mown hay.

And there was her passionate mouth...

Sweet heaven, that mouth transformed her pretty face into a man's secret fantasy!

He swigged the last of his beer down a throat gone suddenly as dry as dust.

Just then she straightened, faced him squarely and smoothed her palms down the front of her dress. "Well, that's the best I can do. What do you think?"

"I think you're beautiful," he said without thinking.

Her startled brown eyes grew as round as her wire-rimmed glasses.

Way to stay out of trouble, Granger.

Obvious disbelief replaced her surprise. "The beer must've gone to your head," she said stiffly.

Forcing back a denial, he set his bottle on the floor and rose from his chair. Best to let it lie.

"Move over and let me see this masterpiece of yours."

He looked down at the canvas and drew in a sharp breath, then exhaled in the form of a long low whistle.

The necklace spread before him was centered by a thin silver oval, the hammered copper bucking bronco on top, a round turquoise stone hovering in the silver sky. A series of geometric shapes flanked the center "buckle," each in hammered copper topped by a silver cutout.

A spur on a rectangle, a Stetson on a square, a boot on a circle, a lariat on a triangle. He peered closer at the realistic coil.

"I braided silver wire," she explained before he could ask.

He touched one of four flint arrowheads wrapped in copper wire interspersing the geometric shapes. Nostalgia twined his heart as surely as wire and squeezed.

"Mary and I used to find these in the draws after every gullywasher. There are about fifty of 'em in a jar around here somewhere."

"Forty-six," Abbey corrected in a guilty tone. "Top shelf in Mattie's closet."

He shot her a surprised grin. "Why, Abbey, you little devil!"

To his amazed pleasure, she grinned back.

"A girl's gotta do what a girl's gotta do. These arrowheads will get a lot more respect on some rich Texas socialite's neck than they would molding in your smelly old jar."

Studying the necklace again, he had to agree.

"Now, all I have to do is sell it to a rich Texas socialite," she murmured.

He straightened, reluctantly empathizing. "It

would sell in a minute at the Houston Livestock Show and Rodeo. The exhibition hall is packed eight to eleven o'clock for two weeks straight.''

''I'm sure it is. But the big rodeos, fairs and jewelry shows have two-year waiting lists to get exhibitor space. And even if I jumped to the top of the list, the rental fees are out of my league.''

''You guessin'? Or you know that for a fact.''

Wrinkling her nose, she sank dejectedly into her chair. ''I know. I've got the inventory, I simply don't have the capital to promote myself as a legitimate designer.'' She looked up earnestly. ''You know how it is. Growing a business and a reputation takes money.''

''Yeah, I noticed.''

They shared a wry look. He moved to his chair, flipped it around and sat properly.

Like someone with manners.

''You seemed to be doin' all right for yourself in Venice. You can always go back there.'' The suggestion left a bad taste in his mouth.

''I could, but I've heard Santa Fe is a good place for new designers to get a start. I'm thinking of heading there, once I get a little money saved.'' She lifted the end of her braid, brushed it back and forth across her chin, dropped the thick chestnut rope and eyed him anxiously.

"You really think my necklace would sell in a big exhibition hall? Based on what you've seen, I mean. I want the truth. You won't do me any favors by lying."

He'd asked for feedback from other riders after every round, learning and adjusting to improve his odds. His respect for Abbey rose another notch.

He struggled to describe his reaction. "Well, it's different from other necklaces I've seen. Anybody wearin' it would get a lot of second looks, 'cause it would almost be like wearin' a piece of sculpture. And anybody seein' it would know they couldn't find the same thing four booths away. It reminds me of you, Abbey. Strong and unique. One-of-a-kind..." He trailed off in horror as her eyes grew suspiciously bright.

Well, hell. "Abbey, I meant that as a compliment."

"I know," she said thickly, removing her glasses. She swiped at a tear spilling free and met his gaze. "Thank you, Matt. That was the nicest thing you could've possibly said to me."

"It was?"

She nodded shyly. Long lashes, wet and

spiked, framed eyes unobstructed for the first time by lenses.

He blinked, then fell into clear brown pools and wallowed in warmth. When her smile slowly gained in strength, becoming the dazzling thing she gave to Mattie freely, his heart surged weightlessly in his chest.

"Abbey...about what happened in the stable, when I kissed you?"

Her smile vanished like a snuffed candle. Wisps of worry drifted through her eyes.

Damn, what could he say?

"I'm sorry," they said in unison, then stared at each other in blank surprise.

Matt recovered first. "I had no right to drag you into that stall like you were some—well, some..."

"Slut?" Abbey provided ruefully.

Huh? "No."

"Bitch in heat?"

Jeez. *"No.* Like some bone I wanted to gnaw in private. I shouldn't have treated you like that."

"I don't see why not. I certainly treated *you* like a piece of meat."

She slipped on her glasses and sighed. "Close your mouth, Matt. I'm the one who should apologize. You took me into a more discreet place to let me crawl all over you, and I nearly broke your nose for it. You never had any warning.''

He'd had a lot of time to relive the whole experience, and he couldn't let himself off the hook that easily. ''I knew something had changed once we were in the stall. Truth is, I was so lathered up by then I didn't want to read the signals right. But I'd like to think I would've stopped myself eventually.''

Rumpling his hair, he looked at his boots, made a sound of disgust, then recaptured her gaze. ''Abbey, I've never forced a woman to do anything against her will in my life. I'm really sorry I scared you. Especially since...''

''Especially since what?'' She looked like a doe in full-alert mode.

Matt shifted in his chair. Why had they steered clear of all personal questions from the moment they'd met? This wouldn't be so damn awkward if he knew more about her background.

He tried again. ''Especially since I'm pretty sure a man has...scared you, somehow, in your past.''

''Scared me?'' She seemed puzzled. ''You think I was afraid of you that day, because a man once abused me?''

Well, hell. "You panicked when I pressed you too hard. What am I supposed to think?"

"I was scared all right, Matt. Panicky, just like you thought. But not because of you. Because of the stall."

The stall. She hadn't been fighting him.

The anvil on his shoulders slipped off.

Before answering, he took time to read her signals carefully. Clenched hands. Taut features. Haunted eyes. "Are you saying you're claustrophobic?"

Her smile was so small and sad it was all he could do not to take her in his arms.

"I once spent four weeks locked up in a dark room about the size of that stall. You might say I'm not anxious to repeat the experience."

CHAPTER ELEVEN

WATCHING MATT'S TAN GROW one shade lighter, Abbey beat back her regret.

All these years, she'd never told anyone but a therapist and Lorna. Why she felt Matt deserved the same honesty was hard to say. Perhaps because he'd shared a painful secret of his own. More likely because she'd grown to...admire him. He didn't need more guilt.

He wouldn't look at her quite the same way after hearing her story. But that would only make it easier for her to leave.

"My God, you're serious," he finally said, his tone incredulous. "Were you kidnapped, or something?"

"Or something." Her stomach rebelled at the memories beginning to swirl up like bile, rank and foul. "Imprisoned is more like it. Solitary confinement."

"*You*, in prison?" Shock streaked through his eyes and skidded to a halt. He spread both hands on his thighs and shook his head. "Uh-uh. That dog won't hunt. You wanna quit playin' games here and tell me what you mean?"

This was much, much harder to talk about than she'd thought. "I mean that when I was nineteen, my father decided to punish me for my sinful ways. We had a storage room in our basement. Just four walls and a door. A *padlocked* door. He cleared out some trunks and Christmas decorations and stored me there for about four weeks."

His shock was back, along with the macabre fascination directed at victims of bizarre crimes. Already he saw her differently. Already he was more withdrawn.

Good, she told herself fiercely.

"Stored you? Alone?" Matt croaked.

"No, I had an air mattress, a chamber pot and a Bible."

Abbey braced herself against his involuntary sound of disgust. "You're horrified," she stated. "You should be. It was horrible, what he did. I pounded on that door until my hands were bleeding, yelled until my throat was raw. And no," she answered the question in his eyes. "He never abused me sexually. He brought me water to wash with and meals twice a day, and prayed with me for hours afterward. Then he unscrewed the lightbulb and took it with him when he left.''

Matt bowed his head and stared at the floor.

He couldn't bear to look at her, Abbey realized, her heart going numb. Curiously detached, she studied his lowered eyelashes. Edwina spent hours gluing on fakes to achieve the same lushness. Matt's natural lashes were much prettier.

Just then his gaze sliced up, mocking her comparison. There wasn't a fingernail of femininity in this man.

''What about your mother?'' he demanded.

Abbey clung to insentience. ''My mother?''

''Are you saying she just listened and did nothing?''

Emotion returned in a painful rush. ''That about sums up her personality, yes. But maybe she left the house until I quieted down. If she didn't...'' Abbey shuddered involuntarily.

She couldn't imagine the horror of listening to Mattie cry out for help and not being able to respond. Loving the child had given Abbey new perspective, transformed her anger into bruised sympathy. Carla Parker had been as much a prisoner as her daughter, padlocked by fear and low self-esteem into a subservient marriage. In the end, she'd intervened as much as her strength allowed.

Understanding, however, and *forgiving* were poles apart.

"My mother loved me," Abbey admitted, "but she thought her first duty was to honor and obey her husband."

Matt shoved his hands to his knees and gripped hard, his forearms corded with tension. "You were nineteen, for cripe's sake. Old enough to put up a hell of a fight. Didn't you try to escape when he brought you meals?"

Abbey flinched, although she shouldn't have been surprised. In California, she'd glimpsed his attitude that victims were as guilty as the perpetrators. She'd *wanted* to make it easier for her to leave.

But, oh, his lack of support hurt. Worse than she could possibly have anticipated. "Yes, Matt, I tried. Twice. My father was...a strong man."

The string of oaths Matt released made his past foul language seem positively antiseptic. He scraped unsteady fingers over his skull. "What kind of monster could treat his daughter that way?"

She offered a travesty of a smile. "A pious Christian monster. The senior minister of a church. You guessed right, Matt. I *am* a preacher's daughter.''

"Your father's a preacher?'' Looking stunned, he lifted his hands in a gesture of helplessness, let them drop back down to his knees. "What did you do to piss him off that much?''

What had *she* done. Obviously when Matt had called her strong and unique earlier, he hadn't meant it as a compliment.

"It's a long story, and you've got a fence to mend.''

"A fence that isn't goin' anywhere.'' He stretched out his boots and propped laced fingers on a flat abdomen. "Neither am I.''

But I am. Soon. Whether you've hired a replacement or not, Abbey reminded herself.

"My father led a congregation in Baker's Landing, Nebraska,'' she began woodenly. "The Eternal Light Church of the Lord and Shepherd. It was founded by fundamentalists unhappy with the new wave of 'liberalism' sweeping the country. The members were mostly farmers. Hardworking, God-fearing, ultraconservative people who approved of my father's literal interpretation of the scripture.''

Envisioning multiple pews of righteous men

and women, wheat-stalk stiff in Sunday clothes, Abbey experienced only cold indifference.

"My father was well respected in the community, and demanded that my mother and I dress, speak and behave modestly. Not a problem when I was little. In my teenage years...well, you can imagine. I wanted fashionable clothes to wear and dances to attend and boys to admire me. Preferably ones who didn't have field dirt under their fingernails."

Beauty had always been integral to Abbey's happiness. She'd admired it in nature, in manmade objects, in the people around her, and at one time, even in herself.

"Of course, Father lectured me endlessly about the evils of vanity and flirtation. 'Honor thy father' was the first commandment in our home. So I wore old-lady clothes and didn't date much or go to 'sinful' dances. The church had picnics and socials—I did go to those. With Jimmy Kane," she qualified, wrinkling her nose.

Matt pressed his thumbs together. "I take it he wasn't a prize catch."

"Jimmy was the son of the most generous financial donor in the congregation. His father owned one of the largest agriculture operations

in the state. *My* father thought Jimmy was wonderful.''

''But?''

''But you could fit a Bible between his front
teeth and plant corn under his fingernails.''

Snorting a laugh, Matt unthreaded his long
fingers and deliberately tucked them beneath his
armpits.

As if Matt's work-roughened hands were in
the same genus as Jimmy's small stubby ap-
pendages, Abbey thought wryly. ''Two weeks
after graduation, a new assistant pastor arrived
at Eternal Light Church of the Lord and Shepherd. Steven Taylor. Fresh from Los Angeles, of
all places...''

Remembering Steven's classic features, his
manicured hands, the cosmopolitan suits so flattering to his blond hair and slender build, she
forgave herself for being dazzled. But not for
being blind.

''I take it this new guy was a prize catch?''
Matt interrupted her musing.

''I thought so. Everyone did. Steven was intelligent, well traveled and a mesmerizing
speaker. He was also as handsome as a Greek
god,'' she admitted. ''Half the women in the
congregation were secretly in love with him. The

other half openly wanted to sleep with him. I decided to be the one he chose." *To be his wife. To have his children and create a warm home. To cherish and love him through sickness and in health.*

But Matt didn't need to know that. Or the way Steven had wooed her with touches that lingered too long, with flattering claims that no one understood him the way she did. Starved for affection and praise, she'd pressed for more.

"I seduced him," Abbey said bluntly. "We had an affair. One afternoon the organist walked into the practice room unexpectedly and caught us in a compromising position." Rejecting the humiliating image, she focused on Matt's lowering brows, instead. "By the next Sunday, everyone in the congregation knew what had happened except my father. He overheard two church deacons gossiping after the service and cleared out the storage room that night."

There.

She'd laid her emotional baggage at his feet and unzipped enough dirty laundry to discourage any man. Especially one already burdened with too much of his own.

She concentrated miserably on the gray speckled linoleum, noting scattered strands of mottled hair. At least Mattie would have Pitiful to comfort her when Abbey left.

"That's your story?" Matt asked tightly.

She peeked up, her heart twisting at his wintry glare. "Yes."

He unfolded his arms, drew in his legs and straightened, emphasizing his impressive size. *"That's* why your father locked you in a dungeon and threw away your chastity belt key? Because you had a little fling?"

"To my father, that was unforgivable," Abbey said carefully. "As his daughter, I was supposed to set a virtuous example. I humiliated him in front of the entire congregation."

"Screw the congregation. Where were they when you disappeared and needed help?"

Cautious fireflies of hope glowed off and on within Abbey. "They were told I was away visiting cousins. Since I was the new town 'hussy,' they weren't sorry to see me go."

"So where the hell was the Greek god all this time? Didn't he try to contact you, or at least take *some* of the blame?"

More fireflies glowed in her chest. She'd waited for Steven to rescue her. As days passed, she'd accepted the bitter fact she'd only been an entertaining diversion. "Steven had no reason not to believe my father's story. And no one blamed him for what happened. I told you, I deliberately seduced him.''

Leaning forward, suppressed violence glittering in his eyes, Matt braced hands that could break a *cholo*'s wrist on thighs that controlled a powerful stallion with ease. "Bullshit!"

Her leaping pulse was more feminine thrill than fear. "Please don't curse."

"I rest my case." He settled back against his chair. "You're no hussy. You may have slept with the jerk, but you didn't do it to cut a notch on your bedpost. You're not the type. And even if you were, it takes two to make music. If the organist caught Taylor harmonizing with his pants down, how come your father locked *you* up and not him?''

Abbey had spent a lifetime fighting her battles alone. Matt's fierce protectiveness was alien and awesome, seductive and sobering. In a last desperate effort to protect her heart, she played devil's advocate.

"Steven was father's protégé. A brilliant disciple of God. I'd led him astray. Father truly believed all women were clones of Eve."

Matt's grunt conveyed a dictionary of scorn. "Your father should be strung up by his balls in the Baker's Landing town square. He's a sick fanatic. A hypocritical bastard using religion to excuse his sadistic nature.''

Abbey gaped, then choked out a laugh. "But how do you *really* feel?''

His eyes narrowed. "Like knocking some heads together. Hard. Starting with your father's and Taylor's. Then working my way through the pious members of Eternal Light Church of the Lord and Shepherd until every goddamn one of 'em answers to St. Peter for turning their backs on you!''

Thrusting up from his chair in a fluid surge, Matt turned and paced the kitchen. Sweat sculpted the hair at his nape into curls, darkened an arrow of cotton down his back, scented the air he stirred in passing with an earthy cologne that flared her nostrils and tightened her belly.

He wore a grimy blue chambray work shirt, dusty jeans and boots bronzed in dried red mud. His hands were callused, his fingernails dirty. Desperado whiskers shadowed his jaw. He looked dark, avenging and dangerous. As different from Steven as Zorro and Prince Charming.

No contest.

"Come sit, Matt. Please. I'm getting dizzy.''

Only a slight exaggeration. A thousand glowing fireflies illuminating one's soul was an intoxicating experience.

She couldn't control her beaming smile as Matt spun around, stalked to his chair and sat in a tense sprawl.

"You think this is funny?"

She thought he had the handsomest scowl she'd ever seen. "Sorry."

"Finish the story," he demanded. "*Please* tell me you reported your parents to the cops when your father finally let you out."

Her smile died. She hadn't been able to bring herself to report them. But neither could she be a part of their lives. Her therapist had advised a complete break from the destructive relationship.

Abbey adjusted the soft pink cotton of her loosely constructed dress. "Father never let me out."

His brows rose. "Come again?"

"One afternoon I heard the padlock open, and then…nothing."

She'd lain on the air mattress, her heart pounding, afraid to test the door because it might not open, because it also *might*. When she'd finally pushed through and no one stood waiting, her knees had buckled. She'd staggered to her feet and searched the empty house.

"I assume my mother unlocked the door. There was about a thousand dollars in cash lying on the kitchen table. No note, but I knew she meant me to take it. I packed a suitcase, walked to the bus station and got on the first express out of town."

He studied her from beneath his lashes a long, uncomfortable moment. "You must've been scared."

So much so she'd emptied her stomach before leaving the house. "Yes."

"Yet you held yourself together and made a new life. Definitely nobody's victim, thank-you-very-much." His faint nod and admiring gaze paid tribute to the sentiment she'd voiced after their mugging.

Abbey released the wad of material fisted in one hand.

He looked down at his shirt and brushed at a streak of dirt. "So why did you lie and say you deliberately seduced Taylor?"

Her heart ker-thumped at his sure tone. "It wasn't a total lie. A few weeks after we met, I started using a little makeup, buying a few form-fitting dresses for church, wearing my hair loose instead of in a braid—" She broke off as his gaze jerked up, keenly alert.

"You wore your hair loose?"

"Y-yes. I wanted Steven to notice me."

"Oh, he noticed."

She cleared her throat. "As a matter of fact, I don't think he did notice. At least, not until I volunteered to type his first sermon. Remember, there were a lot of women—prettier women—vying for his attention."

"Fishin' for compliments, Abbey?"

She stiffened at his mocking tone and insolent appraisal.

"Hell, darlin', unweave that lariat you call hair and squeeze that sweet body into somethin' besides a damn sack, and your face could be so ugly the tide wouldn't take you out, for all it mattered to Taylor—or any other man. He'd still want you in his bed."

So much for choosing Zorro.

Turning blindly to the table, Abbey began disassembling her necklace display. In her peripheral vision, Matt stirred then cursed softly. Her throat constricted.

Ridiculous, this emotional seesaw she seemed stuck riding. That's what she got for letting her guard down. For letting herself care.

"Abbey?"

"I think it's time we both went back to work, don't you?" she asked thickly.

With trembling fingers, she wrapped an arrowhead in tissue paper and set it aside, reached for a tiny silver lariat and paused. Her braid was a no-fuss answer to hair Steven had once called "glorious." She would cut it as soon as she left the ranch.

"Abbey, turn around and look at me. Please."

I will *not* cry, she told herself sternly. Shifting in her chair, she met his remorseful gaze.

"I'm sorry," he said.

Her eyes and nose stung more fiercely.

"I was jealous. That's no excuse for bein' a jackass, but it's the only one I've got. When I thought about the Greek god seein' and doin' what I've only dreamed about, I wanted to hurt someone. You were handy."

The instincts she normally trusted were topsy-turvy. She could scarcely credit her ears.

"I've never been jealous before," he continued, as if anxious for her to understand. "Maybe because you're diffrent from other beautiful women. Not any of the ones I've known would've survived bein' thrown to the wolves like you did, much less had the courage, talent and brains to start up a business. Not any of 'em would've had the heart to take on a neglected little girl and make her feel safe and loved. I never thanked you properly for that, but I want you to know how much I appreciate what you did and what you're doing for Mattie.''

Abbey pressed a hand to the rib cage threatening to crack from internal pressure.

''I guess what I'm tryin' to say is that it's true any man would want you in his bed. But only a fool wouldn't want you in his life...'' Matt trailed off with a look of dismay. ''Well, *hell*.''

Laughing through her tears, the seesaw bobbing like mad, Abbey shook her head helplessly.

''I'm sorry,'' she managed at last. ''Excuse me.''

She sprang up and headed for the roll of paper towels above the sink. He must think her a blubbering idiot.

He thinks I'm beautiful! He thinks I have courage and brains and heart!

Abbey ripped off a section of paper towel just in time to blot a fresh spillover of tears.

The phone jangled, and she turned her back gratefully while he rose to answer. She hardly ever cried. But right now, her emotion was so great she feared she might explode without some release. Matt's conversation faded into background noise.

He all but asked me to share his life!

Dare she consider giving her heart into this man's care? Could she hang that needlepoint picture on the wall permanently? Testing the idea in her mind, Abbey whirled around as Matt slowly hung up the phone.

His manner was preoccupied. An icy premonition doused her cozy warmth. "Anything wrong?"

He shoved his hands into his back pockets. "That was a woman calling about the want ad. Mrs. Fisher, a new widow ready for a complete change of scenery. She's always wanted to live on a ranch, and the salary I quoted is acceptable." He watched Abbey closely, as if waiting for a reaction.

Ask me to stay, she begged silently, years of caution schooling her features into a polite mask.

His lashes swept down, then back up. "We made an appointment on the phone for her to drive here for an interview tomorrow."

So.

Odd, how a crushed heart could go on beating. Abbey wrenched her mask into a brittle smile. "Good. She sounds promising."

"Yeah. She does at that."

Go-away-go-away-go-away before I shatter.

When he moved toward her, Abbey stopped breathing...until he veered left.

He swept his Stetson off the counter and onto his head, tugged down the brim and caught her eye. "Just think. If we're lucky, you'll be able to pack up soon and move on with your life."

If they were lucky?

"Hey, I'm way ahead of you." Pride, plus the chance to finally speak the truth powered Abbey's jaunty glance and flippant shrug. "In fact, I'm already packed."

CHAPTER TWELVE

THE NEXT MORNING, Matt hoisted up his cutting saddle onto the stallion cross-tied in the stable aisle. Mrs. Fisher wouldn't be here to interview for another two hours. Per instructions, Casey would have a full herd waiting in the largest pen.

Tolerating the cinching, buckling and minor adjustments to tack, Doc seemed eager for the job ahead. He gazed alertly out the double doors, his ears pricked forward toward the sound of lowing cattle. A good sign. Matt had recently stepped up the intensity of each session. Boredom was a sure indication of an overtrained horse.

Too bad his own get-up-and-go got up and went some time around dawn.

Sleep had eluded him last night, nipped at the heels by Abbey's words from the day before. *"I'm already packed."* The relentless phrase had worn him down until he'd finally faced the truth. He wanted Abbey in his life indefinitely.

Maybe forever. At the very least for two more weeks.

Then he could release the emotions bundled tighter than hooves in a pigging string, see if they ran like hell...or stood firm and strong. Only two more weeks. Time he desperately needed to focus on Doc's training for the NCHA Futurity. No distractions. No sleepless nights.

No problem, since Abbey would soon be history.

The knot inside Matt's chest tightened.

He unhooked the headstall from his saddle horn, threaded a chocolate ear through the single loop and waited. When the stallion immediately opened his mouth, Matt crooned, "Good boy," and slipped the snaffle bit into place.

Doc's most recent owner, Ben Campbell, had used a wire noseband and heavy Clapper bit to control the "soured" cutter. Matt had used Touch Therapy and lighter tack in hopes of building mutual trust. He knew the locals were skeptical. It was one thing for Charlie's reckless kid to succeed at riding broncs. Establishing a reputable training stable would take more than daredevil skill. And patience, integrity and business savvy weren't qualities associated with those white-trash Grangers.

Doc had surprised and impressed everyone by responding favorably to Matt's unorthodox training. He'd let them stay impressed. But his secret was simple. Some horses, like some people, needed a large measure of freedom in order to flourish.

Hell, look at Abbey.

Abbey, Abbey, Abbey. A half bottle of whiskey at the kitchen table hadn't drowned thoughts of her last night. Frowning now, he fingercombed Doc's long coarse mane and wished she'd never said "I'm already packed."

Abbey loved his niece. She had feelings for him, too, though she fought them, same as he did his own. Yet she'd smiled when he'd told her about Mrs. Fisher, then said those goddamn haunting words. When Mattie and Hal had bustled into the kitchen minutes later with full grocery sacks, Matt had slipped down the hallway and into Abbey's room. There, at the foot of her bed, a large suitcase had stood at the ready. His quick peek inside had confirmed his sick suspicion.

She hadn't been lying. She was sure enough "already packed." Her need to move on with her life was obviously stronger than any hold he and Mattie had on her heart.

The knowledge had hit like a palm in his nose, bleeding slowly throughout the long night, pooling with what he'd already learned about Abbey's past: her parents' unbending rules and moral codes, her first pansy-ass son of a bitch lover, her terrible experience in a dark, locked storage room.

Sometime near dawn, he'd remembered stubbing his toe in her California bedroom on a suitcase. A heavy suitcase. One already packed *before* she'd agreed to travel to Texas.

The facts had congealed into a theory. A girl whose wings had been clipped at the first sign of puberty, who'd been caged up figuratively, and later, literally...a girl like that might easily grow into a woman who feared putting down roots or feeling trapped in one place.

That woman's idea of the Clapper bit from hell might be a small isolated ranch in Texas needing constant year-round attention.

Wincing, Matt released the wiry mane cutting off circulation to his middle and index fingers. He would hire the enthusiastic Mrs. Fisher today. Suitable or not, she was more tolerable than a woman who couldn't wait to be rid of this place...and him. Abbey didn't have much money, but she was smart and tough. She'd do fine on her own.

A dozen horrible scenarios mixed with his hangover to give him a queasy touch-and-go moment. At its peak, he had an idea that might pan out to help her financially. His nausea calmed.

Warm misty air blasted Matt's face. "Hey!"

An upthrust muzzle flipped off his Stetson, butted him a stumbling step backward. "Damn it, Doc, that's not funny!"

Curling up his lip, the stallion nickered his disagreement before swinging his head around to face the front.

"Go ahead and laugh, wise guy. Just wait'll I get you in the pen." Matt yanked out the tail of his shirt and toweled off his face.

A choked noise from behind stilled his blotting motion. Damn. Someone must've entered the back set of double doors. He released his shirt, retrieved his hat and oh-so-casually turned around.

Mattie stood beside an empty stall ten feet away, wearing her favorite Cinderella dress. Her hands were clamped over her mouth and nose, her cheeks ballooned like Satchmo trumpeting a high C, her tummy strained round and tight be-

536   ONE TOUGH TEXAN

neath the pumpkin coach dribbled with maple
syrup. She looked ready to bust a gut or blow
out her eardrums.

Something had to give. And soon.

Settling his hat in a loose fit, Matt deliberately
backed up toward Doc. On cue, the Stetson went
flying to land near Mattie's red cowboy boots.

She flung out her hands, grabbed her bare
knobby knees and let the giggles flow. Gurgling
streams of giggles bubbling up straight from her
belly. The kind you couldn't listen to without
smiling, unless you pulled wings off flies and
kicked puppies for fun.

Matt listened and watched and grinned, struck
by a sudden overwhelming gratitude. His sister's
death had wounded Mattie, sure. Made her
watch him like a skinny pup expecting to get
dumped from his pickup truck any minute and
left beside the road.

But if Mattie could laugh like this, she was
well on her way to healing. Thanks to Abbey.

Of course, there might be a setback after Abbey left.

His grin vanished. Abbey's warning replayed
in his mind. *"She'll be devastated, unless she
can turn to you."*

Scowling, he walked abruptly toward his niece.

Her giggles broke off with a squeak. She stared up as if he pulled wings off flies and kicked puppies for fun.

Gawd.

He leaned down, scooped up his hat and jammed the crown low. "Does Abbey know you're out here, squirt?"

Her eyes rounded innocently. "She says fresh air is good for me."

Hmm. "Did she give you permission to come to the stables alone?"

Mattie thrust out her lower lip. "She's not my mommy."

No. Tough luck for the kid. "Abbey loves you enough to care about your safety. You need to mind her and stay inside the house."

"There's nothin' to do inside but color and bake cookies and watch cartoons and play stupid Candy Land. I'm *bored.*"

At age six, only a year older than Mattie, he'd cleaned Mary's wet bedsheets and Charlie's vomit for fun. "Hell, if you ask me, squirt, you're damn lucky."

Mattie's mutinous mouth pruned up. She

lifted her tiny nose. "Please don't use rude language."

By chewing the inside of his cheek until it blistered, Matt managed not to laugh. Abbey might not be his niece's mother, but her stamp was all over the kid.

"Sorry," he muttered. Then, because the Mary he'd known could singe the ears off a mule skinner, he couldn't resist asking, "Didn't your mama ever use bad words?"

"Sometimes," Mattie admitted. "But she said for me to talk like Abbey, not her or Weena. 'Cause Abbey's a real lady."

Good for you, sis. "So I guess your mama trusted Abbey to take good care of you, huh?"

In answer, Mattie raised a small finger and twined her sleep-mashed hair into blond corkscrews.

Matt set his hands at his waist. "Is that a yes?"

His niece nodded warily.

"Then she'd also want you to mind Abbey, and not sneak out here behind her back. Isn't that right?" He could almost see her agile mind scrambling for a way out of the trap, and found himself looking forward to her answer.

"I had t' go to the baf'room."

He blinked, then waited.

"Abbey says I don't got to have permission t' go to the baf'room," Mattie explained slyly.

Not half-bad, for a raw beginner.

"There's no bathroom out here, squirt. Sorry, but you'll have to go back to the house..." Matt trailed off as a conspicuous spattering sound preceded an unmistakable ammonialike scent. His neck heated.

Damn it, Doc!

Cleaning a cat litter box, even one his niece had witnessed being used, was no preparation for this show. Mattie's fascinated stare said the well-endowed stallion was making an indelible impression on her young mind.

Stepping forward impulsively, Matt grabbed the child and swung her high and around to straddle Doc's back. Her Cinderella dress exposed a glimpse of Wednesday panties, but at least *her* view was G-rated.

"You okay up there?" he asked, knowing Abbey would skin him alive if Mattie started to cry.

His niece nodded vigorously, her blue saucer eyes filled, not with fear, but with pure enchanted awe. As if her fairy godmother had just waved a wand and made her dearest wish come true.

Every true horseman on the planet could relate to that feeling. You were either born with it, or you weren't.

Matt left her where she was.

"Can I ride him, Uncle Matt?" she asked in a breathless voice.

"I dunno, squirt. This your first time on a horse?"

"Uh-huh. But I'm a *good* rider. I promise."

Matt had yet to learn of anything his niece thought she *wasn't* good at. Abbey's influence again. He'd overheard her tell Hal a child couldn't have too much self-confidence, since life would try and whittle it down soon enough.

Still, Mattie was a long way up from the ground.

Doc completed his business and moved into a normal stance, shifting Mattie in the saddle. Her delighted grin shoved Matt off the fence.

"How 'bout you hold on to the horn while Doc and I walk you up to the house," he suggested. "Would you like that?"

Her shining eyes and silent "oh" of wonder fissured another crack in the armor guarding his heart. He and his sister's child shared much more than dimples and an aversion to spinach, it seemed. Abbey had tried to tell him as much. He hadn't wanted to hear.

"Hold on tight," Matt warned, unhooking the nylon cross ties.

He gathered Doc's reins in one hand, led him out of the cool dark stables and squinted a split second too late.

Morning rays drilled his retinas. A geyser of agony mushroomed through his head. Served him right. Whiskey binges were for losers.

Coffee. That's what he needed. Hal's was strong enough to walk into a cup. Matt gritted his teeth and picked up his pace.

"It's so pretty," Mattie said on a sigh, interrupting his misery. "Like Abbey's sparkle stones got spilled everywhere."

Startled, he glanced up and followed Mattie's gaze.

On his forty-yard walk to the stable earlier, he'd added mowing to his list of chores. Focusing again on the overgrown yard, he expanded his frame of view and slowed his steps, then came to a gradual stop.

Rhinestone dewdrops studded the grass and wildflowers skirting the ranch house, emphasizing faded yellow paint, missing shingles and a tilting concrete stoop. The house should've seemed pathetic dressed in sparkles, but instead conveyed dignity and strength. Like an aging country and western singer who'd suffered hard times and survived to triumph.

Three years ago, that "Stand By Your Man" sense of permanence had spoken to the deepest part of Matt. It had told him this house could be the home he'd never had as a child, this land a worthy asset to people who'd once thought him worthless.

Since the day Abbey had challenged him to forgive himself, he'd thought a lot about her advice. Was he overly concerned about the opinion of others at the expense of his niece's emotional needs?

Compromising, Matt decided that after the Futurity, he would repair the roof and repaint the exterior. Maybe build a deck off the back door. Then Mattie could color safely and still see the horses. It seemed cruel, suddenly, to deny her at least that much.

A sharp tug on the reins jerked Matt's attention to Doc.

Muzzle to the ground, his visible eye trained on Matt, the stallion ripped up massive clumps of forbidden clover faster than he could chew and swallow.

"Oh, no you don't," Matt warned, pulling up on the reins and meeting stubborn resistence.

"Aw, he's hungry, Uncle Matt."

"He's greedy. C'mon, porky. You had plenty of breakfast."

Straining against the bit for that last morsel at the salad bar, Doc managed to snatch it up before conceding defeat. He slowly lifted his magnificent head, his nostrils flared in disdain, his luminous eyes focused on mysterious inner visions no mere human could hope to comprehend.

If his overstuffed mouth hadn't looked like a Chia Pet on Miracle-Gro, Matt might even have been impressed.

Choking up on the reins, he headed toward the house and Hal's coffee. The dew-kissed breeze that soothed his hangover bore the tangy-sweet scent of earth, grass and clover. Leather creaked, a calf squalled, an iron-shod hoof clinked against a hidden stone. The familiar sounds were comforting. And oddly companionable.

Matt glanced up to check on the squirt.

Sitting in a near gymnast's split, her ridiculous red boots barely reaching the saddle skirt, Mattie looked shockingly small. A peanut swaying on an elephant. No, a Burmese princess surveying her domain.

Sometime in the space of ten yards her little-girl awe had changed to regal self-possession. Short legs and greenhorn boots didn't change the obvious. She looked as if she *belonged* on a champion bloodline horse, damned if she didn't. Anyone could see she was a natural rider. Maybe he'd look into finding her a smaller, gentler mount. But not a pony. Ponies were for sissies.

At first Matt didn't recognize the emotion expanding his rib cage. Seconds later, when Mattie caught his eye and beamed, he put a name to the warmth in his chest. *Pride?* Hell, no wonder he'd been stumped.

It wasn't a feeling he'd ever experienced before regarding a Granger.

Twenty yards away from the house, the back kitchen door cracked open. A black nose appeared, followed by a scruffy oversize head. The rest of Pitiful wiggled out of the narrow gap like a squeeze of hairy toothpaste.

Matt groaned. Pitiful woofed. Mattie waved and shouted his name.

He leaped off the stoop into Hal's vegetable garden, churning up dirt and a hapless tomato plant in an all-out run toward his new favorite playmate.

Doc's head came up sharply. His ears quivered. His tail swished twice.

"Pitiful, stay!" Matt ordered the goofy dog with more heart than good sense.

Abbey, now on the stoop with Hal, cupped her mouth. "Pitiful, come!"

"Pitiful, go back!" Mattie piped up, adding her two cents to a jackpot of trouble.

The heedless animal hurtled closer...closer. Doc's ears flattened. If Pitiful planted his front paws on the stallion like he did on Matt, Doc would go ballistic. And Mattie...

Cursing, Matt stepped into Pitiful's path an instant before the dog rose.

Two clawed battering rams struck Matt's sternum, knocking him hard into muscular horseflesh that was there—and then wasn't. He hit the ground rump, shoulder blades and hatless skull in jarring succession, his first thought to hang on to the reins, his second to fill his tortured lungs.

Even as he registered the reassuring bite of leather in his palm, an ominous jerking warned him of the horse's series of stiff crow hops. He fought to drag in a breath and willed Mattie to hold on tight.

Seconds later the reins were pried out of his hand.

"I've got her, son," Hal said, his gruff voice gentle.

Blessed air flowed into Matt's lungs. Once the blackness lifted, he raised his shoulders and propped on one elbow. A rush of movement was his only warning before a furry body bowled into his chest.

He went down like a spare pin.

Matt spent the next few minutes fending off an apologetic tongue and Alpo breath strong enough to wilt the spring carpet cushioning his head. Between gasps and sputters, he finally managed a weak "Help."

Abbey laughingly came to the rescue, hauling Pitiful off by his ruff, then kneeling to wrap her arms around him in restraint.

Matt sat up, slapped the pollen and grass from his hair, and cast a worried look around for Mattie.

She stood near the stoop beside Hal, who held the now-docile stallion by his headstall. Luckily she appeared more elated than damaged.

"You okay, squirt?" he asked, just to make sure.

"Okay?" Hal hawked and spit. "Hoooee! I

wish Casey hadn't lit out already for that hay. Mattie rode out those crow hops like a pro. She's a Granger, all right.''

Yeah. And Grangers never let on when they were hurt.

Matt rose, his gaze never leaving his niece's. "You okay, really?''

She sent him a smile to rival the morning sun in brilliance. "I'm fine, Uncle Matt. Really. Can I ride some more? That was fun!''

Fun. His lips twitched. She was a Granger, all right. "You mean you weren't scared riding that mean horse?''

From the mischievous sparkle in her eyes, she remembered asking him the same question a lifetime ago in California.

"Nah,'' Mattie answered right on cue. "I'm too tough to be scared. Just like you.''

The last thing Matt felt right now was tough, and it scared the living bejesus out of him.

"Can I let Pitiful go now?'' Abbey sputtered, drawing everyone's attention.

Her glasses knocked askew, her face scrunched beneath the onslaught of a tongue bath, she crouched with her arms still tight around a dog whose affection would've sent most women into a hissy fit. As Mattie giggled and Hal cackled, Abbey's musical laughter joined in.

Matt's heart contracted. Dangerous to get greedy, to imagine a "what if" that could never be. He'd learned the lesson early, and he'd damn well better remember the pain of loving what he couldn't buy or control. Or keep happy and safe.

When he could trust his voice, he told Abbey, "Go on and let the troublemaker loose."

Then he walked to his niece, lifted her high and deposited her on Pitiful's back. She shrieked gleefully, the dog looked gratifyingly miserable and Matt savored the bittersweet sound of Abbey's renewed laughter.

The Grangers were tough, he reminded himself. Always had been. Always would be. Anybody in Cottonwood would tell you so. But Matt suspected he would soon be tested as no other Granger had in the past.

He hoped like hell, for Abbey's sake, that he was tough enough to let her go.

CHAPTER THIRTEEN

FIVE MILES AWAY at her kitchen table, Bess Campbell watched her daddy clear white porcelain trails through orange egg yoke with a biscuit, then shovel the entire dripping mass into his mouth.

He chewed noisily, his left elbow planted on a folded napkin, his right lifting from polished oak only to help tip coffee into the churning sludge in his mouth. Disgusting. Her hogs had better manners. More appreciation for who fed them and what went down their gullets.

Her vision blurred as a memory surfaced: Matt Granger eating a slice of her apple pie at his own kitchen table.

His bites had been moderate, his chewing silent, his enjoyment lusty but a long way from disgusting. After his last swallow, the virile cowboy had turned his knee-buckling grin on her full force and told her how lucky Ben Campbell was to have her for a daughter.

Bess blinked into focus, then wished she hadn't. Her daddy sat placidly chewing the same huge bite of biscuit. Hiding her revulsion, she nibbled her eggs.

Before her mama died, his temper had been hot, but his smiles were always quick to follow. Bess had thought her stocky father more handsome than a fairy-tale prince. At age forty-five, he was still handsome, and still built like a bull with a temper to match.

Only...the smiles had died with her mama. Without them, his anger was a fearsome thing.

What would've happened if she hadn't made him breakfast, if she'd gone for a walk like she'd wanted while the dew still sparkled and spring smelled best? As Abbey had said, the world wouldn't stop turning. But Bess knew he wouldn't have fixed himself breakfast, either. He would've gotten mad. After that, she didn't know.

She'd never taken the risk.

Abbey had said her parents were strict. The look on her face had told Bess they were worse. But Abbey hadn't stuck around to take whatever ''it'' was. She'd gotten out. And not on the back of some man—though she could have. She had the kind of pretty that snuck up on you and got prettier the longer you were around her. By the time Bess had realized it, she liked Abbey too much to dislike her.

Abbey was strong. She didn't play it safe, she played it her way, no one else's. Bess had thought about that a lot lately.

A grunt from across the table drew her attention. Her daddy had finally swallowed. She waited against all hope for a word of praise. A simple thank-you. A reason to feel worthy for something other than her reign as Cottonwood Festival Queen three years ago.

She got an explosive belch that whipped her head away from the stench.

"Ugh," Bess muttered, frustration and anger and fear rising within her like noxious gas. Like a belch that had been building for days and months and years and only just now climbed to the top of her throat.

Rising from her chair, she placed both palms on the table and leaned forward, capturing startled blue eyes a shade darker than her own.

"Say 'excuse me,'" she ordered, the command a red cape in her daddy's face.

His jaw slackened. "Huh?"

"You belched. Say 'excuse me,'" she repeated. "It's the polite thing to do. It's what Mama would've *made* you do."

A dull red flush rose to the roots of his graying blond hair. "You leave your mama out of this, young lady."

"Why? When will it be all right to talk about her again?"

Not yet, his outraged expression clearly said.

"We all used to talk around this table, remember? Talk and laugh a lot, too. She'd hate the way we are now. Me bowin' and scrapin' to try and please you. You tellin' me I'm too good for the likes of men around here, then treatin' me worse than one of your huntin' dogs."

"What's gotten into you, girl?" Ben thundered.

Abbey's face flashed in Bess's mind. "Maybe some backbone, finally."

Or maybe not, she thought, watching a vein at his temple throb.

Only two people she knew of had ever defied her daddy openly. One of them had died when Bess was fourteen. The other lived five miles away and didn't show much interest in being her white knight, no matter how much she'd tried to fool herself.

"Go to your room!"

"No." Bess straightened, her legs trembling. She'd wielded a meat mallet with less force than her heart pounded her ribs now. "I'm a full-grown woman. Don't treat me like I'm still a girl. Not when I cooked and cleaned and raised chickens and hogs while other 'girls' went to their rooms and listened to music or talked to their boyfriends on the phone."

"Bah! And where are those other girls now? Living in trailers with a kid riding one hip and another baby growing in their bellies. What've they got? No-good husbands, too many bills and squalling brats, that's what. White trash lives no better 'n that Granger slut's who ran off and got herself knocked up. While you've got this big house to rattle around in. This ranch to pass on to your children."

A knife of longing twisted in her womb, made her lash out in pain. "What children? I've turned down three offers of marriage because you thought a Cottonwood Festival Queen deserved better. Well, *I* say I deserve better than your belches in my face!"

He scraped back his chair, but she was through cowering. "I tried to be Mama. I can't help it that I'm not. Quit punishin' me for what I can't change."

"I told you to leave her out of this," he said ominously.

Her pulse leaping, Bess snatched her half-eaten eggs from the table, carried her plate to the sink and glanced out the window. She barely registered the pickup truck approaching the house. All her senses were trained on the man behind her back.

I deserve better, she reminded herself, cramming eggs down the disposal. "I'm through pretending Mama never existed. That won't make the hurt go away."

"Shut up, Bess."

"That won't bring her back to us, or change the fact that we're alone."

"Shut up, I said!"

Bess spun around, feeling oddly detached from his fury, as if she watched him from outside her body. "Why? So you can feel less guilty for fighting with her when you knew she was being treated for blood clots?"

He'd risen to stand with his hands fisted, his eyes as glazed as a maddened bull's.

"Did you think I wouldn't put two and two together, Daddy?"

He stalked forward.

"You were yellin' at her loud enough to start

a stampede. It's no wonder a clot broke loose and—"

Smack!

Her head snapped to the left under the force of his open palm. She cried out and staggered, fell clumsily knees first, then onto all fours. No blessed detachment now. Her ears rang, her vision swam, her cheek throbbed with a pain so intense she nearly lost what little breakfast she'd eaten. The tiny blue flowers in the no-wax floor whirled.

"Bess...honey," her father said brokenly.

His strong hands gripped her shoulders. She screamed reflexively and pulled back, failing to break his hold.

"Bess, listen to me— What the *hell?*"

He released her suddenly and she slumped. His strangled groan brought her head up.

Her daddy's arms were twisted behind his back, held there by a taller man in a beige cowboy hat. She blinked to clear her vision.

Casey? Casey Tannen?

"Can you stand up, Bess?" he asked.

It *was* Casey, though she almost hadn't recognized him at first. No trace of the easygoing boy she'd dated in high school showed in his hard features. His steady gaze both comforted and strengthened her.

She managed a wobbly nod, then rose shakily.

"Good girl."

"Just a goddamn minute, Tannen! You can't barge into my house and—ahhgh!"

Her daddy's face contorted in agony as Casey did something Bess couldn't see.

"Shut up, Mr. Campbell. I *did* barge in here, and I sure didn't like what I saw. Bess, go sit at the table, please."

She made it to a chair without fainting, mostly because she didn't want to miss a second of the amazing scene in progress. Casey was taller than her daddy, but a good forty pounds lighter. She wouldn't have believed he could overpower the heavier man if she weren't witnessing it live and in color.

"Now I'm gonna let up a little on your arm, Mr. Campbell, and we're gonna walk over to Bess, sit down and talk this out. You calm enough to do that? Nod your head if you are."

Ben nodded, and his pained grimace relaxed.

Casey prodded his captive forward to the table, shoved the older man hard into a chair, then sat between father and daughter as if he did this sort of thing every day.

Ben rubbed his left arm gingerly. "It feels broken."

"If you ever hit her again, it will be," Casey promised in a tone that raised the hair on Bess's nape.

He meant it literally, she realized. Even more incredible, her daddy believed Casey would make good on the threat.

A gleam of grudging respect now mingled with the belligerence in Ben's glare. "I'll do you a favor and not call the sheriff like I should. But you can forget leaving with that feed order. Tell Granger he can grow his own damn hay. Now get off my property while I'm still feeling charitable."

"No, I don't believe I will, thank you," Casey said amiably. Then, ignoring her daddy big as you please, turned to Bess and studied her cheek with the gentlest, most beautiful hazel eyes ever shaded by a Stetson. "How are you feeling?"

Like she'd been smacked upside the head by surprise. The smitten wrangler she'd dismissed like a cute but pesky puppy had grown formidable muscles and teeth when she hadn't been looking.

"I'm okay," she said shyly.

"You need to get some ice on that cheek."

She started to rise automatically, but he was up in a flash, his hand pressing down on her shoulder.

"No, you sit. I'll get it. Maybe if Mr. Campbell apologizes to you, I'll get some ice for his arm, too." With a pointed glance at her daddy, he lifted his hand and headed for the refrigerator.

Her shoulder tingling, she blinked at his broad back, then looked reluctantly across the table. Ben Campbell appeared to have aged ten years in the past hour. Yet...

Bess studied her father more closely. Maybe it was the way he seemed to really *see* her, but despite looking haggard, he reminded Bess of the father from her childhood years. The one who hadn't abandoned civil manners and conversation, or anything that might've made him enjoy a world without his wife.

The tears shimmering in her father's gaze stunned Bess.

"Bessie, I...I never meant to hit you. Never! Please believe that." Slowly he stretched out the same hand that had slapped her brutally and turned it palm up on the table.

She stared at the silent apology and plea for

forgiveness a long moment. He'd done a terrible thing. But not without provocation.

She'd *said* a terrible thing, pouring salt on an open wound, implying he was responsible for her beloved mother's death. If she rejected him now, he might never reach out to her again. And she'd missed him so much.

Swallowing hard, Bess met his eyes. "I know, Daddy. I believe you. But I want you to know that I can't—" she shook her head sharply and raised her chin "—no, I *won't* live here unless things—" she shook her head again "—unless *you* change. I'm not invisible. I'm not your servant or one of your horses that's only as good as the trophies it's won. I'm your daughter. I've helped you make this ranch profitable and I deserve your respect."

He looked astonished and indignant.

Her heart pounding, she cleared the wobble out of her voice and took the biggest risk of all. "If you ever touch me again in anger, Daddy, I'll leave. But I'll call the sheriff first. Then everyone will know *you're* the white trash in Cottonwood, not the people in trailer homes, or the Grangers, or anyone else you bad-mouth. Do you understand?"

As he stared down at his outstretched palm,

Bess's stomach dipped. He would pull back any second, and she would lose him forever.

But when he looked up, his eyes swam with shame, not anger. "Your mama would be real proud of you, Bessie. Can you forgive me?"

In answer, she thrust her hand forward. He gripped her fingers in a convulsive squeeze and her heart surged joyfully. She sought Casey's gaze across the room.

His quick approving smile made her stomach turn cartwheels. Her pulse quickened as he walked forward with ice cubes wrapped in two dish towels.

Lordy, what was happening?

Something important, Bess knew instinctively. Something that would change all three of their lives. Something that had been right there for her to grab if only she hadn't been such a coward all these years.

Something better. Something she deserved. Something that swelled her heart in a way Matt's casual attention never had.

Ignoring her aching cheek, she aimed her most dazzling full-wattage parade-float Cottonwood Festival Queen smile at Casey.

His stumble was definitely worth the pain.

FROM HIS VIEW ON THE FRONT porch bench, Hal caught a distant wink of sunlight on windshield and shaded his eyes. Casey back from the Campbell place, probably. Nope. The sporty red convertible now driving slowly over the cattle guard wasn't made for hauling hay.

Didn't look like no nanny's, car, neither.

Hal checked his watch. Eleven o'clock on the nose. Had to be Mrs. Fisher.

Matt would be impressed at her promptness, darn it. And as stinking mad as a wet polecat that Hal hadn't followed orders.

He was supposed to have stopped the training session twenty minutes ago, giving Matt time for a quick shower and change. Good thing the working pens faced the back of the house. Hopefully Abbey and Mattie would stay too wrapped up in watching the cutting action to notice company comin'. Hal had work to do.

Abbey was The One, he was now convinced. The phone conversation he'd walked into that morning was the clincher. After Mattie's ride, Abbey had taken the little girl to pick fresh wildflowers. Matt had tied up Doc and phoned Sam West's wife, of all people.

Hal read the San Antonio newspaper cover to cover. Sharon West was one of them society ladies always getting her picture taken at this or that charity event. Matt had practically sold the woman Abbey's arrowhead necklace sight unseen!

Yep, she was The One, even if neither of the stubborn young 'uns admitted it to themselves, yet. Hal could explain the truth to 'em, but he couldn't understand it for 'em. They needed more time together. And he intended to see they got it.

He pushed up from the bench, walked to the front steps and lifted a hand as the car approached a split in the gravel road. You never knew if a woman's elevator went all the way to the top floor until the doors opened. Looked like this one's did. She steered toward the house instead of the stable, deepening Hal's frown the closer she got.

The red-haired "widow" that parked and uncurled from the low-slung car wasn't much older than Matt. Or maybe she was younger and just harder rode. She wore black pants tighter than a second coat of paint, and a sleeveless white blouse so sheer he could see her lacy brassiere.

And danged if the shadows of her titties weren't showin'!

He wasn't dead yet, so he looked. But he was

old enough to be a little shocked. And smart enough to know she'd chosen her getup careful, not accidental.

It made his mission easier.

"Hello," she called out with a smile, wobbling toward the porch in high-heeled sandals. "The photographs didn't do this place justice. Of course, the wildflowers weren't in bloom, then."

"Photographs?"

"The feature article two months ago in *Texas Monthly* magazine."

Ah, the story on an eligible bachelor and champion bronc rider turned cutting horse trainer, complete with photos of Matt. So that explained her clothes and interest in this job.

"I'm Gloria Fisher. I have an interview with Matt Granger at eleven about a child-care position? Is he here?"

"Somewhere. He's not real good at rememberin' appointments, birthdays, paydays...things like that."

Hal watched her climb the steps stiffly, her movement restricted. She reached the porch seconds ahead of her sinus-clearing perfume.

"You'll need bigger britches if you get the job," Hal warned, stone-faced.

Her smile faltered. "Excuse me?"

"Mattie's a fast little bugger. If you can't run, she'll lose you in these hills in a New York minute. Her uncle got real mad at those other women who couldn't keep up. *Real* mad," he emphasized, letting Gloria draw her own conclusions.

She laughed uncertainly. "I'm sure I'll manage fine. But thanks for the advice."

"Better buy some boots while you're at it, too."

"Mattie already rides?" She recovered her smile. "Of course she does. Her uncle *is* Matt Granger. Fortunately I already have a pair of boots."

"Snake boots?"

Her pearly whites vanished.

"Lots of rattlers out this time of year. If they don't get you, the cactus patches will. Know any first aid?"

"A little," she said weakly, looking as if she could use a good whiff of smelling salts right now. "Mattie is only five years old, right?"

"Five goin' on twenty. She does love to paint her face and get dolled up like a growed woman. If you get the job, you'll let me know if you find—" he scratched his whiskers with feigned innocence "—oh, say a tube of lipstick, an *eye*-talian silk scarf, maybe a sapphire bracelet with a little diamond on the clasp? The others been pesterin' me somethin' awful to mail their stuff back."

"Others?"

"The first three nannies—" Hal bumped a palm on his forehead. "Darn! Don't tell Matt I let on about their missin' stuff, okay, Miz Fisher?"

She lifted a hand to her throat. "Good Lord, did Mattie steal those things?"

"I wouldn't say that around Matt, if I were you. He got real mad at those other women for makin' false accusations. *Real* mad." Hal squinted into the distance a thoughtful moment. "You might wanna buy a lockbox when you get those snake boots, though."

"You're pulling my leg, right?" Her dark eyes narrowed skeptically.

He'd overplayed his hand. Best not to deny her suspicion. "Why, sure I am. You caught me good. Ain't none of that stuff true. Forget what I said. *Please,* ma'am. I think we'd both be better off." That last note of fear in his voice was a stroke of genius. She looked good and spooked.

Her gaze darted to the front door nervously. "Maybe I'll come back later at a more convenient time for Mr. Granger."

Hal struggled not to smile. "You sure? I can try to find him and interrupt whatever he's doin'. 'Course, he might get real—"

"Mad," she finished for him, lifting a brow. "No, I think I'll reschedule my appointment, Mister...?"

Bond. Just call me Bond, little missy. "Bonner. Call me Hal."

"Thanks, Hal. You've been a big help." She smiled gratefully, shook his hand, then turned and started down the steps.

The sound of barking cut short Hal's mild twinge of guilt. *Hurry. Hurry. Hurry.*

"Watch that last step, now," he advised, glancing toward the stable just out of sight. "There's a dip in the ground."

Pitiful burst into his line of vision and galloped straight for Gloria, who tensed worse than Doc had earlier that morning. Seconds later Mattie skipped into sight, followed by Abbey and Matt. The dad-blamed worst timing since Hal had sold his Cottonwood Rodeo, Inc. shares two months before they tripled in value!

Five more minutes and Gloria Fisher

would've driven off never to be heard from again.

Too late now. Pitiful had pinned her against the rail and jammed his nose where it didn't belong. The three trailing behind him closed in fast while she pushed and squeaked at the dog like she'd never been sniffed there before.

Sure thing, missy.

Hal eased backward. It was time to paint his tail white and make like a deer.

"Hal!" Matt bellowed a warning.

Ignoring that tone wasn't good for a body's health, Hal had discovered. He stopped and accepted his fate.

Mattie slowed near the unfamiliar red car, turned shy and ran back ten yards to clutch Abbey's ankle-length dress. A pretty buttercup yellow, today. As loose and ladylike as the redhead's outfit was tight and brazen. Abbey stopped in her tracks as she got her first good gander at the widow. Even beneath billowy fabric, Hal could see her entire body grow rigid.

Matt continued forward, his leather chaps flapping, his matching vest unbuttoned, his gaze fixed on what was staring back like a second pair of eyes. No part of him stiffened that Hal could see, and he checked real close, too. He relaxed

a little. If that wasn't proof positive Abbey was
The One, he'd squat on his spurs.

At least *something* good had come out of Gloria's arrival.

Just then, Pitiful lost interest in humiliating
the woman and loped off to snap at bumblebees.
Matt moved up to prop a boot on the second
step and lean his forearm on his thigh. He'd been
training hard, and looked it. Sweat ringed the
underarms of the denim shirt beneath his vest
and glistened at the hollow of his tanned neck.

"You Mrs. Fisher?"

Gloria opened and closed her mouth. Then
nodded.

Hal snorted. Another one just bit the dust.

Matt flicked Hal a hard glance before tipping
up his hat and grinning. Against a mask of dust,
his teeth glinted extra white. "I'm sorry to keep
you waitin'. And for showin' up dirty like this.
If you'd like to reschedule our appointment, I
understand."

Gloria found her voice, a throaty purr she obviously hauled out special for men like Matt.
"Don't be silly. Anyone can lose track of the
time. I'm ready if you are."

Hal darn sure believed that.

Mission aborted. After coming so close to

pulling it off, too. Ah, well. He supposed he shouldn't feel too bad.

James Bond hisself wouldn't stand much chance against the Granger dimple.

CHAPTER FOURTEEN

ABBEY GLANCED AT THE luminous dial of her bedside alarm clock. Two in the morning. Only fifty-three more hours to endure until her replacement arrived. A spit in the ocean in terms of a woman's total lifetime. Yet Abbey knew each second would drip like Chinese water torture.

Time was her enemy. There was too little remaining for her to ease Mattie's heart, too much left for her sanity's safety.

Drip…drip…drip.

In the two days since Gloria Fisher had accepted Matt's job offer, Mattie had alternately thrown tantrums, cried buckets and pleaded for Abbey to stay. No explanation the adults had come up with had erased Mattie's sense of abandonment. And Abbey's effort to keep from blubbering her eyes out right alongside the child was taking its toll.

Drip…drip…drip.

Matt wasn't unaffected, either. An hour earlier, she'd heard him toss and turn in his creaky bed, then rise and swear softly while dressing in the dark. He'd crept carefully past her door and into the kitchen, where a glass had clinked. Tap water had gushed and stopped. A chair leg had scraped. And the back door had opened and closed.

He was probably in the stable now. As usual. He still devoted more attention to his horses than he did Mattie, despite showing encouraging signs of interest in her recently.

Abbey glared at the ceiling. She never should have come to Texas! She'd failed to facilitate a strong bond between uncle and niece. Yet she'd fused so tightly with *them* that their every breath influenced hers.

Fifty-three more hours wouldn't change that situation. But the prolonged goodbye would slowly tear her apart.

Drip…drip…drip.

A clean break. That was the only answer. A bandage ripped from a wound caused less pain than one slowly peeled off.

She would leave immediately. Matt himself had made it possible by inviting Sharon West to tag along with her husband, Sam, when he came to check on Rio. They'd arrived that afternoon in the middle of Mattie's nap. The horse's settled state had pleased Sam, and Abbey's arrowhead necklace had thrilled his wife. In confirming the price Matt had mentioned over the phone, Sharon named an amount twice what Abbey would have asked.

A kind act on Matt's part? Or an expedient way to insure Abbey had the funds to leave for Santa Fe?

Drip...drip...drip.

Well, she wouldn't stay one more day. Hal would keep an eye on Mattie, protect her from Gloria Fisher's almost certain indifference if need be. The widow's mind was not on child care, that was clear.

Widow. Abbey's bitter laugh ricocheted in the sparsely furnished room. Black widow was more like it.

The woman had taken one look at Matt and started spinning out sultry glances and silken smiles. Her silent invitations had woven a seductive web. Her see-through blouse had lured her prey close. Strumpet! The jealousy Bess had awakened was a molehill compared to the mountain of hate Gloria inspired.

In an ironic twist, the "innocent" fly had invited the spider into his parlor for an interview. Matt had needed less than thirty minutes to make his decision. Bye-bye Abbey, hello Gloria.

Oh, it hurt to anguish this passionately! Hadn't she promised herself she wouldn't care for just this reason?

Only a fool wouldn't want you in his life, Matt had said. Remembering his last words before Gloria's fateful phone call, Abbey kicked violently at the sheet and light bedspread pressing her into the mattress. She couldn't breathe! The air was smothering with spitefulness. Heavy with heartache. Laden with love.

Drip...drip...drip.

When only her chaste cotton nightgown lay oppressively on her skin, Abbey stilled. Of course Hal would watch out for the little girl they both loved. She had to believe that or go mad.

Had to believe, too, that once the NCHA Futurity was over Matt would promote his niece to the top of his priority list. The tough cowboy act was a sham. She'd caught too many disarmed tender glances at Mattie, seen too much evidence of his intrinsic kindness. He was a good man. He would be a loving and responsible guardian.

As for the black widow, Abbey doubted Matt

had any illusions about what Gloria Fisher was or what she wanted. By comparison, Bess Campbell must seem fresh and innocent to him. And Abbey herself?

He'd once called her a sexy prude. She supposed he'd meant a fallen woman who'd been reformed. A woman who would bloody a man's nose for trying to make love to her. Sort of a born-again virgin.

In other words, bo-ring.

Abbey had kissed Matt only once. But she would remember it when she was old and gray, rocking on a porch with a cat on her lap. She would feel the purr under her fingertips and remember the rumble vibrating in a broad chest. She would wonder "what if?" until the day she died.

Drip...drip...drip.

The lovely black widow wouldn't wonder, Abbey acknowleged, the truth a swig of carbolic acid eating her up. The only question was, how long would Gloria wait to make her move? A week? Fifty-three hours? A day?

Resentment kills a fool, and envy slays the simple. Job 5:2.

Rebellion rose within Abbey to kick the caution aside. Matt was out there somewhere in the stable, as wired and unable to sleep as she. And here she lay, spending her last remaining hours on the ranch miserable, driving herself crazy. With jealousy. With yearning. With burning curiosity. It wasn't fair.

She should march out there and give him a taste of his own medicine. Use the innuendo and heated looks that were his specialty to drive *him* crazy! Crazy with lust.

A thrill streaked through her body.

She quivered in the aftermath, her heart thudding to the beat of images flashing in her mind. Matt striding down the boardwalk, his hat bobbing, his buckle flashing in the sun, his loose-limbed power turning every head. Matt placing the ceramic angel high, so Mattie could remember her mommy was in heaven and happy.

Matt pacing the kitchen, his vengeful fury directed at the good folks of Baker's Landing on Abbey's behalf. Matt leading his niece atop the stallion he let no one else ride. Matt's silver-gray eyes. His strong, capable hands. His hard, beautiful mouth.

Abbey dragged the pillow that should've been Matt into her arms.

With an ounce of encouragement, she would've stayed and explored her shockingly strong attachment to this one place. This one man. Unfortunately, he wasn't ready to share his life with any woman. At least, not with her.

But he might share his body.

She clamped the yielding pillow to her aching breasts and groaned at the wrongness of soft against soft. How completely right it would be to press against Matt, to discover more about the body she'd admired in the way that pleased her senses most. She wanted to *touch* him. Every part of him. To savor his multiple textures by degrees, to experience physical joining, not as a naive girl but as a mature woman. One self-indulgent act to remember the remainder of her life. Was that so much to ask?

The pain of leaving couldn't be any greater. What had she to lose but a lifetime of "what ifs"?

Abbey swung her feet to the hardwood floor, reached for her glasses next to the clock and slipped them on. The blurred furniture sharpened. By the dim glow of a night-light plugged into an outlet, she walked to the tall cherry-wood armoire and pulled out her robe. Keds came next. Not exactly a sexy ensemble, but her hair was unbound.

Lately she'd seen Matt look at her braid in a

way that made her glad she hadn't cut the heavy mass. She ran a brush quickly through her one remaining vanity and hoped he would find it attractive. Steven had said he'd loved to touch her hair.

The hallway outside her room was dark and portentous. She knew instinctively that passing through it would change her forever. Yet she stopped only once. At Mattie's door to peek inside.

Abbey's spare night-light illuminated the small lump beneath the bedcovers, reflected in vigilant eyes gleaming from the bed. After a few thoughtful seconds, Pitiful lowered his head back down to the pillow and heaved a contented sigh. Beside him, the sound of light muffled snores continued. Days of crying had left Mattie congested.

Battling a clutch of remorse, Abbey closed the door softly. The child was well taken care of until dawn. Now it was time to take care of her own needs.

If she had the nerve.

"THERE YA GO, BUDDY. Soft as a woman's..." Matt blinked and dropped the currycomb into a plastic caddy in the stall corner.

Well, hell.

That's what had driven him from his bed and out to the stable in the first place. Imagining Abbey's softness. Picturing her asleep in the very next room, her body pliant and warm. Wanting to slip into her bed, into *her,* so bad he'd nearly resorted to a boy's solution and taken the problem in hand.

Matt lowered his forehead onto the stallion's sleek neck and chuckled miserably. He was hornier than a desert toad! The smell of clean horse, fresh straw and new-mown hay usually calmed him. Not tonight.

No, tonight he'd have to gut out this gnawing need like a grown man. Something he'd rarely had to do, once his height and voice headed opposite directions. There'd always been an easy woman somewhere close.

Like Gloria Fisher would be in a few days.

Well, hell.

Matt straightened and distractedly rubbed the crest of Doc's mane with one hand. If all he wanted was easy and close he could've arranged it with a single phone call to the Widow Blanton.

But what he wanted was Abbey, the *hardest* woman to deal with he'd ever met. A woman who, in three short days, would be far beyond his reach.

The thought of her leaving made the ache below his belt a minor annoyance compared with the pain in his chest. Heavy, but hollow. Sharp, but dull. In all his years he'd never experienced the like. It was as if all the physical and mental hurts in his past had combined into one huge lump of misery.

Snap out of it, Granger. You want her because you can't have her, and because that's never happened to you before. Out of sight, out of mind. Just wait. You'll see.

Sighing, Matt stopped rubbing Doc and gave the glossy neck a final pat. The stallion made a low sound of protest, too lazy to be called a nicker.

"You don't want me to quit, huh, boy? Okay. You win."

It'd been awhile since he'd given Doc a full Tellington-Touch treatment. The method of relaxing tension and deepening trust had turned the once unmanageable stallion into a focused athlete.

Matt squared up to the animal's side, his back facing the stall door, and placed both hands over the crest of Doc's neck. Pushing with the heels of his palms on one side and pressing with his fingertips on the other, he began a massaging action he continued up and down the arched crest.

Doc's breathing slowed. The outdoor symphony of crickets played a rusty sweet concert in the distance. The other horses were bedded down, silent, their upper stall hatches closed tight. Some of Matt's tension eased.

All was right—and very wrong—with his world.

Hiring Gloria had been a mistake. A knee-jerk reaction to his hurt over Abbey's eagerness to leave. If only he hadn't found that damned packed suitcase...but he had. And then gone and hired a "nanny" who hadn't asked one question about his niece. A woman whose filmy see-through shirt had been more modest than her Jezebel gaze.

That kind of crap was so boring.

He would have to fire her, of course. *After* Abbey left. No sense dragging out Mattie's suffering. The squirt was taking Abbey's upcoming departure mighty hard.

Scowling, Matt moved on to work the stallion's spine, using the gentle push-pull motion soothing to them both. When he neared the croup, Doc swished his tail sharply.

Matt paused. "That sore, buddy? Let's see what we can do." He positioned his hand in a gently curved cup and stroked light clockwise circles over and near the area. "How 'bout now? Feel better?"

"It must," a feminine voice spoke from behind him. "He looks close to falling asleep."

Matt whirled around and hissed in a breath, his heart bucking hard enough to rattle his teeth.

Abbey stood outside the half door, lit by the incandescent bulbs he preferred over cold fluorescent tubes. The warm light struck red sparks in her mahogany brown hair.

Lots of hair. Masses of hair. Dark wavy cascades of hair framing her delicate face and spilling free over her shoulders. Hair so long the half door hid the ends from view.

He went from semiarousal to the whole banana in three pumping heartbeats.

"Sorry," she murmured. "I didn't mean to scare you."

Matt swallowed hard. "No problem."

None that he wouldn't take in hand later. To hell with dignity. He couldn't seem to take his eyes off that rich lustrous hair. Would it feel as soft and thick as it looked?

She cleared her throat.

He met her hesitant eyes. "I guess you didn't come out here this late for exercise. Did you need me for something?"

A rosy glow crept up her slender throat to stain her cheeks. She resettled her glasses in a familiar gesture. Abbey was either angry...or real nervous.

"I couldn't sleep. I'd heard you leave the house earlier and assumed you'd be out here." A graceful hand rose to fiddle with the top of her high-necked nightgown, pale blue against a white robe. "Do you have a few minutes?"

For some reason she blushed even harder than before.

Curiosity won out over good sense. "Sure, if you don't mind me workin' on Doc while you talk."

"No, of course not. I was watching those circles you made with your hand. It reminded me of a woman on the boardwalk who gives massages to the tourists. Is that what you're doing to Doc? Giving him a back rub?"

Despite Matt's tension, one corner of his mouth lifted. "Sort of. I learned a series of touch techniques at a horse training clinic years ago. The theory is, touching does more than relax muscles and ease soreness."

"How so?" Her hand drifted down to grip the door ledge.

There was a tiny satin bow dead center at the top of her nightgown.

He turned around quickly and continued the circular strokes where he'd left off. "Soft manipulation like this activates new brain cells, releases new nerve impulses. The theory is a horse becomes more alert and learns faster. And his rider understands the animal's personality and spots pain faster."

"Is it true? The theory, I mean."

He began *Chau K'a,* a skin-rolling technique. "When I first rode Doc, he rushed the bit, flung up his head a lot, wasn't interested in cattle. His trainer had changed bits, scenery, riding techniques...nothin' worked. I bought Doc anyway. Cheap. And took him home and started doin' what I'm doin' now."

His concentration was growing fuzzy. Clouded by the gaze he sensed roaming his hands, his hair, his shoulders.

"And?" Abbey prodded.

He pulled his thoughts together. "And when

I got to about here—'' Matt indicated a spot behind the withers ''—it felt hot and a little swollen. Doc dropped his back an inch and jerked up
his head. End of mystery. All horses run instinctively from pain.''

Now Matt's rear end had that prickly sensation of being scrutinized. If she kept this up,
he'd do something real stupid. ''You never said
why you came out here, Abbey.''

A beat of silence. ''You didn't finish your
story. Aren't you going to explain the mystery?''

He opened his mouth to say no, closed it on
a gust of breath. He'd better humor her, or she'd
never leave.

''It's a three-part answer. One, the weight of
a rider hurts Doc, so he rushes forward. Two,
the rider pulls back hard on the reins, so Doc
flings up his head and cramps his neck. Three,
the rider pulls Doc's head to the side to control
the head tossing, and aggravates the cramp more.
A vicious cycle—'' Matt broke off at the sound
of the half door opening behind him.

''Oh, poor baby,'' Abbey crooned, shutting
herself and all that glorious hair inside the stall.
''You were hurting and couldn't tell anyone.
How awful.''

Matt gritted his teeth through a surge of pressure against his zipper. Yeah. It was awful. Sheer hell.

She moved up beside him and smoothed a palm over the stallion's neck. "So did you stroke it and take away the pain?"

He shot her a suspicious glance. Bambi-brown eyes blinked innocently behind her lenses. *He* was the degenerate.

"Doc had been ridden too much and too hard. A little rest and touch therapy let him zero in on the cattle, and not the pain."

Dragging his gaze to Doc's barrel, Matt focused on the folds of skin rolling between his thumb and fingers. If he concentrated hard enough, maybe he'd forget the thick dark waterfall rippling to her shapely rear, the narrow waist cinched by her robe sash, the tiny satin bow at her neckline begging his fingers to delve beneath.

She slid her palm behind the stallion's withers, her white fingers caressing the coat. "Is this where it was hot and swollen before?"

Matt nearly cracked a molar. "Yeah."

"It feels warm, now," she said in a slightly breathy voice. "Hard and velvety at the same time. Is that normal?"

Holy mother in heaven! His eyeballs ached

and his skin felt ready to burst. Did she know what she was doing to him? He cut his gaze down and noted the telltale flush climbing her neck.

"Okay, Abbey, what's goin' on?" His pulse thrumming, he turned and draped an arm on Doc's rump. "What exactly are you doin' out here?"

She kept her focus on her stroking hand while her color deepened. "I'm pretty sure I'm making a fool of myself."

"Why don't you tell me what you're *tryin'* to do, and I'll let you know."

Her nostrils flared in a quick breath. "Never mind. I've reconsidered."

Lord give me patience. "Abbe-e-ey."

She looked up, her expression a mixture of trepidation and sweet yearning. With that one look, she repaired all damage previously inflicted to his ego and raised it to dizzying heights.

He closed his eyes, unable to credit his vision.

"I'm trying to seduce you," she confessed in a small voice.

Matt's eyes popped open like a champagne cork, his blood fizzing at the sight that hadn't changed. An elated laugh rumbled up from his chest and spilled out.

She froze as if he'd slapped her, then whirled around and lunged for the door.

Well, *hell.*

As she fumbled with the latch, he banded her waist and hauled her back into the stall, back against his eager welcome. "Abbey, I wasn't laughin' at you."

"Let me go!"

Her struggling body was warm, sweet torture, her slithering hair cool everywhere it touched his skin. Doc shifted and snorted a warning.

"Damn it, Abbey, quit squirmin' and listen to me."

"No!"

"Then *feel* me," he ordered, snugging her tighter to his groin.

She went completely still.

"I wasn't laughin' at you, Abbey. I was happy to see you. That's not a gun in my pocket, ya know."

His lame attempt at humor only made the heart beneath his forearm pound harder. Not that he blamed her. The extent of his arousal scared even him.

She seemed so much smaller in his arms than

out of them. Her rib cage was narrow and delicate, her head barely reached his chin. It was Abbey's inner spirit that created the illusion of a sturdier frame. He could crush both so easily if he mishandled her now.

Fate had led them to this moment. But *he* could make what followed good or bad. In an instant of stunning clarity, he realized how very much he loved the woman in his arms. Her sudden shiver triggered a strange trembling of his own.

"Let me go," she repeated. But her tone lacked conviction.

Matt lowered his nose and nuzzled aside the soft hair covering her ear. "If you came out here to seduce me, honey, consider me seduced. I'm sorry," he apologized to God as well as Abbey, "but I can't let you go just yet."

CHAPTER FIFTEEN

SITTING SIDEWAYS on padded leather, Abbey hugged her stomach against sinking disappointment. She didn't know what she'd expected, but it wasn't to be lifted atop a cutting saddle and told to stay put. In his arms, spooned against the substantial evidence that her attraction was shared, her thoughts had boiled to mush. But here, awaiting Matt's return, cool rationality returned.

If only he'd kissed her, pulled her into a riptide of passion where consequences had no meaning, doubts no chance for survival. The longer she waited, the closer her attitude moved from "sexy" to "prude."

She was no better than that spider woman, or those buckle bunnies in Matt's past. He was a physical man, his testosterone running close to the surface of everything he did. Of course he would respond to her overture. He would to any woman who'd offered herself on a platter.

Oh, mercy, what on earth had she been *thinking* coming out here like a brazen hussy bent on seduction? The sound of approaching steps whipped her attention to the door...and Abbey remembered.

Wearing beltless jeans and a navy western shirt unsnapped to midchest, a day's growth of stubble shadowing his jaw, Matt ducked inside the room and paused. He brushed a bit of straw from his thigh, reached up and swiped a piece from his tousled black hair, twisted and slapped three times at his backside. A wedge of chest hair played peek-a-boo, sexier by far than the shaved and oiled pecs of Muscle Beach.

Few men Matt's size were as beautifully formed and proportioned, as pleasing to her artist's eye. She'd grown adept at sneaking glances when he was preoccupied.

"Abbey?"

She looked up.

"You keep starin' at me like that, and we might not make it out of this room."

Her heart leaped wildly as he approached, so tall her chin kept rising, so overwhelmingly masculine she felt utterly feminine and completely vulnerable. Unable to hold his gaze, her own skittered over an acre of chest, lowered far enough to confirm he hadn't lost *anything* during their separation, least of all his courage.

His shins bumped her dangling Keds. Rock hard thighs pressed into her knees. Splayed fingers speared into her hair, cupped both ears and tilted up her flushed face.

Beneath sleepy lids, his eyes glittered silver bright. Hot and compelling. Intense and thrilling. Did she only imagine a possessiveness, a desire beyond his natural response to a willing female? She thought so.

But she didn't know.

His thumbs stroked each side of her jaw in feathery windshield-wiper touches. Exquisitely gentle. An arresting contrast to the tension hardening his features. "You have beautiful skin, Abbey. So soft...so clear and fine..."

Raindrops of warmth rolled languorously down her neck.

"...so pale and creamy. Your skin could drive a man to drink, darlin'. Make him want to lap up every inch."

Heat showered onto her breasts, making her breath hitch, her lids grow heavy.

"And this hair..." Matt's low rumble of approval was more eloquent than words. Delving his hands deeper, he lifted and watched the strands trickle through his fingers, scooped up more and washed his face.

Abbey's parched feminine ego soaked up the tribute thirstily.

He lifted his head in a drugged fashion, his hands shifting to cradle her skull. "It's a crime to lock up hair like this in a braid, sweetheart. It's too pretty, smells too nice." His voice deepened to a timbre she'd never heard. "I've been wonderin' what it would feel like wrapped around us both."

Scalding hail swept her from breasts to belly. Her head lolled against massaging fingers.

"You've been wonderin', too, Abbey, I know you have. I can see it in your eyes. Did you know they show everything you're feelin'?" He made a satisfied sound in his throat. "I like what you're feelin', now."

His husky whisper fell like mist; lightning skittered in his eyes. Her lips parted beneath the sudden strike of his gaze.

"I've never tasted a sweeter mouth than yours, darlin'. Thinkin' about it kept me up tonight. That's why I was out here. Because thinkin' about kissin' you, thinkin' about all the other things I want to do to you made me so hot I couldn't sleep."

Heat sluiced downward in an intimate flood. Shyness struck, and she looked away.

"Abbey, Abbey, don't be embarrassed. What you're feelin' is natural and right. The way it should be. A man and woman wantin' each other so much it hurts, easin' the hurt the way nature intended. We'll be good together, darlin', so good." His warm, wonderful fingers moved to her nape and kneaded. "Trust me, sweetheart. This isn't wrong."

He wasn't the first man to say those words to Abbey, but he was the best at verbal seduction. The uncontested champion. He'd had a lot of practice, after all.

Lots and lots of practice.

"Trust me, Abbey."

She met his eyes.

His fingers stilled. "What's the matter?"

I don't want to be a one-night fling. "N-nothing."

He tightened his mouth. "What is it? Tell me."

I want to be special. I want to be...more. "Nothing."

"Nothin', huh?" Huffing a humorless laugh, he withdrew his hands, a charismatic man out of patience with the naive little prude. "You don't have to do this. If you've changed your mind, go back to the house. I'll understand.''

Her chin came up. She opened her mouth for a stinging comeback—and stopped. She'd once boasted of knowing the difference between charisma and character. *Seems to me like what you learned is how to hang a man without a fair trial,* Matt had said. Blinking now, Abbey inspected him more closely. Matt held himself so rigid the cords of his neck stood out in relief. He didn't look disgusted. Or cocky or mad or bored. He looked like someone braced for rejection.

Oh, she'd been so unfair! She'd dishonored not only him, but also herself by doubting for a second that he thought her special. Why else would he offer her the freedom of choice to end with dignity what she'd blatantly started?

''I don't want to go back,'' Abbey told him firmly.

In his eyes emotion flared, then was doused. His shields were less prickly than hers, but equally effective in buffering life's pain.

She reached out, slid both palms up his chest and strung quick kisses from his bobbing Adam's apple to his clenching jaw. When she got to his ear, she looped her arms around his neck and whispered, "Take me forward, Matt."

"Ah, Abbey. You won't be sorry."

Then his arms were sweeping beneath her knees and behind her back, lifting her high against his chest. Abbey twined her arms tighter, dizzy with anticipation, with the sensation of being carried as if she were a precious burden, a hard-won prize. No man had ever valued her for herself. Steven had needed to feel idolized. Her father had needed to feel obeyed. Paul had needed to feel needed.

But Matt appeared to need *her*.

Cradled in his powerful arms, she tucked her face into his shoulder. The smell of horse was strong on his shirt, the scent beneath an earthy mixture of clean skin and aroused male. She gave herself up to the magical moment, dazzled and entranced. When his long strides stopped and she heard the distinctive click of a closing door, it took several seconds for awareness to sink in. She stiffened in shock. Darkness. The rustle of straw. Planked walls pressing the air from her lungs. She was in a stall. *The* stall. The same one that caused her panic attack weeks ago.

"Shh, easy, Abbey. The door's not locked. You can leave anytime. Take a deep breath." She did, his signature cologne instantly calming her frantic heartbeat. "Take another breath. Good. You're safe, Abbey. Nothin' in here but you, me and pleasure, if you'll trust me." He lowered her feet carefully until she stood, but kept his hands on her shoulders. "Trust me, sweetheart."

How she loved his endearments. She would do anything to earn more. Her eyes had adjusted to the dim light. Locating its source, she softened inside. A candle flickered within the corner-mounted feed tub. A *candle*.

"See?" Matt said. "It's not that dark. This isn't a storage closet. Look it over." As if she were a blindfolded child, he turned her around slowly, leaving his fingers draped over her collarbones.

Over freshly fluffed straw, he'd stretched a large Navajo blanket. A smaller bedsheet topped the scratchy wool. He'd obviously made a trip to the house in deference to her skin. Imagine that. Her gaze moved wonderingly to a battered transistor radio anchoring one corner of the blanket.

He'd thought of music, too? Her eyes and

ONE TOUGH TEXAN   597

nose stinging, she glanced to the right...and fell totally and irrevocably in love. A mason jar sat on an overturned bucket, the glass "vase" stuffed willy-nilly with a jumble of wildflowers and weeds. Beads of water still clung to petals and blades, clumps of dirt to tangled roots.

Behind her, Matt made an embarrassment noise in his throat. "It's damn dark out there. Looks like I picked more weeds than flowers. You and Mattie make 'em look a lot prettier."

Abbey's hand drifted up to press between her breasts. The scruffy bouquet swam in her vision. She was quite unable to speak.

"I know it's not the Hilton, but I thought—I dunno. That maybe if you could replace the feelin' you had locked in that storage closet with somethin' else..." His fingers tightened a fraction on her shoulders. "Guess it was a stupid idea."

Abbey swallowed the confession of love threatening to climb her throat. "No, Matt," she said thickly. "It's not a stupid idea. It's perfect."

Pulling free of his grip, she collected her thoughts. He hadn't asked her to stay. Declaring her feelings now would serve no purpose except to make him guilty. He'd experienced too much of that destructive emotion in his life. He deserved more joy.

They both did.

She walked slowly to the feed bin, removed her glasses and placed them next to the tin of saddle soap acting as a candleholder. An instant before she blew out the flame, she thought she saw Matt's eyes widen.

Poof!

Beyond the snuffed candle smoke, Matt was only a vague black shape, but Abbey found him as surely as a homing pigeon. Slipping her hands around his waist, she pressed her cheek against his heart.

"The flowers are beautiful, Matt. Everything is perfect. I've never been quite so touched. I don't know what else to say except that I do trust you. Implicitly. Otherwise, do you think I could leave Mattie in your care?'' He stiffened, and she squeezed him lightly. "She adores you, Matt. Hal loves you like a son. Casey thinks you walk on water. Bess, too. We can't all be such poor judges of character. Promise me that when I leave, you'll trust *yourself,* okay?''

Beneath her ear, his heart thundered with some powerful emotion. His arms came around her hard and swift for a rib-cracking hug.

She gloried in the discomfort, in the gentle ardent wooing of this immanently desirable man. A big tough Texan who hid his tenderness from himself as much as the world.

"You feel so good," Abbey said when she could breathe again. Her bold nestling movement produced a gratifying response.

Matt pulled back just enough to thrust his hands in the hair near her temples. "Abbey, I want you so much I'm afraid—ah, *damn.*" His strained oath was a sweet hymn. "I don't want to hurt you, darlin'."

Exultant, she stood on tiptoe. "Shut up and kiss me."

Control fled. Connecting openmouthed, their tongues greeted like long-lost lovers, plying and playing, plunging and pleasuring in an exhilarating wet, hot tumble. Their bodies met with the same abandonment, flushing and swelling, pressing and seeking. Frenzied to complete the act for which they'd been slowly and steadily aroused.

For Abbey, it was the splendor of their first kiss a thousand times over, for she did trust Matt now. At last, at last she could *touch* him as she'd always imagined. Without reservation, at liberty to explore both him and her own sexuality. She removed his hands from her body three times before he got the message and stood passive, except for his agile tongue.

O-oh, what hair he had, like Lorna's mink coat. Abbey scraped her nails over his skull and marveled at the thick plush resiliency. Ahh, his shoulders—she plucked at his shirt. She needed to feel skin. Her fingers moved to buttons and freed them one by one. Matt found the twist of her belt sash and tugged roughly.

They broke apart to shrug out of shirt and robe, then fell back into the kiss, his chest branding her breasts through her chaste cotton nightgown. Indescribably better than her pillow. Her fingers traced smooth skin over contoured shoulders and arms, moved to his back and found the ridged flesh of old scars. Abbey pulled her mouth free. "Oh, Matt," she crooned, overcome by tenderness for a courageous boy who'd protected his sister.

But he would have none of her sympathy. He dove back into the kiss, obliterating all but the wonderful here and now. She flattened her palms on his chest and hummed approval. Mercy, he was sleek and silky. The gentle tickle formed a narrowing path she traveled eagerly. When she reached his waistband, Matt growled into her mouth.

Cinching powerful arms beneath her ribs, he hitched her high and walked forward, his kiss turning ferocious.

In the slow, leisurely slide down his body, her nightgown bunched up around her hips. Her feet touched down and he tore his mouth from hers. One second she was wearing a nightgown, the next she was clothed in air.

"My turn," he rasped.

The hot wet tug on her left nipple buckled her knees. He caught her fall and lowered her to the blanket, removed her shoes, then sat beside her with a rustle of straw.

A boot hit the plank wall. Another clunked harder than the first. An unmistakable zip preceded a small grunt as he shucked his jeans. He grew busy with something, and it dawned on her that the sheet hadn't been all he'd retrieved from the house. The air above her stirred and heated.

And he was back, kissing the tender underside of her jaw, the sensitive lee of her neck, the upper swell of her breast. He circled the tip of his tongue around the flesh begging for attention. Closer...closer. Chill bumps pebbled her skin.

"Want me to warm you up, darlin'?" His breath fanned a fresh eruption of bumps.

She made a wordless sound of assent, then arched up into his mouth.

Through shock waves of pleasure, Abbey was dimly aware of his rich, satisfied chuckle. She wasn't embarrassed. Trust and love banished the inhibitions of a puritan upbringing. She thrilled to the husky words of praise he slurred between his kisses. She ignited at the warm lips and abrasive beard searing a wandering trail downward. She trembled and gasped at the loving possession she'd never granted to another man. But then, this was Matt, who knew her better than any man. With him, she needn't hold any part of herself back. The tension coiled unbearably tight. She moaned his name, a throaty plea for mercy.

At her shattering point he lunged up and into her body with a single powerful thrust.

Abbey cried out, part startlement, part pain.

"Ahh, Abbey, oh damn, honey, did I hurt you?" Matt braced himself on an elbow to smooth damp hair back from her face.

"No, I'm fine." True. His concerned ecstasy had soothed her discomfort. Tilting up her hips experimentally, she sucked in a pleasured breath.

"Was that a good gasp, or a bad one?" he asked in a strangled voice.

Loving the easy intimacy, loving his labored control, loving him more with every beat of her heart, she reached up and sandwiched bristly cheeks in her palms. "Matt, don't worry. You can't hurt me." *Physically.* "Now shut up and kiss me," she ordered.

Lacing his fingers with hers, he brought her arms high and obeyed her command.

Nothing in Abbey's past had prepared her for the passion Matt unleashed. He was splendidly fit and fiercely aroused, and proceeded to demonstrate both.

She accepted his uncompromising domination joyfully. She'd been alone too long, and lonely longer than that. Her precious independence was all she'd had. But, oh, this was natural. This was right. Each smooth stroke filled her body and her heart, a potent aphrodisiac.

Her senses spiraled higher and higher. Pleasure became sweet agony. Their breathing grew too harsh for kissing. She murmured his name over and over, faster and faster. He gripped her hands tighter and matched the drumbeat of his name. She was dying. She was more alive than she'd ever been. She needed what only Matt could give—

Her climax exploded with rapturous force,

pulsing to every finger and toe. Still shimmering, she heard Matt's choked cry, extricated her hands and draped him in a limp hug.

His replete collapse was a welcome burden, his slowing breath a sweet stir against her ear. Tightening her arms, she embraced the moment just as fiercely. In her future rocking chair, she would daydream and smile.

Right now, she squeezed her eyes shut. Right now, her insulated pleasures of the past seemed mild and slightly pathetic.

Finding beauty only in objects had deprived her of a woman's greatest personal joy and gift: discovering fineness in imperfect humans. Loving the entire flawed design unconditionally. A profound lesson. One Abbey vowed to take with her when she left the ranch.

Even though for agonizing months to come, her heart would remain behind.

CHAPTER SIXTEEN

BESS DROVE OVER the cattle guard separating the Campbell ranch from the county road and headed for Matt Granger's place. For the first time, no baked offering occupied the passenger seat.

Abbey had phoned Bess after she'd finished the breakfast dishes and asked for a "tremendous favor." Could she possibly give Abbey a ride to San Antonio? She needed to leave the ranch today, the sooner the better, and calling a cab was out. She really didn't want to ask Matt or Casey, and Hal had to stay and watch Mattie.

Abbey had sounded close to losing control in a way only another woman could recognize. Responding to the SOS in her voice, Bess hadn't asked questions, just said no problem, she'd be there in an hour.

She'd found her daddy in the machine shed tinkering with a tractor engine. With one arm in a sling, he couldn't do heavy work, and Bess knew that galled him something fierce. Braced for trouble, she'd explained the situation and told him someone else would have to bottle-feed the filly at noon and make his lunch.

He'd opened his mouth, closed it with a click, then finally told her to take her time and watch out for crazy city drivers. He'd even insisted she take his new pickup, since one of the tires on her car was balder than an eagle.

She warmed now at the memory. Since she'd faced him down three days ago, she'd caught him looking at her just like Chad on the soap "Living and Loving" had looked at Mallory when he'd come out of his six-month coma. As if he'd been through something that had changed him, and he saw Bess differently now.

Abbey had been right. Someone could only dominate you if you let them. Bess owed the woman more than a ride to San Antonio for getting her thinking about that truth.

Slowing the truck, she turned left onto a narrow gravel road. The hill blocking Matt's house from view was dotted with trash trees, prickly pear cactus and goat weed. Still, the land was prettier this time of year than her daddy's cleared and mowed acreage.

The bobbing wildflowers gladdened her heart.

Or maybe it was the possibility of seeing Casey. If he was anywhere in sight, she intended to say hi.

She topped the rise and headed down, her gaze scanning the compound. No sign of anyone near the stable or pens, darn it. Sighing, she veered to the right, drove toward the front of the house and parked near the porch. She'd just slammed out of the truck when the screen door opened and Matt pushed through. Pitiful followed and barreled past his master straight for Bess.

She whirled around and pressed against the truck.

As usual, Matt's scolding fell on deaf ears. By the time he reached Bess, the dog had frisked her thoroughly and backed off. She turned around and smoothed her jeans, a lifetime around hunting dogs helping her take Pitiful in stride.

"I'm sorry, Bess. I've been tryin' to teach him some manners—" he shot a dark look at the mutt now peeing against a tire "—but hell, neither one of us is worth a damn in that department." Blowing out a breath, he resettled his hat.

"I think you have real nice manners," she

said sincerely, a little intimidated by his grim expression. "Um, would you happen to know if Abbey's ready?"

He laughed bitterly. "Yeah, she's been packed a long time. I tried to talk her into lettin' me or Casey drive her to San Antonio, but she is the *stubbornest* woman."

Startled, she studied him more closely. He looked awful, the kind of awful that starts in a person's spirit and moves out from there. Like he'd lost whatever it is that makes a body get up in the morning to face the day. Bess blinked.

So *that's* how it was.

Just then Abbey came out on the porch and held the screen door open. A large green suitcase nosed through, followed by Casey and a matching bag. He shifted both pieces of luggage to the proper position and carried them easily, his gaze finding Bess.

Her heart thrummed like a Singer stitching full speed. The hazel eyes beneath his hat brim were still the most beautiful she'd ever seen. She smiled shyly.

He stumbled, nearly pitching forward off the top step. Pitiful ran to the bottom step and barked excitedly. Abbey rushed to fuss over Casey and try to take a bag. Hal pushed through the door, rolling two carry-on bags into the confusion.

Bess simply enjoyed the dark flush on a lean handsome face.

Matt kneed Pitiful aside, climbed the steps and yanked the bags from Casey's hands, telling the younger man to get the other two. Then he stormed back down the steps and swung the luggage up and into the truck bed, looking as if he wanted to take a swing at someone's face while he was at it.

Bess shrank back a few steps.

Casey moved up to fill the void, hoisted the smaller bags into the truck and turned to study her face intently. "Your cheek looks much better. How's everything else?"

He meant was her daddy treating her right. Lordy, he still seemed to actually care! "It's good, Casey. Better than since Mama died."

His smile put the wildflowers to shame. "I'm glad. And your dad's arm? Is he back to full speed?"

Uh-oh. "Almost."

"You mean he's still hurtin'?" Casey scowled. "Damn, I didn't mean to put him outta commission during the busiest time of year."

His jaw firmed. "You tell him I'll come over and lend a hand first chance I get, hear?"

Bess nodded, the emotion swelling her heart making what she'd felt for Matt seem puny and childish. Needing time to adjust, she averted her eyes and sensed Casey turn around.

The curious silence caught her attention first. Beside her, Casey stood unnaturally still. She emerged from her dazed glow and looked up at the porch, her view front row and center stage.

A little girl, the niece named Mattie, had entered the scene. Her arms were wrapped around Hal's leg, her face hidden against his baggy jeans. He patted her blond curls awkwardly, his wrinkled face so gentle and sad Bess wondered how she'd ever thought him mean.

Six feet away, Abbey's chin was up, her body rigid, her hands fisted at her sides. She caught the old man's gaze and offered a wavering smile. "I'm going to miss you, Hal. You be sure and take as good care of yourself as you do everyone else, okay?"

"Don't you bother your head none about me. I ain't the one you need t' worry about." At the sight of her trembling mouth, he looked ashamed. "I'll miss you, too, honey. But there's nothin' that says you can't come back real soon an' visit us...is there?''

Abbey surged forward into his open arms. They exchanged a long rocking hug. She pulled back, crouched down in a puddle of denim jumper and swayed beneath the impact of the little girl's body. Abbey's reassurances of love and promises to write and phone were drowned by repetitive shrieks of ''please don't go.'' The shrill litany turned incoherent as shuddering sobs racked Mattie's body. The gruesome drama tore at Bess's heart. Her throat thickened. She didn't dare look at Matt. Somehow her hand found Casey's and she took comfort in his warm squeeze.

Abbey tried to free herself but couldn't. Mattie was hysterical. Inconsolable. Pitiful galloped up the steps and nearly bowled the two over seeking a patch of Mattie's face to lick. Hal pulled the whining dog back and Abbey stood, the sobbing child's legs and arms wrapped around her in a death grip.

She walked down the steps, her gaze dismissing Casey and zeroing in on Bess. *Please, please help me get through this.*

Releasing Casey's hand, Bess moved forward, grasped two thin arms and pulled gently but firmly. The little girl's strength was amazing, but no match for a grown woman used to lifting foals. The looser Mattie's hold became, the louder she screeched.

Knowing the second she let go of Mattie the child would reestablish her grip, Bess looked beyond Abbey to Matt's stricken gaze.

"Come here and take your niece," Bess ordered.

He obviously wanted no part of it, but he came. With his large hands completely encircling the child's ribs, he made easy work of pulling her locked legs free. Mattie bucked and writhed in his implacable arms, her wails degenerating into terrible garbling noises.

It was awful. Bess shook worse than after her daddy had hit her. Matt had gone pale beneath his tan.

Abbey looked up, her eyes dark and anguished behind her glasses. "I'll call later to make sure she's okay. Goodbye, Matt. And remember, trust yourself." Ducking her chin, she lifted her long jumper and fled to the truck's passenger door.

More than ready to leave, Bess mumbled goodbye to the remaining actors, climbed into the cab and started the engine. She drove away considerably faster than she'd arrived. In her rearview mirror, Mattie still struggled in her uncle's arms.

When the truck had almost reached the top of the hill, a keening moan lifted the hair on Bess's nape. Alarmed, she slowed her speed.

"*Go. Go. Go!*" Abbey choked out.

Bess pressed the accelerator and seconds later they were traveling down the backside of the hill.

Abbey pulled off her glasses, tossed them onto the seat, and lost control.

Listening to the wrenching sound of crying held in too long, Bess had never felt so helpless. She stood it until she'd reached the county road, then stopped the truck and shifted into park.

Abbey had drawn her legs up and sat hugging her knees, her face buried, her shoulders shaking with the force of her grief.

"This is crazy," Bess stated. "You don't want to leave. They don't want you to leave. I'm taking you back."

"No!" Abbey raised a ravaged face. "I c-can't go b-back. Give me a m-minute. I'll be f-fine." She lifted a fold of denim and roughly wiped the tears falling faster than she could blot.

"Is it Matt?"

She nodded, blotting like mad.

"But he especially doesn't want you to go. Abbey, I've never seen a man look so miserable. Why should you both be miserable when you can stay here and be happy?"

"Because he d-didn't *ask* me to stay! So if I s-stayed, I'd be m-m-miserable. O-oh, I *hate* to blubber like this! It's s-so *female!*" Abbey gathered up some drier denim and scrubbed her red splotchy cheeks.

Stretching across the seat, Bess popped open the glove compartment and pulled out a small box. She sat back, plucked a handful of tissues and extended them wordlessly. They weren't going anywhere until she got some more answers.

"Thank you," Abbey murmured, releasing her sodden dress and accepting the offering. She blew her nose twice, then took a shuddering breath. After drawing three more, she regained a measure of composure and looked at Bess squarely. "I appreciate your concern. You were wonderful to just drop everything and come to my rescue. If I'd had to stay there much longer, I might not've had the strength to leave."

"And staying would've made you miserable? Even though you want to stay so bad you're cryin' your guts out?"

"I'm glad you understand."

Bess didn't understand at all. But she knew firsthand that holding feelings in could mess up your life. "Why don't we just go back and talk it all out? Get everything into the open so Matt knows how you feel and you know he wants you to stay."

"No!" The wad of tissue twisting in Abbey's hands shredded.

Bess handed over the box.

"Thank you. Look, I know you mean well, but Matt had his chance to talk. The last thing he wants to know now is that beneath all her bluster, Miss Unconventionality is really Miss America in disguise."

Bess knew her pageants, and she was more confused than ever. "Miss Unconventionality?"

"Miss Independence, Miss Entrepreneur—take your pick."

"Are those local California titles? You know, like Cottonwood Festival Queen here in Texas?"

"No, they're all a sham. I just didn't know it until now."

Bess gave up. "I'm lost."

Abbey's laugh was close to a sob. "I'm sorry for rambling. The point is, I don't want to be simply convenient for Matt. I want to be...more.'' The wistful yearning on her face was a universal language women had spoken across the world and throughout time.

At last Bess understood. ''You want to be loved, not simply desired.''

''Yes.''

''You want to live in your own home, not simply a house.''

Eyes welling, Abbey nodded.

Bess swallowed hard. ''You want to be a mother, not simply a baby-sitter.''

Abbey's nod released a tear.

''You want a husband, not simply a fling,'' Bess finished huskily. Plucking two tissues from the box, Abbey kept one and handed the other to Bess.

They blotted and blew, then exchanged a misty smile.

When Bess could see clearly again, she shifted the truck into drive and cast her friend a decisive glance. ''Buckle your seat belt, Abbey. Those crazy city drivers are dangerous.''

KNOCK! KNOCK! KNOCK!

Matt lowered his fist and wished the trailer house door were Hal's head. Maybe a good pounding would knock some consideration into the mule.

What a yellow-belly stunt, after the trauma of Abbey's departure the day before, to announce he was driving to Gonzales to visit his sister for the day. He'd hightailed it straight from the breakfast table to his trailer before Matt could react.

He reached out and turned the knob. Locked.

Knock! Knock! Knock!

"Open up, you coward, or I swear you're gonna need a new door. And I'm not payin' for it, either!"

"Hold yer britches, I'm comin'," Hal called, his voice muffled.

A fumbling noise confirmed he'd arrived. The weathered door opened. Matt moved back as Hal stepped purposefully outside then turned, without making eye contact, to shut the door.

He'd shaved and was wearing his good hat.

Matt panicked. "You can't do this, Hal. Not ten days before the Futurity. Not with Casey helpin' Ben Campbell today. Wait until Gloria gets here tomorrow, then find another way to punish me."

The old man hadn't forgiven Matt for letting Abbey drive off and out of their lives.

"Gloria." Hal hawked and spit, his opinion of the woman clear. His gaze swept the immediate area, then flicked to the stable, which blocked his view of the house. "Where's Mattie?"

"Still sittin' at the kitchen table. I told her not to move until I came back." Matt winced beneath a glare of such disgust and disappointment it was all he could do not to hang his head—which reminded him.

"She's not alone. Pitiful is with her," he added lamely.

"Son, if brains was leather, you couldn't saddle a flea! Now you kin get back there and take care o' yer niece, or I can whittle a switch fer yer backside. Which will it be?"

Matt's frustration roiled up and out. "How 'bout I just fire your ass? Now *there's* an option."

Pain pulsed once in faded blue eyes.

Through the sound of his own agitated breathing, Matt heard a bobwhite whistle goodmorning to its mate.

Hal looked away and dug his keys stiffly out of his pocket. "You do what you have to, Matt. I'll do the same."

He turned and limped toward the ancient Ford

pickup truck parked beside the rose bed he'd planted so proudly two years ago. A riot of pink, red and yellow blooms attested to his loving care.

This time Matt did hang his head.

Hal had helped pour Charlie into bed too many nights to count. He'd flown to Vegas with money he couldn't spare to see Matt compete in the PRCA National Finals. He'd stood beside Matt as Charlie's coffin was lowered six feet under, offering comfort and the unspoken love that had gotten Matt through some rough childhood years.

"Hal, wait!" Matt loped to the truck. "I'm sorry. That was a rotten thing to say. You know I couldn't get along without you."

Grunting noncommittally, Hal clambered into the cab and reached for the door handle.

Matt's arm shot out to stop the slam. "*One* day. That's all I'm askin' you to postpone your visit. I'll call Harriet myself and explain how important every hour I spend with Doc is right now."

Matt had gone with Hal a number of times to visit the fragile old sweetheart. She'd understand.

Hal's scowl slowly relaxed. "Did you know Harriet was married once?"

Matt couldn't hide his start of surprise.

"She don't advertise it none. She run off with a no-account drifter when she was seventeen. Back then, divorce was more shameful than lettin' someone use you fer a punchin' bag. She took it till I got wind of things."

A gleam of remembered battle entered Hal's eyes. "Then me 'n' him had a little…discussion, and he signed the papers."

The wiry chute boss had obviously done right by his sister. Matt fought a quick, familiar skirmish with guilt.

"Harriet always wanted kids," Hal continued, "but after the divorce, she never got hitched again. So her 'n' me, we're all we got, family wise. She'd be the first to say every hour is important, and you shouldn't waste 'em."

He tugged forcefully enough on the door to dislodge Matt's arm, then held his gaze. "When you're as old as us, do you really want your time with Doc to be the hours you remember?"

The door slammed shut. The window rolled down.

"I'll be back by nine tonight. There's fixin's for sandwiches in the fridge. You're on your own for supper.'' Hal lifted an arthritic hand for a beauty queen wave. ''See ya, Uncle Matt.''

The window rolled up on his rusty cackle. He started the engine with a roar.

Matt jumped backward as the rear bumper swiped the air he'd just vacated. Damned old coot would be lucky to make it to Gonzales and back in one piece! Watching until the truck drove out of sight, he wiped his clammy palms on his jeans.

Hal's heart was in the right place. But he didn't know that Matt had waited for a sign, a slipped word, anything to convince him Abbey didn't want to leave. He loved her. Even more incredibly, she loved him. He'd known for sure after they'd made love. No woman had ever been as tender, passionate and, well, *loving* in his arms as Abbey. Yet she feared his hold on her so much she'd hustled Bess into cab service rather than risk being talked into staying.

So he'd given her the freedom she craved, praying silently that time away would make her heart grow fonder and not erase him from her mind. He'd grimly held his hysterical niece and walked her through the wildflowers until she'd stilled and fallen into an exhausted sleep. She hadn't awakened until that morning, and had been listless and docile at breakfast.

Matt glanced toward the house.

He didn't have the time for this. He didn't have the patience for this. Who was he kidding? He didn't have the guts for this.

But it wasn't like he had any choice.

Much as he'd like to, he couldn't spend the next thirteen years avoiding time alone with his niece. It wasn't rational, much less realistic.

Resigned to his day of baby-sitting, he walked past the stable and on to the house, already counting down the minutes until Mattie was tucked safely into bed for the night. He swiftly climbed the concrete steps and opened the kitchen door. His gaze swept the room.

Empty.

He strode forward and bellowed, *"Mattie?"*

A shattering crash was followed by a canine yelp.

Matt covered the short distance to the living room in record time and skidded to a stop on the varnished wood floor. He took in the ottoman dragged over to the fireplace, the child in her nightgown standing on tiptoe high enough to stretch and reach the mantel, the ceramic shards that had once been an angel scattered amid ashes on the floor.

Mattie lowered her heels and directed a huge stricken gaze at Matt.

He read her intention a split second too late.

"No!" he yelled as she stepped off the ottoman onto the floor.

She sucked in a breath and looked down, let it out in a pained terrified, "Ow! Ow! Ow! *O-o-o-w-w-w-w!*"

Pitiful rushed closer and barked in distress, his tail thrashing.

"Don't move," Matt ordered, noting sickly the trace of blood beneath one of her heels. A step in any direction would mean more cuts.

"Abbe-e-e-e-y! I want Abbe-e-e-e-y."

The dog's barking grew more frantic.

The din was ungodly. He could barely think.

In two long strides he was close enough to reach down and scoop her up. She clung to him like a tree frog, wailing for Abbey the whole time, while he walked to the kitchen and mentally reassured himself.

It's only a cut. Clean the wound first. Check the damage. She'll be fine. She'll be fine. She'll be fine.

Pitiful whimpered and crowded close to Matt's knees, causing him to stumble.

He shot the dog a savage look and roared, ''Move!''

Mattie tightened her arms and bumped up her volume a notch. ''Abbe-e-e-e-y.''

His ears ringing, he hurried to the counter, set Mattie down next to the sink and unpeeled her arms from around his neck. She stopped cater-wauling and tried to peer at her dangling feet, but he sandwiched her face with both hands and steered her head up.

Wild eyes looking anywhere but at him trig-gered his sudden calm.

She was frightened, in pain, and reacting very much as a horse would.

''Mattie, look at me,'' he said, switching to his trainer's voice. A low, unruffled croon that filtered through equine fear and confusion.

''Look at my eyes. That's right, now listen to what I'm saying. You cut your foot, and I know it hurts. I know you're scared, but you're gonna be fine.''

''I want Abbey,'' Mattie said in a choked whisper, followed by a hiccupy little sob that caught at his heart.

Me, too, squirt. "You know Abbey's not here."

"I want Hal."

Matt's chest tightened with perverse jealousy. "Hal went to visit his sister, just like he said at breakfast. It's just you and me, kid. But I'm gonna fix you up good as new. Trust me. I wouldn't lie to you. You're gonna be fine, okay?"

Her blue eyes appeared magnified by the tears glimmering between curly blond lashes. He felt her begin to nod and removed his hands, but continued holding her watery gaze.

"That's good, darlin', 'cause I need to get something out of the bathroom medicine cabinet, and I want you to stay still until I get back.

"I'll hurry," he promised, stemming the rise of panic in her eyes. "Why don't you start countin' and see if I can make it back before you get to twenty five? Can you count that far?" He'd overheard her chanting to fifty for Abbey once.

A spark of interest sharpened her fear-clouded gaze. "I'm a good counter," she said, taking the bait.

"Okay, then. When you say 'one,' I'll take off."

She plunged right in. "One...two...three..."

Matt pounded toward the bathroom, his ears tuned in to the singsong voice behind him. Pitiful bounded alongside, woofing happily at this fun new game of chase and trip Matt.

He nearly went down twice in the hallway, but made it to the bathroom in good time. He lost audio contact while yanking items out of the medicine cabinet, lost seconds while searching for the sterile gauze. Back in the hall, he picked up Mattie's voice at number twenty.

Using every inch of his long legs, he managed to reach the kitchen just as she said twenty-five.

Giggling, she clapped her hands. "You did it, Uncle Matt! You run *good*."

Grinning triumphantly through his wheezes, he walked forward and dumped an armload of supplies on the counter. Her fear was gone. No blood had dripped to the floor. And if she could laugh like that, she couldn't be in too much pain.

He motioned to the sink. "Put your feet in there, squirt, and let's wash off that heel."

She sobered instantly.

Scrambling for inspiration, he remembered she was finicky about spit. "Hurry up, before Pitiful washes it with his tongue and gets germs in your cut."

She glanced down at the rubbery nose near her dangling feet. Sure enough, that did the trick.

Swinging her skinny legs over as ordered, she pulled up her Little Mermaid nightgown until Ariel's tail bunched around her knobby knees. Mattie leaned over and stared at the blood smearing the heel of her peanut foot. Fascination obviously warred with returning fear.

"Seemed like every time I turned around, your mama needed doctorin'." Matt moved close to turn on the faucet.

His niece's head whipped up.

"Yep, she got cut or busted a finger or something damn near almost every week."

Mattie's puffy eyes were huge and guilty. "I busted all of Mommy. I didn't mean to. I was gonna give her a hug, but she fell."

"A hug?"

"Uh-huh. Abbey says a hug is the best cure for feeling sad. Only she wasn't here."

Matt's heart twisted. "Remember that the angel only reminded us of your mama. She's really in heaven where nothin' can get busted or hurt, and where she'll always watch over you."

"I like Abbey to watch over me. Is she ever comin' back?"

Matt cupped the back of his niece's head. "I

hope so, squirt. Right now she needs some time by herself to think about things. But if she doesn't come back, it won't be because she doesn't love you." Dejected, Mattie leaned into his hand a little, the way a cat seeks to be petted. He massaged the silken curls gently, his own heartache eased by the contact. Whatever else he did wrong, from now on he would not shirk his responsibility to this child. He owed Mary that much.

"You know, Mattie, *I'm* not goin' anywhere."

Her startled gaze met his.

Flustered, he pulled back his hand and realized the water had been running all this time. "Now, how 'bout we get that foot cleaned up? You ready?"

"Okay." Her voice decidedly lacked enthusiasm.

"Good girl." He lifted Mattie's foot and held it under the stream of cold tap water, flinching at her involuntary jerk and hiss. Her lips quivered, her eyes glistened. "I know that stings, darlin'," he said hastily. "But it looks like you're just as tough as your mama was. Mary never cried."

But maybe she should have.

The idea erupted forcefully in his brain, as if it had simmered for years waiting for exactly the right conditions to bring it boiling up.

Maybe, just maybe Mary shouldn't have been so tough all the time. Maybe if she'd told Matt outright in words—or through rare tears—that something was very wrong in her life, he wouldn't have ignored her need for help. Wouldn't have given their dad the benefit of the doubt. Matt considered the theory for all of five seconds.

No maybe about it. He would've protected Mary with his life!

So maybe Abbey had been right after all, and blaming himself for the actions of his father was self-indulgent behavior. He certainly couldn't change history. But he could affect the future. *Remember, trust yourself,* Abbey had said.

A tiny whimper drew his focus back to Mattie's foot. She was being a brave little thing. The cut was shallow, thank God, but needed attention.

He turned off the tap water, tore off a paper towel and patted the tender skin dry. Lifting her feet from the sink, he guided them to dangle once more toward the floor.

"You ever had iodine put on a cut before, squirt?"

"Is it that orange stuff that really really hurts?"

He had his answer. "That's the stuff. Hurts like hell for a few seconds, but it kills those nasty germs. And I promise to blow real hard while I put it on."

He reached for the iodine bottle and unscrewed the cap. The pungent odor triggered a flare of fear in her eyes.

Damn, he wished he could take the pain away. "Ready?"

When she slowly lifted her foot, he didn't feel panic at the trust she revealed. Instead, he experienced a soft bloom of wonder, the emotion unfurling quickly into rich contentment.

He wrapped his hand around his niece's ankle and removed the iodine wand. "It won't hurt long, darlin'."

Her little chin firmed. In that instant, she was a dead ringer for Mary. "I won't cry, Uncle Matt. I'll be tough."

Now he felt panic.

"You cry all you want," he said urgently. "That doesn't mean you're not tough. From now on, you either tell me with words, or with tears, when you're hurtin', so I can help. Will you promise me that, Mattie?''

She nodded shyly. ''I promise.''

''Okay. Here goes.'' He slathered the cut with iodine, then blew fiercely as she whimpered.

Matt was still blowing his guts out when a small hand patted him on the head.

''I don't hurt anymore, Uncle Matt. You can stop blowing if you want.''

''Oh. Yeah.'' Flustered, he busied himself opening an adhesive bandage. She swung her injured foot idly.

''Uncle Matt?''

''Hmm?'' Damn, did you have to be a mechanical engineer to figure out how to peel off the wrapping?

''I'm glad it's just me and you, today.''

His hands stilled. His throat swelled along with his heart. He looked up at her shy smile and Granger dimple, and matched it with his own.

''Me, too, darlin'. Me, too.''

CHAPTER SEVENTEEN

"As you can see, I incorporate a number of different materials in my designs," Abbey said, referring to the jewelry spread out before her on the conference table. "I've used gold sparingly, but quite frankly, it's a decision based on prohibitive cost rather than personal taste. I intend to use more precious stones and metals as my finances improve."

And she hoped that would happen soon. She'd spent half the money from her arrowhead necklace sale updating her appearance from flower child to professional businesswoman.

The jewelry buyer for Neiman Marcus, Houston, an elegant gray-haired woman in her fifties, straightened up from inspecting the array. She wore exquisite silver and gold Durant earrings and a matching brooch. Very pricey. Very exclusive.

Abbey struggled not to defend her use of eclectic materials again. She pulled out three mounted photographs from a small portfolio.

"I've also done a few custom-ordered pieces. Here you can see the finished design. Below I listed the specifications given to me by the client, along with a phone number where each can be reached if you'd like to confirm their satisfaction."

She reached automatically to push up her glasses and flip back her braid before remembering that she no longer had them. Her cheeks heated. She'd never felt so vulnerable and exposed.

Mrs. Lawrence studied the photographs, her expression revealing only polite interest, then raised a gaze that seemed to assess Abbey and find her lacking. "Is this all you have?"

With tremendous effort, Abbey kept her dejection from showing. "I only brought selected samples that represent my style. But if you don't like these, I'm certain you won't like the others."

Cool blue eyes warmed several degrees. "My dear, you misunderstand. I love the samples. If the rest of your work matches these in quality, I'd like an exclusive agreement to sell Free Bird designs in all our stores."

Abbey blinked, not sure she'd heard correctly.

Mrs. Lawrence smiled and became, not an intimidating businesswoman wearing expensive designer jewelry, but simply a woman.

"Abbey...may I call you Abbey?"

You can call me a-ny-thing you want. "Of course."

"Good. Please call me Linda. I have a feeling we'll be seeing a lot of each other."

Abbey groped beside her. "Excuse me, Mrs.—Linda. I need to sit down." Without further ado, she collapsed onto a black leather chair.

Laughing, Linda sat with much more dignity. "You seem surprised."

"That's putting it mildly. I'm competing against *that*." Abbey gestured to the other woman's brooch.

"No, you're not." Excitement crept into Linda's eyes. "What intrigues me about your jewelry is the fact it's in a class by itself. I've never seen such innovative use of materials. Some designs are whimsical, some clever, some stunning. But they're all unique.

"Texas women are friendly, confident risk-takers. Given a choice between ho-hum me-too gold jewelry, or something that will set them apart, they'll go for individuality every time. I think you'll be an instant hit."

Abbey began smiling. This couldn't be real.

During the next hour, Linda convinced her it was. They shook hands and agreed to finalize details in two days, after Abbey had absorbed the information and could consult with a lawyer.

By this time bonded, Linda asked her a few personal questions. When she found out Abbey had no car and was riding the bus, Linda offered to drive Abbey home after work. She could shop in The Galleria until five.

Declining the gracious offer, Abbey was ashamed of her earlier assumption that the woman was cold.

She left the administrative offices in a daze, pulled her wheeled carry-on through the store and past the jewelry department in a numb fog, pushed through an exit and into the bright sunlight, blinking like an animal emerging from hibernation.

A blast of heat brought her fully awake. She stopped, her elation swelling. Mercy, she'd done it! This was a *huge* triumph. Unable to help herself, she smiled broadly at several customers heading for the bank of glass doors.

An expensively dressed young woman with a preoccupied expression breezed past without making eye contact. A middle aged couple looked a bit startled, but offered a tentative smile in return.

"I just heard some great news," Abbey told them, bursting to elaborate on the subject. Nodding politely, the man opened a door with one hand and hurried his wife through with the other. The door eased shut.

Abbey was left staring at her reflection in the glass. High heel pumps and a red crepe wool Evan Picone suit. Dark wavy hair barely brushing her shoulders. An overall image of chic professionalism at odds with eyes so stark with loneliness Abbey had to look away.

Was this, then, what she would be forced to do from now on? Seek strangers kind enough to stop and listen whenever she had personal news?

The last of her elation drained. She grabbed the handle of her carry-on and walked lethargically toward the bus stop in front of The Galleria. She supposed she could phone Hal with her news when she got home.

Home.

A laugh caught in her thickening throat. Her tacky furnished apartment made the one in Venice seem like the Ritz. She hadn't told Hal, of course. They'd spoken a few minutes last night, and she'd been purposefully upbeat, mentioning her meeting with Neiman Marcus today. If she called and told him her news, he'd be happy.

She wouldn't feel so alone. But she might have to speak with Mattie again.

Hearing her sweet voice, answering the same heart-wrenching questions, risking Matt answering the phone! She couldn't bear that pain.

Abbey's vision blurred. How could one person produce so many tears? She'd wash away her new contact lenses if she didn't stop crying. Struggling for composure, she moved to the nearest parked car, set her purse on the hood and pulled out a bedraggled tissue.

Once upon a time she'd gloried in her ability to walk away with a single suitcase from any place and never look back.

Now she longed to return to the people who'd earned her love and shown her what "home" could be. A sanctuary instead of a prison. A place where imperfections were accepted with laughter and forgiveness. A refuge of the heart she might never experience again.

She blew her nose. The irony was too cruel. Surviving alone would be harder than ever now that she knew what she was missing.

Unless you quit feeling sorry for yourself and make new friends, an inner voice scolded.

Astonishment stopped Abbey's tears. A surge of resentment flowed powerfully, ebbed slowly.

Convictions that had been adrift for weeks settled, begging closer examination.

In the past, isolation had been her choice. But here in Houston, she didn't *have* to be alone.

She'd met Linda, hadn't she? A woman Abbey already liked a great deal. There were probably dozens of organizations and causes begging for volunteers, a city full of strangers to meet and get to know. Most people would feel fortunate to call her a friend.

Yes, she thought in amazement, they would feel fortunate. Because she would make a true and worthy friend. There wasn't a doubt in her mind. Another irony.

Somehow, as she'd counseled Matt to reject responsibility for the sins of his father, he'd convinced her to do the same.

A curious peace settled over Abbey. She tucked the soaked tissue in her purse, slipped the leather strap over her shoulder and pulled her luggage the rest of the way to the bus stop benches.

Inside the Plexiglas shelter, an elderly white woman clutched a shopping bag in her lap, a black woman in her thirties read a paperback, and a teenage Hispanic girl smacked her gum and stared dully at passing cars. They sat equidistant, but in their own separate worlds. All three glanced up at Abbey's approach.

Their double takes were as clear as a mirror.

She managed a small smile. "Don't worry, I'm not contagious. I always get splotchy when I cry."

The reader scooted closer to the teenager and patted the gap she'd created. "Whoever he is, honey, he's not worth it."

Just like that, Abbey's tears returned. "Yes, he is." She settled on the bench and wiped beneath her eyes.

"Here you are, dear." An age-spotted hand thrust two clean tissues under her nose. "Some men should be horsewhipped."

Abbey accepted the tissues gratefully. "Thank you, but you don't understand."

The teenager extended a pack of Wrigley's gum. "Want some?"

Shaking her head, Abbey dried her blasted tears. "He's a good man," she insisted.

"If he's so good, how come you're crying?" the girl asked.

Here were the strangers, kind enough to listen, that Abbey had sought earlier. Like Forest Gump without the box of chocolates, she found herself telling her skeptical bench mates—and the three others who wandered into the shelter later—

about the tough Texan with a heart as big as the state who'd changed her life forever.

By the time her bus rolled up to the curb with a squeal of brakes and noxious exhaust fumes, more tissues had been passed around.

Abbey stood, helped Emma rise stiffly, handed Leah her book, cautioned Rosario not to forget her backpack.

"Call him tonight," Frank advised as they all formed a line at the open bus door. "He can't read your mind."

"Yeah," Don seconded. "Tell him you love him and can't live without him."

Leah poked Don in the back as he climbed the steps. "Do you have cotton in your ears? She told you he let her leave without a fight. Why should she crawl back to him?"

Emma sighed. "Pride won't keep her warm at night. Oh, thank you, dear," she said to Rosario, who carried Emma's shopping bag for her up the steps.

Abbey followed the older woman's painfully slow climb, then paid her fare and found an aisle seat next to Leah at the rear of the bus.

To crawl...or not to crawl? Abbey wondered.

The answer would have to wait. She'd never felt so emotionally and physically exhausted.

Leaning back, she closed her eyes and heard the hiss of the closing door.

Bang! Bang! Bang!

"All right, all right," the driver grumbled. The door hissed open again.

"I'm lookin' for a passenger," a deep voice drawled.

Abbey's heart jolted. Her lids snapped open.

"Long braid, glasses, probably wearin' a pretty flowered dress. She get on this bus?"

"Mister, I just look at the road and my watch. Right now I'm running late. Either climb all the way on, or step off so I can close the door."

"Can I take a quick look before you leave?"

"No time. Step down, please."

"One minute. That's all I'm askin'."

The driver reached for the door lever. "Watch out."

"But—"

The door began closing.

Slam!

Abbey jerked, every cell on red alert.

"Touch the door or the gas pedal, and you'll regret it," Matt promised in the tone she'd once seen spark fear in a kickboxing bodybuilder.

Heads craned toward the front and murmurs broke out. A black Stetson rose from the stairwell, followed by plenty of muscle to back up the threat.

The driver shrank against his seat, then cleared his throat. "Okay. You've got one minute," he said weakly.

Matt nodded and turned to straddle the center aisle, looking tired, dangerous and every inch a rodeo champion in a black shirt, jeans and boots. Beneath the low hat brim, his silvery eyes gleamed.

An awed hush fell over the passengers.

"Abbey Parker?" he called, his gaze systematically sweeping left to right.

Beside her, Leah stiffened. "That's him?"

Abbey nodded.

"Start crawlin', girl."

Four rows ahead, Rosario twisted around to give Abbey a thumbs-up sign. One by one, the rest of the bus shelter occupants turned to gape or grin.

Tracking their focus, Matt walked forward—and stopped as if poleaxed. "Abbey?"

She'd lived with the man for weeks, shared the most spiritual and carnal of intimacies, and he didn't *recognize* her? "I'm sorry. You must be mistaken."

Leah chuckled.

His mouth thinned. "Get off the bus, Abbey. It's important."

Oh, God. "Mattie?"

"She's fine. Hal's fine. Everyone's fine except us. We need to talk."

She ruthlessly squelched a leap of hope. "My phone's been connected for a week."

He spared a frustrated glance for their avid audience, blew out a breath, studied the floor. "I'm sorry I didn't call. I had a few things to work out."

"I see." But she didn't. And she was terrified of what she might learn. "So now that you've worked your way down the list to my name, I'm supposed to be grateful, drop everything and come crawling?"

He looked up, his gaze thrillingly intense. "Crawl, walk, run…I'll take you anyway I can get you, darlin'."

Her jackhammer heartbeats made speaking difficult. "Why?"

His eyes darkened. "You know why."

A maelstrom of emotion swirled within Abbey, joy at its core. "No. I don't. Tell me."

"Get off the bus, and I will."

"Tell me now."

A slow grin cut the Granger dimple deep.

"You really want your pound of flesh, don't you?"

He'd put her through hell. "Sixteen, twelve, eight ounces...I'll take whatever I can get, darlin'."

Her blood beat in her ears as she held his glittering gaze. Oh, how she'd missed this! The exhilaration, the challenge, the wondering what his next move would be and when she could surrender, as they both wanted.

He'd missed it, too. His lean face was alive as it hadn't been minutes ago.

In complete safety, she made one last goading remark. "Obviously you don't have the guts to take what you want."

Matt slipped his thumbs free of his pockets.

"Uh-oh," Leah muttered.

One second Abbey was holding her breath, the next she was being scooped into powerful arms and lifted, her shriek lost amid the cheers and applause of passengers.

"Put your arms around my neck," Matt ordered.

She obeyed blissfully.

He faced the front and started walking, heedless of her feet bumping against those heads too slow to duck.

"Sorry," she said over a broad shoulder.

"Oops, sorry. Mercy, are you hurt? Sorry—oh! Matt, my shoe fell off!"

"I'll buy you a new pair."

"I left my purse in the back!"

"Leave it."

"It's got my license and keys and—oh, stop!" She wriggled futilely. "My luggage!"

"When we get home, Abbey, I'm unpackin' every goddamn piece of luggage you own and throwin' 'em in a bonfire."

Home? Abbey started to smile, then panicked as a new thought struck. "My jewelre-e-e!" she wailed.

Matt stopped.

Behind them, Abbey watched her shoe, purse and carry-on luggage get passed cheerfully from hand-to-hand toward the front of the bus. Her friends from the bus shelter were beaming. She smiled mistily and waved.

"Okay, my stuff's here," she told Matt. "Let me down."

"Not until I get you off this bus."

True to his word, he somehow squeezed the two of them down the stairwell and lowered her to the pavement outside. She balanced on one foot as he retrieved her shoe, purse and luggage, set them beside her, then went back to shake the grinning driver's hand.

As Matt stepped off the bus, more cheers and applause broke out. Abbey slipped on her shoe. The door closed. Smoke plumed from the exhaust pipe.

Seconds later, they were alone.

His gaze traveled slowly from her new haircut to her high heels, came back up heated and yearning. "What happened to the prude part of sexy?"

"I ditched her a week ago. Do you mind?" Raising one hand, she traced the textures of his beloved face, her eyelids drooping in sensual pleasure, a feminine hum escaping her throat.

With a strangled sound, he grabbed her luggage with one hand and her arm with the other, then took off as if running a footrace.

It was all she could do not to stumble. "Where are we going?"

"The truck's not far from here."

His long legs ate up the ground. They were headed toward the parking garage.

"How did you know I'd be on the bus?" She was panting now.

"Hal knew about your meeting. Some lady named Linda told me you'd be out here waiting for the bus." A grin hovered in his smoldering glance. "Said to tell you again what good taste you have."

Cocky cowboy. He'd probably flashed that Granger dimple and melted every woman in the office.

"Not far now."

Mercy, she hoped not. They entered the shaded parking garage and she sighed at the cooler temperature. Amazingly, he'd found a space on the first level. She watched him throw her carry-on in back, unlock the passenger door and hold it open.

Climbing in took some fancy doing. By the time she'd settled on the bench seat, her skirt had risen several inches. She caught him staring at her legs and reached to tug down her hem.

"Leave it," he ordered, then slammed the door.

He loped around the bumper, unlocked his side, slid in and jammed the key in the ignition. The engine roared to life. His hand moved to shift gears.

"Matt."

He paused, his profile grim.

"You said we need to talk."

"I changed my mind. That's not what I need to do."

She squeezed her eyes shut and tried not to scream. "You're driving me crazy."

A faint rustle and wave of body heat were her only warning.

Long fingers speared into her hair, thrusting her head back. "You're driving *me* crazy. I need to get you somewhere private. *That's* what I need to do."

His mouth fused with hers.

They were as wild for each other as they'd been in the stable, but with a difference. No secrets, no emotional cages barred their deepest feelings from each other.

The unfettered meeting of hearts, minds and souls took Abbey soaring to a new level of pleasure. He didn't have to say the words, but she wanted them anyway.

She broke the kiss with a gasp.

He leaned his forehead against hers. "Oh, God, Abbey, I can't sleep, I can't eat, I can't concentrate. Tell me it's not too late. Tell me we still have a chance."

Have a chance? She stifled a laugh. "That depends on what you tell *me*."

He pulled back and looked into her eyes. "I want you ringside when I compete in the Futurity. I want you picking wildflowers every spring. I want you making terrible spaghetti and beautiful brown-eyed babies. I love you," he said gruffly. "Mattie loves you. Hal loves you."

Joy exploded in her heart.

"Marry us, Abbey."

She laughed, her heart too full to contain her love. "Are you sure?"

"I'm sure."

"Absolutely cert—"

He cut her off with a kiss. Long and searing enough to steam the windows. When it ended, they were both breathing hard.

"Do you believe me now?"

"I don't know..." Cuddling against his chest, she smiled dreamily. "My apartment's not far from here. You think maybe a little privacy might help you convince me?"

He chuckled. "I'll sure as hell cowboy-up and give it a go."

Is it possible to be any happier than this?

"Abbey?"

"Hmm?"

"Later...after you're good and convinced...I'm takin' you home, darlin'."

Mercy. I guess it is.